DESTRUCTION ISLAND

DESTRUCTION ISLAND

A Novel

By **FREDRICK COOPER**

Copyright © 2014 by Fredrick Cooper

This novel is a work of fiction. With the exception of Christian Zauner, the great-grandfather of the author who served as the first keeper of the Destruction Island lighthouse from 1889 to 1899, his wife, Hermine, and Abigail, Hermine's daughter from a previous marriage, the names, characters, and events are the products of the author's imagination or are places or historical events that have been used fictitiously. Any resemblance to actual events or persons, living or dead, is entirely coincidental.

ISBN:-10: 0988198339
ISBN-13: 978-0-9881983-3-3
Library of Congress Control Number: 2014903936
Fredrick Cooper, Portland, OR
Printed in the United States of America

In Memory of:

Mary Jane Armstrong Smith

AUTHOR'S NOTE

By far, the most frequent comment by readers of my debut novel, *Riders of the Tides*, other than it was a page turner and complaining about keeping them up all night, was *when are you coming out with a sequel*? I had not given the idea of a sequel to *Riders of the Tides* much thought and was working on the storyline and character descriptions for another novel set in Southeast Alaska. Then four months after its release, I got word that it had received an IPPY award for best regional fiction. This turned out to be the motivation I needed to get busy with writing a sequel involving my principal character, Earl Armstrong, and *Destruction Island* became my sole focus. This second novel was an absolute thrill to write. As with the *Riders of the Tides*, I found that I needed to do research about places I wanted to use for settings—places I had known about or visited many years ago but didn't know much about their history. For example, the lighthouse on Destruction Island is one of six on the Washington coast. My great-grandfather, Christian Zauner, was the very first keeper for this lighthouse, as well as the Grays Harbor Lighthouse. Destruction Island lies off a remote section of the coast of Washington and few residents of the Pacific Northwest even know of its existence. Since a person can no longer visit this lighthouse due to the island's designation as a marine reserve administered by the U.S. Fish and Wildlife Service, I turned to several interesting sources for information. The first was my Aunt Mary Jane Armstrong Smith, who lived with "Papa" Chris as a young girl and published a small recipe book entitled *Herminia by the Sea, Favorite Family Recipes and Stories.* It is filled with little anecdotal stories about the life of the Zauner family while living on Destruction Island. I visited the U.S. Coast Guard museum in Seattle to examine photographs and lighthouse memorabilia and appreciated the able assistance of Capt. Gene Davis, USCG retired. The Westport Maritime Museum, which is featured in the novel, has a fabulous exhibit about Destruction Island, its keepers and displays the actual Fresnel lens removed from the lighthouse after it was closed. I visited the communities of La Push and Forks, with its interesting Visitors Information

Center, the Olympic National Park's Kalaloch Ranger Station, and the Hoh and Quileute River regions.

The book's cover design is by a talented Northwest artist, Debra Faast. Also, I owe much gratitude to my stalwart critique team who read my early manuscripts several times and offered many helpful comments—Ann-Marie Bruhn, who suggested the idea of a female villain; Larry Rogers; dear friend and librarian Jody Westerman; Peter Leonard, also a librarian; my sister Karen Engel, an avid reader of mysteries; and the person who puts up with me retreating to my office to write, and traveling with a computer, my companion and wife, Joy.

"And only the enlightened can recall their former lives; for the rest of us, the memories of past existences are but glints of light, twinges of longing, passing shadows, disturbingly familiar, that are gone before they can be grasped..."

Peter Matthiessen
The Snow Leopard

PROLOGUE

Destruction Island off the Washington Coast;
August 16, 1888

The sailing vessel *Cassandra Adams* was thirteen days out of San Francisco, bound for Tacoma in the Puget Sound, as First Officer Michael Bauman was completing his watch. He strode back and forth near the huge wheel manned by two sailors who, like himself, were enduring the early-morning chill of what looked to be another gray, unwelcome day. He raised his ever-alert eyes to the ship's sails taut in the brisk breeze and then gazed forward along the broad deck past the canvas-covered hatches to the bow, where another sailor stood watch.

Bauman had proudly served on the *Cassandra Adams* under her first master, Captain Gatter, for five of the ship's eleven years since being launched. With three masts, the *Cassandra Adams* was the fastest ship on the West Coast. However, on this particular trip to San Francisco, she had not lived up to her reputation. The ship had a new owner, the Tacoma Mill Company, which had hired a new master, Captain F. F. Knacke. The mill superintendent was pleased to have the 197-footer available as a lumber carrier for the California market and had insisted that Captain Knacke add extra lumber to her decks at the sacrifice of some of her speed. Their return trip had been slower as well because they were heavily laden with new mill machinery. Under full sail, the ship responded sluggishly to course changes, but, fortunately, they were able to maintain safe passage northward by remaining three to four miles off the Northwest's treacherous coastline.

Bauman had been concentrating on a broad bank of fog a mile distant on their current heading when the captain himself came on deck to relieve him at eight bells.

"Captain Knacke, sir, the ship is making seven knots and our course is north by northwest, 335 degrees," the officer reported as the captain buttoned his great coat tightly under his bearded chin.

"According to the logbook entry, sir, we should be about fifty nautical miles north of Grays Harbor and just south of Destruction Island. So we should reach Cape

Flattery and the Strait of Juan de Fuca in another eight hours."

"Only seven knots?" the captain asked with a frown. He thrust his hands deep into the pockets of the heavy coat. "This ship is supposed to be the fastest in these waters."

"Sir, if I might comment, we laid on a considerable amount of heavy equipment, and there is a strong southerly current this time of year. We could sail further offshore and avoid the current, but your standing orders were to maintain the shortest course possible."

"Yes, I did so order. I guess we'll have to tolerate it for another eight hours. Where will that put us for the prevailing tides once we enter Puget Sound?"

Before he responded, the first officer glanced to port and starboard and grew increasingly concerned with the fog that was settling around them. Despite his concern, he said, "Should still be good, sir. While we are more than a day behind schedule, we should have an incoming tide as we round New Dungeness."

Captain Knacke grunted and watched two sailors make their way toward them. He acknowledged their arrival with a slight nod as they assumed their stations at the ship's wheel. The two men who they had relieved trotted amidships and scampered down a hatch to the first deck, where mugs of hot coffee and a chance to get warm by the cook's stove awaited them.

"Anything else to report?" the captain asked, his face still baring a frown.

"Yes, sir! I was about to make a course change ten degrees west. Destruction Island lies ahead of us, and with this fog bank we are approaching, I thought it would be prudent to hold well off. There is a new lighthouse under construction on the island, but..."

"Yes, I know," interrupted Knacke. "That silly Congress in Washington can't seem to come up with enough money to get a new lighthouse built. Then that blasted Lighthouse Board hires some fly-by-night contractor who says he needs another two years to finish the project. I tell you, Mr. Bauman, the shipping industry in the Northwest has got to have a stronger voice with our elected officials."

Knacke shook off the annoyance at how slow they were traveling and lack of better navigation aids and added, "By the way, do you know why on earth this damned island came to be known as Destruction Island? Seems like an odd sort of name for a lonely spot."

"I have heard a number of stories about the island's name," answered the first officer. "I believe that the one closest to the truth is based on an incident that occurred about a hundred years ago when a British exploration ship called the *Imperial Eagle*, under command of a Captain Barkley, had its crew massacred by Indians at the mouth of a river close by. It was called Destruction River back then. There have been other engagements with hostile Indians as well, giving this island quite a tragic history."

The two men stood side by side for a few minutes, peering into the fog that was now rolling over the deck of the ship. The first officer slapped his arms in an attempt to stay warm.

"Sir?" he asked. "My watch is over. May I take my leave now?"

"You are relieved and I'm certain you're headed for the galley, right? Then have the cook send up my coffee."

"Yes, will do, sir," answered the first officer as he hurried forward.

The fog was now condensing on the sails and drops of moisture were spattering the deck. As he started down the ladder, First Officer Bauman took one last look toward the bow. The fog had become so thick that he could no longer see the sailor who stood there on watch. Whether Captain Knacke forgot about Bauman's proposed course change or disregarded it, the *Cassandra Adams* was about to become another chapter in the tragic history of Pacific Northwest shipping. The captain had been on his watch for about ten minutes when the bow watch fearfully shouted an alarm.

"Rocks off the bow! Breakers immediately to port! My god! We're going to…"

Bauman and the crew heard the captain frantically issue a series of ineffective commands as the two men at the helm spun the wheel hard to starboard. The *Cassandra Adams* veered to starboard, but it was too late to avoid striking the rocks. A terrible cracking sound pierced the air, and a violent shudder ran through the hull, throwing the two steersmen to the deck. The ship's keel had struck the reef at the southerly tip of Destruction Island. The wooden hull uttered a dying groan as thirty feet of the port side was ripped open. In the galley, Bauman and other men were tossed about the room like rag dolls. The cook was struck and burned by his stove as it ripped free from a bulkhead and flew forward. The bow watchman miraculously avoided being thrown overboard but suffered several broken ribs when he collided into the port rail. Captain Knacke had grabbed one of the safety lines along the starboard rail and somehow kept his footing. The rudder of the *Cassandra Adams* was ripped clean off its mountings as the doomed ship slid along the reef. Having lost steerage and listing rapidly, the vessel hove to, her massive sails and lines flapping wildly. The ocean's swells began to lift her off the reef and pull the *Cassandra Adams* toward her grave in the cold depths of the Pacific. Captain Knacke gave his final order to abandon ship, and, minutes later, sixteen men in two long boats were struggling to reach the lee side of Destruction Island, just a short distance away from where the foundation of the new lighthouse was being laid.

CHAPTER 1

Norika Edo paced back and forth next to one of the huge picture windows of her apartment that offered a panoramic view of the Roppongi District of Tokyo. She spoke loudly into a satellite phone and then tossed it onto a couch as she stopped pacing and stared for a long time at the carefully manicured gardens five floors below her. The fifth floor of the Izumi Villa Tower was entirely leased by the Edosan Corporation, an international import company dealing principally in precious stones and gold. There were actually very few employees, as most of their buying and selling was arranged by telephone and computer. Norika Edo was tall for a Japanese woman, in her early forties and still possessing the exquisite features of a woman in her twenties. Due to the sudden death of her husband she had recently become the sole owner of the company. The fifth floor of the tower served both as the corporate offices and her residence. The phone call she had just received did little to alleviate her frustration, a feeling that she unrelentingly passed on to all of her employees and others in her hire.

Norika was making very little progress in resolving a problem that had consumed her every waking moment of the last four months—from the day that the island of Honshu had experienced a major earthquake. The fact that nearly 20,000 people had died, 400,000 people had been left homeless, and a nuclear power plant had leaked radioactivity and caused a meltdown did not bother her. Her concern was for a very small, unmanned watercraft—an escape pod that had been lashed to the aft deck of a freighter that just happened to be anchored in the Miyako Harbor at the time of the quake. The *Kanji Maru* had turned on her port side and had been pushed under a bridge by the receding tsunami wave, drowning most of the crew as the boat sunk just outside the bay. One of the survivors reported that her husband made it into the ship's lifeboat which may have remained attached to the ship.

When Norika heard about the tragedy, she immediately ordered a salvage crew to find the sunken vessel and to retrieve her husband's body and a certain item of cargo, only to learn that they were missing and presumably had become part of the massive raft of floating debris consisting of houses, docks, vessels, vehicles, toxic chemicals, personal possessions, and, of course, thousands of corpses.

For weeks after the tsunami, Norika dispatched search team after search team to find the small escape pod from the vessel amongst the debris that continued to drift eastward across the Pacific. Other teams searched inland in the event that scavengers had already salvaged the pod and secreted it away for later resale. Each day the reports were the same—the pod had not been found. She kept the real reason for the search a secret, leaving Edosan employees and the search teams mystified as to why she wanted so desperately to find the boat, knowing that her husband was most likely dead. Only she and one of her most trusted employees, who had just made a report to her, knew that the little pod contained one hundred million dollars in bearer bonds from an offshore bank in the Marshall Islands and another one hundred and fifty million dollars' worth of diamonds that belonged to her now-dead husband and his business associates. What the rest of her employees did know was that their boss, like her dead husband, was a Yakuza—a crime lord—and they dare not fail in their search.

Her personal cell phone rang again. Norika retrieved it and looked at the number on the display. It blinked "Unknown Caller." Her tone was terse as she took the call. "This is a private number. Who's calling?" she demanded.

"Now, Norika that is no way to greet a longtime associate of your husband."

"Yuri Matasuba! Even if you had called through my personal secretary, I have no reason to offer any pleasantries to you. And in case you are thinking of hanging up quickly, watch your ass. You may get stuck with a needle filled with puffer-fish toxin."

"Oh, a most unpleasant lady making such violent threats," Yuri replied with a voice that was even icier than her own. "So I am pleased to respond in kind. Your dead husband was involved in a certain business transaction with myself and another associate whose identity I cannot reveal. It involves a large sum of bearer bonds and diamonds that now seem to have disappeared from our account in the Marshalls. My source informed me that your husband was the person who withdrew, shall we say, these joint assets. He covered his tracks well, but not well enough! Before he most unfortunately died, the young clerk who assisted your husband told us everything. We would like to receive our share—with interest, of course. You have ten days to make arrangements for the transfer. You will be contacted as to the details. Have a most pleasant day, Norika."

Norika Edo was both furious and frightened as she threw the phone across the room. She turned to the window facing the east side of the city and beyond. Somewhere out on the Pacific was the escape pod with her husband, the bonds and diamonds. It had to be there, and she had an impossible ten days to find it.

CHAPTER 2

It was the first day of summer and the tenth day without rain—the beginning of a summer that raised the spirits of everyone along the otherwise rain-soaked coast of the Pacific Northwest. The mountains of the Olympic Peninsula were the home of snowfields and hundreds of glaciers. In its rain forests, giant trees filled the valleys of the Sol Duc, Hoh and Quinault Rivers. Its small towns, such as Forks and Queets, were often cited as the wettest places in the United States. Snow-fed streams in the rain forests ran clear and fast and were considered sources of some of the best salmon and steelhead fishing in the world.

On a remote island four miles off the coast, the environment was radically different. This rugged island, not much more than a half mile long and a quarter mile wide, was sparsely covered with grass, scrub brush and wind-shaped cedar trees that struggled to survive in a storm-swept world. It was officially named Destruction

Island, although historically it had also been known as the Isle of Sorrow because of its tragic history. Both were apt names for such a forbidding place.

On this marvelous summer day, a lone man sat hunched over the tiller of a small skiff as he approached the island from the mainland. Steering his skiff toward the rocky shoreline, he smiled as the island's cliffs burst through an opening in the drifting fog like the opening scene of an epic film. There it was, with its windswept grassy-green slopes and rugged rock cliffs shining brightly in the early morning sun with a deep blue, summer sky above.

Will Pence had a confident look about him. He had just crossed four miles of ocean in a sixteen-foot aluminum skiff, using nothing but dead reckoning. He reduced the throttle on his old Honda outboard to let the bow of the skiff level out so he could scan the south end of the island. He was seeking one of the narrow channels that led to a small cove with a driftwood-covered beach. The air overhead was filled with seabirds—gulls, boobies, puffins and auklets. By the hundreds, they rose into the endless sky from the low cliffs, circling and swooping in every direction. Others flew fast and low over the water, quickly landing on the guano-covered rocks and grassy slopes above him, their attention fixed on feeding their young. It was a raucous scene, one that Will Pence had witnessed many times as a young Indian boy growing up on a coastal reservation and later as a commercial fisherman.

The majestic white tower of the old lighthouse rose above the island's crest off to his left. It had proudly withstood the ravages of the violent coastal weather for over 120 years but now stood abandoned, its purpose rendered obsolete when an automated light was installed. Near the base of the lighthouse, and obscured from Will's view by the cliffs, was a cluster of building foundations that had once served as warehouses, workshops, and accommodations for the keepers and their families. Will's grandmother had told him stories about Christian Zauner, the first keeper, and his wife, who had befriended the Hoh and Quileute people. On cold and rainy days, Mrs. Zauner would welcome them into her kitchen and offer them freshly baked cookies and mugs of hot chocolate. Will Pence smiled as he remembered these stories. His grandmother and her sisters must have enjoyed their trips to the island and its many wonders.

When the ocean conditions were suitable, Will made this crossing in an open boat just as past generations of his family had done in seagoing canoes from the Indian village of La Push, located at the mouth of the Quileute River. Will's mother and his two aunties had brought him and his brother Leon to this lonely island as young boys to collect eggs from the thousands of seabirds that nested on its shores, but now the women were too old to make the trip to the island and climb the cliffs. They relied upon Will or Leon to gather the eggs several times a year for special feasts.

Time had changed how local Indians could use the island as well. In the old days, the whole island provided a wide variety of traditional food, from chitons and mussels to seabird eggs to berries. Now the island was administered by the Fish and Wildlife Service as part of a marine reserve, and entry was restricted.

Will recalled climbing the long flight of steps up from the old boathouse to the lighthouse complex high on the south cliff, where the principal keeper and his assistants had lived. After the lighthouse was abandoned, the boathouse and stairway gradually deteriorated, damaged by storms off the Pacific, and never repaired. Many of the original buildings, including part of the keeper's quarters and other buildings constructed on the island during World War II, were not built of stone or concrete like the lighthouse itself and were long gone, with only a few foundations remaining. There was an old helipad not far from the building complex that was still used periodically by federal employees conducting surveys and inspections.

A young male sea lion emerged from the kelp beds close to Will's skiff, barking and splashing as he rolled and then slipped once more below the surface. His actions brought Will's attention back to his need to watch for submerged rocks guarding the narrow entrance to the cove he sought. He slowed the old outboard motor to near idle and deftly slid the skiff first left then right, following a channel between the rocks up to a small pebble beach. He revved the motor to increase the skiff's forward momentum, and then he hit the kill switch and raised the motor as the bow slid up onto the shore. He grabbed the painter, a line he had attached to the bow, and played it out as he stepped onto the beach and walked up to one of the closest logs just above the tide line. He secured the line and then dragged the boat as far up on the shore as he could so that the incoming tide would not push it against the logs or rocks farther along the beach.

Once he felt that everything was secure, Will grabbed an old khaki knapsack for collecting the eggs, slipped it onto his back, picked up a small ice chest, and walked to the foot of the cliffs. He shielded his eyes as he scanned the slopes that rose nearly a hundred feet above the beach. Most of the seabirds were in flight and avoiding their nesting sites as though alarmed by some hidden predator. As Will climbed over the last few logs, two black furry animals bounded away and disappeared into a small, dark burrow. They were part of a rabbit population on the island that now numbered in the thousands and were descendants of domestic rabbits turned loose by the last lighthouse families when they departed the island in the fifties.

Will tucked his ice chest under a large log. He avoided the old wooden stairway off to his left and instead climbed quickly up the steep slope. Near the top, he had to grab tufts of guano-covered grass to keep from slipping back down. Next to one of the larger tufts was an opening to an auklet burrow. He reached inside and found several deep chambers and two small nests, each containing two eggs. Not wanting to disrupt the adult auklets in their chick-raising, he left two of the eggs and removed the other two, dropping them into a deep pocket of his knapsack. He expected to make several trips back down the cliff to transfer eggs to the cooler before returning to the mainland.

Will resumed his climbing; his laboring breaths becoming more rapid as he struggled to reach the broad plateau that stretched across the island to an abrupt rock cliff on the westward side. The auklet burrows were concentrated mostly on the flatter ground above him. Will paused for a moment to glance back at the beach. His skiff was there, safely pulled well away from the water. A flash of color drew his attention to the beach in the second cove. Another boat, larger than his, was moored in the center, tied off to several rocks to keep it in the deeper water. Will looked up and down the shoreline but saw no one. He studied the boat for a minute. It was not familiar to him. Whoever the boat belonged to must have climbed to the top and perhaps was exploring the old lighthouse grounds. He frowned, shook his head as if puzzled, and resumed his climb.

Lifting his head to peer over the top of the slope, he caught sight of two men several hundred feet from him who were busy digging with long-handled shovels. Will was shocked in disbelief as he stood upright and walked toward them.

"What the hell is going on here?" Will shouted at them. "This is a damn marine reserve. You idiots shouldn't be disturbing this ground!"

The two men, who had their backs to the cliff, turned quickly at the sound of his voice, as if the approaching figure had fired a gun. One of them stumbled backward and dropped his shovel and then retrieved it after regaining his footing. The other man, the bigger of the two, eyed Will up and down and made a slow swing of his head, checking to see if there was anyone else. Neither man uttered a word in response to Will's angry outburst. After stepping around several deep holes, collapsed burrows, broken bird eggs, and a few dead chicks, Will stopped a few feet from the men.

"Who the hell are you guys? Not Fish and Wildlife, that's for damn sure."

The men just stared at him without uttering any response.

"Look at the damage you have done to these nests," Will said in disgust and he turned his head to survey the disturbed ground. Before he could say another word, the bigger man swung his shovel hard against Will's left knee. There was an audible crack. Will let out a scream as he grabbed his injured leg and crumpling onto his right knee. The second man hesitated and then, looking at his partner, raised his shovel and brought it down hard on Will's skull.

The big man looked around once more and then dropped his shovel and grabbed one of Will's wrists with both hands. His partner hurried to assist, and together they dragged Will's body back toward the cliff and shoved him over. With his arms spread out like the wings of a seabird, Will flipped over backward several times as he tumbled down the slope. He crashed into the jumble of drift logs at the base of the cliff, breaking his neck, but it didn't matter by then. Will Pence was already dead.

CHAPTER 3

As he paddled just outside a line of gentle waves breaking along the broad expanse of sand beach, Earl Armstrong scanned the nearshore waters south of Grayland State Park. He was searching for evidence of tsunami debris reaching the coast of Washington. Even with a calm sea, he kept a lookout for the ever-present sneaker wave rising in the ocean swells farther offshore. Earl was an experienced kayaker and enjoyed the special challenges of ocean kayaking as well as the relaxed solitude offered by the bays and inland sloughs.

On this early July day, the ocean was calm and presented little difficulty. In fact, in his forty years of living on the Washington coast, he could not remember an early summer period when the weather had been this fine. The warmth of the sun penetrated the front of his wet suit and inflatable life vest, creating beads of sweat on his brow. He wore a wide-brimmed hat and polarized sunglasses to protect his vision from the glare off the water surface. His arms and shoulders were well muscled from many days spent kayaking. His long, dark brown hair, which held a few greying streaks, was pulled back into a pony tail. His complexion held a perpetual tan which his mother had told him at an early age was due to his degree of Indian blood.

Earl kept up a steady rhythm to his paddling, dipping first one blade into the glassy water and then the other. The day was so gorgeous that it was hard to keep a focus on why he was there in the first place. A firm voice emitting from the small VHF radio pinned to the front of his vest reminded him.

"Armstrong! Do you see anything from out there?" said the voice on the radio.

The voice was that of Lieutenant Eddie Shaw, the head detective for the Pacific County sheriff's office and a team leader for a volunteer beach cleanup program.

Earl dropped his paddle onto the front of the cockpit and used his right hand to squeeze the push-to-talk button. "It's been clear so far," answered Earl.

Eddie Shaw could hear Earl chuckling before he let loose of the talk button and came right back with a more direct question. "I know you are having too good a time playing around out there. I meant any sign of debris, big or small?"

"Well, nothing big; that's for sure," Earl replied. "I don't think we're going to have to deal with a concrete floating dock or a boat washed up on the beach today like they've experienced down on the Oregon coast."

Eddie's voice came back on the small marine radio. "Yeah, I sure hope not. We can do without those kinds of contaminated debris problems. They can be an enormous disposal issue—one monster environmental problem."

Shaw was in his third year in a position that Leo Patterson had held for decades but had been forced to retire because of his wife's health. Both Shaw and Earl respected Patterson for his leadership style and dedication to law enforcement in a county made up of small coastal communities. Eddie Shaw was an enrolled member of the same Indian tribe as Earl, as well as being Earl's closest friend. Earl was quite confident that Eddie would someday make a great detective like Patterson had been. For one thing, he was thorough beyond a doubt in his investigations, and he was also a true friend who had saved Earl's life not once, but twice. Eddie Shaw had recently been appointed by the County Commission to be the South Coast team leader for the Miyako Project, a recently created organization formed to survey and clean up tsunami debris from the huge earthquake and resulting tidal wave that had hit the island of Honshu in early March. It was only a matter of time before a massive amount of debris came ashore somewhere along the Pacific Northwest coast.

"Hey, we're volunteers, Eddie," Earl said through his radio. "We can leave the big jobs to the professional cleanup types."

"True, true—but one of the facts they shared with those who attended the tsunami cleanup training up in Olympia was that there are supposed to be four of those docks, and they can only account for three of them."

"So there's a ghost dock out there somewhere?" Earl answered.

"Maybe; I don't need folks going ballistic due to a ghost dock or some other big chunk of hazardous tsunami debris washing up on our beaches. I've got enough real work in the sheriff's office with my homicide investigations."

"Since when have we had a murder here in Pacific County?" Earl replied. "The whole damn south coast hasn't had an interesting case in what? Fifteen years?"

"OK, OK, but I still have to investigate any death— like last week, when some guy fell off an oyster barge and drowned after getting tangled up in his own oyster strings. Drifted around out in the bay for three days."

"That had to be a pretty sight. Well, enjoy your day off to play in the sand, Eddie," replied Earl. "It's a pretty doggone nice day out here, so I'm going to try to make it all the way to the point before coming into the beach. Might take me another hour, I guess."

Earl shielded his eyes and scanned the beach. "I can just make out you and your team up near the drift logs. Have those transects you laid out turned up any tsunami debris?"

"Not that we can positively identify," answered Eddie. "Nothing with Japanese letters on them, if that's what you mean."

"No radioactive stuff?" Earl asked.

"We're testing a few things with a Geiger counter, but I'm not expecting any positives. Nobody along the coast has found any radioactive debris resulting from the reactor meltdown yet. But it's only a matter of time before our beaches get hit."

"With 1.5 million tons of debris coming our way, it's going to be a god-awful mess."

"Yup. By the way, Earl, I appreciate you being out there and volunteering for the Miyako Project. Our little team here on the South Coast is only a small part of an army of cleanup volunteers that is going to be needed when we get socked with all that debris."

"Glad I can help. Actually, it's a great excuse to get out on the water. I can see a lot more from a kayak than you can from the beach or aboard a larger boat that has to stay farther out. If I can get another day off from my forestry work, I'll cruise along some of the shore at the Willapa Bay bar and inside the mouth of the bay itself."

"That would be great. We need lots of people watching. Those Coast Guard H-65 helicopters can't be everywhere. I hear they're making daily trips out of Astoria to see how close the stuff is getting."

"Yeah, makes me sick to think about when it gets here. Hey, maybe you can mention it to some of the tribal fishermen," Shaw commented. "They could help report any sightings, too."

"I'll do what I can. Maybe the tribe would be interested in forming its own Miyako Project team of volunteers. They have about a mile of beach on the reservation. Do you have some PR materials?"

"Can do," replied Shaw.

"Great! I can get them to the person who puts out the tribal newsletter, plus leave some copies in the tribal library."

"See you on the beach," said Shaw. "I'll be monitoring channel 10 if you need assistance or have something to report."

Earl picked up his paddle and began propelling himself forward once more. The predicted offshore breeze had not increased, and Earl was able to remain close to the surf line. It was rare when he could paddle this close to the beach. He wished that his wife, Sally, could be enjoying it with him, but she preferred the flat water of the bay—and, besides, she had received a call from the hospital, asking her to come in and handle a couple of difficult patients, just before he had left home.

He and Sally had been married for fifteen years; after finishing her postdoctoral work at the University of Washington, she had been fortunate to get the job of chief psychiatrist with the local hospital in South Bend. She could have made a lot more money working in the Seattle area, but the couple was reasonably content with life on the coast, away from the urban bustle and the traffic congestion in the I-5 corridor. Sally sometimes mentioned how she missed the activity of the university hospital scene and the invigoration of doing research. The saving grace was that, even in a small town, Sally had a professionally challenging job, was able to go back to work after having two children, and didn't have a time-consuming commute. She was able to devote a lot of time to raising their kids.

Their daughter, Christine, was now twelve years old and already a charmer. Two years behind her was little brother Bernie. Bernie already liked the outdoors and loved to fish, and Earl looked forward to teaching him to kayak. Earl smiled as he pictured Bernie holding up his first trout for Sally to photograph last summer when they were picnicking on the Palix River.

Earl had nothing to complain about. He had held his job as a forester with the Shoalwater Bay Tribe for seventeen years now. He got to spend a lot of time outdoors, appraising timber, managing reforestation work, and being responsible for the tribe's wildlife management program.

Earl corrected his course to stay close to the beach. He was still a little more than a mile from Washaway Beach. Tokeland Point, which marked the entrance to Willapa Bay, his favorite kayaking spot, was maybe another three miles farther. The bay had been once known as Shoalwater Bay, and many of his ancestors had grown up around it. True to its name, the bay was shallow, with a large tidal exchange, but the tidelands were ideal for oyster growing and harvesting, an important local industry. There were also tens of square miles of marshes to explore, including the Willapa Bay National Wildlife Refuge. If the tide flats and refuge were to become covered in plastics and other debris from Japan, it could be likened to an oil spill and require a great deal of human effort to clean up.

Earl's double-ended paddle dipped and lifted alternately in a steady rhythm—left, then right. The paddle blades made almost no sound as they dipped and cleared the surface of the water. After another thirty minutes of gliding just outside the breaking waves, Earl noticed a large bundle of kelp surrounded by white foam up ahead of him. There was something about the bundle that didn't look natural.

Looks like a piece of sailcloth or a fisherman's jacket. Earl was maybe fifty yards from the object when a bad feeling swept over him, instantly darkening his mood. As he got closer, he dug in his paddle and veered off to one side of the kelp patch. Earl hit the talk button on his radio.

"Shaw? This is Armstrong." Earl spoke into the small mike and then waited for Shaw to grab his own radio.

"This is Shaw. What's up?"

"You better break off whatever you are doing and get down the beach to my location. Put on your other hat. I just found a body in the surf zone."

CHAPTER 4

Juno Betar had chosen to build his mansion in the gated community of Glen Estates in West Bellevue not because it was very, very exclusive, but because of the privacy he required and its added security. Glen Estates was located on a peninsula on the shore of Lake Washington and consisted of only fifteen homes. The only street entrance had a guard on duty twenty-four hours a day, and another guard patrolled the shoreline by boat. Juno Betar's mansion was the largest of the homes at 17,000 square feet, with over 1,000 feet of waterfront, and was one of the most expensive homes ever built in West Bellevue.

The national tabloids had run a few articles showing an aerial photo of the mansion and mentioning Betar's secretive lifestyle, but they revealed very little factual information about the man himself or his many businesses. He was the only son of Lebanese emigrants who had operated a small grocery store in north Seattle. He had received a degree with honors in electrical engineering at the University of Washington when he was only eighteen. Immediately after graduation, he had moved to Europe to start a telecommunications company when cellular-phone systems were in their infancy. Within ten years, he owned cellular companies operating in eight European countries, was the majority owner of a fleet of Panamax oil tankers, and had built a large resort/casino on the coast of Lebanon, north of Beirut. At forty-five years old, Betar could be one of the youngest men on the world's list of top billionaires. That is, if he bothered to disclose his wealth, something that had never crossed his mind.

A select group of people knew Juno Betar for another reason: he was a private collector of antiquities. Collecting was a passion of his—whether it was expensive cars, early Egyptian sculptures, or Islamic jeweled art objects. But his greatest obsession was masks from ancient and primitive cultures. His West Bellevue mansion had a basement vault of more than 3,000 square feet in size to house his extensive collections, including dozens of masks that were considered rare and highly sought after by museums.

While Juno would sometimes make personal appearances at art auctions in New York, London, or Istanbul, most of his purchases were conducted anony-mously through emissaries or representatives in the art world. He maintained a network of informants who investigated items in which Juno might be interested. Such was the young man who had visited him a month ago and was again waiting in his sitting room just off the main foyer. The man was Halid Merzat, one of many nephews of the wealthy owner of a Turkish auction house that Juno frequently used for purchases. Juno had a complete dossier on the young man, who was studying primitive cultures at the University of Washington and supported his social extravagances of enjoying the company of young American women by doing research and selling information to wealthy collectors. Juno was pleased that Halid never asked what he did with the information or how he acquired his art. Halid probably was not even aware of the outcome of one of his earlier transactions with Juno, which had turned out to be extremely useful. The young man had informed him of the whereabouts of a collection of Kwakiutl ceremonial masks in a small native village in northern British Columbia. Not more than a month later, the collection had been stolen.

Halid Merzat fidgeted in his chair in the foyer, crossing and re-crossing his legs and tapping his laptop case with his fingers. He tried to calm his nerves by studying the beautiful furnishings around the room. It reminded him of an art gallery. This was his third visit with Mr. Betar. Halid's uncle in Istanbul had informed Halid that such a man could be an important client, willing to buy good information regarding obscure antiquities at an excellent price. Juno had paid well for the information on Halid's first visit. His second visit resulted in only a small retainer and a request to verify what was secondhand information.

The opening of the main entry to the mansion startled Halid. His jaw dropped when he saw the figure in the doorway. A young woman, her arms loaded with shopping bags, closed the front door. As she crossed the room, the clicking of her high heels matched Halid's heightened heart rate. She glanced at him without saying a word, gave him a sexy smile, and proceeded up a spiral staircase to the second floor. He could not take his eyes off of this dark-skinned beauty with long legs and swaying hips. When she disappeared at the top of the stairs, he remembered to breathe again.

"Yes, she is quite a sight, isn't she?" Juno Betar commented from where he stood in the open door to his study. "She is one of my most prized possessions."

Halid's face flushed bright red with embarrassment as he jumped to his feet to offer his apology. "I...I am deeply sorry, sir. I could not help it. She is so beautiful. You are a very lucky man, Mr. Betar."

"Luck had nothing to do with it, Mr. Merzat," replied Juno. "She likes to spend money, and I have more than I require. Some men would say that she is a trophy wife. I cannot dispute that. Let them say what they want as they wallow like pigs in their jealousy."

"I am not jealous, Mr. Betar. No. Someday I will be like you. I will have my own."

"Maybe. Insha'Allah! God willing," replied Juno. "Let's go into my study."

Juno beckoned Halid to follow him. "You have confirmed the information from our previous meeting?"

"I have," Halid said as he followed Juno into the study and stopped to stare in awe at its furnishings. There was a beautiful Renoir painting on a wall opposite a row of windows that looked out onto the grounds of the estate and the lake beyond. The other walls were lined floor to ceiling with bookcases filled with antique leather-bound volumes interspersed with fine glass perfume bottles and Islamic brass pieces heavily decorated with glittering jewels.

"Like Samara, my wife, they are beautiful, too. Are they not?" Juno commented, waving an arm in the direction of the shelves. "Many of these objects were purchased through your uncle's auction house. Now, please take a seat and let me hear your story. If I like it, you will be rewarded accordingly. If I have no interest, then you will have enjoyed your brief visit to my humble home and will go away with some memories and nothing more to satisfy your own passions."

Halid took a seat in one of the large leather chairs that faced Juno's gigantic desk. He sat upright on the edge of the chair afraid to appear too relaxed. He took a deep breath and began at the beginning. "When we previously met, I told you about having several close friends at the university who are doing studies in the same field as I am, but their specialties are quite different. One friend, in particular, told me over many glasses of wine about his interest in the early history of the State of Washington just after it obtained statehood. My friend was raised on Puget Sound, and his father was involved in shipping lumber to Japan and other countries. He became interested in the history of the lighthouses that were important to the early shipping enterprises."

Juno's mannerisms showed signs of boredom as he interrupted Halid. "I remember you telling me all of this about your friend, including something about an island with a lighthouse that he was studying. Please get to the point: were you able to verify what he told you?"

"I...I am getting to that. My friend came across several very old journals that were kept by the men who operated the Destruction Island lighthouse. You urged that I look at these logs myself and locate the entry about discovering a strange artifact and a message contained inside it."

"Yes, the message in a bottle, but on land!" Juno exclaimed. "That bottle and its message are what interest me. Did you read about the message as I requested?"

"Oh, yes. That is what is *most* interesting," Halid stated as he began again. "The message, written in Spanish, was signed by a Lieutenant Juan Francisco de la Bodega y Quadra in 1775. His ship was the *Sonora*, and he was exploring the northwestern coast of the Americas. The message was an account of what happened when he put a crew ashore to find fresh water and they were attacked by savages. All but one man were slaughtered. The lone survivor told his captain how fierce the natives on the island were and about them possessing a *mascara del oro*, a..."

"...a golden mask. Yes, you mentioned this mask at our last meeting," Juno added as he leaned forward and stared intently at Halid. "Did this Lieutenant Francisco de la Bodega, or whatever his name was, try to find the mask? What else did the lighthouse keeper write down in his journal? What did he do with the damn bottle? Having found it, what was done with it? Did he search for the mask? These are the things that might be useful to know."

"I'm sorry, sir, but the museum staff person was suspicious of my intentions," answered Halid, lowering in eyes. "I was only able to confirm what I was told by my friend, which I just reported... And t...there was nothing more said in the document about anyone searching for the mask. However, the entry was quite clear about the bottle. It was found in a garden, and that was where it was reburied."

"Well, maybe that is the good news," said Juno, rubbing his chin. "There is a chance that the bottle, and therefore the mask, still exist, but it appears there will have to be additional research to confirm this one way or another. Perhaps some family letters mention this incident." Juno was silent for a minute and Halid waited with expectation as to what the man was going to decide.

"And where, may I ask, are these journals? Juno finally asked.

"The keeper's logs for the Destruction Island Lighthouse are part of a collection at a maritime museum in the town of Westport," replied Halid with a smile. "My friend told me that the lighthouse is no longer active and is abandoned. This museum has many artifacts and materials from it. You might learn more there."

"Well, that is a starting point. We will see where it leads—hopefully to learning more about this golden mask, right?"

Juno relaxed and turned to stare at the gathering clouds on the horizon above the lake, avoiding letting the young man see the gleam in his eyes.

Halid sighed in relief, and his smile broadened, erasing his earlier disappointment. He now knew that he would soon be rewarded, possibly very handsomely, for this information.

Juno smiled too, as he escorted Halid to the door, assuring him several times that he would indeed be offered a nice sum for the information. As he watched Halid drive away, his expression agreeable no longer. The gleam in his eyes darkened, like a thick cloud passing in front of the sun. His lips were tight and his jaw moved to one side. Juno had already initiated a plan to find the golden mask but the first attempt had failed miserably. It did not matter. The mask would soon be his—the culmination of all of his years of collecting.

Juno took out his cell phone and hit a speed-dial number. A hard, husky voice answered on the second ring: "Dixon."

"Get me some pictures of the island. When you get back, call me and we will meet at Chaser's," Juno replied and hung up.

*

An hour after Earl had called Eddie Shaw about finding the body of a man in the surf, the stretch of beach at North Cove became a center of activity. The SAR truck from the fire department in South Bend had driven down the hard sand beach from one of the access roads and was now parked where Earl had come ashore in his kayak. Several beach access points had been closed off and were manned by deputy patrol cars to keep gawkers away.

From a secluded spot along the highway, two men with binoculars watched the activities from a distance as Eddie Shaw, now without his Miyako volunteers, directed the search and rescue operation. The two men were Asian and oddly dressed—wearing suits with new black rubber boots caked in mud. Their curiosity held them even though they were anxious to move on, as the county rescue crew waded out to the object in the surf, placed it on an aluminum basket stretcher, and then started back towards the beach. Eddie's four-wheel drive pickup was parked next the truck with Earl's kayak now lashed to a rack over its bed. The observers watched as the two men who remained by the trucks gesturing and presumably talking about what had been discovered in the offshore water. They were as puzzled over the discovery as were the two men by the truck. The observers knew everything about Eddie Shaw and Earl Armstrong, where they lived and worked, and all about the efforts of the Miyako Project. This new development with the Miyako Project needed reporting to their employer so they retreated to their rental sedan and drove back to the main highway and from there, headed north towards Aberdeen.

Eddie Shaw was leaning against the side of his county vehicle talking to the coroner's office in South Bend. One of the patrol officers was ordered to look for fresh auto tracks on the nearby beach. It was popular to drive on the sand beach near Grayland but vehicles were not allowed beyond North Cove. He slipped his cell phone back into a shirt pocket and turned his attention to Earl.

"You do have a knack for finding bodies under interesting circumstances, Armstrong. I still remember the one you found some years back that we pulled out from under a pile of logs over in Raymond."

"I've tried to forget that one," replied Earl. "I nearly got killed myself in connection with that murder. And I still owe you for rescuing me from a watery grave, not once, but twice."

Earl struggled to take off the wet suit that he wore when ocean kayaking. He placed it along with his life jacket in the bed of the Eddie's pickup and then pulled on a hooded sweatshirt with a large red 'B' on the back. The two men walked down the beach towards the water anxious to take a closer look at the body being brought in. As they met the SAR crew, Eddie asked to them to pause for a minute. A backpack was dangling off one side of the stretcher.

"Hmm, male maybe 200 pounds and just under six feet; facial features pretty messed up from being in the water and exposed to seabirds. But by the hair and complexion, I'd say the person is a Native American."

He took a vinyl glove from a pocket put it on and patted the body until he felt a wallet in a pocket. The backpack slipped some more and twisted as Eddie pulled out the wallet causing some blue particles to drop onto the beach below the stretcher.

"When we put the body in the basket, the head rolled around." One of the rescue team stated. "His neck appears to be broken."

"I called Gupta. He should be here shortly," said Shaw. "He might be able to tell us if that was the case but the actual cause of death will have to wait until the autopsy. Might as well take the body on up to the truck, guys."

As the crew continued up towards their truck, Eddie checked the wallet for an ID or driver's license. Earl stood back watching. To him, the man on the stretcher had appeared to be Indian but most of the pigment in the hands and face was bleached out from being in seawater. The facial features were badly ravaged by predation from birds. The man had black hair made into a single long braid. Earl guessed that the person might have been in his forties or fifties.

"Damn, this is getting interesting by the second." Shaw exclaimed. "Got a driver's license here belonging to a William Pence with an address in La Push. Back at the office we have an MPR on him that says his vehicle and boat trailer were found parked at the mouth of the Hoh River and his boat had washed up on a beach near Moclips. That's over one hundred miles north of here."

"What's an MPR?" asked Earl.

"That's a missing persons report. It did mention that Pence could have drowned since the boat had been found. There are no reported witnesses however."

"The currents could explain what happened." Earl commented. "In the fall and winter, the currents along the coast of Oregon and Washington flow north. In the spring and summer they flow southward."

"That could explain it alright." Shaw added. "But it's surprising that the body hadn't washed ashore before here." Shaw started to follow the rescue crew back to the truck.

Earl began to consider the possibilities. "Maybe he was on another boat and had some trouble or slipped getting off his own boat. I never heard of anyone breaking their neck getting out of a skiff unless it was a fall onto a rock or a dock or something."

The fact that the man had not been wearing a life jacket but was wearing a backpack struck Earl as odd. *If he had been in a boat wouldn't the backpack have been just lying in the boat?* He was about to join Shaw when he remembered the blue stuff that fell out of the knapsack. He looked at the spot where the men had stopped and saw several pieces visible on the sand. Picking them up, he realized that they were eggshell, pale blue in color. *Seabird eggshell?* Earl thought as he pocketed the eggshell pieces in his sweatshirt and trotted after Shaw. Another vehicle had joined their little gathering. It was Ajit Gupta, the part time county coroner.

CHAPTER 5

The summer tourist traffic was heavy on the coastal highway, which also served as the main street of Forks, Washington. The small town of less than 4,000 residents was full of wannabe *Twilight*ers; family sedans and SUVs crawled through the town while teenage girls peered at every building. Shiny silver Airstream trailers pulled by pickups tried to avoid being run off the road by fully loaded log trucks. The prediction that Pacific Northwest beaches would be covered in toxic waste and tsunami debris did not deter the desire of the tourist to visit vampire territory.

From a small table next to the front windows of the Salmon Berry Café, Leon Pence stirred three packets of sugar into a cup of black coffee and waited for his grilled cheese sandwich to arrive. His hand shook as he continuously stirred his coffee. Minus the six years serving as a marine, Leon had lived all his life in La Push, located at the mouth of the Quileute River, just fifteen miles west of where he sat. While he considered it silly that the town of Forks had become a favorite tourist spot for young girls because of that vampire movie, there was a time as a young boy when he believed in such myths. His grandmother used to tell him and his twin brother Will about the Q'waeti, a mysterious and powerful medicine man who roamed the Olympic forests, changing animals into people. According to his grandmother, some of the Quileute people were actually wolves turned into humans as well. Leon smiled as he remembered how scared his brother Will had been after hearing those stories.

He looked at his watch and then back out at the traffic on the highway. *Where is he? Damn Indian should have been here by now.* Oscar Persson was supposed to meet him at the café during his off-duty break. Oscar was a patrolman for the Quileute Tribal Police and worked out of the tribe's center at La Push. One way or another, Leon wanted more information on his missing brother, and nobody was saying anything. The newspaper reports were vague and, after reporting that Will was presumed dead, there hadn't been a report in over a week.

Leon knew about Will's boat being found down on the Quinault reservation near Moclips, but it had been impounded for some damn reason and he couldn't even go get it. His mother and aunties were worried sick and blaming themselves for asking Will to make another trip out to Destruction Island. *Why hasn't anyone gone out to the island? Oscar, you better tell me something.* Oscar Persson was known to be a talker, and Leon intended to draw him out.

He glanced out the window again and saw that a black-and-white pickup truck with a light bar on top and the logo of the Quileute Indian Nation stenciled on the door had pulled into a parking spot on the curb. Officer Persson hefted his bulk out of the driver's seat, slammed the door, and headed for the café. He saw Leon and nodded as he passed the window.

"Mornin', Leon," said Oscar, as he took off his hat and sat down heavily, putting his thickset arms on the edge of the table. Leon's cup rattled, and some coffee spilled onto the saucer. "Sorry to keep you waitin'. Dispatch asked me to check a few housing areas for a missing bike. Belongs to the chairman's son. I told dispatch he probably left it on the beach, but he told me to go look anyway. How you been? I hear you quit your job at the fish plant."

"Not so good, Oscar. Figured I'd take some time to take care of things for my brother, our mother, and her sisters."

"Damn shame about your brother. He was a good man. Respected by the tribal elders and a real decent guy."

"Sure, sure. Then why can't I get nobody to tell me nothin' more than I read in the newspapers? Like it's an investigation or something. He's my brother, for Christ's sake! And our mother has been fretting about him for two weeks now, ever since he didn't come back from the island. Didn't anyone bother to go out there and check? I've been a good citizen and waited patiently for the law to do its job—to find my brother."

Oscar's head rolled from side to side as he leaned back and settled into his chair. He looked like he was trying to put a little more distance between him and Leon. "Geez, I don't know if I'm the one to tell you this, Leon, but they found Will this morning."

"What?" Leon straightened up. "Where? What do you mean you're not the one to tell me? He's dead, isn't he?"

"Well, I…I thought you might have heard already. His body was found washed up on the beach down near the entrance to Willapa. The county sheriff's office down there called the tribal office maybe two hours ago."

"Willapa Bay? Why shit—that's over a hundred miles down the coast. He was supposed to be going out to Destruction Island. How the heck did he end up way down there?" Leon dropped his head to the table, covering it with his arms. "Ah, Will, what happened to you? Did you do something stupid?"

"Wh-what was that you said, Leon?"

Leon raised his head and looked at Oscar. There was anger in his eyes.

"Something's not right here. Will knew how to take care of himself out there better than anybody. Spent his whole life on one kind of boat or another. He has been goin' out to that island since he was a boy and was familiar with every inch of it. Besides, it was good weather." Leon hit the table hard enough with his fist that it startled Oscar and spilled the rest of his coffee. "If no one is gonna bother to check on what happened out there on the island, I'm gonna do it myself."

"Leon...listen to me," Oscar replied, his words hesitant. "I...I know you served as an MP in the marines and did two tours in Iraq. I did one myself. But this is best left to law-enforcement types. If it was an accident, they'll determine that. If...if it was somethin' else, they'll deal with that, too."

"Somethin' else? Like murder? Christ, Oscar what are you trying to tell me? That someone up and killed my brother? If I find the son of a bitch first, there sure won't be no arrest and trial."

Oscar stared at Leon for a minute, not knowing anything else to say. He finally slid his chair out and rose, hitched up his equipment belt over his large belly, and said, "Sorry to be the bearer of this news. I...I gotta get back on patrol. Is there anything I can do? You gonna break the news to your mom and aunties, or do you wanna have someone from our office do that?"

Leon was silent for a moment. He ran his hands through his hair and looked up at Oscar. "Thanks for the offer, but I guess it would be better for me to tell them. I do want to know when we can bring him home, though."

"Sure, I'll call it in, Leon," Oscar replied as he fidgeted with his equipment belt. It was clear that he was anxious to leave. "I can have the dispatcher get the information from South Bend and give you a call, OK?"

Leon turned away and stared blankly out the window before answering. "I'll go get him and hold a wake. But sooner or later, I'm goin' out to that damn island."

"We...we can't help with that, I'm afraid. That island is federal land, and the tribe don't have no jurisdiction. Maybe the feds will look into it if there is some evidence of foul play. But the department would be glad to help with Will's wake and burial. Just let us know." Oscar pulled on his police cap and raised an arm in a weak good-bye. "You take care of yourself, Leon."

*

Lieutenant Robert "Bo" Phillips chatted with his copilot as he brought the H-65 air-sea rescue helicopter down for a closer look at the mass of tsunami debris they had been monitoring for the past several weeks as it slowly drifted toward the Washington coastline. The debris mass was so large and dense that it calmed the surface of the sea for nearly thirty miles north and south of their position—about fifty miles off the coast. The debris extended out to the west as far as they could see.

"I've never seen anything like this, Dave," Lt. Phillips remarked as he tilted the helo to get a good view from his side. "It boggles the mind, the sheer size of it."

Lt. Dave Ramsey, the copilot, scanned the debris with his binoculars. "Where did all this stuff come from?"

"A port on the northern island of Japan—Miyako, as I recall," Phillips replied.

"That figures. There's one hell of a lot of steel drums in that mess. Once this debris mass gets inside the twelve-mile territorial boundary, the US of A is going to have two humongous hazards to deal with—a navigational hazard and an environmental hazard. No telling what might be in those drums. Some of them are floating pretty low in the water."

"Yeah, I heard last week that a few drums are already washed up on beaches from here to Alaska. We should be in the cleanup business. Somebody is going to make a lot of money. Then there was that concrete dock that hit Agate Beach down in Oregon; it was expensive to get rid of because of the possibility of invasive species clinging to it."

Bo brought his aircraft around and headed for the easterly edge of the mass. "Time to take our GPS readings so the district office can update their models on where all this crap is going to come ashore."

Dave reached down and grabbed a camera from under his seat. "The light is pretty good here. Can you swing right so I can snap a couple of pictures, Lieutenant?"

"Roger, coming around again."

The shadow of the H-65 glided over the mass, which was a kaleidoscope of colors—oranges, blues, reds, and yellows, mixed with browns from the algae and kelp that clung to pieces of lumber and larger objects. Dave snapped a few pictures with his digital camera.

"Looks like a few small boats made it this far. I can make out a couple of upturned hulls," commented Dave. He pointed ahead of them on his side. "See that orange one up ahead? Could be an escape pod off of a freighter or something."

Lt. Phillips peered out the cockpit's front window to where Dave was pointing. "There's writing on the side, but it's too faded to see the name of the boat it belonged to. Wonder if it has any passengers."

Dave let out a good laugh. "I don't see anyone waving at us. Then again, after four months of drifting across the Pacific, the only ones on board would be stinking corpses."

The Coast Guard helicopter swung back to the south, toward their air station near Astoria, the steady beat of its rotors echoing off the eerie seascape below it. Battered and half-covered in algae and sea growth, the escape pod of the *Kanji Maru* bobbed gently in the thick mass of debris as it drifted steadily toward the Washington coastline.

CHAPTER 6

The Pacific County medical examiner's domain in the basement of South Bend Hospital was not a place that Eddie Shaw particularly enjoyed visiting. Fortunately, there were few deaths in the county that required autopsy reports to be filed with the sheriff's office. But with his promotion, verification of all ME reports had become one of his responsibilities. About the same time that Shaw had become head detective, the county had hired a new medical examiner. He seemed to be a pretty capable fellow, but he had some quirks. Maybe it was because he was Hindu and looked at death differently.

Shaw guessed that Dr. Ajit Gupta had been out of medical school for about ten years. Prior to taking the pathologist job at South Bend Hospital, he had been employed as a morgue assistant with Harborview Medical Center in Seattle. Harborview was the King County public hospital, and its morgue performed at least ten autopsies per day, seven days a week. Many were pretty gruesome—victims of building fires or homeless people found weeks after death. One thing Shaw could say was that Dr. Gupta's work was thorough, efficient, he didn't have to cajole the man for a fast turnaround on a report.

It was Monday morning, and Shaw was thankful to find Dr. Gupta in his office. Stacks of journals, report folders, loose papers, and specimen jars were strewn about. Gupta's office organization skills seemed to directly contrast his thoroughness and accuracy in cutting up a cadaver.

"Good morning, Ajit," Shaw said as he stuck his head in the door. "Do you have the report on William Pence yet?"

"Yes, yes," replied the man, peering over his reading glasses and gesturing with his left hand toward a folder on top of his "out" basket. "Cause of death was blunt force trauma by unknown source, possibly a fall, but it could have been some type of broad object. There were multiple contusions—some pretty significant—a broken neck, a fractured right arm, and a crushed left kneecap. The latter injury was odd in that it is uncommon to a fall. There was no water in the lungs, meaning that he didn't drown. The body had been subject to immersion in cold water for some time, and to predation, so the source of the injuries is impossible to determine. I also found some pebbles in the pockets of his pants, his socks, and under the clothing. You found the corpse in a sandy beach area, so the pebbles had to have come from wherever the body was before being discovered. There were also bits of grass and traces of some kind of fertilizer underneath the fingernails of the left hand which had been bound inside his jacket sleeve—possibly bird guano. His left wrist showed bruises, which is another sign that the body may have been moved. Those facts led me to conclude that the man probably did not fall over-board unless maybe he took a serious fall before getting into a boat, which would have been pretty difficult unas-sisted with a broken neck, arm, and kneecap. As I stated a moment ago, the kneecap injury is unlikely to have been the result of a fall. I will review some journals to verify the frequency of such an injury."

Shaw flipped through the pages of detail, which were handwritten in a fine, neat script. Each page was signed and dated. "Damn, I had a hunch this would not be an ordinary drowning."

"Yes, yes, you have much work to do yourself, I think," Gupta said, simply as a matter of fact. "Plenty of work for a mortician as well. I would suggest that his coffin remain closed."

"Yeah, I took a quick look when the body was pulled out. Not much flesh left on his face. Were you able to get any fingerprints so we can confirm an identity?"

"I could not obtain any from the right hand, but the left hand must have been rolled up in part of his clothing. Therefore, I was able to obtain some fair prints. They are on the back of the report."

Shaw closed the folder and started for the door. "Well, from you what have found, it looks like I might have a potential homicide to investigate. I appreciate you working a shift on the weekend to have a report for me. Thanks, Ajit."

"Anytime, but please make the next one a simple gunshot to the heart. And make sure the body is still warm. My wife complains when I come home smelling like my morgue." Gupta adjusted his glasses and went back to reading one of his medical journals pulled from a stack on the edge of his cluttered desk.

"Glad to know I am not the only person with a dislike for the smell of this place," Shaw said with a smile. He closed the door and walked swiftly to the stairs that led to the main floor in a hurry for some fresh air.

*

Earl Armstrong arrived at his office in South Bend a little after 8:00 a.m. As usual, Sally had to leave earlier for work, so getting the kids off to their summer-school science program had become his task yet again. It was not particularly difficult, as they both loved the class. Sally had agreed to try to get away from the hospital for lunch so she and Earl would have some time to talk. All she'd had time for while they shared a cup of coffee before work was to explain that a couple of people had been admitted early Saturday morning with symptoms of paralysis and delirium. The doctor on duty in the emergency room said it looked like paralytic shellfish toxicity or maybe hallucinogenic mushroom toxicity, but he wasn't sure and was waiting on test results. Sally had been asked to monitor the cases since he was exhausted from working nearly 36 hours. While Earl did miss having more time with Sally, he was proud of the work she did.

Earl's secretary, Latonya Baker, was already at work, efficiently organizing the Saturday mail and forwarded messages from the tribal office in Tokeland. Latonya was also a member of earl's tribe and full blood Indian. She was a few year's younger than Earl, married with three children. By the time Earl arrived, she was making arrangements for him to attend a quarterly forestry conference in Port Angeles and had coffee brewing. Earl went straight for the pot.

"Mornin', Earl," Latonya said as she pulled some copies out of the printer's tray. "How did the volunteer job go with Eddie and his tsunami-project team?"

Earl had filled his coffee cup and approached Latonya's desk to take a peek at what mail had come in. "Well, it started out being a whole lot of fun. The conditions for kayaking couldn't have been better. But the debris-survey effort kind of fell apart about midday. You remember hearing about that fellow who was reported missing from up near La Push a couple of weeks ago?"

"I think so," Latonya answered. "A man with the Quileute tribe?"

"Yup, that's the one. We found him—dead, unfortunately. His body washed ashore at North Cove. I actually spotted the body in the surf and called Eddie Shaw, and he took charge. Had to send the rest of the volunteer's home and close the beach. The guy's name is William Pence. Do you know him? I think he was quite a bit older than you, but you've attended powwows up that way, right?"

"I didn't know him, but I've met his mother. She and his aunties are well-known basket-makers with the Quileute people. I took a class with his mother several years ago. She's goin' to take her son's death pretty hard, I think." Latonya was quiet for a minute and kind of stared at her hands. "I guess I need to spread the word around to some of the women down this way who studied basket-makin' with her. Maybe we can provide a little comfort or support. I know I would need a lot of support if I lost Ed. It was bad enough that time when he got hurt and had to go through months of physical therapy. What really helped us was the support we got from Johnson Wewa, the shaman. Do you see Johnson much?"

"I try to spend a day with Johnson once or twice a year. We usually meet in his sweat lodge and just talk. I guess I haven't mentioned it; it's kind of a private thing. Gets my head back on straight, especially when Sally and I are having a difficult time in our relationship."

"Ah, a guy thing," said Latonya. She frowned. "Do you remember that Indian basket at the maritime museum up at Westport—the one with your great-grandfather's name on it?"

"Yeah, Christian Zauner?"

"That basket was made by Big Rosie, Pence's grandmother."

"Really? Latonya, you are a wealth of knowledge on Indian families. How did you know about that? That basket was given to me by my mother. Neither she nor I knew anything about it except that it was made for my great-grandfather when he was the principal keeper for the Destruction Island lighthouse. My mother told me that he was a friend of the local Indians. That's about it. Do you know anything else about my relatives?"

"A little bit—we women like to talk while we do the twining for our baskets. You know, like men—tell stories. Most of them are not for your ears," Latonya responded with a slight giggle.

Earl refilled his coffee cup and then sat down next to her desk. "OK, OK, so tell me more."

"The Hoh and the Quileute people opposed the construction of the lighthouse on the island, you know. It was a special place for them and important to their subsistence. When your great-grandfather moved to the island with his family, it was a time of difficult adjustment. But somehow things all settled down, and the Zauner family became very good friends of the Indians. Big Rosie and her children used to go out to the island to gather eggs, mussels, and abalone." Latonya raised a hand and wagged her forefinger at Earl like an admonishing mother would. "Some of the keeper's records are stored at the museum up in Westport. You might want to read them some day. How else can you tell stories to your children? That's all I have to say right now. So take this stack of things to your desk and get to work."

"Latonya, you are a gem. Thanks." Earl picked up the stack of papers and headed for his desk. The office phone rang and Latonya answered. "It's for you—Detective Eddie Shaw."

*

Earl was still pondering his conversations with Latonya and Eddie Shaw while he waited in the café for Sally to arrive. Eddie had said that his department was starting a homicide investigation based upon the ME's statement that there were suspicious circumstances surrounding William

Pence's death, and that the man had not drowned but had
died of blunt force trauma, possibly in a fall. Somehow his
body had ended up in the ocean. Eddie was trying to construct a timeline and pinpoint where Pence may have been
when he died, and right now he didn't have much evidence.
Shaw thought that Pence may have been near a bird nesting area at some time just before his death. Earl suddenly
remembered the eggshells that had fallen out of Pence's
backpack. He dug out his cell phone and was about to call
Shaw when Sally arrived.

"Hi, kid," Earl said as he rose to greet her. He
slipped the phone back in his pocket and gave his wife a kiss
and a hug. "How are your new cases doing this morning?"

Sally took a seat across from Earl and let out a sigh.
Her face was slightly flushed, and Earl suspected that she
had walked down the hill from the hospital. "Not so good,"
Sally answered as she slipped off her jacket and let it slide
behind her. "Their symptoms have not subsided and maybe
are even slightly worse. Most mushroom toxicity cases
begin to recover in six to eight hours. But some of them are
showing signs of a hyper-allergenic reaction, which could
be a result of the body's response to dozens of things. So
I've starting doing some epidemiological investigations to
see if there are any similarities between the patients—foods
ingested, where they live or have been in the last 72 hours,
that kind of stuff."

"Looks like you have some detective work to do, just like Eddie Shaw does," Earl added.

"Yeah, but Eddie does it every day. I haven't had to collect this kind of information since my research days at the university hospital. Speaking of Eddie, have you heard anything more about the body you found in the surf?"

"He called me this morning and said that they've opened an investigation since there are some suspicious circumstances surrounding the cause of death. Latonya and I were talking about it this morning in the office, and you know what?"

"What? I'm supposed to know something about this?"

"Not really. What I mean is, there's a connection between me and the dead guy—my great-grandfather."

Sally's eyes widened as she exclaimed, "Christian Zauner?"

"Yup, old Chris Zauner. Remember the Indian basket I donated to the maritime museum in Westport about five years ago when they were adding the exhibit about the Fresnel lens? William Pence's grandmother knew my great-grandfather and made that basket with his name on it. Latonya told me her name was Big Rosie. Latonya took basket-making classes from Pence's mother."

"Huh, that's interesting. I'd like to hear more, but first you have to feed me. I've got less than an hour to get back to work." Sally grabbed a menu and noticed that the soup of the day was clam chowder—one of her favorites. "Want to share a bowl of chowder and a large mixed salad?" Sally asked just as the waitress arrived at their table with two steaming cups of coffee. Sally stared out the window while they waited for their lunch. Across the street, she noticed two Asian men get out of an SUV and walk up the street to City Hall.

*

Judy Lange was on receptionist duty when the men entered through the two sets of doors to the small lobby of South Bend City Hall. What caught her eye first were their tattoos—the arms of both men were covered in them. On the shorter of the two, there was something scaly-looking that wrapped around the man's neck and ears. They didn't approach her desk immediately but stopped and studied the public announcements posted to a bulletin board just inside the main entrance along with framed photographs of the mayor and city council members that were mounted on one wall. One of the men pointed to the picture of the mayor. They nodded to one another and then walked toward Judy's desk with exaggerated grins setting off their very white teeth. The taller of the two men held his business card out to Judy with two hands. Judy started to reach for the card but hesitated. *Great white sharks have white teeth too. Will I lose my hand?*

The man extended his hands closer to her as he spoke. "Good afternoon. I am Hiroko Takahashi with the Edosan Corporation. I telephoned earlier and asked to meet with your honorable mayor, Mr. Justin Murray."

The man's gesture surprised Judy, who was now fixated on their tattoos. The man nodded in a most respectful Japanese manner with a quick jerk of his head and repeated his request. "Mr. Murray, he is in his office, yes?"

"Oh, I mean yes. Mr. Murray is in. Please wait here one minute, Mr....ah...Takahashi," Judy replied as she read his card and handled it as if it might burn a tattoo on her hand. She turned and fled down a short hallway to the mayor's small office.

Hiroko Takahashi smiled and then turned to his partner with a changed expression. He spoke to him sternly, "We will offer the services of our employer with the cleanup of the tsunami debris as we have done in other communities, but we do not mention what we are looking for. Remember that."

The other man nodded and answered, "Of course, Takahashi-*san*; our employer wants to help in any way she can."

"Yes," added Hiroko. "She is prepared to make a generous monetary offer to the cleanup effort and to contribute special teams to deal with hazardous materials. We must convince this man and the others in authority along the coast to accept the generosity of the Edosan Corporation and to be a part of the solution to this disaster. We also need someone to be a mouthpiece—to mobilize the public to assist. Mr. Murray is trying to be elected to a higher government position and therefore may be easily convinced to undertake this role. These Americans are self-centered and need motivation to serve the public."

"But why were we told to pour a chemical onto the mud in the bay not far from here and leave the barrel behind? Was that not to make the public take notice and report any strange containers they find?" the younger man whispered as they waited for the receptionist to return.

"Silence your tongue, or you will lose it!" Hiroko hissed.

*

Earl and Sally finished their lunch together as they chatted about their children's summer activities. Sally was putting on her jacket when Earl asked her about something he had been thinking about since his conversation with Latonya earlier that morning. "Sally, how about tomorrow I take the kids up to Westport? I'd like to see what they've added to the lighthouse exhibit about Chris Zauner.

Latonya said the museum might have the early log books that the lighthouse keepers were required to maintain. I'd love to look at some of the entries made by Chris Zauner when he was on Destruction Island."

"Sounds like fun. I will have to work, but a visit to the museum might stimulate Christine regarding her summer science project. She's been struggling with deciding on a topic."

CHAPTER 7

L eon Pence had a very determined look as he eased his 26-foot troller out of its moorage slip at B Dock of the La Push Harbor. The wooden-hulled fishing boat had belonged to his father and, after getting out of the marines, Leon and Will had rebuilt the motor, then the trolling gear, together. The hull was sound, but the cabin had some rot and restoring it had been planned as a winter project. Leon cruised close to the drift boom and then out into the Quileute River. He passed a few set nets and the new village site on his port side. The old village was just upriver from the small harbor. The parking spot on the point was empty but probably would not be for long. It was popular with tourists who drove out from Forks to enjoy the picturesque view of the islets now off his starboard side—James and Little James Island and several other rocky islets that were draped in a bright morning sun.

Leon's thoughts were about his dead brother and the good times they'd had together, exploring the shores of these islands when they were young. They would seek out the most difficult climbs to the tops of the cliffs and challenge each other to see who could make it to the top of the island the quickest. Will had always been stronger and usually won. They were always testing one another's physical skills, whether scaling rock cliffs, swimming, or fishing.

Leon recalled a day just after he had returned from his first tour in Iraq. The brothers were sitting on a log along the edge of the river, and Will challenged Leon to a race across the river and back—the last one to touch the log bought a case of beer. It was a tie, so Leon suggested that they test their skills at knife throwing, not revealing that he had been practicing nearly every day. An old wooden fishing float hanging on the wall of a shed behind them became their target. Will threw first, and his blade embedded itself deeply in the boards, inches from the float. Leon threw his knife quickly and with such force that it split the float into two pieces. Leon smiled at the memory—Will paid for the beer that time. He clenched his right bicep and then his left. They were firm, but not like they had been in those days.

The boat took a few rollers as Leon rounded the end of the jetty. Once outside James Island, he turned south and, using his chart, set a course for Destruction Island. The trip to the island was about eighteen nautical miles and

would take about two and a half hours as he followed some
of the most beautiful shoreline on the Washington coast.
Its broad, sandy beaches; rocky promontories; and in-water
rock formations provided a very serene setting and made
Leon feel as though he was hundreds of miles from civi-
lization. Some of the formations off the coast had Indian
names, while others had English names, such as Quileute
Needles or Devil's Graveyard. Leon thought that the latter
fit its description well, with scattered rocks that looked like
giant tombstones protruding from the water.

Leon wondered what the masses of tsunami debris
steadily coming eastward would do to these beautiful
beaches, islets, and coves when they arrived. It was a worry
to everyone living along the coast. Arnie, a friend who he
had run into on the dock this morning, had said something
about a company from Japan that had offered to help pay for
the cleanup. Aside from agreeing that there could be temporary jobs for the locals, Leon thought that some places
would be hit harder than others and would need considerable effort to gather up and dispose of the stuff. There were
coves and beaches that tended to collect and concentrate
driftwood, plastics, and, more than once, the contents of a
boat lost at sea. Leon was now headed for one of these natural traps at the north end of Destruction Island.

CHAPTER 8

It was nearly noon when Earl and the kids got to Westport and found a parking place along the promenade near the museum. The historic building used to be a Coast Guard station and had been turned over to the town to serve as a maritime museum. It had become a very popular tourist attraction. A new section had been added to house the Fresnel lens from the abandoned Destruction Island lighthouse.

Earl was admiring the renovated building when he heard his son's voice. "Hey Dad, can we go down on the docks first?" Bernie was halfway to one of the ramps when Earl answered.

"Sure, let's do that. We're making a day of this. We'll take a look at the boats first and then get ourselves some lunch before exploring the museum."

An hour later, Christine and Bernie had run off some of their energy by exploring every dock along the waterfront and looking at the fishing boats and whale-watching charter vessels. They had a lunch of bowls of oyster stew at a small café across from the promenade, and then they walked back to the museum. Inside the entrance, Earl spotted an elderly woman at an information desk. He smiled and approached her.

"Excuse me. My name is Earl Armstrong, and I am wondering if you can assist me with two particular things today."

"That depends," the woman replied. "I'm the only docent working today, and if a lot of visitors show up, I have to remain here at the desk. What type of help do you need?"

"I was told that the early log books kept by the keepers of the Destruction Island lighthouse might be here in the museum. The first keeper was my great-grandfather, Christian Zauner."

"Why, Mr. Armstrong! Now I recognize you. I'm Ann Clemons. I served as a volunteer on the day they dedicated the new room to the Fresnel lens and keeper display that includes your great-grandfather. I believe you were here that day?"

"Yes, I was. I donated an Indian basket to the museum that was made for him while he was on Destruction Island. The basket has his name on it, which is my middle name. In fact, that's my second request—to hold the basket and show it to my children."

"For you, I can arrange that. You'll have to wear some gloves because it's an archived artifact now. And we do have some of the early log books. I believe we have all of them for 1889 through 1910. We've had those logs on loan from the National Archives for more than ten years, and no one has ever looked at them—that is, until about two months ago. I can certainly understand why you would like to see them, but the previous visitors were quite unusual."

"Really? Why is that?" Earl asked.

"There was a nice young man, a student at the University of Washington, who inquired about them and spent several days reading through the entries. He was working on a master's thesis about early lighthouse operations or something of that nature. Then, maybe a week or so ago, another young man showed up and said that he knew the first fellow and was following up on some information but was pretty secretive as to why. I had to keep an eye on him. When the first young man happened to come back right after that, I asked him about his friend, and he told me that he hadn't asked anyone for assistance. When I showed him the name in our sign-in log, he became furious and made a call on his cell phone. He sounded really upset at first, and then calmed down and finally spent the rest of the day going through some more of the logs. As I said, he was a nice young man—not like the other one."

"Sounds like the logs must be interesting reading. Have you read any of them?" Earl asked with interest.

"Most of the entries concern the maintenance of the lighthouse, adding oil to the light, cleaning the mirrors, getting fresh supplies from the mainland—very mundane things like that. Sometimes there is an entry concerning the families, a child being sick, harvesting things from their gardens, slaughtering of livestock—more living history type entries. There is a very humorous incident about a bull in the first log. You should look for it."

"I will," Earl replied. "That was his second year in charge of the lighthouse?"

"Yes and no. Captain Zauner arrived on the island in 1889, but the new light was not lit until two years later. You will find that the entries, while brief, are quite precise. Keepers had to be very disciplined and make an entry every day. It must have been a very lonely existence out there, even with one's family present, so they spent quite a bit of time doing maintenance and organizing things. The supply tender only made visits every two or three months, and the intervals were even longer during the winter when there was no access due to rough seas."

"Quite a life Christian Zauner had," Earl said.

"It probably was," Ann said. "So, do you want to take a look at them now?"

"Sure do! First, let me show the kids the exhibit area," answered Earl. "Which brings up a question—anything new?"

"As a matter of fact, there is. We recently added a diorama of Destruction Island, that includes a very informative display on the nesting birds and an environmental problem on the island—the wild rabbit population. The information on the rhinoceros auklet should be very interesting to your children. Destruction Island is one of the few places on the coast where they nest, and they build their nests on the ground in burrows."

"I'll be sure to have them look at it," Earl replied. He gathered up Christine and Bernie, who were now looking at a restored doubled-ended lifeboat that had to be launched off the beach and rowed through the surf on rescue missions. Earl left them in the exhibit area after explaining to them where he would be. He pointed out several things for them to explore while he was busy.

Ann Clemons took Earl to a small room with a long table and two chairs. "Are you going to be taking any notes like the young man from the university?" she asked.

"No, I'm afraid my visit is not for scholarly purposes. I just want to see how my great-grandfather might have spent his days on the island and to get a feel for his writing. It's kind of exciting to have an opportunity to connect with him."

"Okay." she said. Ann walked over to one of the shelves to retrieve several of the keeper's logs and then placed them on the table beside Earl. "Then I'll leave you alone for a while and keep an eye on the children for you."

Earl spent the next hour reading the entries. While it was stimulating to run his fingers over words hand-written by his great-grandfather, most of the daily entries were very mundane, as Ann had warned him.

> *05/29/1891—Mail and supplies were delivered by the Columbine this morning. Contractor began installation of the new fog signal.*
>
> *06/06/1891—Hermine was able to harvest our first lettuce of the season from the vegetable garden.*
>
> *07/21/1891—Sighted two ships southbound and one northbound.*

Earl continued flipping through the pages, reading an entry here and there, when he finally came across the humorous entry that Ann had mentioned. He had a good laugh, and he read it again so he could relay the story to Bernie and Christine. Reading about the event was almost as if his great-grandfather were speaking directly to him.

11/15/1891—The contractor tested the new fog signal today. Taurus, our bull, became very upset when he heard the first sounds. He proceeded to run amok, breaking down the fences to Hermine's vegetable garden, and did his best to destroy the walkway to the outhouse. Taurus must have thought there was a competitor on the island, seeking out his cows. We finally corralled him at the west point after stopping the test. Then we got him to calm down so we could lead him back to his pasture.

Earl chuckled once more and put the first volume aside. He was opening the second book when he noticed a small strip of paper marking a page near the end. He turned to it and scanned the page, wondering why it had been tabbed. At first, he did not see anything unusual—just more short, ordinary entries. But the last entry on the page continued on to the next and was considerably longer than most entries. Earl read it carefully.

05/20/1893—Hermine came to me this morning with an unusual find. She was working in our garden when she unearthed an old ceramic vessel. I took a rag and cleaned it. It was light brown in color, glazed, and ten inches in length. There was the faint outline of a crest engraved on one side, and Hermine stated that it might be an apothecary jar. On removing the sealed stopper to examine its contents, I discovered a piece of parchment. I was able to translate most of the message, which stated:

"In the seventeen hundred and fifty-fifth year of our Lord, my ship suffered a terrible fate. I put ashore on this island a crew of seven in search of fresh water and to gather firewood. They were attacked by savages, and only one man managed to avoid this fate by hiding. His companions were murdered in a ceremony in the presence of a tall savage wearing a mask of gold—a 'mascara del oro.' Upon departure of the savages, we recovered the bodies of my men from a cave which was filled with their possessions. Due to the ill nature of the place, we left them untouched. I have placed this message in a flask and

left it at the base of a cross that we raised on the island, which I shall name the Isle of Sorrow, as a testimony to their bravery."

Juan Francisco de Bodego y Quadra
Captain of His Majesty King Ferdinand's
ship, Sonora

Out of respect for the men who died on this island and the Indian people who are my friends, I have reburied the flask where it was found.

Earl could not believe what he was reading. A Spanish explorer had landed on Destruction Island, a fact that had been discovered by his great-grandfather. He wondered who had flagged this page with the strip of paper—one of the college students? Thinking that the person might have marked other entries, Earl looked for more slips of paper. He found none. He flipped through several of the pages of entries that followed the mention of the flask's discovery, but saw no further information about it.

His search was suddenly interrupted by Ann.

"Are you finished reading the logs?" she asked from the doorway, "Your children are anxious to show you some things in our exhibits."

With his hands hidden from her view, he slipped the page marker back in place and closed the log. "Yeah, very interesting; I liked the incident with the bull."

*

"Hi, Dad!" Both kids said in unison when Earl found them in the exhibits.

"Look at these cute little birds!" Christine shouted to her father, beckoning him over to a large glass case.

Earl looked where she was pointing. It was the new display about the Destruction Island bird colonies that Ann had described when they arrived.

"This is the new exhibit, guys," Earl said, as he took in the large glass display case. In the foreground was a terrain model of the rocky island, showing the cliffs and coves and, of course, the lonely lighthouse and remains of the support buildings. Behind the model was a replica of a rocky cliff and steep grassy slope with nests, complete with chicks and eggs. From one of the burrows, a rabbit was emerging.

"Are there rabbits on the island, Dad?" Christine asked.

Before Earl could explain, Bernie started reading aloud from part of the display narrative. "It is believed that the last lighthouse keeper families released their domestic rabbits, which, having no predators, have increased their population to over 2,000 and have created a serious environmental problem. The rabbits threaten many of the nesting seabirds that use the island, particularly the rhinoceros auklets, which prefer to raise their young in burrows rather than on the ledges of the rocky cliffs."

Christine stared at the adult birds that were scattered over the terrain model. "Cute little guys. Look at their orange beaks with that funny-looking lump. It must be the source of their name. It might be fun to do my summer science project about these birds."

"Sounds like a good idea, Christine," Earl replied, remembering Sally's earlier comment. He read from another part of the exhibit. "There are three colonies of rhino auklets in Washington State—two on protected islands in the Strait of Juan de Fuca and one offshore on Destruction Island. This seabird colony on Destruction Island is administered by the Fish and Wildlife Service. Public visits to the island are prohibited." Earl frowned, remembering the eggshell particles he had picked up. "Huh, I wonder if that was what William Pence was doing when he died. Could he have been on Destruction Island?"

"The man you found last week?" Christine asked with a surprised look.

"Yeah. I remember when they were putting him in the ambulance that he was wearing a small knapsack, and a couple of bits of eggshell fell out. I picked them up and was going to give them to Detective Shaw later, but I forgot. They looked a lot like these rhino auklet eggshells in the exhibit. I've got to remember to call him when we get home," said Earl. "Hey, kids, let's go find the lighthouse exhibit!"

Earl led the kids into another room, which housed the huge Fresnel lens and lighthouse display. One of the exhibits was devoted to the keepers. He stopped at Ann's desk on the way.

"I think I'm ready to show the kids the basket. Can you spare a moment to get it out of the display?' he said to her.

"I'd be happy to, Earl," replied Ann. "You will have to wear these gloves."

She handed Earl a pair of white, cotton gloves as she put on a pair herself and led them into another part of the exhibits. Earl was putting on the gloves when he felt an odd sensation in his hands. He held up his fingers and stared at them.

"What's the matter Dad?" Christine asked, noticing his peculiar actions.

"My fingers are tingling. Hasn't happened to me in years."

CHAPTER 9

Leon Pence arrived at the north end of Destruction Island a little after 1:00 p.m. The sea remained calm, and he was able to maneuver his boat into the cove at the north end of the island and set the anchor. He lowered the inflatable that he kept secured to the top of the cabin, took some dried beef jerky and a bottle of water out of a small ice chest, and rowed to the shore, dragging a stern line from the *Mary Lou*. He tied the line to a drift log to keep his boat from swinging. The depth gauge had shown ten feet under the keel, and the tide was in flood. It would be fine for another six hours, enough time to explore the forty-acre island thoroughly.

Leon planned to start his search near the lighthouse, then climb down to the two coves at the south end, where his brother usually beached his skiff, and finally crisscross the terrain back to the north end. The problem was he didn't know what he was looking for. The cliffs on the west side were impassable; the sheer drop to the rocks below was nearly always awash due to a westerly swell. There were a few places where Leon would be able see the bottom of the cliffs, but he needed to search the cove where he was anchored first. It was a natural trap for flotsam. All sorts of things drifted in and could get trapped there. Leon checked out the drift line as he walked from one end to the other. There was no sign that Will might have been there. He noticed that there was more debris than usual and spotted an unusual fishing float with Japanese characters on it.

Leon climbed to the plateau and followed a small trail along the westerly cliffs through thick patches of salal, tall brush, and blackberry bramble. As he approached the abandoned lighthouse complex, he was able to use one of the old concrete sidewalks, then the brush gave way to a well-cropped grass clearing. A couple of rabbits that had been grazing near the edge bounded into the brush as he walked out into the open area. On the far side of the clearing, he noticed a patched of disturbed ground, as though someone had been digging. The seabirds and rabbits both dug a lot of burrows, but this looked different. When he reached the spot, it was evident that the digging had been done by someone with a shovel. The holes were deep and had actually uncovered a number of burrows; in several places, the holes had caused the burrows to collapse.

Leon shook his head in dismay and made his way over the uneven ground to the edge of the slope at the south end of the island. Below him were the two small coves. There was no sign of any human presence. He hesitated, looking for an easy way to the bottom, when a red object near one of the large drift logs caught his eye. He half-climbed, half-slid down the slope until he got to the bottom and then worked his way along the base of the slope and over several drift logs. Tucked under a large log was a small red-and-white ice chest. Leon pulled it out. Printed in rough black letters on the top of the cooler was the name "W. Pence." Still breathing rapidly from the descent, Leon swore out loud. "Son of a bitch! Will *was* here."

He opened the cooler and found it empty except for two cans of Diet Coke, which his brother always drank. *No eggs, and his cans of soda are still full. And the cooler is still here where Will must have put it, so he never finished his egg gathering. What happened to you, Will?*

Leon closed the cooler, picked it up, and began his climb back to the top. Within thirty minutes, he was untying the boat's shore tie and putting his inflatable into the water when he heard a faint thumping sound overhead. He scanned the sky, but the aircraft's position was blocked by the crest of the cliffs. He rowed out to his boat, pulled aboard the inflatable and tied it down. Then he started the engine and walked to the bow to manually pull up the anchor. The thumping sounds of the helicopter grew louder, and Leon saw it appear to the south, along the rocky cliffs. It swung in a wide arc out to the west of the island.

Leon could not tell who the chopper belonged to— only that it was small and silver. It was definitely not the orange and white colors of the Coast Guard. He secured the anchor and hustled into the small pilothouse. He put his engine in forward and surged out of the cove as quickly as he could and then, turning the wheel hard over to starboard, he headed back toward the La Push harbor. The sound of the chopper grew even louder, and he knew that it was going to buzz him for sure.

*

Jake Dixon waved a gloved hand, motioning for the helicopter pilot to swing wide around the island so he could get a good feel for the terrain and take the pictures his boss had requested. He had seen the tall lighthouse at the south end from some distance away and needed close-up shots of all of the buildings. The rugged rocky shore that surrounded it looked formidable, and he could only imagine what it looked like with a storm and high waves. Besides Dixon and the pilot, there were two other men on board. While Jake Dixon, an ex-marine Special Forces sergeant, was shrewd and had a special knack for organizing any mission handed to him, the other two men were hired to just do what they were told. Mirko Rifi tended toward using his brute strength rather than his brain. The fourth man was a new recruit by the name of Knute Watkins. Mirko knew him from a past job and assured Jake he was okay, but Jake saw him as a braggart and had directed Mirko to keep a sharp eye on him and that Knute should keep his mouth shut.

Mirko and Knute had spent several days on the island doing a random search for the flask from the Spanish ship. Jake had aborted their work when a person had discovered them. Jake had to do some things to cover their tracks and so far there had been no signs of an investigation even though the body had been found several weeks later. Now, however, the search had to somehow be finished quickly before the island was linked to the death.

As the helicopter swung around the westerly side of the island, the pilot pointed a finger at a boat just off the north end. Jake quickly motioned for him to check it out. As they got closer, they could see that it was a small fishing boat that was motoring very close to the shore. From the wake of the boat's stern, it looked like it could have just emerged from a cove inside a line of rocks. Jake raised his binoculars and read the name of the stern—*Mary Lou*. He would not forget that name and would check out its owner. He needed to know about that boat and why it had been at the island.

*

Leon's boat was moving at full speed when the chopper came up on his stern. There were three or four men, he wasn't exactly sure, in the craft. A bald-headed man with a short-cropped, dark beard, sitting beside the pilot was watching him with a pair of binoculars. Leon gave a little wave as the chopper swerved off and headed back toward the island. They were close enough to see their faces. The bald man looked grim-faced and no one aboard the chopper acknowledged his wave.

CHAPTER 10

Arriving at the South Bend hospital at 8:15 a.m., Dr. Sally Armstrong was immediately informed that an emergency meeting would start in fifteen minutes to discuss the patients suspected of having PSP. Sally was included because she had recently assisted with examinations of the patients. She grabbed a cup of coffee and hurried to the small conference room next to the office of Dr. Samuel Reynolds, the hospital administrator. The man was speaking as she entered.

"Please everyone, may I have your attention? I know you all have busy schedules ahead of you, but we have an extremely urgent matter to address. First, let me brief you on the status of the patients admitted to this hospital three days ago and were tentatively diagnosed as having paralytic shellfish poisoning. These patients continue to be nonresponsive to treatment, and four more patients, two adults and two children, with the same symptoms were admitted last night. The hospital in Aberdeen informed us early this morning that it has admitted four patients—three adults and one child—with similar symptoms.

Two of our initial patients have experienced respiratory difficulty, and if their condition worsens, may need ventilation support. Our lab tests have been inconclusive for ingestion of the biotoxin *Alexandrium catenella*, the dino-flagellate typically associated with red tides in our area of the coast. My office checked, and the state health department in Olympia has not issued any red tide warnings on its shellfish safety hotline for the Puget Sound or anywhere for Pacific coastal waters. The prognosis for the recovery of the patients at this point in time is uncertain—they have many of the symptoms of PSP, but we have no sure evidence of its presence through laboratory testing. As a result, we have a serious matter on our hands that must be reported to the state health department and the public."

Dr. Reynolds paused to focus on each person in the room. He had everyone's attention, so he continued. "Here is what else we need to do immediately: I want Dr. Catino to compare our patients' records with those of patients admitted at Aberdeen. I want us to go back over all epidemiological data and expand it to include all known friends and family members. At least one cognizant patient said that he had ingested bay clams that had come from near Smith River, here in Willapa Bay.

We may need to inform the public about avoiding harvesting and consuming clams from Willapa Bay and to report any illness due to ingestion. My office will get this announcement prepared and out to all radio stations and newspapers. And Dr. Catino, as the attending physician, I want round-the-clock observation for the patients who may require ventilation support. Also, we need to continue to collect data to confirm a diagnosis and determine the most effective treatment. Dr. Armstrong, I need you to perform additional neurological tests and further examinations with particular attention to the newly admitted patients. We need answers, folks, or we are going to lose someone to respiratory failure."

Once Dr. Reynolds had finished, Sally turned to John Wadsworth an intern who worked in the emergency room. "Wow, this has gotten really serious. Were you working when the new cases came in, John?"

"Yeah, we were pretty busy and triaged them for high-priority treatment. They were all vomiting, with severe stomach pain and diarrhea, and were only semi coherent. I think Dr. Reynolds is correct. We need to assume that the problem is from eating bay clams. It is a little early for harvesting, and maybe this area hasn't been inspected for red tide recently. It isn't going to be very good news for coastal tourism when people hear about the warning. Tourists will assume this applies to oysters, too."

"Well, I've got to see if I can confirm any symptoms with my examinations. You staying here or headed home?" Sally could tell that John was exhausted.

"Gotta hang around a little longer, I'm afraid. Bill Catino is going to want my full report."

"Good, then go home and get some rest, John," Sally said. "If there hasn't been any public warning yet, we may be seeing more cases. I sure hope we don't lose anybody."

She left John and headed for her office and what was going to be a very, very busy day.

*

The phones in the mayor's office in South Bend had been ringing constantly all day. Since announcing to the public that the Edosan Corporation had offered to assist in cleaning up tsunami debris, Mayor Murray had been responding to all kinds of reports. One woman said that there was a dead sea lion on the beach near the jetty at Tokeland. It smelled awful, and kids were playing around it. She wanted the Edosan folks to come and get the damn thing. Among all of the crazy calls was one from his partner, Sam Reynolds, informing him that the hospital was about to issue an alert about possible shellfish contamination and to avoid clam-digging. With that bit of news, the mayor wasn't in a very happy mood—this was going to be very bad for local businesses.

After taking one more call, Mayor Murray picked up the phone and dialed the extension for the receptionist.

"Hey, Judy! Get one of the guys in maintenance and operations to take these calls, will you? I can't get anything else done."

He slammed down the phone and sat back in his old wooden executive chair. *Damn it. Maybe I should have said no to that guy from Edosan Corporation wanting to help with cleaning up the tsunami debris. Let someone else coordinate what they want—maybe the county road department or sheriff's office. There isn't any good press from getting rid of dead sea lions that can help my election campaign. What we need is our own Japanese fishing boat or dock, something that will really make the news. One of those would have reporters from all over the country down here and wanting to interview me.*

Mayor Justin Murray picked up his copy of the morning newspaper, which he hadn't had the chance to read yet. The headline read, "Foul Play Suspected in Death of Indian Fisherman Found near North Cove." He tossed the paper in his wastepaper basket, grabbed his jacket, and headed over to the café for a cup of strong coffee with lots of sugar. While he walked, he made a return call to his partner, Sam. Maybe they needed a vacation.

*

Earl had arrived at his office later than usual and found a note stuck to his desk phone that Latonya had to make a run for office supplies and to the post office. Earl looked over at the coffeepot by the window. *Bless that woman, she started the coffee.* He walked over and poured some of the black liquid into his favorite cup. Latonya had washed it out one time, and he had complained loudly about destroying its character as well as the flavor that the old coffee stains provided. Latonya had thrown up her hands and told him that it would be his own fault if he got sick from the mold.

Earl looked out the office windows, which faced the bay and its exposed tide flats. Row upon row of poles used to mark the corners of oyster beds were driven into the mud like giant toothpicks. A few old metal racks used by some of the oyster growers were scattered about. Most of the growers dredged their oysters from a barge, but some of the smaller growers used wire baskets on racks set directly on the mud that got covered with each tidal exchange. Earl shuddered, recalling a time nearly fifteen years ago when he got stuck in that bay mud and almost drowned when the tide came in.

On the street below him, Earl noticed an SUV with the county sheriff's insignia on the side drive by. It was

Eddie Shaw. Earl picked up his phone and called Eddie's cell number, but it went straight to voicemail. He left a message for Eddie to call him back.

CHAPTER 11

J uno Betar and Jake Dixon sat at a table in the back of Chaser's Lounge, an upscale establishment not far from Payne Field, the center for Boeing's airplane production operations, and the site of a large hangar where Juno kept his helicopter and two private jets. He liked Chaser's because it was a pleasant environment in which to have a Grey Goose martini or two and was an "in" spot frequented by beautiful women in the late afternoons and evenings. The lighting was subdued, and the seating offered some privacy despite the large number of early evening customers. The two men went over the day's flight out to Destruction Island.

"I made a few calls on my way here regarding a boat we discovered next to the island, boss," Jake Dixon said. The look on his face showed that he clearly was not pleased with what he had learned. "The owner of that frigging boat, the *Mary Lou*, is a guy named Leon Pence. Lives in La Push. According to newspaper reports, he's a relative, maybe a brother, of the person whose body washed up on a beach south of Grays Harbor—the fellow my men killed a couple of weeks ago when they were caught digging on the island. We didn't think anyone would be out there. If Leon Pence went ashore, what he might have been seen is a real concern."

Jake paused, taking a large swallow of his drink. "I'm worried about something Knute Watkins mumbled to me apologetically after we landed. Said he thought he saw a red and white ice chest on the back of the fishing boat and it could be the same one that was on the beach where they set the dead guy's boat adrift. He admitted that they forgot about the ice chest in their hurry to leave the island while the tide was still high. So this Leon Pence could have been on the island and found the ice chest."

"Well, you may have to deal with the brother or whoever he is. We can't draw any more attention to the island and our search for the bottle," Juno stated. "But whatever you do, it has to look like an accident." Juno paused for a moment while a gorgeous young woman with long blond hair and wearing a little black dress that showed off her flawless long legs and bare shoulders brought them another drink. Juno followed her back to the bar with his eyes as he took a sip of his martini and savored it for a long minute before saying anything more.

"Did you get some pictures?" Juno asked.

"Yeah!" replied Jake, as he brought up his photographs on his digital camera.

Juno studied the pictures for a minute.

"That island is bigger than I realized," he said. "This haphazard digging could take a long time, and putting more men on it only increases the risk of discovery. We've got to have more information that can narrow our search."

"How are we going to do that for something that happened over 250 years ago and has never been documented?" Dixon asked.

"We go to the original source, Jake. Maybe I didn't get the whole story from my informant, just a watered-down version of the facts."

"I take it this is another assignment where you need some special talents?"

"This one will be a piece of cake. All you have to do is steal a few books from the archives of a small museum down near Aberdeen. You can be down there and back in one night and enjoy a dinner of oysters at the same time."

"And where, pray tell, is this museum, and how am I supposed to recognize these books?" Jake asked.

"It's a maritime museum in Westport. However, to make your job even easier, you're going to take along the idiot who told me about the books. He can identify the right ones so you can be in and out quickly."

"I'm supposed to use an amateur? He could do something stupid, and we might get caught."

"Correction, *he* might get caught. In fact, he very likely will, as the museum staff probably has a record of his earlier visit which will make him a suspect. Why not make his crime complete but one that goes terribly wrong? That way, he will not lead anyone back to you or me."

Juno picked up his cell phone, scrolled through his lengthy list of contacts, and hit a number. He talked quietly to whoever answered for a minute or two and then broke off.

"Okay, he'll be ready to go at 8:00 p.m. Pick him up in front of the grocery store north of the University District. His name is Halid Merzat, and he is anxious to help in any way he can because of the big reward I promised him."

Juno threw a fifty-dollar bill onto the table and rose to leave.

"One last thing: inform Knute that he better be more careful in the future if he wants to stay in my employ."

CHAPTER 12

Sally arrived home from the hospital late and exhausted. Earl had already fed the kids, who were now watching TV in the living room. Her nose led her right to the kitchen, where Earl was cleaning up. "Mom's mac and cheese? I'm starved."

"You're late and very lucky there is still some left," Earl replied as Sally gave him a quick kiss then reached for a plate off the drying rack.

"It has been nonstop work for everyone," Sally said as she sat down at the kitchen table. "Reynolds called a staff meeting first thing this morning. Did you hear about the PSP alert that went out over the radio stations?"

"Yeah! Did that originate with the hospital? I thought the state issued the alert. They usually do that after having some positive tests for a red tide. A little early in the season, isn't it?"

"That's the strange thing about having suspected PSP cases. There are no reports of a red tide anywhere. The hospital up in Aberdeen has some cases, too, and they are just as dumbfounded as we are."

Sally paused to take a couple of bites of her mac and cheese. "This is great! You have your mother's recipe down perfect." She took another bite before continuing, "I spent the whole day going over the diagnostic reports for every case. I interviewed the ones who were able to talk and ran some neurological tests of my own. It looks like paralytic shellfish poisoning, but the tox screen tests are negative. After a lot of reading in the medical journals, I'm convinced that it's not caused by the dinoflagellate associated with red tide. Our patients have the symptoms of diarrhetic shellfish poisoning, but they're remaining sick for a prolonged period. The lab found high concentrations of okadaic acid, which is associated with DSP rather than PSP. These people positively ate bay clams, yet water samples from the area where the clams were dug showed no harmful algal blooms. I think that somehow they were poisoned with okadaic acid."

"Poisoned?" Earl frowned. "Eddie Shaw told me that one of the reasons everyone needs to watch out for the tsunami debris when it washes up on the beaches is that there can be hazardous materials or toxic chemicals. Maybe a chemical drum that was part of the debris is the source."

"Certainly could have happened. It's worth checking out for sure, Earl. Can you ask Eddie if he could get some guys from the county to conduct a search of the North Cove tide flats for chemical containers right away?"

"I'll give him a call first thing in the morning. I need to talk to him about something else anyway."

"What?" Sally asked with a puzzled look. She had finished her dinner and was stretching her back and shoulders, trying to release some of the tension of the day.

"It may not be important, but if I'm right, there are some peculiarities with his homicide case that have to be checked out. When Shaw had Pence's body taken away, some eggshells fell out of the backpack that Pence had been wearing. When I saw the rhino auklet exhibit at the maritime museum, I noticed a similarity with the eggshell pieces that I had picked up to the eggs in the exhibit."

"I'm not following why that is so important," Sally said.

"What it means, Sally, is that William Pence had to have been on Destruction Island sometime before he died. It's the only location on the whole coast where these birds have their nests. It could be sufficient evidence to involve the FBI or another federal law-enforcement agency with jurisdiction. Eddie is pretty frustrated with having to handle what might be a murder case, and it may have occurred in another jurisdiction where he has no authority."

Earl was silent for a minute and Sally saw him staring at his hands.

"By the way," Earl said in a more serious voice. "While at the museum, my fingers started tingling. It was right after flipping through the pages of the logs and reading some of Christian Zauner's entries."

Sally looked at him intently. "Does this mean that you might have another of your dream stories? You haven't had one in fifteen years."

"I...I didn't bring it up earlier in case it didn't amount to much. Besides, there hasn't been any time in your busy schedule to discuss it."

"What you are avoiding telling me is that you already had a dream. Am I right?"

"Uh...yes, I did—after returning from Westport, I dozed off on the couch. It was about Chris Zauner."

"This is incredible. If I had not been with you the first time it happened I would have brushed it off as just another vivid dream. Do you think this one is similar?"

"I think so. I remember every detail," Earl replied.

"Your ability to remember in detail things about the life of one of your ancestors that you dream about is really amazing," Sally replied, shaking her head. "I've wondered if this might happen to you again, but I've avoided the subject with you because I didn't want to trigger another episode. You know, there has actually been a lot of recent research documenting these types of experiences? My own doctoral studies on tactile-induced memory recall were only one small part of the research on the whole mystery of consciousness. There's been recent studies on what happens to it when a person dies. Most cases that are documented are with very young children, and they lose this ability as they get older. We both know that at one time you had a similar ability, but I was hoping that you were over your episodes, particularly since they were a source of trauma."

"Sorry to disappoint you Sally, but it looks like that's not the case. Something did trigger them again, and it wasn't you. It was the logs."

"Okay, so now that it has happened again, I'm very interested in the details. Let's start with what happened at the museum."

"As I said, the museum has the actual logs from the Destruction Island lighthouse, Chris Zauner was responsible for making the daily entries during his years as lighthouse keeper. I looked through the books for maybe an hour while the kids explored the exhibits. Then the museum volunteer let me show Christine and Bernie the Indian basket that I donated, so I handled the basket as well. But the tingling in my fingers started before I touched the basket, so it must have been a result of handling the logs. That's all that happened."

"Alright, you have my total undivided attention. Tell me about the dream. Do you remember any details? Like when I hypnotized you while I was doing my research at the University?"

"Just the same. I can remember everything—names, places, even conversations. I know that sounds weird, but..."

"It's not weird, Earl—not anymore. I just told you—there are a lot of occurrences of past-life memories that have been documented. I read a recently published book on the subject by a professor of psychiatry. He mentioned one case concerning a very young child who could identify details about the life of a person who had died more than fifty years earlier. His parents were adamant that there was no other way that their child could know things about this person. In this case, the long-dead person wasn't even a relative."

"Really? But I'm an adult. Like you said, shouldn't I have lost this ability as I got older?"

"Who knows, Earl? Maybe the more we understand consciousness and memory, we'll find out that it's not so unusual. With you, there's always something that triggers a past-life memory, like touching the logs or maybe the basket. So your dream was about Chris Zauner? Did he speak to you in the dream, or was it just a place that you visualized?"

"He spoke to me. My mother and her two sisters used to call him Papa Chris. They lived at his home in Westport after he retired from the lighthouse service. But the event that he told me about occurred earlier in his life and was something that he had kept a secret."

Earl paused and took a sip of his coffee. "Yup, clear as day—as if I were there and living his life. I experienced a presence like the last time. Only it wasn't a ghostly figure; it was Christian Zauner himself. He seemed to be bothered by this secret, and it was important for him to tell me about it."

"Something important that you, Earl Armstrong, needed to be told one hundred years later? Must have been pretty important. So what was it he needed to convey?" Sally asked.

"Well, he didn't exactly say. The way he put it, I needed to know some background first. It was not a simple matter. He made a fateful decision that bothered him for the rest of his life."

"Wow!" Sally exclaimed. "This is super-interesting. Do you think that his fateful decision was connected with the logs you were reading at the museum?"

"Gosh, Sally, you're asking a lot of questions, and I don't have all of the answers, okay? So listen to what I learned, and maybe you can help me understand it. Captain Christian Zauner—at least that's the rank he held in the lighthouse service when he retired—had just been assigned to the new lighthouse on Destruction Island as the principal keeper, meaning the highest ranking person. He had two assistants, and all of them had their families with them at the station, including Zauner," said Earl. He took hold of one of Sally's hands as a means of security.

"It's a strange feeling, Sally. Remembering the dream, I feel like I have been on the island. But I never have. Until seeing the museum display, I haven't even looked at any pictures of the place. Yet I can describe the island completely to you—every cove, cliff, and rocky point; every building; and every detail about the lighthouse itself. My secretary knows more about that island and the Zauner family than I do. He moved out to the island before the construction was being completed—at a time when there was a lot of trouble with the local Indians. They didn't want the light built. The island was important to them for subsistence and was even considered sacred. When Zauner arrived, Indians were blocking the main landing beach with canoes so that the workers couldn't unload construction materials."

Earl paused and then continued. "You know what, Sally? According to Latonya, it was actually his wife, Hermine, who was responsible for solving the problem with the local Indians. Whenever they came out to the island, she let them into her home to get warm, and she gave them flour, sugar, and other supplies to take back to the mainland. They never had another problem after that."

"Are you sure it wasn't what Latonya said and your trip to museum that led to this dream?"

"I guess it's possible. Ann Clemons, the volunteer at the museum, told me a lot about my family too. But it was during my dream that I learned about the dilemma that confronted my great-grandfather."

"OK, let's assume it really was one of your dream experiences. If this dilemma wasn't the Indians, then what was Christian Zauner concerned about?" Sally asked.

"I don't know. I woke up."

"Do you remember the procedures that I used in the lab when you were having dreams about your great-great grandfather?"

"Sure do. You hypnotized me and did some kind of brain stimulation; then later you recorded everything I could remember. You were able to verify through university archives that things I remembered were factual.

"Do you want me to try this again?" asked Sally.

"Let's wait. I don't know what's going on. It might not amount to anything."

"I hope so. I remember the last time all too well. You tended to act very irrationally after one episode and almost got yourself killed. Even under the controlled conditions in the lab the emotions you experienced were severe. I thought you might require post-trauma treatment. I was really scared more than once."

"This afternoon's dream wasn't the same, Sally. Nothing happened. Like I said, I experienced a person talking to me, and I learned a little bit about what it was like living on a remote island, taking care of a lighthouse. It was a hard existence."

"Well, if you dream again, I want you to tell me about it. If you get all wrapped up in this like last time, you could become involved in something that might be dangerous. The fact that this spirit of Chris Zauner had something important to say bothers me."

"Sally, you'll be the first to know. Besides, talking to you about a dream helps me make sense of it. I'm bothered by this, too."

CHAPTER 13

At 2:00 a.m., the streets of the small bayside town of Westport were deserted except for an occasional car leaving one of the dockside bars at the far end of the waterfront promenade. There was traffic in and out of the twenty-four-hour Quick Stop, but it was more than a mile from the museum. Jake Dixon had arrived around midnight and spent a couple of hours figuring out the patrol route of the local police. He watched as the lone police car pulled into the Quick Stop for a break.

"Wake up. Time for work," Jake said as he prodded Halid, who had fallen asleep shortly after leaving Seattle.

"Huh? Where are we?" Halid mumbled as he stared out at the dark streets.

"We're not far from the maritime museum. I've already looked the place over and plan to leave the car near the promenade, where it won't draw attention. There's a bunch of vehicles left there by owners of boats in the marina. We'll approach the main museum building from the west side where there's an adjoining building and some kind of shelter. It's a good location to find a way to get inside without being observed."

"We're going to break into the museum at night?" Halid asked. "Won't they have an alarm system? We'll get caught."

"Not if we're quick. That's why you're so critical to this operation. You know where the logs are stored and which ones we're going to take. Besides, the local police patrol officer is over a mile away, having coffee. We should have four or five minutes to get in and get out."

"I…I don't want to get arrested. I'll be deported and bring shame on my family in Turkey."

"You should have thought of that before engaging in criminal activity," Jake stated frankly.

"All I've done is sell information. Maybe I've been dishonest, but it's not a felony."

"It is if it leads to a valuable collection of masks being stolen, which happened recently up in Canada. Selling such information makes you an accessory and is the same as doing the stealing."

"You know about those masks?"

"Of course! I stole them," Jake answered as he pulled into a parking space between a four-wheel-drive pickup and a camper van. He didn't let Halid have a chance to respond. "OK, let's go."

Jake locked up the car and pulled on some gloves as he walked across the street to the lawn around the museum. Halid stumbled after Jake and followed him past some kind of shelter next to the old museum building as they approached a series of first-floor windows on the west side. Jake looked at the first window they came to. It was painted shut and looked as though it had not been opened in a long time. He moved on to the second window, which looked into an office. Jake noticed cracks around the window frame, revealing that it had been opened frequently. Furthermore, the floor just inside was clear of furniture. He pulled out another pair of disposable gloves and handed them to Halid.

"Put these on so you don't leave any prints. After all, you don't want to be deported, right?" Halid struggled with the neoprene gloves and got one on just as Jake broke one of the windowpanes with a small hammer and then handed it to Halid. Without thinking, Halid took the hammer with his ungloved hand and stuck it part way into a jacket pocket. Jake reached in, unlocked the latch, and lifted the lower section of the window. It slid up easily. No audible alarm sounded. Jake was inside before the real shock of what they were doing hit Halid.

"Come on," Jake said. "The clock's running. There's probably a silent alarm to the police dispatch office. We have maybe five minutes."

Halid climbed over the windowsill and bumped into an office chair while crossing the room. Shaken, he failed to notice the hammer slip out of his jacket pocket and drop onto the carpet. Jake was already in the exhibit area when Halid caught up with him.

"All right, where are the books stored?" Jake asked.

"There's a room behind the receptionist desk. That...that's where a woman took me to see them," Halid answered, his voice clearly showing his nervousness.

Jake flicked on a small flashlight. The beam lit up the hall, reflecting off several glassed-in exhibits, and then fixed itself on a short counter at the far end of the room. He switched off the light, trotted quickly to the desk, and then tried a door just behind it. The door was locked. He put his hands behind him on the counter, lifted his legs together, and thrust them hard against the door. There was a loud crack, and the doorframe splintered.

"Inside, quick!" Jake said. "Now, show me the books!"

The small room was lined with cabinets and open shelves filled with various objects not on display. Halid seemed unsure and disoriented in the wavering beam of Jake's flashlight.

"Over there—on those shelves to the left," Halid stated. "There's a bunch of old leather-bound books that look like ledgers. I think those are the logs."

Jake held his flashlight steady on the spot that Halid had indicated, moved quickly over to the shelves, and pulled out the first volume. He smiled. Halid was correct. They were the logs.

"Which one mentions the bottle? It looks like there are six of them."

"The flask was first mentioned in second volume. That's the one you want to look at. There should be a marker for the page. It…"

"We aren't going to look at any of them right now," Jake said. "Here, take these."

He grabbed two of the logs and shoved them at Halid. Then, he took the last three logs himself, leaving the first one, which Halid had said didn't have the information they wanted. Within another minute, they were lugging the books across the street to the vehicle. There was the sound of a siren in the distance. A silent alarm must have interrupted the late-night coffee break of the town patrolman. Jake set his volumes on the pavement and then opened the trunk of the car and pulled out a tarp with a tire iron wrapped inside it.

"Put the books in here and shove them against the back as far you can reach. I'll place the tarp over them."

Halid dumped his books in the trunk, and while he was shoving them back, Jake brought the tire iron down as hard as he could in a crushing blow to Halid's head. There was a soft thud as the heavy metal bar connected. The back of Halid's skull caved inward and his body fell limp on the edge of the trunk. Jake removed the books and placed them on the back seat of the car; he then came back and lifted Halid's body into the trunk and closed it. The first stage of Jake's plan was over; next was the disposal of the body. He drove slowly away from the waterfront without his headlights and taking a back street through a boat storage area to avoid the police patrol car with flashing lights that he could see speeding along the main street to the museum.

The coast highway back toward Aberdeen was sparsely traveled. No other car passed Jake as he pulled over by a culvert to a tidal slough and shoved Halid's body over the bank, where it rolled into the water and cattails. He yawned as he started the long drive back to Seattle and Betar's mansion.

*

Juno Betar poured himself a glass of fine burgundy wine and walked over to one of the alcoves that held part of his rare book collection. He touched a hidden panel on one of the shelves, exposing a key pad, and entered a security code. A section of shelving slid to one side, revealing an elevator door, which opened simultaneously. Juno entered the elevator and took it down to his basement, which was built like a bunker but had an interior design that would rival any exhibit area in the best museums in the world. He touched a panel of light switches, and row after row of museum-quality lighting illuminated the large room.

There were rows of waist-high glass display cases, each with its own humidity- and temperature-control system. The cases contained Juno's personal collection of Islamic and Mesopotamian jewelry and ceramic art. A series of Middle-Eastern sculptures lined one wall.

Further into the room were two rows of floor-to-ceiling cases that held his collection of primitive masks. Juno approached the case that held his newest additions— the Kwakiutl masks from north of Vancouver Island. They were old, beautifully carved and painted, with several adorned in mother-of-pearl shell. Some were trimmed in white ermine fur along with human hair. The paints were faded with age but obviously had been applied by superior artisans of their time. One mask in the center of the display showed more signs of age than the others. It had several cracks across the face and was missing many of the pieces of shell around its perimeter. It was a sun mask, one of the rarest of the Northwestern ceremonial masks.

After receiving this mask, Juno had carefully researched all of the old Kwakiutl sun masks known to still exist. The sun mask held a place of high rank or chiefly status, was the center of many legends, and was a symbol of supernatural power, both creative and destructive. This one had a round human face in the center and four smaller human faces around the perimeter, along with several painted human hands. The face in the middle had the lips, eyes, and nostrils of a man but a beaklike nose—like that of a raven. It was a big mask, measuring some twenty inches in diameter, and was made of yellow cedar that had been painted with red, black, green, and yellow pigments, though they were now extremely faded. Even in its poor condition, this mask was likely to be priceless. The Johnson Museum at Cornell had a slightly smaller one in much better condition. It had sixteen small panels of hammered copper around the perimeter instead of hands and faces.

Juno Betar had one thought as he stared at the mask: *What if there existed a Kwakiutl sun mask with gold panels, a* mascara del oro, *and it hung in the place of this one? I would have a one-of-a-kind—a mask that no one else alive possessed or had even seen. If there was a lost mask on Destruction Island, could it be Kwakiutl?*

Betar stood there for quite a while, dreaming about discovering and possessing such a treasure. Finally he turned, walked back to the elevator, and turned out the lights.

CHAPTER 14

Earl Armstrong lay awake for a long while after he and Sally had gone to bed. He kept thinking back to their conversation and wondering whether he really would have another dream like those he had experienced many years ago. Back then, he could remember vivid details of his dreams after he woke. Those earlier memories were hard to forget, like other major events in his life. He thought about Sally's concern and whether he might be putting himself or others in danger. Years ago, his dreams had caused him to get involved in a murder and coming very close to drowning, not once but three times. Earl shuddered. He hated the thought of death by drowning and maybe that was why he liked kayaking. It was his way of challenging fate.

After turning over several times, he finally drifted off to sleep. Someone was there and calling his name: *"Earl, Earl, I want you to know my story..."*

CHAPTER 15

Destruction Island; May 1893

From their bedroom, Captain Christian Zauner smelled the pleasant morning aroma of frying bacon and boiling coffee on Hermine's cook stove. While he was hungry and looking forward to eating the breakfast she was preparing, he was frustrated. There were too many stubborn buttons to his uniform pants and jacket, and the brass insignia for his jacket appeared to be missing. "Hermine, come here for a minute!" he hollered toward the kitchen of their small cottage.

His wife appeared in the doorway. "What's the problem now? I know that tone of voice, Chris. You sound like your father with his army command voice."

"Sorry, my dear Hermine, but as much as I like wearing this uniform, it is such a pain. And I can't find the jacket insignia."

"I removed them last night when I pressed your uniform. I gave them a good polish, and they are in the little box on top of your dresser. You just have to look."

"I stand in front of you, duly admonished for my transgressions."

"Well, it's all right to speak to your men that way, but not in this house," replied Hermine. "Anyway, why you insist upon wearing your uniform every day is beyond my understanding. You should wear work clothes like the others. No one would mind, and we seldom have any visitors here on the island."

"That's just it. Someone has to provide a degree of order and discipline on this godforsaken island."

"Watch your tongue, Chris Zauner," Hermine stated.

"Sorry, but you know that the Lighthouse Board inspectors take note of these things when they come. Discipline and organization starts with me. They also keep us sane. Each day must have its order, what with maintenance of the light, making my entries in the log, and keeping things in proper repair. As much as I respect the other men, the work is my responsibility, and I truly love my job.

My only regret is the hardships it puts on my family. We have lived out here on the island for almost four years, and it's just not the place for you or our daughter. Abigail needs to attend a real school, and the work that you do is too hard."

"Nonsense! I quite love it here; no busybody women asking me to tea or to play cards every afternoon or talking about trifle affairs. I like my kitchen and taking care of the garden and my man, despite his German stubbornness. And such a handsome keeper you make in your uniform, my dear."

"Well, if I don't get my breakfast," Chris stammered, "I'll waste away and not be too handsome. I'm starved."

Chris followed his wife to the kitchen and poured a mug of fresh coffee from the pot on the stove. Outside the window of their cottage, he could see the waves breaking high on the rocks at the south point of the island. He knew the story of what had happened there. *If only this light had been operating, the* Cassandra Adams *might not have shipwrecked on that point.*

"Looks like it's going to be a bit breezy today. Maybe some sun later," Chris commented. "There's Olle on the way down to the lighthouse. He's having a tough go in the wind."

He watched as Olle Olsson, one of his assistants, walked along one of the boardwalks that led to the lighthouse entrance. The big Swede held his cap tightly on his head as he leaned into the wind.

After finishing his breakfast of bacon and eggs, Chris donned his long coat and officer cap and stood at the door. "It will take us the usual time to clean the lens and refill the lamp. Is there anything you need help attending to?"

"I will be fine," said Hermine as she cleared the breakfast dishes from the table. "After starting Abigail on her lessons, I plan to work in the garden this morning. Despite the wind, I have to pick the last of our cabbage and turn over some soil for planting potatoes. The *Columbine*, brought me some nice seed potatoes along with our three months' worth of supplies last week, and I need to get them in the ground."

"You sure you don't want me to send up one of the men to help you till the garden?"

"Certainly not! I need my exercise, and I like doing it myself. You might ask Olle to bring me a bit of seaweed that I can use for fertilizer, though. Would you please?"

"I will tell him. See you for the noon meal, dear," Chris replied as he exited the cottage. He headed down the same walkway that Olle Olsson had taken, his mind fixed on pleasant thoughts. He had a wonderful, uncomplaining wife who he loved very much. He enjoyed the solitude offered by his position on the island. Abigail, their nine year-old daughter, seemed also to enjoy living on the island and explored it at every opportunity. She was as curious as a cat, and with her talent for drawing, she had created some good sketches of some of the island's interesting features.

It was several hours before Chris Zauner had the opportunity to take a break from the morning routine of taking care of the light. The men had to be disciplined in their duties; the proper operation of the Fresnel lens each night demanded it. They had to climb the circular staircase several times, carrying buckets of whale oil, trim the wicks, and clean the mirrors and the windows around the lens. Chris had completed the latter chore and was watching the waves break on the rocky shore from the outside balcony when he noticed Hermine hurrying toward the base of the lighthouse and waving for him to come down.

When Chris reached the foot of the staircase, Hermine was waiting for him, out of breath and holding a small object in her soiled hands.

"Chris! Look what I found while digging in our garden. It's beautiful and yet so strange. How on earth did it get there?" She handed the object to her husband to examine.

Chris took it over to the light from one of the small windows and studied the object. He had a puzzled look on his face as he took a cleaning rag to it, rubbing its sides.

"It's a flask. Hmm, this is interesting, Hermine. Look here on the side of the bottle—there is a very ornate coat of arms and some wording." He rubbed the area again with his rag and read what it said. "Here, above the coat of arms is the word *Sonora* and below it is a date written in Spanish. It appears to read 1770."

"1770? What is a bottle dated 1770 doing in my garden?" Hermine asked.

"That is a very good question, and I have no idea how to answer it," Chris replied as he shook the flask. He heard something shift inside and inspected its top. "There is some kind of stopper still in the bottle. I wonder if we can remove it." Chris took his pocket knife and gently ran it around the top, cleaning some sealing wax from the groove between the stopper and the lip of the opening. He held his breath while attempting to twist the stopper and remove it. "I don't want to break anything. Ah, it's coming loose." He removed the stopper and tipped the flask upside down. A small roll of parchment fell to the floor...

*

Earl woke, bolting upright in bed, disturbing Sally, who was snuggled up against him. "Wow, he told me how he discovered the bottle containing the message!"

"What are you talking about, Earl?" Sally said in a sleepy voice. "Are you dreaming again or just talking in your sleep?" She rolled over to face her husband.

"Chris Zauner! I know how he found a message in the bottle."

Sally slid over to her side of the bed, got up, and put on her bathrobe. "Oh, oh! You had another dream? Let's go make some coffee. You're going to tell me everything," she said quickly. "By the cheerful tone of your voice, I can assume that nobody died and I don't have to call for a trauma team. What's this bottle you are talking about, and what message?"

CHAPTER 16

L t. Eddie Shaw sat in his office in the basement of the old court house and read through the previous day's incident reports—a task he tried to get done before noon each day. The reports were consolidated so that all law-enforcement units for the western part of the state outside of the Seattle and Tacoma metro areas could familiarize themselves with crimes reported in the prior twenty-four hours. Seattle and Tacoma had their own reports, which tended to be lengthy when one considered all of the minor arrests or calls made by every police unit.

Aside from a few DUI arrests and traffic accidents, Eddie's county had been quiet. Not so with Grays Harbor County to the north. There were two reports that caught his attention, and he read them in detail. One was the report of a body found in a ditch along Highway 101 west of Aberdeen. It was a possible homicide—that of a young man. The other report was a burglary at the Westport Maritime Museum.

There was a broken window used to gain entry and damage to an interior door. There were no witnesses to either incident. Eddie thought about the crimes as he walked to the coffeepot for his first cup. His cell phone rang. It was Earl Armstrong.

"Morning, Earl. What's up? Got another body to report?"

"What? No. In fact, the one from last week is actually why I'm calling."

"Really?" Eddie responded. "What have you got for me, Earl?"

"I should have told you this earlier. When you walked up the beach to the van with the recovery team, I noticed something that fell out of Pence's backpack. It was some pieces of eggshell."

"Eggshell? Like he had a hard-boiled egg as part of his lunch or something?"

"No, it was pieces of eggshell from a rhino auklet, a seabird. I saw the same eggs in a new display at the museum in Westport. I'm sorry, Eddie. I should have told you sooner, but I forgot about them until I recognized them in the display. They could be evidence."

"I'm not sure I'm following all this, Earl. Some eggshells fell out of the dead man's backpack. And this means what?"

"It's really quite simple, Eddie. Will Pence was gathering seabird eggs sometime before he died. It's a traditional thing for some Native Americans to collect eggs. It used to be a subsistence practice. But, here's the interesting part—according to the information in the museum's display, the only place that these eggs are found on the coast is on Destruction Island."

"Good point, Earl. Now it does make sense. Pence's family informed us that he was going to Destruction Island to collect eggs. This could further help pinpoint his whereabouts before he died. Can you bring the stuff in to my office? I'll need to interview you for the record. This could help convince the feds to assist in the investigation or at least authorize a visit to the island."

"Sure, I can drop them off later this afternoon."

"That would be fine," Eddie replied. "Leon Pence is coming down from La Push to take his brother's body back for burial sometime today. I will be asking him some more questions about what his brother was supposed to be doing."

"Leon Pence? Would you mind if I met Leon? Seems there is an old family connection. When his grandmother was a very young girl, she met my great-grandfather. I'd like to offer my personal condolences."

"I guess that would be all right. He has to come by the office to sign some papers in order to have custody of the body, and it will take a few minutes to ask him some questions. I can interview you at the same time. I'll have the dispatcher give you a ring when he arrives."

*

The old log books sat on a table in the middle of Juno Betar's study. He had spent over a day reading them while Jake got some much needed sleep in one of the guest bedrooms. Juno poured himself a single-malt scotch while he pondered about what he had read. He took a sip, savoring the strong smoky peat flavor, hesitated, and then dialed Jake's cell number. "Meet me in the study. We now know a bit more, and I have a plan."

Jake arrived a few minutes later and slumped into one of the large leather chairs by the picture window. He yawned. "Okay, so my night's work has something to show for it, you say?"

"Indeed, it does," Juno said. "It seems as though Halid was a little brief about just what the message stated. The bottle apparently was found in the vegetable garden plot of the keeper's residence. That is also where it was reburied, according to the entry in the log. I did some Internet research of old photos, and the keeper's residence was removed a bit from the others on the west side of the island. The foundation of that building still shows up in your photos."

"So, the search area could be reduced? If the spot was close to this old building, we might have an area of just a couple hundred square feet to dig up."

"Yes; except my plan is to be in and out quickly. Instead of more digging by hand, we'll drop a small excavator on the site and dig up the area in a few hours rather than days. I'll locate a helicopter and a pilot who will keep his mouth shut. We'll need a chopper that can lift a stripped-down machine. You can plan on taking it out to the island one day and bring it back the next. Make it look like an archeological dig or something in case there is a flyby and somebody gets curious and reports it."

"Sounds like a good plan. Want me to set it up for tonight, Mr. Betar?"

"Unfortunately, we are going to have to wait a few days. The weather on the coast has changed, and a storm is moving in off the Pacific. But find a place for a staging area and take a machine down from here and get it ready. We don't want to raise any suspicions by renting this kind of equipment on the coast. Hire some innocent jerk to rent one, put it on a trailer, and haul it down to whatever location you pick. Say you want to fix up a site for a mobile home or something like that."

"Sure," Jake said as he stood, stretched, and started to leave. "I'll arrange it. Let me know when you plan to have that helicopter available. We'll be ready for it." He stopped at the doorway. "Do you want me to dispose of those books?"

"Drop them in a Dumpster down near Aberdeen. If for some reason they are found and turned over to the authorities, they will think it was just the unfortunate Mr. Merzat."

*

It was early afternoon when Earl received a call from the sheriff's office. It was the dispatcher, and she told Earl that Mr. Shaw and Mr. Pence were meeting at the Coast Café for coffee before going up to the courthouse and that Earl could meet them there or at the office in about thirty minutes. Earl thanked her and grabbed his jacket to walk across to the café. The lunchtime crowd was gone, and most of the tables were empty. Earl found Eddie and another man seated in one of the booths.

Eddie saw Earl, waved him over, and made the introductions. "Hi, Earl! Glad you could make it. This is Leon Pence. Leon, meet one of my friends, Earl Armstrong; he's the guy who found your brother."

"Sorry for your loss, Leon," Earl said. "It is a pleasure to be able to meet you, though, and to express my sympathy in person."

Leon stood up and took Earl's extended hand, accepting his words of friendship and sorrow. "Armstrong? I've heard of you. You're a Shoalwater, correct?"

"Yup," Earl replied, "but I prefer to recognize my family as being Lower Chehalis Band."

"That's alright. We all have our family bands, which are more important," said Pence. "What I meant to say is that I know of you because your family's been friends with Indian people for many generations. I have heard stories about the Armstrong's from my mother and my grandmother—stories about how your people were always generous and would welcome my family whenever we traveled along the coast to hunt and to fish. That we never went away from your home hungry. I want to thank you on behalf of my family and myself. You are welcome in our home any time. If you can make it, I would like you to be present for my brother's wake."

"I'd like that, Leon."

"Can we finish our coffee and then maybe head up to my office, guys?" Eddie said, butting in.

Leon and Earl smiled at each other and sat down. Earl had something to get off his chest. "Eddie, I know you are conducting an investigation into the death of Leon's brother, but can Leon, you and I talk about it? Maybe just a little, like off the record?"

"Go ahead. I'll decide what can be said and if Leon or I can answer any questions, OK?" Eddie replied.

"I learned from my secretary that my great-grand-father probably knew Leon's grandmother. She and her mother used to visit Destruction Island when he was the keeper at the lighthouse."

"Yeah, that would be Rosie," said Leon. "My grandmother used to tell Will and me stories about those trips to the island. Rosie loved to sit by the cook stove in their kitchen to get warm after collecting a basket full of chitins and mussels. Mrs. Zauner would give her a mug of hot cocoa to drink and fresh-baked cookies."

"I don't know if you are aware of it, Leon, but when she learned to make baskets herself, she made one for Christian Zauner. My mother gave it to me because my middle name is Christian, after my great-grandfather. It's now in the museum in Westport."

Leon relaxed a bit as they chatted, sipped his cof-fee, and even smiled as they traded stories. Earl finally got around to the question that he was just burning to be asked. "Leon, did your brother, like your grandmother, ever go out to Destruction Island to collect eggs from the seabird nests?

As this point, Eddie interrupted the conversation. "Ah…this is about as far as we can take this without sworn testimony. Will's death is still an open investigation, and I don't want any speculation about where and how he may have died."

Earl reluctantly nodded that he agreed.

Leon looked like he wanted to respond then checked his watch and remarked. "Ah, I've got to get back to La Push, guys. Mr. Shaw, I understand that you need to ask some questions, which I'll be glad to answer if I can. And I do need the papers for my brother's body. Earl, I appreciate havin' a few moments to just talk. It has made the job of bringin' Will home a little easier. Please come up for the wake. It should be the day after tomorrow. Can't say what time it will start—Indian time, you know."

Earl grinned. "I'll be there and I would like to bring my wife, Sally," he added.

"She would be very welcome," replied Leon as they shook hands.

CHAPTER 17

Every Thursday night at the community center in Raymond, the Miyako Project volunteers held a meeting to coordinate their efforts and hear reports from the watch teams that had been assigned various stretches of the beaches of the South Coast from Cape Disappointment at the mouth of the Columbia River to Grays Harbor. While the project had been organized for only two months, the turnout for the meetings increased every week. It was volunteerism with a devout purpose—no one wanted to see their beaches destroyed by the approaching menace of tsunami debris.

There were teams of people who simply walked short stretches of beach, those who used four-wheel drive vehicles, sea kayakers who patrolled offshore and within Willapa Bay, and other teams who were trained to survey and quantify the amount of debris against baseline data and check for any radioactive materials. There were teams whose job it was to pick up and bag materials, and others who would haul debris from collection points to designated disposal sites. The collection points even had volunteers who would segregate anything considered as hazardous for special handling and disposal. Social organizations were represented, as well as churches, Little League teams, high school clubs, state and county highway departments and businesses big and small. Members of a local Cub Scout troop were stationed at every entrance to the hall, handing out flyers about how to report any unusual debris seen on the beaches.

On this particular night, representatives of the Edosan Corporation were present. While few people knew it, Edsosan paid for rental of the center, supplied the plentiful refreshments, and covered the cost for local government officials to be there. Mayor Justin Murray, one of the officials who had all expenses paid, worked the crowd, shaking hands with strangers and slapping those he knew on the back, and thanking everyone for being part of the Miyako Project. Even the telephone call center was a service hired by the Edosan Corporation. It ensured that they would be the first to hear about what was being found on the beaches and be able to dispatch an Edosan crew to examine it.

Sitting near the back of the audience, Hiroko Takahashi was pleased with what he saw—organization, teamwork, enthusiasm. Two days earlier, he had hired a local pilot to fly him and his partner out over the tsunami debris. He was sure that few people in the room realized what was about to hit them. This was not an annual beach cleanup that might collect a few tons of fishing nets, plastic, Styrofoam, and various other flotsam. Thousands upon thousands of tons of debris were about to wash ashore and would continue to come, one tide cycle after another, quite possibly overwhelming the enthusiastic volunteers that were now smiling at each other. And when the escape pod was reported, like any other potential source of hazardous materials, Takahashi and his men would be the first to know where it was and would quickly pick it up and disappear. Their mission for Mrs. Edo would be over.

Mayor Murray bounced up onto the stage and tapped the microphone at the podium. There was a series of loud clicks over the speakers in the room. "Is it on? Can everyone hear me?" the mayor asked the assembled room. A rousing acknowledgement rose from the crowd. "Great! Then let's get this meeting's agenda rolling. We have two guest speakers tonight: Dr. Reynolds from the Willapa Harbor Hospital and Joe Rawlins with the State Highway Department. They will be followed by another round of training. But before we get to our speakers, there are a few introductions. I'm Justin Murray, mayor of South Bend. Also present is Ann Southern from the governor's office and John Rice, a Pacific County commissioner. Thanks for coming, folks. And if you all did not sign in, be sure to do so and tell us how you think you can help. We have several tables manned by Miyako volunteers like yourselves out in the main lobby, ready to assign you to one of the many roles needed to tackle the cleanup. Oh, and be sure to report and debris sightings but leave any dead sea lions alone, Okay?"

The mayor offered a big smile and paused. There were some chuckles in the audience as he continued.

"I talked to the FEMA guys in Seattle this morning, and while the federal government is thinking about how to plan and manage this catastrophe, they don't live here on the coast and don't see the urgency. It's up to us to get it done. Now let's get Joe Rawlins up here to tell us about all of the collection points we'll be using."

Joe Rawlins, overweight and a bit unsteady on the series of steps to the stage, walked over to an easel with a map that had big dots stuck on it in a half dozen places. "Uh...good evening, everyone. I'm Joe Rawlins, Southwest District in Chehalis. We put this map together to provide the public with the location of the designated tsunami debris collection stations. Each one will have several large Dumpsters, which will be replaced by local refuse haulers whenever they are filled. These stations will have some of you as volunteers to inspect materials brought to the sites that might be hazardous—things like chemical drums, paint cans, bottles with unknown liquid content, and so on.

Let them decide what Dumpster to put things in, OK? By the way, the state wants to extend its thanks to the Edosan Corporation from Japan for funding these collection sites. Our legislature hasn't authorized any funding for tsunami cleanup yet. So we thank Edosan for stepping up to the plate and offering their financial assistance."

After a round of applause, Joe rambled on for another ten minutes regarding safety measures when handling debris, using disposable gloves, and bagging everything. Dr. Reynolds from the hospital in South Bend spoke next. His message was pretty much the same as what had gone out to the media about possible contaminated shellfish in Willapa Bay that could have resulted from toxic chemicals that were part of the tsunami debris. He spoke about the seriousness of the problem and assured people that as long as they didn't eat stuff that they picked up off the beaches, they would be fine. That comment brought a lot of laughs, which helped relax many of those present who were becoming nervous about what they had volunteered for.

Earl Armstrong sat on one side of the audience with Eddie Shaw. Eddie wore a team-leader badge like quite a few others in the room. To identify what each team was responsible for, each team wore a badge with a specific color and a large letter. Eddie's team, of which Earl was a part, had green badges with the letter "G," meaning that they were a response team for a stretch of beach that included Grayland, north of the entrance to Willapa Bay. Once the meeting was over, Earl and Eddie walked out to the parking lot together.

"It was pretty obvious that Justin Murray is running for election. The guy sure knows how to work a crowd," Earl commented.

"Bought and paid for by the Edosan Corporation, like everything else," replied Eddie. "I sure hope it works out as planned. It's got me nervous, though. You probably haven't seen the tsunami debris reports from the Thirteenth Coast Guard District, have you?"

"Nope. I'm not on the need–to-know list like you are. What do they say?"

"That there is one hell of a lot of debris out there, maybe fifty miles from the beaches. I talked to Lt. Phillips at the Coast Guard Air Station in Astoria yesterday. He's worried. He thinks that there are two really bad situations about to develop, one being the beach cleanup and the other being navigation. The nearshore zone and some of the entrances to inland navigation channels, like the Columbia River bar, may become impassable. He doesn't know what the Coast Guard is going to be able to do about it."

"I sure hope that all these volunteers don't get demoralized with the beach cleanup effort. This could be a real disaster," Earl added as the two reached Eddie's SUV.

As Eddie got behind the wheel, Earl took the moment to say to Eddie what had been on his mind. "On

Saturday, Sally and I are going up to the funeral for Will Pence. Is there a reason why you didn't bring up your suspicions of foul play with Leon?"

"That's all they are at this point, Earl. I don't have any suspects, and I'm not sure I have a crime scene. Might be Destruction Island; then again, it might not. Then there's the fact that the island is federal land and out of my jurisdiction. I need strong probable cause to bring in the federal marshals. But one of the reasons I didn't divulge any of my department's findings is that I don't want Leon going off on his own—trying to find out who might have killed Will. He could get all worked up about seeking revenge and end up hurting or even killing an innocent person. That a good enough answer?"

Drops of rain started to spatter all around them as Earl turned to head for his own vehicle. "Yeah, good enough for me. Take care, Eddie. I gotta get home and talk to Sally about getting someone to look after the kids. Looks like it will be a wet summer weekend, too."

CHAPTER 18

The drive Saturday morning up the coast to Leon's hometown of La Push was both wet and windy. The predicted weather change had indeed taken place. The pleasant early summer weather had been interrupted by a typical southwestern storm of intense rain, but the weather was expected to clear in another 24 hours. Sally and Earl stopped in Forks and checked into a motel that Earl had reserved, placed their bags in their room and then drove on to La Push.

Upon entering the small town, the magnitude of the funeral ceremony for Will Pence became quite evident. The funeral was being held in the gymnasium of the Quileute Indian School. There were no parking spots left around the school, and vehicles were parked in every possible pullout along the road, all the way to the marina. Leon had left Earl a message telling him to drive down to the marina, where his cousin was keeping several spots reserved for close friends of the family. There was a town taxi that was providing shuttle services up to the school.

At the school gym, Earl and Sally saw that the chairs set up on the floor were all occupied, so they climbed up several rows in one of the bleacher sections. They had just sat down when a procession of elders entered the gym and led by an honor guard made of military veterans. The elders were wearing traditional blanket robes in red and black. Wearing his military uniform, Leon Pence followed the elders. The whole procession moved with a slow shuffling pace to the rhythm of several drums while the drummers sang a death chant.

It took several hours for Will's friends and family members to come forward and speak at the gathering. Several of them spoke only in their native language. Earl was quite moved by the whole event.

Afterward, everyone was invited to take part in a huge traditional feast served in the school cafeteria. Because the rain hadn't stopped, everyone ate inside at long folding tables which were quickly set up by a bunch of young men. The drummers continued to sing songs of honor, and a group of young people in fancy dress performed traditional dances.

Leon was part of a receiving line near the entrance to the cafeteria, and when Earl and Sally finally got up to him, Earl introduced Sally. "Thanks for inviting us to share this moment with you, your family, and your friends," Earl said. "Leon, I'd like you to meet my wife, Sally." To Earl's surprise, Leon smiled, made a slight bow, and kissed Sally's hand. Sally gave him a sisterly hug and said to Leon, "We are truly sorry for the loss of your brother."

"Then please join us for some food," Leon said with a smile as he pointed to the crowd of people that was gathering at the cafeteria doors. "It's our way of celebration in a time like this. We should not be buried in our grief, and I'm sure that this is what Will would have wanted."

"Where will the interment be, Leon?" Earl asked as he took Leon's extended hand.

"There will not be one. He's being cremated this evening, and if the weather improves, which it's supposed to do, I plan to take his ashes out among the islets in the morning and spread them on the ocean. Say, would you and Sally like to join me? It's a short boat ride, and the spot is very scenic, especially with the early morning light."

"Well, since we are staying over until tomorrow afternoon, we would love to assist you. Wouldn't we, Sally?" Earl answered. Sally nodded in agreement.

In the dense crowd that had gathered near the food tables, a white man with a close-cropped beard and a Mariners baseball cap listened to their conversation while those around him began filling their plates with food. He hesitated and then abruptly broke from the food line and slipped out of one of the gym exits. He walked briskly to a black SUV parked several blocks away, ignoring groups of people both arriving and leaving the gymnasium. Jake Dixon had work to do.

Jake was sure that he could find Leon's boat, the *Mary Lou*, down at the small marina, but first he had to drive back to the old farm he had rented nearby. The farm was an isolated place, located just upstream of the mouth of the Hoh river, with a steep, dead-end gravel road. There was a large parking area that was perfect for landing the helicopter and for use as a staging area for their trips out to Destruction Island. Jake had brought a few other tools of his trade down from Tacoma, and he needed to assemble them before finding the *Mary Lou* later that night.

CHAPTER 19

As Leon said it might, the rain squall was short-lived and moved inland. The early Sunday morning weather on the coast, while slightly cool, was sunny and calm winds. Sally and Earl found Leon at the docks along with an Indian friend who he introduced as Arnie. The man was short, skinny and wore a grimy baseball cap with a beaded eagle design on the front. When he grinned, Earl noticed the man had lost several teeth.

"Arnie will be drivin' while you and Sally help me perform the simple ceremony at the stern to release Will's ashes over the side," stated Leon. "Welcome aboard the *Mary Lou*. She ain't much to look at, but I'm proud of her and she's seaworthy."

Earl and Sally sat on the hatch to the engine compartment near the stern while Leon went into the small pilot house to start the engine. Arnie busied himself bringing in the dock lines. A few minutes later they were leaving the harbor. They remained on the back deck while Leon and Arnie were in the pilot house, which was far too small to hold four people. On a trip several years ago, Earl and Sally had driven down the highway to La Push and enjoyed the view of the mouth of the Quileute River from the point next to the jetty. It was a magnificent setting, and it was even prettier from the water.

As the *Mary Lou* motored toward the mouth of the river, terns took flight from in front of the boat and gathered again behind them, diving to catch their breakfast from a school of juvenile salmon.

Along the beach, drift logs, bleached white by the salt water, lay stacked like a giant's game of pick-up sticks. Behind the beach, sparkling with sand, shell and pebbles rounded by ceaseless rolling in the surf, stood the dark green forests. Earl gazed at the nearshore waters just beyond the bar and pointed out several of the islets and slender sea stacks that had names.

"As I recall, that is James Island out there, and the smaller one just inside it is Little James," Earl said to Sally, pointing to one of the closer islets. "I think that's where we are headed."

The *Mary Lou* made a southerly turn just in front of James Island and crossed the bar. The weather front over the past several days had been weak, so it was an easy crossing with very little ocean swell. The *Mary Lou* began a wide swing back to the north around the larger island and back toward the shoreline. As the boat approached several of the smaller sea stacks, Leon joined them on the back deck. While entering the lee of James Island, Earl sniffed the air and smelled something that alarmed him—gasoline.

"Leon, I was wondering: did you ventilate the engine compartment this morning? I think I can smell gasoline."

"Shouldn't be any; I always run the exhaust fan for at least five minutes before startin' the engine. Let's take a look."

Leon pulled a hatch cover off the inboard engine, and he and Earl peered into the compartment. There were several inches of fuel shining in the bilge, and a small stream of gasoline was spurting from a slit in a hose to the carburetor. On the side of the engine, Leon saw something that alarmed him even more than Earl's concern—a detonator made from a cell phone and a bundle of C4 explosives had been taped to the fuel line. Leon glanced toward the shore and saw a man standing next to a black SUV in the parking lot, staring at them through a pair of binoculars. The man let the glasses drop to his chest and put a hand into a backpack lying on the hood of the SUV.

"Bomb!" Leon yelled. "Over the side! Now!"

Leon, Earl, and Sally all turned toward the starboard rail and were clamoring overboard when the engine compartment exploded and a ball of fire rose above the cabin. A loose hatch cover hit the back of Sally's head as the blast propelled her over the rail and into the cold water. Leon and Earl were thrown clear of the boat with the blast. When Earl broke the surface, he could see that the back of the boat had been torn to pieces and was totally engulfed in flames. The *Mary Lou* lurched onto her port side and quickly slipped below the surface. Scraps of burning wood hissed, and smoke and air bubbled on the surface of the water where the boat had been moments before.

Earl looked around frantically and yelled, "Sally! Sally!"

"I'm with her Earl—over here, behind you. She was blown clear but she's unconscious. I'm having trouble holdin' her head above water. You've got to swim over and help me if you can. Are you OK?"

"I…I think so, Leon. I'm coming to you."

Earl did a full circle, looking for Leon's friend Arnie who had been driving the boat, but he saw only Leon and Sally bobbing in the waves. He swam toward them.

"I haven't seen…any sign of Arnie," Earl said as he got close to Leon and Sally. "I…I don't think he made it off the boat."

Both men kicked and struggled to keep Sally's head up. Earl glanced at Sally and then towards the beach with a worried look.

"Her head is bleeding. Can we get to the beach or maybe one of the islands?"

"Too much current—it's best not to waste our strength," replied Leon. "Someone on shore surely saw the explosion or heard it," replied Leon. "We're only a few hundred yards from the beach."

No sooner had he spoken when the town's siren started to wail. Leon and Earl hung on to Sally and watched the shore. The black SUV that Leon had noticed just before the blast was now gone. There were people rushing to the beach and to the marina. They watched as the bright-orange Coast Guard rescue boat left the small harbor at full speed. Minutes later, the boat was alongside and one of the crew jumped in the water to assist them. Together, they thrust Sally into the arms of two other crewmen on the craft.

Both Leon and Earl were rapidly losing their strength, unable to climb aboard the inflatable on their own. While it had been less than fifteen minutes from the time they had jumped clear of the boat, the cold Pacific water was taking its toll. Earl's hands were numb and his feet were like lead weights when he men pulling and pushing him up and over the side of the boat. He began shivering uncontrollably. Once everyone was aboard, the craft made several circles around the site of the explosion, looking for Arnie but without success. The rescued trio was bundled inside space blankets as the inflatable headed for the docks and the waiting town ambulance.

"They'll take her to the tribal health clinic," said Leon. "It has an urgent-care facility, and the doctor lives here in town. Once she is stabilized, she'll be transported to the hospital in Aberdeen. I'm really sorry about this. How are you doing?"

"Well...we're alive," Earl answered, still shaking. "Damn! Was that really a bomb in the engine compartment? Someone was trying to kill us. I'm using up my nine lives way too fast. This has happened to me before."

"It was a bomb all right. I saw lots of them in Iraq with the Marines. I think someone was tryin' to kill *me*," Leon stated. "Someone knew I'd be takin' my boat out but probably didn't know that others might be aboard. Or maybe he just didn't care. I think I saw the bastard on the beach just before he set it off. Whoever he was has just raised the goddamned stakes."

CHAPTER 20

After being stabilized at the clinic in La Push, a helicopter flew Sally Armstrong to the emergency center at Grays Harbor Community Hospital in Aberdeen, where she was transferred to the intensive care unit. It was over twenty-four hours before she regained consciousness, and, when she did, Earl and the kids were at her bedside.

Her hair singed by the explosion had been trimmed close to her scalp and her head was bandaged. There was some bruising on her face and her eyes were puffy. Her doctor had informed Earl that Sally would have to remain at the hospital for several more days for observation and periodic CAT scans to make sure that there was no swelling around her brain. His prognosis was for a full recovery.

There were already lots of flowers from friends and Sally's coworkers at the hospital in South Bend. Christine had taken it upon herself to look after all of the cards and gifts, and she was delighted to read the messages to her mother.

The following morning, Earl sat patiently in Sally's room, waiting for her to be brought back from some tests, when a familiar face appeared in the doorway to her room.

"How's our favorite doctor doing, Earl?" the man asked.

"Hey, Johnson! How are you?" Earl replied, jumping up to grab the short, stocky man and give him a hug. The man had a dark complexion, deep hazel eyes, and graying hair tied in braids that hung down to his big belly. "Sally is doing pretty well, I guess. At least her doctor thinks so. Still looks terrible, though."

"Well, she'll get back that outer beauty soon enough," the man added with a wink as he struggle to free himself from Earl's bear hug. "If the doctors here can't fix her up, I've got some special herbs that will do the job."

Johnson Wewa was an Indian shaman, a profession still practiced among Native American tribes on the coast. Earl and Johnson had been friends for over fifteen years, ever since Earl's secretary, Latonya, had urged him to seek Johnson's help when he first started having dreams about one of his ancestors. After the period of strange dreams had ended, Earl continued to visit with Johnson every couple of months. They would sit in the hot, moist air of Johnson's small sweat lodge on the beach and talk for hours. After Bernie was born, Earl's life was busier and their sessions were less frequent. Sometimes the old shaman would show up at the Armstrong' home, have dinner with Earl and Sally and afterward play with the kids or tell them stories. Johnson Wewa had a master's degree in psychology from the University of Washington, yet he was trained in the old traditional ways and was a great storyteller.

"Johnson!" Bernie and Christine shouted in unison as they rushed up to the little man. They had been visiting the vending machines in the visitor's lounge. Once they spotted Johnson, they each grabbed an arm and pulled him into the room.

*

Although he was madder than hell, Leon Pence felt very lucky to have survived the explosion on his boat. After being treated for minor burns and some cuts at the health clinic, he immediately filed a full report with the tribal police, including a description of the man and vehicle he had seen on the beach just before the blast. They assured him that they would look into it, but Leon didn't let it drop there—he spent the next two days asking everyone in town about the SUV that had been parked on the point Sunday morning. A few folks noticed the vehicle but had not given it any thought. The few descriptions he did get were of no help in making a better identification.

Leon was working on a mug of hot coffee early Tuesday morning when his cell phone rang.

"Mornin' Leon. It's Oscar Persson. How you doin'?"

"Not great. Lost my boat; Arnie got killed; and my best shirt got ruined by an explosion. At least I'm still kicking," replied Leon.

"Sorry to hear 'bout Arnie. Damn shame 'bout your boat, too."

"When I find the son of a bitch who blew it up, I'm gonna put his lights out permanently. So is this just a call to offer regrets, or have you got somethin' to say?"

Oscar responded in a low voice, as if he were trying to lower his voice so that no one would overhear what he was about to say. "It might be nothin', but one of the Jefferson County patrol officers told me while we were havin' a drink after our shifts that he seen a black SUV like the one you're lookin' for. He seen it at one of the service stations in Forks. The driver had a short dark beard, like you told the department, and didn't dress like no local. Later, he seen the SUV turn off the coast highway onto that old road that runs down to Oil City. Everyone knows there ain't nothin' down there anymore. So he thought it was strange to see such a well-dressed guy in a flashy vehicle take that road."

"Did he happen to run the plates or write them down?" asked Leon.

"Uh-uh. The officer didn't see no cause. Guy hadn't committed a violation. Just looked out of place, that's all."

"Well, I appreciate the information, Oscar. Thanks for the call." Leon ended the call and thought about the report of a vehicle still in the area that matched the description of the one he was looking for. Then an idea came to him, and he made a call himself.

"Good morning, Earl." Leon said. "How's Sally doing?"

"Hey, Leon. She's doing OK. So far there's been no swelling. She spoke a bit yesterday and her speech seems fine, too—both good signs."

"Good to hear." Leon replied then paused for a few seconds. "Say, I hear you spend a lot of time in a kayak. Have you ever kayaked down the Hoh River?"

"Uh, no I haven't." Earl replied. "Beautiful country up there though. You planning a trip down the Hoh?"

"Yeah. I need somethin' to take my mind off what's been happening. Wanna go along? I'm kind of new at white-water kayaking and could use some pointers."

*

With the passage of the summer storm, Juno Betar pushed his men to expand the search of the ground around the old lighthouse on Destruction Island. This time, they were instructed to focus their attention closer to the old foundations. If the old bottle left by the Spaniard captain had been reburied where it had been found, it would be in the area that had been used as a garden by the keeper's wife—at least that was what the entry in the log alluded to. Betar told his men to restrict their digging to within two hundred feet of the old foundation and the top twelve inches from the surface. His men and their equipment were flown out to the island before dawn and back to the old ranch each day just after dusk in order to avoid attention from fishing vessels or private planes. Even with the small excavator it was slow work and taking longer that Betar had planned. By the end of the third day, the crew had failed to turn up anything resembling the bottle described in the keeper's log. They had uncovered old whiskey bottles, beer bottles, and pieces of discarded kitchen trash, but no bottle from 1775 with a note inside.

*

By evening, Earl Armstrong was bone-tired. His back still ached from being thrown from Leon's boat by the bomb blast. He had been driving to the hospital from South

Bend each day with the kids and usually ended up falling asleep for short periods in a chair next to Sally's bed. The hospital finally provided him with the room next to Sally's. Latonya Baker offered to keep the kids at her place for a couple of days, and Earl accepted her offer. Christine and Bernie had tried to hold Sally's attention until dinner, but the drugs kept her drowsy. After Latonya left with the kids, Earl finally decided to call it a day, and he collapsed in his own room and fell into a deep sleep. For the third night in a week, he dreamed. It was no ordinary dream, and two images stood out: a lighthouse and Chris Zauner.

CHAPTER 21

Destruction Island; May 1893

Christian Zauner relit his pipe and sat back in a chair, thinking about the letter that lay in front of him. It had taken the better part of the previous afternoon and this morning to translate the message into English. He had studied Latin and the Romance languages as a student, but the message was handwritten in script, and parts of the writing had faded. Hermine approached his side from time to time, but Chris refused to describe what the letter stated until he was finished. Now that he had done the best he could, the content of the message bothered him. And he was perplexed as to what to do next. He stretched and ran his fingers through his wavy hair.

"Hermine, my dear, may I have a piece of that rustic pie you just baked? Then come and sit with me. You have made a remarkable discovery, and I am ready to share with you what has been written and the problem that it presents us."

Hermine brought over two plates of her freshly baked apple pie, and they sat silently for a few minutes, enjoying this treat that Hermine had made from their store of apples from the mainland. Finally, Hermine spoke up. "I am dying to hear what kind of message was left on this island. Do you think it is real and not some recent hoax from one of the men who built the lighthouse?"

"I doubt it is a hoax," Chris replied. "It would have taken a highly educated person to concoct such an elaborate tale. First, the message was written in Spanish, and second, it appears to have been associated with a cross left on the island, a common practice for early Spanish explorers. Such actions usually were to make a declaration in the name of their king. This one is unusual because it is a memorial. You asked whether it was a hoax. No, I believe it to be authentic and was left for someone to discover."

"Fascinating! And to construct a memorial in such a lonely place." Hermine replied. "Does it say why or who wrote it?'

"Yes. The writer signed the message, and his name was Lieutenant Juan Francisco de Bodega y Quadra. He was in command of a Spanish ship that came to this area as part of an expedition to explore the Pacific Northwest. His ship needed fresh water, and he sent a boat with seven men ashore to find it. Why he chose the island rather than the mainland, he does not say. Perhaps there was danger, the winds were wrong or there was a storm. Either way, a tragedy found him nonetheless."

Chris took a moment to take several bites of the piece of pie that Hermine had placed in front of him. Then he sat back and read from his notes.

"The lieutenant describes his crew being far out-numbered by some savages. They were captured, taken into a cave, and systematically sacrificed. One man man-aged to escape by slipping out of the cave and hiding until the savages departed the island. He told the lieutenant how his shipmates were slaughtered by a half-animal, half-man wearing a golden mask and that the cave was some type of ceremonial place. The surviving seaman was crazy with fear and urged that they sail away from this dreadful island as soon as possible, lest the savages return and attack the ship. The lieutenant did so after removing the bodies of his men from the cave for a Christian burial later at sea. He then wrote this letter and left it to warn others who might come to the island. The bottle was placed at the foot of a large cross that his men placed on the island. He gave it the name 'Isle of Sorrow.'"

"Such an awful fate—to be sacrificed by savages," Hermine responded. "How horrible to know that your shipmates died like that. To him and his men, it certainly was an island of sorrow." She shuddered. "But, Chris, you have never mentioned there being a cave on the island. If that part of the story were true, why wouldn't the cave have been discovered by now? And these savages the lieutenant referred to—do you think that our Indian friends are their descendants?"

"I have never seen an entrance to a cave in all of my wanderings about the island nor have I heard mention of a cave from any of the workmen who spent time here building the lighthouse. That's not to say there is not a cave. The entrance could have been covered over or may be now underwater," Chris stated matter-of-factly. "As to our Indian friends who visit us on occasion, I suppose I could ask one or two of them innocently when they come again. But that is not where my concern lies. It is the very idea that early savages in these parts made sacrifices of human beings. A story, or even a rumor, of such a monstrous act could have dire consequences on the livelihood of the local Indians. Their existence is pitiful now. Could you imagine how they might suffer if they were labeled with such a notion of murdering people in one of their cultural ceremonies? To our Indian friends, it would also become an island of sorrow."

"I...I see what you mean." Hermine replied, her face showing signs of alarm. "What do you plan to do? Will you have to report about what we have learned?"

"Before telling you about the message, I gave some thought to what has to be done. First, I have to make some kind of entry in my log. It is required; no matter how routine or unusual, it must be reported. So I will report that an old bottle containing a message was found and very briefly summarize the contents of the message. But the fact that the men of the *Sonora* were sacrificed while the savages were engaged in some type of ceremony will not be mentioned. This could open an investigation, lead to curiosity seekers and unending stories with no good ending, especially for our Indian friends."

"But what about the message itself and the bottle?" Hermine asked.

"I see no way that we can possibly keep them. I think the best thing to do is to bury them where they were found. If they are ever discovered again in the future, the circumstances at that time and how they might affect the local Indians can be dealt with by others more capable than you and me. My superiors in Seattle would not be sympathetic to the local Indians after all of the grief they caused during the construction of this lighthouse. That in turn would make my position very difficult."

"I suppose that is the right thing to do," Hermine added. "Go make your log entry, my dear, and I will melt some candle wax so we can reseal the bottle after replacing the lieutenant's letter. It's an amazing story, and I certainly hope getting rid of the bottle will be the end of it. Although I can't imagine I will ever forget it myself."

"Nor will I, Hermine," replied Chris, as he carefully re-rolled the piece of parchment and slipped it back into the bottle. Then he got up, put on his coat, and readied himself to walk down to his small office at the base of the lighthouse. While doing so, one thought crept into his mind and would not go away. *If there is a cave on this island that contains a golden mask, I wonder where it is. I must try to find the cave.*

It was midnight before Chris finally retired. He had left many of the daytime duties to his two assistant keepers while dealing with the message and offered to do a double watch so his two associate keepers could have a few more hours of rest. He was tired and cold as he slipped beneath the covers, but Hermine moved closer to warm his body and he quickly fell asleep. As he dozed off, though, the contents of the mysterious note continued to bother him.

*

A strange noise outside a window woke Chris Zauner. He got up and peered out into the semidarkness. A full moon had risen, and he could make out the edge of the cliffs along the western side of the island and the glittering sea beyond. Four silhouetted forms moved quickly along the top of the cliffs, disappearing and then reappearing as they traveled northward over the rough ground. Chris rubbed his eyes and stared at them, only to see them slip over the edge of the cliff. He grabbed his shirt and slipped on his pants, shoes and cap as he rushed to the door.

Moments later, he was outside and trotting in the direction of where he had last seen the four forms. Reaching the precipice, he stared down, expecting to see whoever it was on the rocks below. He was standing at the top of a narrow defile maybe two hundred yards long and fifty feet wide. The end of the defile, over a hundred feet below him, was blocked by the sea.

The shoreline was deserted.

He stood there for several minutes searching every foot of the steep cliffs, which shone snowy white in the moonlight in contrast to the dark shadowy recesses. There was no movement or other sign that someone was there.

He was about to return to his home when he saw a series of notched steps leading downward into the recess. He had never noticed them during daylight and would have missed seeing them except for the full moon reflecting on several treads in the path. *The cave! Whoever came this way must have proceeded down the cliff and into a cave!* Chris hesitated, wondering if he should seek help from his assistants, but one of them had to remain on duty, and the other was sleeping until his early watch.

Chris shook his head, took a deep breath, and cautiously started down the rough path. As he neared the midpoint of the descent into the defile, a cloud passed in front of the moon and the way was plunged into darkness. He had to keep one hand on the side of the rocks to avoid slipping. Out of the darkness, he heard something hurl toward him. Suddenly, he felt a sharp pain surge through his head. His world went black.

*

Chris came too slowly. His head was spinning and his vision was blurred. There was a dim, flickering light and strange sounds reverberating all around him. He tried to move an arm to feel the right side of his head, which was pounding and burning as if it were on fire. But his arm—in fact, both of his arms—was trapped underneath his back. He tried to move his legs and roll over, but they, too, were immobilized.

Chris closed his eyes and took several deep breaths. As he regained full consciousness, he realized that the sounds were voices singing to the soft beating of several drums. He tried to speak to whoever was there with no response. He struggled again, trying to move his arms and legs, but to no avail. His heartbeat raced faster and faster, matching the rhythm of the drums. As his vision cleared, he could see a tall form standing close by, chanting louder than the others. Chris blinked again and again, trying to see the strange form. Finally, it came into focus.

His eyes widened as he saw clearly the grotesque shape beside him. It had long, dark hair like a bear. Where its head should have been, there was a brightly painted mask, a man's face but with the beak of a bird and rimmed in something that shone in the flickering light—like gold. He moved his head and caught sight of one of the drummers close by, a large woman who was sitting cross-legged. He recognized the woman. It was Big Rosie, Hermine's Indian friend.

The drumming and the singing suddenly stopped and the bear figure moved next to Chris's side. He nearly choked on the smell. Then a man's arm appeared from the side of the beast. The hand was holding a long, bone knife. As the arm and the knife descended toward Chris's chest, he screamed again and again, his terrified voice reverberating off the walls of the cave.

"Chris! Wake up! What's wrong?" Hermine screamed at him as she pressed her hands against his heaving chest...

*

Earl woke with a start and suddenly felt claustrophobic. Trying to move, he found that he had wrapped himself up in his bed sheets and couldn't move his arms and legs. The unfamiliar room was totally dark, and he had the sudden fear that he was trapped in a pitch-black cave. His heart was beating fast and his breathing was ragged. Gradually, he heard the quiet sounds of the hospital ward outside his room and could recognize his surroundings. As he lay there, he mumbled to himself, "Another dream! Why did you disclose these things to me, Chris Zauner? Man, there's sure a lot more to that message than Chris wrote in his keeper's log. Destruction Island—the Isle of Sorrow. Wow!"

CHAPTER 22

Hiroko Takahashi and his partner, Yuki, got out of their car in the parking lot of a restaurant, called the Edgewater Diner, located just under the south end of the Megler Bridge in Astoria. They were tired and hungry, having spent a week hiring local contractors and organizing them into cleanup response teams. They had rented trucks and affixed signs with the Edosan corporate logo to trucks of all sizes, drop boxes, and loading equipment. They had established staging areas along the entire coast of Washington State and the northern coast of Oregon, and they had dispatched men and vehicles to be ready to move on a moment's notice when the newly established call center received public reports of debris sightings.

"I wish for some real Japanese food, not this inedible fried stuff that the Americans call breakfast," Yuki grumbled.

"Most unlikely," replied Hiroko. "This place smells unclean and we are not even inside. But I am afraid it must do. This is the place where the men from the Coast Guard air station come to have their morning meal."

"Why is this so important to us that we must consume such dreadful things as hotcakes and greasy bacon?"

"During my morning phone conversation with Mrs. Edo, she ordered us to learn more about the status of the tsunami debris and when it may come ashore. As we heard in the meeting last week, the Coast Guard pilots stationed here are the people who are responsible for this task."

"But are we not ready for this?" Yuki asked his partner. "When the debris does come ashore, we now have contractors hired as special cleanup crews who will be able to retrieve the pod."

"True, Mrs. Edo has even sent my sister to manage the call center. She will monitor all of the messages received and reports of large objects will be given priority for our first responders to check. Their response time is critical to ensure no one opens the pod. The rest of the debris will be left to the efforts of the beach-cleanup volunteers."

The two men entered the café. A television on the wall was showing the morning FOX sports news. Most of the booths were occupied, as were the stools at the counter, with local fisherman and cannery workers having coffee or breakfast. Hiroko spotted four men in uniform in one of the booths, drinking coffee and waiting for their orders from the kitchen. Two men who had been sitting in an adjacent booth were getting up and taking money from their wallets. Hiroko and Yuki quickly slipped into the booth after the men left even though the table had not been cleared. Yuki looked at a menu and frowned as he searched for some American food that he considered edible. Hiroko picked up the *Daily Astorian* newspaper left by the previous customers, but he was actually listening to the conversation of the Coast Guard men behind him.

"Are we taking the chopper up this morning, Bo?" one of the men asked.

"What did you say, Dave?" Bo replied. "I was watching the commentary on the White Sox game on the news. I swear, some sportscasters have more opinions than my all of my past wives put together."

"Are you implying that they're going to spend the whole day talking about the White Sox's season?" Dave asked, poking fun right back at his flight commander, Bo Phillips. "I said, are we going to make another flight over the tsunami debris today?"

Bo laughed. "Yeah, if the weather holds. Could be a bumpy ride, though. The district office wants its update. They have started issuing notices to all mariners. Looks like the shipping lanes to Seattle, Tacoma, and the Columbia River are going to be seriously impacted. So I guess we'll be making the trip a couple times a week for a while."

"Can't they just use satellite imaging—like NOAA does for the weather?"

"The district has asked Washington for authorization, but it hasn't been approved yet. I guess the East Coast folks don't feel it's that big of an emergency."

"Looking at the pictures I took during our last flight, I'd say there is a mighty serious problem." Dave replied, as he pulled an envelope out of his flight bag and set it on the table. "I got some really great pictures. Take a look at these shots, guys. Kind of colorful in a weird sort of way when you think about what kind of hazardous junk might be floating out there. Remember that bright-orange pod we saw, Bo? Captured it in one of my photos. Look here—it's a big son of bitch." Dave stuck a forefinger on one of the photos spread out on their table. "Looks like a big orange coffin. Could have a bunch of dead Japanese sailors in there."

Hiroko's brain sounded an alarm when he overheard what the airman just said. *They saw a rescue pod in the sea of debris! It's here—the* Kanji Maru *rescue pod has been seen. Mrs. Edo must be informed immediately.* Hiroko turned and stole a look at the photos as he rose and left the café without ordering breakfast. Yuki tossed his menu on the table and followed. They both smiled, but for different reasons.

CHAPTER 23

Earl slipped quietly into Sally's hospital room from the one adjoining where he had spent the night. "Sally, Sally, how are you this morning?" he whispered. The early morning sunlight shone directly through the hospital window onto a human form burrowed deep under a pile of rumpled sheets. Then a bandaged head appeared, uttering a weak response. Sally's head had been freshly bandaged sometime during the night and the gauze wrappings on her hands replaced. She had been slower to leap off the boat, and the searing heat of the explosion had caused minor burns.

"Please pull that damn window shade closed." Sally winced as she pulled her pillow over her head. "That bright globe reminds me of that awful fireball."

Earl shuffled over to the window in his slippers and pulled down the blind. Then he sat on the edge of her bed and peeked under her pillow. He received a feeble smile, but it was enough to give him some encouragement.

"How are the kids holding up?" Sally finally asked in a muffled voice. "Can you bring them again today? I felt so bad yesterday not being able to talk to them. I hardly knew they were here."

"It would take two hospital security guys to keep them away from you. Yes, they are coming. Latonya is bringing them up later. You've been on some pretty strong painkillers, Sally," Earl said as he looked over at the empty drip bottle now hanging loosely from its hook. "Looks like they took you off the morphine drip last night. Are you in any pain?"

"My head is throbbing like a bad hangover," Sally croaked as she rubbed the center of her forehead just below the bandage.

Earl moved closer and removed her hand. He began gently massaging her forehead with two fingers.

"Mmmm. God, that feels good. Don't stop until they bring coffee."

"I'm not sure that they will allow you to have coffee yet, but when a nurse comes with our breakfast, I'll ask."

"I want to hold those kids and never let go."

"You'll have your opportunity; they will be here. First, the doctor has to come by and see you. One of the nurses told me he wants to discuss the results of the first

MRI. All they have told me so far is that we should expect you to have a number of tests so they can see if there are any changes—blood clots, internal swelling—things like that."

"The way you are talking, I might be staying here awhile and not going home," Sally pouted as she removed Earl's hand and turned her head to look at him.

"That's a pretty good assumption, especially being that you're a doctor who has studied the brain, including mine," answered Earl. He resumed his massage as Sally lay back, with her hand caressing his strong forearm.

"You know, I had another dream last night—more like the ones from years ago when I was your guinea pig."

Sally managed another smile, noticing that her memory was functioning fine. "You were a research subject—not a guinea pig. But, yes, I do remember you all covered in wires and sensors, lying on a cot in my lab. One of my cutest subjects, too."

"Sally! What I meant is that I had another dream last night, and again it was about Chris Zauner."

"What? I'm sorry. I guess I'm not fully awake yet. Your massage is so soothing I could purr." She lifted his hand away. "So why are you still dreaming about Chris Zauner? I thought you already had a dream, which we felt was triggered by handling his logs at the museum."

"There must have been more to the story. Maybe I was too startled and woke up too soon. I don't know," Earl added as he left her side and sat down in a chair beside her bed.

"I think you need to talk to someone about these dreams besides me. There has to be something pretty important about what is going on. You haven't done this in years."

"Yeah. Maybe Johnson Wewa can help me understand why they are occurring. That old shaman sure figured it out last time. By the way, he dropped by to see how you were doing yesterday."

"That was nice," Sally replied sweetly. "Johnson really cares a lot for our family."

"Yeah, Christine and Bernie were all over him. They wanted to hear a story or two, but he had business here in Aberdeen and couldn't hang around. I sure appreciated him coming by to check on you."

The door burst open, and a gray-haired nurse with a pleasant smile pushed a cart loaded with plates with plastic covers into Sally's room. "Breakfast time!" She set plates for both of them on a stand next to the bed. "I see that our beautiful patient looks a lot better today. Can I get you anything else?"

"Sure could use some coffee," said Earl.

"A mocha for me," added Sally.

"Hardly! But I can bring you a decaf tea," Billie replied.

"Billie, you have been a doll," Sally said with a pout. "I love you. Then could you brush my hair before we eat?"

Billie Taylor, the nurse who had been caring for Sally every day since she arrived at the Aberdeen Hospital, stared at Sally and began to laugh joined by Earl. Sally broke into a weak smile and added, "But since my hair seems to have been clipped off by a mysterious hairdresser and I'm all bandaged up, there wouldn't be much improvement. I must look terrible."

Billie popped off the hot covers, and put them back on the cart. "Let me see if I can find a wig somewhere as soon as my remaining patients get their breakfast," replied Billie as she whisked the cart around and pushed it back out the door.

They ate in silence and were picking at the remains of their hospital meal when Earl spoke up. "Leon has asked me to accompany him on a river kayaking trip this afternoon. He thought it might be good to get his mind off the death of his brother and the events that have happened since. Be good for me, too. He wants to kayak down the Hoh River up in the national park."

"Leon's a nice guy and all, but do you think that it's wise to be around him right now?"

"What?" Earl replied.

"What I mean is, for some reason somebody tried to kill him, and we just happened to be in the way. I don't want you to put yourself in danger again."

"Nah, it's a small river. Has a few whitewater rapids, but the flow should be pretty low this time of year. Leon said he doesn't have much experience at it and felt I could give him a few pointers."

"Don't ignore my concern. It's not the river I'm worrying about. It's the men that blow up boats."

"You're worrying a little too much about this, Sally. We can each keep an eye out for any mad bombers. For Pete's sake, we're going to be in a national park."

Before Sally could express her concern any further, Billie entered the room again in her usual flurry. She had a cup of coffee for Earl and tea for Sally. "I hate to rush you but this lady has a busy day ahead of her, young man. So get dressed and find something to do. Your wife is about to get a bath, and her doctor will be making his rounds shortly."

Earl quickly gave Sally a kiss and then smiled at Billie, who stood impatiently with a bundle of blond hair tucked under one arm. Before either one of them could say anything more, he was gone. After getting dressed, he called Leon Pence.

"Hey Leon, This is Earl. Looks like I have the afternoon free to join you. Where do you want to meet?"

"Great, Earl!" Leon replied as he was finishing his morning coffee. "I can borrow another whitewater kayak and have them loaded and ready to go in an hour. How about we meet at noon? There's a small parking area and launch site just north of the bridge where the Hoh River crosses the coast highway. We can meet there."

"OK!" Earl replied. "Do you have helmets and life jackets?"

"Yup, we're all set. I've got a buddy with a pickup who will meet us at the Oil City beach at the mouth after he gets off work at the fish plant. I'll have time to pick us up some bottles of water and lunch stuff in Forks on the way 'cause it's a shorter drive for me."

"Did you say Oil City?" Earl asked. "I haven't heard of the place."

"That about sums it up. It's just a place," replied Leon. "Never really got developed. It was part of some speculator's grand development plan when oil was discovered on the Washington coast back in the early 1900s. I'll tell you about it while we're paddlin' down the river."

"See you there," Earl replied." It should be fun."

"Good. The river's got a couple of great whitewater runs just below the bridge and a small waterfall a couple of miles down where it drops through a canyon."

Leon didn't dwell on the scanty information he had on the black SUV and whether its owner might be somewhere downriver, but he hoped that their little exploration would hide the fact that they would be snooping around and shed some light on what the driver of the SUV was up to. His fists clenched involuntarily every time he thought about what happened to his boat, how lucky they had been and how unfortunate for Arnie. The image of the man wearing sunglasses standing by the SUV kept coming back to Leon. There was something familiar about the guy.

CHAPTER 24

The small parking area by the Hoh River Bridge was easy to spot. Earl arrived a little before noon. Leon already had the kayaks unloaded and was kneeling beside them where they rested on a gravel bar. Earl almost didn't recognize the man beside the boats because Leon was wearing sunglasses and a baseball cap. His long, black, braided ponytail was recognizable, though. The water flowing under the bridge was clear, a sign that the river had cleared quickly of silt after the rain. Looking downriver, Earl could see the start of the whitewater running through a broad wild floodplain.

The Hoh was an undammed river and went wherever it wanted to during winter high water. Logs and piles of dead brush dotted this year's freshly formed gravel bars. A few hundred yards downstream, there were some large boulders, and then the river took a sharp bend to the south and dropped out of sight. Old growth forest came right down to the broad riverbed on each side. To Earl, it was a beautiful sight. The paddle should be a lot of fun. Leon saw him coming down the bank, stood up and waved.

"Hi, Leon! We all set? I forgot to ask if you have skirts for the cockpits. You never know when a stretch of whitewater will put you into a roll."

"I've got a helmet and a skirt right here for you, Earl."

"By the way, you said you haven't done much whitewater kayaking?"

"I've kayaked a few rivers. The lower Hoh should be pretty easy today. It's up a bit with the recent rain but shouldn't give us any problems. Lock up your car, put on your life jacket, and we'll get on the water!"

A few minutes later, the two men were entering the first rapids. In addition to the helmets to protect their heads if they rolled over, they wore vinyl skirts around their waists that stretched over the edges of their cockpits to keep water out of their kayaks. They let the current take them as they steered with their paddles left and then right to avoid spinning and to keep their kayaks in the deepest water to avoid submerged boulders. The first set of rapids had some whitewater that bounced them around a little bit with a few waves letting them know that the water was cold but refreshing. Leon caught up with Earl in the next stretch of calmer water where they could paddle side-by-side.

"Woo hoo! That was a super start," Leon exclaimed as he pulled close to Earl's kayak.

"Yeah, the Hoh sure is a nice river. Any idea how long it will take us to reach the mouth?"

"I'm guessing about three hours. We'll stop for some lunch after another few miles or so downriver. There's a nice gravel bar just before the river drops through a canyon that has a few nice drops. We can have a chance to rest before tacklin' that section. After the canyon, the river gets pretty slow, and we'll have to paddle more."

"Any log hazards or sweepers?" Earl asked.

"They're just about everywhere, but the water is pretty clear, so we should see them. Now, if a couple of logs are hung up in a whirlpool, like the one below the last drop in the canyon, they can be trouble. There are usually a lot of big logs in the last half-mile before the beach, too. Gotta watch out for the ones still in the river. They come downriver during the winter high flow period or get pushed upriver by the bigger tides. So we need to be on the lookout for any because the tide should be in flood when we get there."

"How are we getting the kayaks back up to the vehicles?"

"Otis, a buddy of mine, has a new pickup, and will meet us at the beach." Leon responded. "He's gonna drive down the Oil City Road to the beach which is about fifteen miles from the main highway. If we reach the mouth before he gets there with his pickup, we can paddle out around some of the sea stacks just offshore, as long as it's clear and a fog bank hasn't settled in. It's one of the prettiest places along this part of the coast—even better than the mouth of the Quileute."

"Sounds good all around. Let's go!" Earl said as he increased his paddle strokes. Around the next bend of the river, they hit more whitewater. As Leon had cautioned, about halfway through there was a huge log that had grounded and was lying across several large boulders. It was causing more than half of the river flow to be diverted toward the north bank, which was being eaten away by the current. There was a pretty big eddy just downstream. Earl went first, shouting to Leon as he steered his kayak toward the north bank.

"Do what I do!" hollered Earl. "Stay right and paddle hard as you shoot out to avoid the back eddy. If you get sucked in, it can be really dangerous. You could get flipped upside down and held there."

"That doesn't sound good. I'm going to stay wide right for sure!" Leon shouted back. "Let's go!"

Both men maneuvered their kayaks through the whitewater and around the log perfectly. They came out grinning after avoiding the big back eddy by paddling hard. Around the next bend, they faced some quick runs with small standing waves that doused them heavily as they ran through. Earl heard Leon sputter a few times as the waves broke over them, but he was handling the river quite well.

When they got a chance to relax again by drifting through a reach with a lower current, Earl asked Leon, "How long did you say you've been whitewater kayaking? You looked pretty good back there."

"I wasn't entirely truthful with you, Earl. I've kayaked all of the rivers along this part of the coast and some up in Canada. But I needed to convince you to come on this trip. There's something downstream that I have to check out, and I needed somebody like you along."

"That's okay, Leon. I would have come regardless. I really did need a little time to get away and think about how Sally and I are going to handle things while she is recovering from her injuries. She could be hospitalized for another few days and may not be able to go back to work for some time after that."

"I'm glad to hear you were comfortable making this trip. But you may change your mind when I tell you more about what we might be facing. There's a nice gravel bar up on this bend up ahead. There may be a spot of sand at the lower end. Let's pull in there and have our lunch, and I'll tell you about it."

Earl and Leon slid their kayaks into the small beach and secured them to a big log with lines. They stripped off their life jackets and cockpit skirts and used the log as a backrest as they ate their lunch. Leon took out some ready-made sandwiches and sodas and handed one of each to Earl. "All they had at the Quick Stop in Forks was roast beef. Hope that's all right with you."

"My favorite, actually, and I'm hungry," Earl responded as he unwrapped his sandwich. "So what are you talking about that might be so interesting downstream?"

"Just before that bomb exploded on my boat, I noticed a guy on the beach that could have been the trigger man. I saw the same thing happen more than once in Iraq. He was standin' next to a black SUV, one of the bigger ones—like a Lexus or Mercedes. Well, I got a report this morning about one being seen in the area. One of the Jefferson County deputies saw a vehicle matchin' the description take the road down the north side of the Hoh River. There's an old platted town at the mouth—Oil City."

"Oil City, huh? Made me curious when you said there's a place here in Washington State with that name."

"Sure enough. No more than five or six miles from where we are right now. My brother and I explored that whole area back when we were in high school. Our science teacher told us about the area 'cause of its geology. There was a surge of interest back in the early 1900s to drill for oil along the coast and inland around Tenino. The first well was drilled just north of the mouth of the Hoh at Jefferson Cove. There must have been over 500 wells drilled, but they never found enough oil to go into commercial production. It created a lot of speculation, including building an oil export port at the mouth of the Hoh River. The developer called it Oil City. Most of the lots never sold. The forest grew back and now there's just rotting foundations and some rusty machinery from the drilling."

"Nobody lives there now?" Earl asked. "That's incredible. Like a mining ghost town but on the coast instead of up in the Cascade Mountains."

"It's more like an abandoned town site. There's a small farm on the river. Some old guy, maybe a descendent of the original developer, lives there. Never seen him myself, but I hear he's kind of a recluse and not at all friendly. He could be smuggling dope for all I know. That kind of thing does occur at remote locations along the coast."

"Yeah, I've heard a few stories from Eddie Shaw about guys using their fishing boats to ferry in drugs from vessels offshore."

"Yup. Anyway, the place has got an interesting history, but what I want to see is what might be going on down there right now. Why would a guy in a black SUV be hanging around a remote place like Oil City? I needed you to make this river trip with me so it wouldn't raise an alarm if someone sees us. If I were to drive down there in my truck, it might raise suspicion. This guy knew my boat. So he probably knows what kind of truck I drive. If we just float past in whitewater kayaks wearing our helmets, we're just two outdoor types having a good time on the river."

"It sounds pretty easy, but what are we looking for—just the black SUV?" Earl asked.

"I don't really know—maybe it's at the farm. I have a bad feeling that it somehow involves my brother. I can't imagine him being involved in any illegal activity like drug smugglin'. Will told the family he was going to collect bird eggs out on Destruction Island. That was the last we heard from him."

"That fits what I discovered when the body—sorry, I mean Will—was found. He had some eggshells in his backpack, which he was still wearing. I think they were auklet eggs, and auklets are the predominant nesting seabird on Destruction Island."

"I've collected eggs out there myself," Leon replied. "Were they light blue?"

"Yup," Earl answered.

"I went out last week and found Will's ice chest, but there were no eggs in it, which means that he never got to finish collecting."

"Then something or someone must have interrupted what he was doing," Earl said. "Could he have fallen off a cliff?"

"Maybe. The island has lots of them. That's where you find eggs." Leon set about stowing the remains of their lunch back into a bag. "He could have slipped and fallen into the water, but that doesn't explain his boat driftin' away and washin' up on a beach down near Taholah. He would have secured it high up on a beach—most likely right close to where I found the ice chest tucked under a drift log."

"Well, then, Oil City here we come. Let's get through that canyon and check out this farm. Do you think we can see it from the river?" Earl said as he stood up and reached for his life jacket and skirt to put them back on.

"I'm not sure," Leon replied. "We may have to stop short of the farm and get out of our kayaks to do some snoopin' around."

The rest of the trip was an exhilarating ride and fun for both men as they responded to the changing water conditions with ease. Entering the canyon, the rock walls arched above their heads, almost shutting out the sky. They shot through the drops, disappearing in the white spray of the outwash and popping up like corks. Once they cleared the canyon area, the river slowed again, and they marveled at the wilderness along its forested banks. Earl was convinced that the only way to experience this area was from the seat of a kayak. But, the closer they came to the mouth of the river, the more both men became focused on what lay ahead of them at the farm with an unfriendly owner and potentially unfriendly guests.

CHAPTER 25

The black Mercedes sedan turned into the Minato-Ku district and traveled several more blocks before pulling to the curb in front of Vinoteca Restaurant, one of the premier dining establishments in Tokyo and one of Norika Edo's favorites. Her personal secretary had made a dinner reservation for her and her mother, who would be meeting her there. A number of valets in crisp uniforms and white gloves stood in a group on the sidewalk, waiting to assist the guests of the restaurant. Just as her driver stopped the Mercedes, one of the valets who had been standing at the rear of the group burst forward and opened her door the instant her driver unlocked it. He forced his way into the vehicle and slammed the door. In his white-gloved right hand was a 9mm Glock.

He barked two orders: "Drive away now!" and "No cell phones!" Norika's driver drove quickly away from the restaurant, obeying the intruder who held the automatic at the base of his skull. Norika had shrunk into the far corner of the back seat, frozen in fear. The driver was ordered to make two more turns and enter a small alley away from the bright lights and nighttime activity of the Minato-Ku district.

"Stop the car!" the intruder ordered. As the vehicle halted, he fired one round into the base of the driver's skull. His body slumped forward onto the steering wheel with a dull thud. Before Norika could react, the door next to her opened, and two men in black clothing grabbed her. They dragged her roughly from the car and stretched her body over the hood on her back. Her arms and legs were pinned down by strong, firm hands. A familiar face appeared close to hers.

"Norika, you have been disobedient to the Yakuza. This is the tenth day, and the debt has not been repaid. You know what the punishment is. It is not pleasant, especially for a beautiful woman such as you."

"Yuri Matasuba! Release me this instant!" Norika screamed as she struggled in vain to escape the grip of the men holding her. "I can repay the debt of my husband, but I need more time. Ten days was not nearly enough."

"That may be, but you need some encouragement. You are not working hard enough. The old Japanese technique of *yubitsume* encourages one to work harder and to be faithful," replied Yuri as he removed a small knife from his pocket and gripped her left hand. In one stroke he sliced off the tip of her pinkie finger. Norika screamed and began to cry.

"You have ten more days to repay the debt in full, with interest, or you will lose more of your finger. As long as the debt is not paid, you will continue to be punished until, bit by bit, you have no fingers. Then I will take your toes. Savor the pain of your first *yubitsume*, Norika. Neither fleeing nor praying to Buddha will do you any good, for the pain will only stop when I have my money."

Yuri Matasuba and his men disappeared into the darkness, leaving Norika Edo curled up on the blood-smeared hood of her Mercedes, holding her disfigured left hand—her sobs drowned out by the street sounds of glitzy Tokyo beyond the alley.

CHAPTER 26

The late afternoon shadows of the forest were stretched across the river as Earl and Leon quietly paddled the last several miles of the Hoh River. They no longer spoke to one another, and even the forest had become quiet. There were no bird calls, and the squirrels ceased their chatter. Bleached stumps and logs dotted the gravel bars, and others that were waterlogged slipped silently by—remnants of countless winter storms and high flows. The only sound that the men heard was the faint roar of the Pacific Ocean waves breaking on the pebble beaches, which were now less than two miles ahead.

The forest began to give way along the north bank to open farm fields overgrown in blackberry and tall ferns. A sign nailed to a fence post on the north bank offered a warning: "Trespassers will be shot, and survivors will be shot again."

"I'm not so sure I want to come across your local landowner," Earl whispered to Leon, reading the sign as they paddled past it. "You sure you want to go ashore and look around?"

"The information I got from a buddy of mine is that he may be over on Puget Sound right now, doing some salmon fishing or something," Leon said quietly as he pulled into the shallows and lifted himself from the kayak. "He left about a week ago with a boat and trailer. But there could be someone else around. That's who I want to know about."

Earl followed Leon to the shore. "I guess it's OK to stop then, as long as *they* don't shoot trespassers, too."

"The old farmhouse, with a barn and some small outbuildings, are at the west end of this field, just beyond that row of trees," Leon told Earl. "If we can skirt around the field, staying just inside the timber, we should be able to get pretty close without being observed. Once we've had a look around, we can double back and then continue down to where the river enters the ocean. There's a beach on both sides. On the south side is the Hoh Indian Reservation. There's a good road to it, but there was a landslide two days ago, and the road is still closed. So we have to pull into the beach on the north side, where our ride back to the highway will be waiting."

Leon opened a small waterproof bag and took out a cell phone. "I'm going to give Otis a call and tell him to meet us at the end of the road in two hours. That should give us time to check out the farm and then finish our trip."

Earl was glad to be out of the kayak and walking. The cramped muscles in his legs loosened as he and Leon picked their way through the blackberry vines and ducked through a broken-down, rusty barbed-wire fence and entered the forest above the field. Inside the tree line, they found a faint game path that paralleled the fence and followed it toward the buildings.

The old farmhouse was in poor condition; its roof was covered in moss, and dirty white, with paint peeling from the clapboard siding. The barn looked sturdy but showed its age with bleached lumber and some missing shingles in its roof. It sat away from the farmhouse. A few smaller buildings and a clutter of old rusting farm machinery, partially covered in blackberry vines, lined another fence down to the river. There was a large, graveled parking area between the house and the barn.

Leon chose to climb over the vine-covered fence to move closer to the barn. There were several vehicles parked close to the farmhouse. One of them was a black Mercedes SUV. Leon raised a hand and stopped. The two scanned the area for human activity.

There was none.

"Pretty quiet here," Leon whispered, taking a small pair of binoculars out of a pocket in his trousers. "Don't see anyone around. Do you have a pen and something to write on, Earl? I think I can make out the license plate number on that SUV."

Earl checked a shirt pocket and discovered that he had a pen. He took out his wallet and removed an old gas receipt. "Read off the number," he replied. "I'm ready."

"It's 323-ACF." Then Leon noticed something very interesting. Next to a large door at the end of the barn were a half-dozen large drums. "Hmm...you see those drums over by the barn?"

"Yeah. For refueling farm equipment, I suppose," Earl responded as he squinted in the late afternoon sun. He scanned the area himself looking for signs of farm activities. "I don't see any working tractors or other equipment, though. Maybe in the barn?"

"I don't see any, either and no one has cut the grass in this field yet this year." Leon commented.

A faint thumping sound echoed off the hillside above them, causing both men to glance upward and then toward the ocean.

"Oh oh! I think I know what the fuel is for—a helicopter," exclaimed Leon. "And it's coming back. We better get back to the kayaks—fast."

Earl hurriedly stuffed the pen and paper back into a pocket, and Leon put away his binoculars. The two men stayed low as they hustled back to the forest game trail. Leon hoped the helicopter would come straight in and land without circling upriver; if it did, the pilot would certainly notice their beached kayaks.

They were lucky—the helicopter swooped straight toward the house and barn and began settling onto the parking area between them. Minutes later, Leon and Earl were back in midstream and paddling toward the ocean. At first they were screened by the barn but when they got abreast of the farmhouse they were in plain view a couple hundred feet away. The helicopter was sitting on the ground with its engine winding down, and several men had climbed out. Leon and Earl drifted quietly by in the current of the river. If any of the men who were busy at the helicopter looked toward the river, they would be spotted.

Earl glanced sideways at the men. They appeared to be unlashing a large piece of equipment that was slung underneath the helicopter. One man glanced toward the river and pointed in their direction. Another man, standing next to the pilot, raised a pair of binoculars and looked at Earl and Leon and then twirled his arm, motioning to the pilot to restart the engine. The rest of the men hurried to get the equipment free from underneath. As the two kayaks rounded the last bend in the river and disappeared from view, Leon and Earl heard the whine of the helicopter engine coming to life. With the ocean now in sight, the two men paddled as fast as they could.

"So what do you think caused them to go airborne again, Leon?" Earl yelled over the noise of the chopper.

"My guess is not what we did, but what we saw," Leon hollered back. "I think they aren't happy that we saw them unloading that equipment from their helicopter. Did you see what it was?"

"Yeah—looked like a mini backhoe," Earl answered, breathing hard as he dug in the blades of his short paddle.

"I'm worried whether they recognized me, too. Kind of easy to notice that I'm Indian with black hair below my helmet."

"Why?" Earl asked as he glanced back and saw that the helicopter had gained some altitude above the tree tops and was slipping around to follow the river out to the ocean.

"Because I'm pretty sure that it's the same helicopter I encountered when I was out at Destruction Island. I think we're in serious trouble. That sign concerning trespassers being shot is no longer a joke. I sure hope they left their rifles at the farmhouse."

Earl's and Leon's kayaks breached the ocean swells over the bar, and, after ducking through a couple of waves, they turned the boats north, along the beach. The thumping of the aircraft's rotors and whine of its turbo engine grew louder as it closed on the two men, a clear indication that they were of prime interest to whoever was using the old homestead as a landing area.

"We've got to ditch these guys!" Leon yelled. "We'll never make it to the beach and get the kayaks into Otis's pickup. Besides, we're early anyway. He won't be here for another half-hour, if I know Otis!"

"There's some fog gathering just offshore around those islets," Earl said. "Do you think we can reach them? The fog might be thick enough that they won't be able to tell where we are, and the pilot can't get close enough without risking hitting one of the rocks."

"Just might work," Leon called back. "Maybe they won't hang around. That chopper could be low on fuel if it just returned from somewhere, carrying that equipment and men. They didn't take the time to refuel."

Just as the helicopter was bearing down on them low to the water, Earl and Leon were enveloped in the low fog bank, which was getting thicker by the minute. At any other time, it would have made a Kodak moment—the sun setting behind a low fog bank, silhouetting the rocky islets and two colorful kayaks disappearing in its grasp. The helicopter rose up over the fog because the presence of taller islets made it hazardous to remain low over the water. Earl and Leon drifted in close to one of the islets, which was covered in storm-twisted trees, where Leon took out his cell phone to call Otis and delay his arrival.

It was a standoff. The kayaks could not move out of the fog and go to the beach, and the helicopter could only circle overhead until forced to return for fuel.

CHAPTER 27

Detective Eddie Shaw leaned back in his chair and propped his feet on the edge of his desk. He had been studying the Pence file and the tribal police report from up north concerning the sinking of Leon Pence's boat. Three people had been rescued by the Coast Guard and one person was confirmed missing and most likely drowned. Eddie picked up his phone and dialed an extension number for one of his department staff.

"Danny, you got a minute to talk? I need to discuss the Pence case."

A few minutes later, Daniel Green entered Eddie's office and took a seat opposite him. Danny, as Shaw liked to call him, was in his early sixties and had been employed as a county patrol officer for most of his career with the county sheriff's department. He had been born in Aberdeen and lived on the Washington coast all his life except for a couple of years when he served in the navy in San Diego during the first war with Iraq.

Danny's short hair was white with a buzz cut, and he had the usual paunch of a police officer who spent too much time at a desk. He didn't play golf, nor did he fish or hunt. However, he was an expert marksman and loved guns—particularly handguns—to the point of addiction, some would say. Danny Green was an avid gun collector, and he and his wife operated a shooting range as a side business. He set a copy of the latest issue of the *Shooting Times* on a table next to his chair and waited for Shaw to say what was on his mind.

"I've been trying to connect some dots on the Will Pence case. Did you see the report on the explosion on his brother's boat a couple of days ago?"

"Yeah," replied Danny. "Will Pence dead, and now Leon Pence almost killed. The way it happened makes you wonder what these guys might be mixed up in—drugs?"

"Neither of them has any prior arrests. I made a call to the tribal police up at La Push and learned that Leon Pence worked at a fish plant but quit his job just after his brother was reported missing. Will Pence was unemployed. Both of them did commercial fishing off and on. The tribal police know that there are drugs moving through the area somehow, but they don't have any reason to suspect the

Pence brothers—but maybe they're just careful and haven't been caught."

"Attempted murder by use of explosives sounds like a drug cartel activity, but who knows," Danny commented.

"Whatever it is," said Shaw. "My friend Earl Armstrong and his wife Sally were almost killed, and I don't see them being mixed up with some illicit activity.

"Maybe they were just in the wrong place at the wrong time," replied Danny. "So we don't have any definite motive for either incident?"

"That's right," replied Shaw. "One of the tribal patrolmen, an Officer Persson, stated that Leon Pence has been asking a lot of questions about his brother's death. It was his opinion that Leon is pretty broken up about it and might be doing a personal investigation into why his brother died. There are rumors that he made a trip out to Destruction Island a few days ago to look around. If he did go out there, then he may have confirmed that Will Pence was on the island, and it could have been the last place he was before his death."

"Our own evidence is a bit like scrambled eggs— literally—meaning pieces of eggshell. According to his family, Will Pence was on Destruction Island just before he died. It was Earl Armstrong who put two and two together that the eggshells in his pocket could have come from the bird colonies on Destruction Island."

"If the man was there solely to gather some darned eggs, why did he die?" asked Danny.

Shaw paused, sat up, and opened a file on his desk. "If we look at it from the standpoint of being a plain and simple homicide, we have a victim but no crime scene. I asked the coroner to take a look at his notes on the injuries that Will Pence had incurred, and he concluded that several of the wounds could have been inflicted by some blunt object and not the result of a fall. One of his kneecaps was shattered, and the wound to his head may have been caused by some kind of rounded object."

"Maybe Will Pence stumbled into something illegal, like a drug transfer. Might be interesting to take a trip out there. Do you think the Fish and Wildlife people will let us on the island if we tell them we're investigating a possible homicide and a drug deal?" Danny asked.

"That may not be easy to arrange. I could get cooperation from Jefferson County, but it's out of their jurisdiction, or even the state's, for that matter. We would need to bring the federal marshals in on the case, but we don't have enough good evidence at this point to sway their interest and persuade them to authorize a visit. No one except the Fish and Wildlife folks or the Coast Guard is allowed on the island, which leads to the question of why Will Pence went out there in the first place. Then again, I don't know whether there may be some traditional hunting and gathering rights that local tribes have. I'd like to schedule another talk with both Leon Pence and Earl Armstrong. I understand Sally is still in the hospital up in Aberdeen, and Earl's been staying with her. Call the hospital and tell Earl that we want him to come in and talk some more, will you? I'll call Leon Pence."

"Will do. Tomorrow morning okay?" Danny asked, getting up to walk back to his office.

"Yeah!" replied Shaw, glancing at his wrist watch. It's late but I think I'll try to get someone from Fish and Wildlife down here as well."

A few minutes later, Danny stuck his head in the door to Shaw's office. "Couldn't reach Armstrong. A person at the hospital told me that he drove up north this morning after taking a call from Leon Pence. I called the county sheriff's office for Jefferson County and gave them a description of Earl's vehicle. Guess what? His vehicle was already written up in a report as of midafternoon. One of their patrol officers reported a green and black Toyota 4Runner parked at the Hoh River Bridge along with another vehicle. I asked him to run the plates on the other vehicle. It's a pickup truck belonging to Leon Pence. The pickup truck has a rack over the bed for two kayaks—both empty."

"Damn!" Shaw spurted out. "If Leon Pence and Earl are working together on this investigation, they have a lot of explaining to do. And we could have a problem—Earl has a knack for getting into trouble."

*

It was nearly dark when Earl and Leon dragged their kayaks through the surf and up onto the broad sand beach a half-mile north of the mouth of the river. The sound of the helicopter had faded away nearly a half hour earlier, and Leon had reached Otis by phone and told him to get his butt down to the end of the road fast to pick them up. Otis stood by his four-wheel-drive pickup with its headlights shining down through the drift logs as the two men lugged their kayaks up from the beach and dumped them into the bed of the truck. When they got within earshot of Otis, the man started firing questions.

"What's going on? Why did you wave me off? My old lady expected me home almost an hour ago, man. You guys in some trouble or something? Did you get lost?"

"I guess you can call it trouble," Leon answered. "Some unfriendly people were trying to find us using a helicopter. We'll explain as you drive, but right now we gotta get out of here. Even though it's dark, and they can't use the helicopter, they've got vehicles and could drive over here to check out the beach."

"OK, but you're gonna owe me more than gas and a case of beer for pickin' you guys up this late," said Otis. He got behind the wheel and started up his new Ford 150 pickup truck. Earl and Leon loaded the rest of their gear into the bed and got in. As Otis turned the truck around and left the small parking lot he started asking more questions. "What's with a helicopter messin' around down here on the beach?" Then he shook his head and uttered, "Oh, man, I bet they're runnin' drugs!"

"Maybe, maybe not. Anyway, these guys sure like their privacy," replied Leon.

"Yeah, these guys were using that old farm over by the river for something, and they sure didn't like us watching them," added Earl. "We saw a helicopter land and unload some equipment and a couple of guys. When we tried to slip by in our kayaks, they spotted us. They lifted off again and started after us like a bunch of mad bees."

"Yeah, one big bee with a turbo engine, flying ten feet above the water right at us, with a guy with a rifle hanging out the door," said Leon.

In the headlights, they could see a truck blocking the road near the tree line. Two men leaned against the side of the truck. Both were holding automatic rifles.

"Cripe!" shouted Otis when he saw the guns. He slammed on the brakes. "They're gonna shoot holes in my new truck!"

"Do you think they would shoot at us, Leon?" Earl asked. "We didn't do anything but look at them. Maybe they just want to make sure we stop so they can check us out."

"I think it best we not get checked out," Leon added. "Back up a few yards, Otis, and take the side road that goes off to the left. It goes north about a mile to a trailhead and the site of one of the old drilling rigs. There's lots of old logging roads that used to go all of the way back to the highway and connect to a back road into La Push. They're not on a map anymore, so I hope the way is still open. As a last resort, we can take the beach trail."

"You're not referring to the Third Beach Trail, are you?" Otis yelled as he backed up his pickup and turned onto the side road. As he was turning, Earl could see the two men jump in their truck and its headlights turn in their direction. Otis stood on the gas pedal, and the truck charged up the narrow track with its tires throwing dirt and rocks. The four-wheeler climbed a short hill into the forest. Earl felt for his cell phone, pulled it out, and found that he had only a weak signal, but a call might get through. He searched for Eddie Shaw's number. As it rang, he explained to the others. "If this road isn't open, we're going to need some help or a mighty good backup plan."

"I've hiked that beach trail between here and La Push. It ain't much of a backup plan," Otis stated as he shifted into second and watched his mirrors for headlights to appear behind them. "It's hell in daylight and damn near impossible to attempt it in the dark. There are forty-foot ladders with ropes to get up the steep cliffs at Hoh Head.

When you can't use the beach, you have to go inland. There are blowdowns, mud holes that suck your shoes off, and streams to ford. This is the damned rainforest, Leon!"

Earl's call went through. "Eddie, boy am I glad you picked up!" Earl shouted into the phone over Otis's jabbering. There was another lurch due to a sharp turn that Otis took too fast, and Earl almost dropped the phone. "I'm kind of in some trouble, Eddie."

"Why am I not surprised, Earl?" replied Shaw. "You down that Hoh River Road somewhere?"

"Yeah, how did you know?" Earl asked.

"There's a Jefferson County patrol car parked next to your rig up by the bridge. We've been trying to locate you."

"Sally? Is it Sally?" Earl asked.

"Nah, she's fine. I just need to talk to you about the Pence brothers. Leon with you?"

"Yes again. Say, would you mind sending that patrol car down the Oil City Road as fast as he can go? And have him put on the siren."

"I can do that. But just what type of trouble are you in? Someone hurt?"

"Not yet," Earl replied. "But we've got guys chasing us with guns."

In another half mile, the road ended at the trail-head parking area. Otis slammed on the brakes again. In the headlights, they could see a concrete barricade placed across the old access road leading to the derelict drilling rig.

Their escape route was blocked.

Leon's backup plan was their only option.

The three of them scrambled out of the truck and headed down the trail toward the beach. They could hear the other truck coming up the hill. Not wanting to risk being exposed on the beach or breaking their necks by falling off a cliff, they scattered. They left the trail after a hundred yards or so and took up hiding places in an area of tall ferns and waited. They heard car doors opening and slamming along with voices. The voices got further away as the men searched up the old road beyond the barrier then got louder again. One of the searchers was on the trailhead when the wail of the siren on the patrol car could be heard. Earl let out a sigh of relief when he heard a truck engine start and beams of its headlights showed it was heading back down the road.

CHAPTER 28

J ake entered the office and walked over to a coffee service sitting on an ornate side table. The table was mid-18th century from Eastern Europe, like many of the expensive furnishings of Betar's mansion. He poured himself a cup of coffee and added some milk then a healthy amount of rum from a decanter next to the pot. Juno Betar liked his morning coffee Turkish style—strong and bitter. It was not Jake's favorite, but the rum and milk helped. He was lounging in one of the large chairs, facing the office windows and enjoying a view of a small sailboat moving across the lake, when Juno joined him.

"Our operations were a success. The flask you found is undoubtedly the one we have been looking for," Juno stated as he poured himself a cup of the strong coffee.

"Once we knew where to concentrate the digging and had something other than shovels, it was easy." Jake said. "You were right. It was not far from what used to be the keeper's residence. It was down maybe a foot below the surface and covered with pieces of wood—maybe cedar boards—and some of them were still intact. Was there a message inside? I left that for you to look for."

Juno's eyes were sparkling, and Jake could see that he was pleased about something. "Yes, indeed there was," he answered excitedly. "I have already scanned the document and sent it to a friend of mine in Madrid. Unfortunately, the writing is in old Spanish, and I'm waiting for a translation. Maybe in another hour or so at the most. Time enough for you to give me a report on last night. You removed everything from the staging area for your little operation?"

"We did. We had to rush after being discovered by two men who came down the river. One of them looked a lot like Leon Pence, and the other like a friend of his who survived the bomb blast on his boat."

"I'm disappointed, Jake. You failed, and if you are right about this Pence guy snooping around, it has raised attention about what we are doing."

"Nothing will be found at the farm, I assure you," Jake added. "I personally checked everything, even the refrigerator and bathroom. We removed everything we brought in, our equipment, even the garbage."

"What about the fellow who rented the place to you?" Juno asked. "Did he see any of your people or might inform the police about you?"

"Not likely. I used a drop to pay him in cash. Told him we wanted some privacy and to take an extended fishing trip in Alaska or something. Besides, he's sure to keep his mouth shut since he uses the place from time to time for drug trafficking from vessels off the coast. The place is still available to us if we need it again."

"So what about these two guys who were spying on you? You sure that's what they were doing?"

"When I recognized them, we put the chopper back in the air and followed them. They were already out of the river on the ocean and attempting to evade us by hiding in a bank of fog. We were short of fuel, and it didn't look like the fog would lift until the following morning, so I aborted the search. I thought it best to concentrate on clearing out. I had a couple of guy's watch them on the road and they took a side road and avoided us again. No matter, whatever they might report as suspicious activities to the authorities would just be hearsay."

Juno's cell phone beeped. He took the call. He listened for about five minutes, nodding several times, and then a slight smile crept across his face. "Thank you, Lucio," he said to the caller. "I appreciate your quick attention to the translation. Send me a copy, OK? And my secretary will see that you have a nice bonus for your services. Adios!" Juno put his phone back in his shirt pocket and smiled at Jake. "We now move on to the next phase."

"What's that?" Jake was anxious to know what Juno had just learned.

"It seems that there was a lot more information in the message from the commander of the Spanish ship. Our keeper, who reported finding the flask, failed to mention quite a bit about the incident. The ship captain's crewmen were killed in some kind of ceremony led by a man wearing the golden mask in a cave on the island."

"Damn, there's a cave somewhere on that island?" Jake uttered with a surprised look. "We walked all over that island in the last few weeks. Never saw anything that looked like the entrance to a cave. The island is barely above sea level; there can't be a cave."

"That's what the message said. There is a cave, and it is full of things used for rituals—capes, masks, drums, and some weapons. If they are still there, this would be a fabulous find. Finding them is exactly what we are going to do, starting immediately, before anyone else starts nosing around on the island. Get your team ready. I want every inch of that island searched again, even underwater if you have to. Just find me a way into that cave."

CHAPTER 29

Five people sat silently in the Pacific County Sheriff's office. Earl Armstrong sat next to Leon Pence, who fidgeted impatiently. Across the table were three law-enforcement people. Earl recognized Danny Green, who had been with the county sheriff's office for as long as he could remember. Next to Danny was a tribal police officer from the Quileute Tribe. The other person, a young woman, wore slacks and a khaki short-sleeved shirt. Her hair was pulled tight into a ponytail, and she wore no makeup. She was also wearing body armor as if it were part of the uniform she put on each morning before eating a bowl of cereal. In addition to the bulletproof vest, she wore a side-arm, as did the tribal officer, but on him it seemed natural. Earl found it difficult to picture any woman drawing and using an automatic weapon, particularly one as beautiful as the one sitting across from him. The badge pinned to her vest was that of the United States Fish and Wildlife Service.

The door to the conference room opened, and Detective Eddie Shaw entered. He took a seat at the end of the table, tossing a thin file folder down in front of him. He laid his cell phone alongside the folder and stared at it for a minute before speaking.

"Sorry to keep everyone waiting. We've had over a hundred calls this morning about tsunami debris, which began washing up on the beaches last night and again with this morning's high tide. Commissioner Rice called an emergency meeting of all departments. It looks like law enforcement, along with public works, is going to be short-handed and working overtime."

Shaw leaned forward on his elbows and glared at Earl and Leon. "I am not happy with you two interfering with an active case in my department by conducting your own little investigation. I can sympathize with the fact that both of you had your lives endangered—and Sally's, too—and could have been killed when Leon's boat blew up. By the way, I hear your wife is doing better, Earl."

Earl Armstrong acknowledged Eddie's words with a weak smile as he mumbled a response. "Yeah, she was able to come home yesterday afternoon but won't be able to return to work for a while. She won't like missing out on helping with the tsunami cleanup."

"We'll all be involved soon enough, Earl," responded Eddie. "The way the Coast Guard puts it, there's going to be so much debris to remove from our beaches, it could fill the crater of Mount St. Helens. But let me get to the point of this meeting. There have been two deaths and an attempted murder, and I want to know what the hell is going on here. Seems you and Leon know more than I do. So starting right now, I want to know everything."

Earl looked at his hands and said nothing. Leon fidgeted some more and a frown had formed on his brow.

"Let's start with you, Leon. Sorry I had to threaten to have you arrested in order to get you down here, but for the moment this is my investigation. Officer Persson is here from La Push because his department conducted an investigation into the sinking of your boat. Special Agent Lori Williams is here from the Pacific Regional Office in Seattle because Destruction Island keeps coming up as a possible crime scene, and the island is under Fish and Wildlife jurisdiction. She's a forensic specialist and investigates cases involving protected wildlife. Last year, Ms. Williams single-handedly took into custody three men, all twice her body weight I could add, who were illegally taking sturgeon on the Columbia River. So if something illegal is occurring out on the island, she's the go-to federal officer unless a marshal is required."

Lori Williams nodded ever so slightly to everyone in the room during Shaw's remarks, but she didn't smile when he mentioned her exploits. Shaw paused and stared at Leon Pence. "I want to...ah...be up front in saying since there are others present today, this is not an interrogation. But I have to warn you, Leon, I can require you to be interrogated and will issue a warrant if I have to. So, let's get started."

Leon raised his hands as if he were fending off Shaw's words like they were rocks. "As long as you are being so up-front, Shaw, I want an answer to one question before I say anything. Is this a murder investigation? Do you think my brother was murdered?"

Shaw hesitated before answering and took a few seconds to look around the table at each person present. "OK, I'll give you a strong maybe. We have some evidence that indicates that his death may not have been from natural causes. For the record, the autopsy report showed that he did not drown, and there is some evidence his body may have been dragged. That a good enough answer, Leon?"

"Fine." Leon said quietly. He bowed his head and ran his fingers through his long hair before continuing. "Will didn't deserve dying like this. He was a good man. He volunteered to serve his country in the military. He adored his mother and her sisters and tried to do everything he could for them—things they could no longer do for themselves. Our family has been goin' out to Destruction Island for generations for subsistence purposes. The trips have been as much a part of our culture as it is for you white people to go to a grocery store. That's what Will was doin' when he disappeared. He was gatherin' eggs from the cliffs on Destruction Island.

"There's another name for that island—the Isle of Sorrow. That name certainly takes on a bit of truth with our family. In the days after Oscar informed me about Will's body bein' found washed up on a beach, which I later learned was by Earl Armstrong, I felt like nothin' was being done to investigate his death. So I took the *Mary Lou*, that's my boat, and went out to the island. After anchoring in the small cove at the north end, I walked the entire length of that damned island, lookin' for clues that Will had been there. And I found one. The cooler that he used to keep his collected eggs in was tucked under a drift log at the south end of the island. It's sittin' right here behind me."

Heads turned to stare at the battered red-and-white cooler sitting against the wall behind Leon. On the top, in faded letters made by a felt-tip marker, were the letters W.-P-E-N-C-E.

"I carried that son-of-a-bitch cooler up the cliff and back to my boat. But what got me steamed up more than confirming that Will had been there were a couple of things that didn't fit."

"What didn't fit?" Shaw asked Leon.

"Along the top of the cliff, east of the abandoned lighthouse, the ground was disturbed from fresh digging.

At the time, I figured something had been digging out the burrows. Everybody knows the island has too many goddamned rabbits."

Lori Williams interrupted Leon. "Excuse me, but you're saying there has been digging on the island? Destruction Island is a no-entry area due to its status as a seabird nesting site. You and your brother aren't supposed to step foot on the island. But since apparently you did, what was the extent of this digging you saw? Are you sure it wasn't caused by rabbits or maybe just erosion?"

Leon turned his head toward the woman and smiled. "It was quite widespread, and some of the holes were pretty deep—maybe a foot or two. If it's rabbits doin' the digging, they sure have to be big suckers." Leon turned back to Shaw. "Can I continue? I'm not finished."

Shaw looked at Lori as he said, "Sorry, Lori, can you hold your questions until later?"

Leon rubbed his hands together and continued. "Then, when I was gettin' ready to pull up my anchor, I heard a helicopter. It was flyin' over the far side of the island, and then, as I got my boat underway, it turned my way and buzzed me real close. There were several men in addition to the pilot inside, and they looked me over pretty good before turnin' back to the island. I think they landed, but I didn't stick around. I went straight back to the harbor at La Push. Maybe it was just a coincidence seeing that helicopter, and maybe they were just curious about some old fishing boat next to the rocks along the north shore of the island. At least that's what I thought at the time. But not more than a week later, my boat was blown to pieces and is now at the bottom of the ocean. Earl Armstrong, his wife, and I were damn near killed. One of my buddies went down with that boat. He didn't have a chance in the world to get out of the cabin before she sank. I sure hope he died instantly from the blast. We were lucky to notice the detonator in the engine compartment and spotting a guy on the beach who looked like had activated it."

"I'm sorry for the loss of your friend, but why do you think someone set off a bomb on your boat?" Shaw asked Leon as he thumbed the edge of the file folder in front him. "I have a copy of the report on the incident. Officer Persson brought it with him this morning. There is only a brief mention regarding your statement of just you seeing someone do it and no one else. The report identifies your fishing boat as showing its age and is not well maintained but makes a lot of trips in and out of the harbor. The report also mentions an increase in contraband coming ashore along the north coast in recent months."

"That's a bunch of BS. Neither Will nor I have had anything to do with drug runnin'. And I know what I saw 'cause I was looking for that somebody. While on active duty as a Marine in Iraq, I saw dozens of IEDs that either were set off by cell phones or had failed to detonate for some reason. It was my damn job to clear them."

"Ok, Ok! The report is a bit brief," Shaw added. "But the tribal police were unable to find any witnesses who saw a suspicious man on the beach. Nor were there any reports of strangers, except for Earl and his wife, visiting the La Push marina prior to the incident. So we have just your word on that, Leon."

Oscar Persson looked nervous and shifted in his chair. He kept his arms folded over his extended stomach.

Leon continued to talk. "It was a black SUV, one of the larger models—like a Lincoln or a Lexus." Leon stared at Oscar and his voice was beginning to show his irritation. "And there is a report of one being in the area. I owe this bit of information to Oscar here. One of his friends who is a county patrol officer reported seeing an SUV matching my description turn off the Pacific Highway at the Oil City access road."

Oscar made a slight nod at the mention of his call to Leon. Leon relaxed a little and continued his story.

"Well, Earl and I checked out this black SUV report ourselves, and we found it along with the same damn helicopter that I saw out at Destruction Island."

All eyes were on Leon as he paused to let that comment sink in. He had their attention, especially Lori

Williams who looked like she was about to leap over the table at him.

"We sure as hell did. We found both of them at Oil City. There's an old homestead near the mouth of the Hoh River. From what we saw, the helicopter had probably been using the place to fly back and forth to the island. We spotted a bunch of barrels of aviation fuel they used to re-fuel it next to an old barn. When we saw the helicopter return, there was a small backhoe lashed to the undercarriage. They noticed our presence on the river as they were unloading it, which apparently they weren't happy about 'cause we got chased by that helicopter. Earl and I were able to duck into a fog bank, and after dark we went into the beach, where a friend of mine picked us up. When we tried to drive out, they had blocked the road and were waitin' with guns. You know the rest of the story—your call to the Jefferson County patrolmen apparently scared them off."

Lori Williams couldn't sit quietly any longer. "Mr. Pence, are you speculating that someone would actually fly earth-moving equipment out to a bird colony and commence digging? That is reaching a bit. Did you see anyone digging? I admit that there is an excess population of rabbits on Destruction Island, which my agency is studying, and they are known to be destructive to the vegetation and turf, which leads to erosion of the topsoil. Could it have been soil erosion?"

"The Fish and Wildlife Service is studying the rabbits?" Leon shook his head and was ready to laugh but instead responded angrily to the young woman. "You think I can't tell the difference between soil erosion and potholing? My god, woman! You folks better get off your asses and get the hell out there and see what's going on. Seems your no-entry area is gettin' mighty popular."

Lori was about to respond when Earl raised a hand and spoke quickly to relieve the tension in the room. "Uh... can I say something here?" No one said another word, so he continued. "Leon just mentioned potholing. It very well could be that something like that is going on out on the island. Let me tell you about something that happened with my great-grandfather when he was the keeper of the lighthouse on the island back in the late 1800s. His wife, Hermine, happened to find a very unusual object in her garden. It was a flask with a document sealed inside, which my great-grandfather discovered had been left on the island more than one hundred years earlier—in 1775, to be exact. The document from the flask reported a tragedy that befell the crew of a Spanish vessel and the presence of artifacts somewhere on the island."

"Is this true?" Shaw asked Earl.

"Yes. How do you know about this story?" Miss Williams added.

"It has been documented. Only I don't suppose anyone has ever read the report—at least until recently. And that includes myself."

"Where is this report, and who did you say wrote it?" asked Shaw.

"There is a set of log books for the Destruction Island lighthouse at the museum in Westport. They have a collection of things from the period when the lighthouse was still active. You can find his report in the log for 1893–94."

Danny Green abruptly got up from the table and left the room while Earl continued to describe the early years, when there was a staff stationed at the lighthouse. He paused when Green rushed back into the room and handed a piece of paper to Shaw. Shaw raised a hand, asking for silence, and read what was in the report. He nodded to Danny and then spoke to everyone present. "Mr. Green just remembered a recent police report from the City of Westport. It would appear that Earl is not the only one interested in what the Destruction Lighthouse logs have to report. Two weeks ago, someone broke into the Westport Museum. The only items removed from the museum were the logs, which were recovered several days later from a Dumpster on the outskirts of Aberdeen—not far from the body of a University of Washington graduate student who died from blunt force trauma. The young man's fingerprints were later confirmed to be found on a hammer used to break a window at the museum, and sign-in records indicated that he had visited the museum to examine the logs."

"Wow!" Earl remarked. "I knew other people had read the same entry I did, but one of them was murdered?"

"Gentlemen, I think some pieces are starting to fall in place." Shaw stated. "The evidence is pointing to multiple homicides, all leading back to Destruction Island."

CHAPTER 30

The skipper of the *Crystal Blue Sea* adjusted the autopilot ten degrees to starboard to pass just outside Buoy 6 off the entrance channel to Grays Harbor, putting the bow into a three-foot southerly swell. The wind was light, creating only a ripple on the surface of the water, which was good for whale sighting. Wendell Carter had been part of the whale-watching boat's crew for eight years and had gotten his "6-Pack" captain's license three months ago, which meant that he could skipper a vessel under sixty-five feet in length, carrying no more than six passengers.

Today, he had nine people on board for the first three-hour trip of the day. A family of four from Montana had arrived just before sailing time and pleaded with him to take the whole family, so he ignored the Coast Guard rules. The former skipper had been known to do it all the time, and it helped ease the pain of burning a full tank of expensive diesel fuel. There was some fog lying farther off-shore, so Wendell decided to run fairly close to the shore-line. He increased his rpm a few notches so that the boat was traveling at twenty knots. He was anxious to get to a spot where his boatload of tourists from the day before had enjoyed watching a pod of gray whales.

Wendell picked up the mike to the PA system, faced his little tour group, and started describing the gray whale migration and what they should be able to see today. He was a few minutes into his presentation when one of the Montana family's kids, a girl about eight years old, started running back and forth across the seats, looking for a whale on either side. He was starting to smile and make a remark about her antics when he was suddenly thrown back against the helm with such a force that he hit his head before slip-ping to the deck of the pilot house. The Montana girl liter-ally flew across the salon and crashed into the cabin bulk-head next to him. Every one of his passengers was thrown forward and out of their seats.

The entire hull of the *Crystal Blue Sea* shuddered as it slewed to starboard with the twin engines whining at a high rpm as the propellers were sheared off. Everyone was screaming as Wendell Carter struggled to his feet and shut off the engines. Then he grabbed the microphone for the marine radio and started hollering, "Mayday! Mayday! Mayday! This is the *Crystal Blue Sea*. Mayday! We just hit something. I'm activating our AIS signal now." He reached up and punched a button on the front of the radio.

"*Crystal Blue Sea*, this is Astoria Coast Guard. We have your Mayday call and your location. Are you in any immediate danger?"

Wendell answered back. "I've lost engine power. We have a list and there are injured. There are ten souls on board, including myself." Wendell shouted at a man who was attending to the little girl, who looked to be unconscious. "Get everybody to put on life jackets, right now, and put one on the girl!" He saw no sign of the two passengers who had been smoking cigarettes on the back deck.

He punched the radio mike again. "Correct my previous transmission. I may be missing two people. They could be in the water."

"This is Astoria Coast Guard. Roger that. We are sending a rescue helicopter now. Can you determine what you might have hit? Was it a whale?"

Wendell glanced out the windows of the pilot house. There was a long flat object barely above the surface of the water, floating about a hundred yards off. The water surface as far as he could see was covered in flotsam of all description—plastic, wood, Styrofoam. "Shit! There's debris everywhere. I think we hit a damn floating dock! Where did that come from?"

*

The message light on Mayor Justin Murray's telephone was blinking when he got to his desk at City Hall after a morning breakfast meeting with the owner of the South Bend Oyster Company. The owner wanted to expand his oyster snack bar to add a brew pub and was hoping that the mayor would help speed up approval of his building plans. He threw a set of plans and pictures that the man had given him onto a pile of papers behind his desk, sat down in a hurry, and grabbed the phone. The receptionist said that the call was from Sam Reynolds at the hospital.

"Hi, Sam. Sorry I left in such a hurry this morning. I had a breakfast meeting." Murray said as he glanced at the top letter on a stack of mail on his desk. "What's up?"

"You haven't heard the news?" Reynolds shouted into the receiver. "Jesus, Murray! A whale-watching boat just hit something and is aground on a reef south of Grays Harbor. The Coast Guard rescue boat from Westport is also on the scene, trying to locate two missing passengers. There's a couple of badly injured people. One's a little girl. A Coast Guard H-65 is taking them off the boat. We may be getting some of the people here at my hospital."

"Do you have any idea what happened to the boat? It's a beautiful day." Justin sat upright and gripped the phone hard.

"What I'm hearing is that the boat hit some kind of floating dock. One of our emergency-room staff heard on his police scanner that it may be one of docks that broke loose with the Japanese tsunami and believed to be part of the debris. We're going to be busy today, I'm afraid. I...I won't be able to have lunch with you, Justin."

Justin rubbed his forehead and thought for a moment. "This couldn't get any worse, Sam! This is going to be a public-relations nightmare."

"What is going to be a nightmare? We can handle it. I've got more emergency-room staff reporting for duty."

"I'm not referring to the victims. I know you will do everything you can for the injured. I'm referring to the nightmare that this tsunami debris is going to cause me. First, that threat of shellfish poisoning, and now a whale-watching boat hitting a dock where there shouldn't be one. No one is going to want to come to the coast this summer, and if people panic, we'll lose the volunteers needed for the cleanup."

Murray hung up without so much as a "see you later," only to have the front desk receptionist buzz him with another call waiting. He took the call with a more brash voice.

"Mayor Murray—who's calling?"

"So sorry to interrupt your busy day, honorable Mayor, but we have important business to discuss," stated the caller, purposely not identifying himself.

"Mr. Takahashi? My apologies, please," replied Murray. "I...I was not informed as to who was holding for me. Is this about the floating dock that was just found under unfortunate circumstances?"

"In a manner of speaking, yes. If you recall, our agreement was that you would do everything in your power to inform the public and have sightings of major debris from the tsunami reported to our call center. Edosan Corporation has contributed many hundreds of thousands of dollars to support the cleanup. We intend to do our job. Must I remind you to also do yours? We have made sure that there were certain donations to your reelection campaign, which total over $50,000 to date. In return, you offered the full cooperation of your public office. We heard your speech at the public meeting in Raymond last week. All Edosan is asking is that we work together. Now you wouldn't want things to suddenly go terribly wrong, would you, Mayor Murray?"

"No! No! Nothing like that!" Murray replied. Beads of sweat were forming on his brow and starting to drip onto his desk.

"Then we understand one another. I expect to see your face and hear your voice on TV by this afternoon, showing great enthusiasm and encouragement for the public to go out and help with the beach cleanup and to promptly notify the tsunami call center of any unusual pieces of debris and to not in any way attempt to handle them."

Without another word, Hiroko Takahashi clicked off, and Mayor Justin Murray was left to sweat all the more profusely.

*

When Mayor Murray appeared on the midday news, he looked and acted like the fatherly figure that his campaign PR person wanted him to portray. He was a Miyako Project leader, pleading for help in ridding our precious beaches of tsunami debris. It pleased Hiroko Takahashi that the man was convincing. His speech was so good that it could have persuaded people by the hundreds, young children and grandparents alike—anyone who could walk—to head for the beaches and help with the cleanup effort.

And they came. Within hours, businesses closed and schoolchildren were let out early, and buses full of volunteers were headed for the coast from nearly every community within a hundred miles. Families, church groups, scouts, students from the local community college—all loaded up with bags and buckets—and headed for the beaches. There were traffic jams at every beach access

from Westport to Ilwaco. People were parking and walking more than a mile to offer their help. Huge piles of collected debris began accumulating everywhere, overwhelming the ability of state and county public-works equipment
to haul it away. And the tsunami debris kept coming. With
the afternoon's receding tide, hordes of people descended
on the sands to pick it up, only for the next incoming tide to
bring tons more.

CHAPTER 31

The rattle of the anchor chain signaled to everyone on board the *Centaur* that the search for the cave and the golden mask was about to begin. The eighty four-foot cruiser had left Victoria the evening before and now lay a quarter mile off the west shore of Destruction Island. On the top deck, two of the crew hoisted an inflatable dinghy over the side while a dive master readied the dive gear on the aft deck. He laid out two tanks along with dry suits. Inside the luxurious cabin Juno Betar waited impatiently to begin his briefing. A young woman in skinny jeans and a tank top was gathering up breakfast dishes and coffee cups. Six pairs of male eyes watched her hips as Juno ordered her to leave until he was done.

"We have a single mission today—find an entrance to a cave on this island that has eluded discovery for over one hundred years." Juno paused and looked over the men who Jake Dixon had recruited and were now gathered in the salon. They were a tough-looking group. All of them had spent much of their lives outdoors, engaged in logging, mining, or construction. Two of the men were experienced rock climbers. Most had a record of felonies."

"Our search will be on land and underwater," Juno continued. "We will start both searches at the south end of the island, which has the highest terrain but is also the most rugged. There are crevices that drop down to the shoreline in almost sheer cliffs. Most of the island is overgrown with thick brush, but it will not deter any one of you. I want every inch of the island's surface above the water and under the water searched."

One of the men who was putting on a climbing harness looked out at the cliffs not far from the boat, where a slight swell was breaking onto a rocky shoreline. He gave Juno a questioning look.

Juno noticed this and continued, "Given the fact that sea level has changed over the last one hundred years, the entrance to this cave could lie just below the surface. Jake Dixon and Knute Watson will be our underwater exploration team. Their job won't be easy, again because of numerous underwater canyons and crevices. Now I want to emphasize to each man here that this isn't a picnic or walk in the park. You will work in teams of two and coordinate using the radios and GPS location devices that everyone is carrying. If you find anything that looks promising, call it in along with your GPS coordinates. You have four or five hours, so make every second count. That's about all the time we have; we have to pick up the anchor and haul our asses out of here before the weather turns. Any questions?"

The six men looked at each other, but none of them spoke. They all knew that in addition to being paid well, there was a nice bonus for the one who found the cave.

"Fine. Then let's get to work," concluded Juno.

Within minutes, the drone of the outboard motor on the dinghy could be heard as the first team headed for the shore. Jake Dixon and Knute Watson went out on deck and began putting on their dive suits. Knute was slower and a little unsure about adjusting his tank straps and the position of his regulator. Jake, who had spent four years of his life as a Navy SEAL, showed a little annoyance with Knute and finally assisted him in getting ready to dive. "I thought you said you had lots of experience at this."

"Yeah…uh…I've done a couple of open-water dives up in the San Juans. It's been a while, but I'll do okay."

"Sure, but what are you going to do if I get into trouble and need help? Call for the Coast Guard? You're not showing me any signs of being a good dive buddy."

"I'll manage, all right? I…I won't let you down. I want that bonus as much as anyone here." Knute busied himself by putting on his fins and face mask, testing his air, and finally giving a thumbs-up sign. Jake gave him a slight nod and dropped over the side. Knute climbed out onto the swim deck and jumped.

He had to swim hard to catch up with Jake, who was halfway to the shore and headed for the south point of the island. Both men were pushing surface debris out of there way. They would start at the point and then work their way north, exploring a couple of underwater slot canyons. Jake had studied the coastline and estimated that they could complete a search of two of the slots before going back to the boat for a brief rest and to exchange air tanks. One of the slot canyons looked pretty large on the charts and went deep, but Juno Betar had said that they probably didn't have to go deeper than fifty to seventy-five feet.

They were bounced around some with the swells as they explored the underwater terrain up close to the rocky shore. Visibility improved as they moved north, away from the surge at the end of the island, and began exploring the first slot canyon. The walls on each side were steep and smooth. Jake used his dive-mask communication unit to tell Knute to take the north side while he took the south. They probed small crevices and, other than surprising a few ling cod and small morays, did not discover anything that looked like a cave entrance. There were huge colorful anemones in the shallower water and large pale sponges as they went deeper.

"Man, this is an amazing area for a dive," Knute mentioned over his communication unit. "There's nothing in the Puget Sound that comes close in comparison."

Jake had to agree that even he was impressed with the abundance and diversity of sea life. He took his time and was methodical in his search, moving up and down the side of the canyon. He also kept an eye on Knute and noticed that the young man was moving far too quickly, using a lot of energy as well as air.

"You better slow down and control your breathing. I can tell by your bubble stream that you're using too much air. If you keep it up, we'll have to go back to the boat before finishing the next canyon."

Knute slowed a bit.

"Sorry, I keep thinking about the bonus for the first person to find the cave."

"Just focus on doing a thorough job. You get careless, and it can put one of us at risk." Jake checked his depth gauge. "I think we explored this one deep enough; let's move around the point and into the next canyon. It's quite a bit wider and is going to take more time."

The two men swam side by side around the underwater point between the two canyons. A large gray grouper hanging off the point in the current moved slowly out of their way and into deeper water. As they moved into the second canyon, they could see that the walls were more uneven with numerous dark areas, suggesting deeper depressions.

Jake spoke again to Knute over their underwater communication devices. "We'll go all the way in and work our way back out. You take the north side again."

They began to search once more. After checking the shallow surf zone, which was filled with boulders, each started going deeper on their respective sides of the canyon. Jake was right about his first impression. His side had several dark areas, but on closer inspection they were just overhangs and not deeper than a few feet. Glancing over at Knute, he noticed that the man was swimming down toward a fairly large dark depression on his side of the canyon. It looked promising, and Jake decided to abandon his side. He swam toward Knute, who was maybe another ten feet deeper.

"Damn! I found a cave, Jake," Knute announced excitedly. He waved both arms and then pointed down below his position just above the upper rim of a large opening.

Jake swam deeper so he could get a better look. There was a large amount of whitish rubble just below the opening, which looked to be maybe eight to ten feet wide based on Knute's height. He was twenty or thirty feet away when he noticed movement in the semidarkness of the cave opening.

"Knute! Get the hell away from there!" Jake hollered into the mike in his mask.

"What? What do you…" Knute's response was cut short.

A huge gray mass had emerged from the dark void. Before Knute could move away, a long tentacle wrapped itself around his right foot and started pulling him downward. Another tentacle reached up and grabbed his right arm. Knute struggled to free himself as he shouted to Jake. "Jake! For God's sake, get it off me!"

An ear splitting-scream came over the communication system, followed by a large stream of air bubbles spewing from Knute's face mask as it was ripped away. Jake was close enough to hear Knute's final screams underwater as the young man was dragged down and back into the cave entrance. He knew what the creature was, and there was nothing he could do. This was the largest Pacific octopus Jake had ever seen. Its tentacles must have been ten feet in length. He quickly backpedaled away from the entrance of the underwater cave, and, as he swam, he couldn't help but recognize that the white rubble that littered the slope below the cave entrance was the bleached remains of the victims of the huge octopus.

CHAPTER 32

After two days of managing beach cleanup efforts, the volunteer leaders of the Miyako Project were exhausted. High tide after high tide brought huge quantities of debris onto the beaches of the South Coast, and each time was like starting the cleanup all over again. Earl Armstrong was dead tired after managing a collection station for the debris. He was helping an older couple from Bay Center place bags of debris in a drop box that had just arrived at the beach access when he got a call on his radio from Eddie Shaw at the command center for the cleanup.

"Earl, this is Shaw. We've got a relief crew coming to your location. They're from one of the fire stations up in Olympia. As soon as they get there, tell your crew they can go home to get some rest. We will let you know if we need you again."

"We are being relieved? Thanks. We're about dead on our feet. It's like standing in the middle of an unending garbage dump out here. Plastic bags filled with picked-up debris and larger pieces that my volunteers have dragged in are piled everywhere."

"Yeah, the reports are pretty much the same all along the coast. Not too bad in Willapa Bay except for a bunch of oil drums that drifted onto the tide flats near the mouth of the bay. Some of the oyster growers are real worried about leaking chemicals and are trying to gather them up using one of their barges," Shaw said. 'Have you had a radio to listen to where you are?"

"A couple of the volunteers have been listening to the reports," responded Earl. "I've been too busy. Is this going to be over anytime soon?"

"According to the Coast Guard reports, the worst of it could last another couple of tide cycles. But there could be stuff coming ashore for months. This morning they had to close the Columbia River bar to all but commercial navigation under the command of the river pilots. Too many hazards. They're dispatching a salvage tug to try to get a line on that large concrete dock that the *Crystal Blue Sea* hit. Reports are that the boat sank and two people were still missing, presumably drowned."

"Wow," exclaimed Earl. "What about you? Is the county going to let you get back to being a crime fighter?"

Eddie laughed. "I'm being relieved as well. Believe it or not, the Governor asked for FEMA support and more help is on the way. Fortunately, crimes of passion seemed to have taken a holiday with the waves of tsunami debris attacking our coastline. Hasn't been one homicide reported. Couple of people died trying to pull some weird contraption out of the surf up north. It rolled and crushed two guys."

"They should have reported it for special handling on the hotline funded by that Japanese company. What's their name?"

"Edosan Corporation. I have no idea what their line of business is, but they seem to be spending a lot of money helping. Funny thing about their cleanup teams, though."

"What's that?" Earl asked as he pulled off a pair of work gloves and walked toward his car.

"I don't know what kind of weird stuff is being found in the other zones, but in the one assigned to me, we have had maybe a half-dozen sightings of suspected hazardous materials. Each time a cleanup crew has been dispatched by the Edosan call center to take care of it, my volunteers have reported that their crew took a look at the object, declared it nonhazardous, and left. It gave me the impression that they were looking for something specific."

"Maybe they have information about some really bad stuff that they aren't sharing with us or the public," Earl said. "We had that toxin scare a couple of weeks ago. Sally was working on that before the accident. She didn't think it was associated with shellfish, like the press reported. Her investigation showed it to be an industrial chemical compound that is similar to one found with shellfish poisoning."

"If they are looking for something like that, they certainly are being secretive. Maybe they want to avoid an international incident or something that might further embarrass the Japanese government."

Earl groaned audibly as he slumped into the driver's seat of his car. "Gosh I'm tired. Might sleep for two days. Don't call me, okay?"

There was a chuckle on the other end from Shaw. "Thanks for your help, Earl. But I almost forgot one of my reasons for calling you."

"And that was?" Earl asked.

"I got a call from Lori Williams, the Fish and Wildlife cop."

"Yeah. She's one tough gal. I would never want to be caught by her without my fishing license."

"She doesn't check licenses, Earl," Eddie replied. "She is a federal agent, not state. Just don't try poaching a species where the feds have jurisdiction, or she will have your neck under one of her shiny, black, special-ops boots with your hands zip-tied. *Then* she will ask you what the heck you were doing."

Earl laughed. "OK, OK, we can agree that she's one of the good guys, Eddie. So why did she call you?"

"Lori is gonna take a helicopter out to Destruction Island tomorrow. She wanted to know if I was interested in going along as part of the investigation team. Since I'm being relieved of my cleanup duties, I didn't hesitate in saying yes; in fact, I asked for two seats. She gave this cute laugh when I told her who I wanted to come with us. That's you, Earl."

"Me? No kidding!"

"Really, I do. Like Lori said—you are kind of an odd duck. But you know more than the rest of us about what someone might have been looking for out there. We're not sure how, but maybe your eyes will see something we can't."

"Did I just say I was tired?" replied Earl. "Man, I sure would like to see that place."

"Okay, you're going. I'll call you early tomorrow morning with the arrangements. Get some rest."

*

The truth was that Earl was dead tired after working so long on the beach cleanup. He struggled to stay awake while driving home. Sally seemed better, but the doctor had given her strict instructions about no lifting and no chores for another few days. It was not that difficult to prepare dinner because friends had been dropping off all kinds of prepared dishes. All Earl had to do was heat one up. He cleaned up the kitchen and collapsed into bed before eight o'clock. He slept soundly for six hours. Then the dream started...

CHAPTER 33

Destruction Island; June 1893

I t had rained steadily for five days. *Summer will be over before it started,* Chris Zauner thought as he shook the water from his black wool jacket and hung it near the woodstove in their small kitchen. His frown quickly dissipated with the smell of a freshly baked apple pie made from a barrel of apples that had arrived on the supply boat two days ago. The transfer from the *Columbine* had been exhausting for everyone, including the boat crew. First, the supplies had to be unloaded from the tender into a long boat, which two men struggled to row through the treacherous rocks to the small boat dock below the lighthouse. Then, the boxes and barrels were hauled up along a long wooden tramway to the top of the cliff and finally stored in a small building that served as a warehouse. The winds were never under 15 knots, and at times the rain whipped at the men with such force that it stung their faces and necks. Chris's devoted wife, Hermine, spent long hours in the warehouse, unpacking and taking inventory of the supplies as they arrived from the tender. The ship would not return for another two months.

Chris retrieved his mug from a plain breakfront where all of the china was stored and filled it with brewed coffee from a large pot warming on the back of the huge woodstove. It served as their source of heat as well as the source of Hermine's delicious meals. Even when they were down to their last few potatoes and dried beef, Hermine found things in her small root cellar under the floor of the kitchen to add to a stew that even a cook at the best hotel in Seattle would envy.

Abigail, who had just celebrated her ninth birthday, sat at the large dining table next to the window. She paid no attention to the rain that battered the panes and rolled down in large rivulets. With a lead pencil in her small hand, she was concentrating on something in front of her, probably copying letters from a page in one of her school books. Hermine was busy cleaning the dishes and pans from the evening meal. Chris took his mug of coffee over to the table and sat down across from Abigail. He stared at her soft curls of dark brown hair that Hermine had cut to just below her ears. Abigail sensed his stare and raised her sparkling eyes, smiled, and went back to her work. Chris turned his head toward the window and unconsciously studied the shifting pattern made by the rivulets of water.

He was having difficulty concentrating on his duties. They had been living on the island for nearly four years. He had to admit that those years had had their difficult moments, but he could not remember when he was not able to give 100 percent to his job. The Board recognized him as a keeper who could be counted as responsible and fastidious in his duties.

The Destruction Island post demanded such diligence. It was a difficult and important post on the Pacific Northwest coast and he had been selected to hold it. Now this cursed bottle with its message had come to light. He didn't like having to put its discovery in the lighthouse log, but it was required of him. It was the details he had failed to report to his superiors that bothered him. Maybe this was why he kept having the same dream—finding the cave, only to be held captive and involved in some kind of ritual. *Was there really a cave somewhere on Destruction Island?* The Spanish captain of the Sonora had specifically mentioned rituals being performed in a cave where his men had been sacrificed. Yet the presence of a cave on the island had never been revealed.

His thoughts were always on the cave that had appeared in his recurring dream. The dream had been unusual in that he had remembered every detail. He recalled the tall figure of a man wearing a cloak fashioned from some type of animal skin and his bright, shining mask—a golden mask. He could still hear the beat of the drums that reverberated off the dark walls of the cavern as the figure in the mask towered over him. He remembered the trail from the top of the cliff, which had been revealed by the moonlight. A few days after the first dream, Chris had explored the westerly edge of the island where he thought the trail started. Sure enough, he had found crudely shaped steps chiseled into the rocks that led down through a crevice in the steep walls of the cliff, only to discover that it ended just above the water. *Was the cave now underwater?*

His thoughts were interrupted by Hermine. "Chris, would you mind stowing the new potatoes and onions in the root cellar?" He walked over and pulled up the hatch in the floor. A cool breeze touched his face. He picked up one of the sacks of potatoes and climbed down the short ladder to store them in the cool, dry space below. He glanced at the crack in the hard rock floor, which was the source of the cool air. *The air must come from the cave! It's right under us! So there really may be a cave.*

After stowing the rest of the items from the ship, he took another sip of his coffee and tried to remember more

of the details from his dream. He had been knocked unconscious while descending from the top of the cliff and woke
up to discover his plight of being bound, lying on a rock in
what appeared to be a cave. *So how did I get from the path
into the cave? Surely I wasn't carried back up the trail to
the top of the cliff.*

Near the end of the path in the crevice was a
blowhole. Everyone knew about the blowhole because it
often entertained the island families during periods of
large southwesterly swells. It would boom loudly as a big
swell hit the rocks, and on rare occasions it would release
a spout of water. Chris thought about the blowhole and
how it might function. The thunderous thumping sound
it made must require some kind of a chamber in which
the water became trapped and then was forced upward
and outward. *A chamber!* Chris thought. *Could there be
an exposed chamber when the water level is low? Could
there be a cave that is accessed through a chamber within
the blowhole?*

Chris glanced at a calendar on the wall. There
would be a full moon in three days. The tides were already
in their extreme highs and lows. He decided to resume his
search for the entrance to the cave with the early morning
low tide when the blowhole would be dry.

Chris stood and walked around the table to see
what his daughter had been working on. He smiled. Instead

of numbers or letters, in front of Abigail was a sketch of the lighthouse and a small house.

"Well done, Abigail. It looks just like our home."

"I like to draw, Papa," Abigail replied. "Pictures can tell a story, too. See, by our house is mother's garden where the old bottle was found."

"Yes, I see that. But the bottle is gone now. We reburied it in the garden."

"Why, Papa?" Abigail asked.

"It represents a mystery, and maybe someone else will find it again someday and try to solve its mystery."

*

Chris rose early the next morning. Hermine did not stir; he often rose early to relieve one of the men on watch at the lighthouse. There was no sound from Abigail, whose small bed was curtained off from the main room of the keeper's quarters. The easterly sky bore a thin orange tint as the rain clouds moved farther to the north. The board-walks and tall grass around the buildings were wet from the night's rain.

Chris put on his cap and a short rain slicker and then picked up a lantern he kept just inside the door to the house. Chris gave it a shake and was satisfied that there was enough kerosene to last him if he needed it to enter the cave.

He set off in the direction of the narrow defile that led down to the blowhole below the westerly edge of the cliffs. The way down was slick from the rain, so he proceeded carefully. It took him ten minutes to reach the bottom near the blowhole, where he checked his pocket watch. He had two, possibly three, hours before the tide turned and came back up. To be safe, he would stay for only two hours and give himself a safety margin. It could be disastrous if he stayed too long and the blowhole filled with surging water while he was inside.

Except for the calls of a few feeding seabirds just off the shore, it was quiet. The ocean was calm, and there was very little wave action on the rocks. This meant that he could probably enter the blowhole and explore it without much danger of water entering and trapping him inside. Chris climbed up to the level of the top of the blowhole and peered inside. He had never studied the interior of the blowhole before and now looked at its construction from the standpoint of its geology rather than with curiosity as to how it functioned. He knew that a blowhole had to have a narrow opening to the sea and that the wave action would force water up through it and out the top of it when the blowhole was submerged.

Some blowholes acted like geysers. Others made a deep booming noise due to the water's surging action as it filled an empty underwater pocket. The one he was looking at had a broad opening at the top, like a bathtub with a too-small drain. Most high tides simply flowed over the top with a lot of foam. It did make a drum-like thumping sound when there was heavy surf, which could mean that it was connected to a chamber where air was trapped and compressed.

Across from where he stood, peering into a now-empty basin, was a deep, dark slit in the rock. Chris was pretty sure that this was where the water entered with a rising tide and drained out on an outgoing tide. When a large wave hit the shore, it forced water up through the slit repeatedly until it spilled over the rim of the basin or drained back out.

The interior walls were covered in barnacles but had fewer mussels than rocks just outside the blowhole, probably due to the violent surges it experienced. On the wall opposite the ocean was a dark area under a protruding ledge. It was large, and from where he squatted on the rim, he could not see whether it was a chamber or just an overhanging ledge of rock. The bottom of the foreboding cavity was about five feet below him, and he would have to climb down to investigate. As he slid down into the blowhole, a small figure at the top of the cliff watched him disappear.

CHAPTER 34

As Chris examined the dark chamber in the back of the blowhole, his excitement grew. What could have been easily mistaken as smaller ledges were actually several steps at the bottom of the blowhole hewn into the stone surface just like the path at the top of the cliff. While he lit the lantern, he glanced anxiously over at the dark slit in the rock behind him, imagining the sea water gushing into the blowhole. Then he cautiously used the steps to approach the opening, holding up the lantern to see how far back it went. The yellow light from his lantern showed a cavern with a gentle incline leading back into the bedrock of the island. He proceeded into the cavern and had to stoop over because of the sloping roof. The first few feet were covered in barnacles, small crabs, and copepods that skittered away from him as he proceeded. He estimated that he may have gone about forty feet and climbed a little over ten feet when the walls and floor of the cavern became dry.

There were no more barnacles underfoot. The sloped surface was smooth. Up ahead was a black void that the lantern light could not penetrate, and the sound of his rapid breathing was magnified by the rock walls as he moved deeper into the passageway.

A huge figure of a man suddenly appeared in front of him. Startled, he stumbled backward, knocking off his cap on the ceiling of the passageway. He instinctively raised the lantern to protect himself, and its beam revealed a painted petroglyph of a fierce-looking man with an oversized head. The figure held a knife or club in one hand. The red pigment that had been used to paint the figure was bright and looked like it had just been applied.

Chris lowered the lantern and moved on. The cavern made a slight turn to the left and, after a few more steps, he found himself in a large chamber. He thought about kicking himself for not bringing a second lantern as he began to raise and lower the one he carried in an effort to see more of the chamber. The last thing he wanted to do was to fall into a shaft or hole that he could not see.

Waving the lantern to his right, he noticed a number of slender objects next to the wall—some leaning, some fallen over. He walked toward them, shuffling his feet so as not to stumble and to be able to detect whether the floor dropped away. He reached the objects without incident. He let out a low whistle when he discovered that they were spear shafts—dozens of them. Mixed in with the fallen shafts were shorter, heavier objects, which he assumed were war clubs.

Chris sniffed the air and recognized a familiar scent lingering in the air. He should have recognized it right away—the smell of burned whale oil. He raised the lantern again and saw a stone bowl sitting on a rock about waist high. He approached it and let the lantern play on the object. There was a sheen coming from the contents of the bowl. Setting his lantern down, Chris pulled out his kerchief and ripped off a piece, stuck it into the flame of his lantern, and then dropped the flaming cloth into the bowl. The contents burst into flame, and the chamber brightened. He turned to his left and saw two more bowls. Each contained a small amount of whale oil, so he lit them the same way.

Chris was shocked beyond belief as surveyed the cavern. It was roughly one hundred feet long and much taller than he could reach. In the semidarkness, he could see that the back of the cavern narrowed. Part of the wall was smooth and in one corner was a jumble of boulders possibly with a connection to the root cellar under his house. What drew his attention next were the sides of the chamber. Along each side were low platforms made from rough wooden planks. Stacked on the platforms were dark bundles that appeared to be secured with rope.

He walked over to the closest platform and ran his hand over one of the bundles. The surface was smooth and slick. *Some kind of tanned hide, and this isn't rope but braided cedar bark!* Chris had noticed that some of the Indians who visited the island in their canoes wrapped things in sealskin to keep them dry and used rope braided from cedar bark. He searched for a knife in his pocket and used it to cut the bindings on one of the bundles. Rolling it open, he discovered that he was correct. It was sealskin. Inside was a wooden mask, a cedar robe, and a round drum with an eagle design painted on the stretched leather. The objects were in beautiful condition. Chris made another guess. *Wrapping these things in sealskin must have preserved them!* He cut the bindings on a second bundle and opened it. Inside was another robe and a beautiful rattle shaped like a bird with the figure of a man lying on his back on the top.

Chris coughed twice and realized that it was starting to get smoky in the confines of the cavern. He quickly rewrapped the objects that he had examined and turned to look at the rest of the chamber. In the center, and closer to the rear wall which had no platforms, was a large flat stone. Arranged on top of the stone were several human skulls. He almost dropped his own lantern as he stumbled backward, as if his body had been shoved by some unseen force. *Oh, my God! This is the stone in my dream. This is where someone in a mask was about to kill me!*

Suddenly, Chris felt his chest tighten and found the air in the cavern difficult to breathe. He had to get out. Chris panicked and ran back down the passageway to the blowhole. Once outside, he scrambled up the side of the blowhole, where he leaned over and vomited. Chris sat there for several minutes in the cool, fresh air until his hands stopped shaking. He looked around and noticed that the ocean's waves were building and crashing onto the rocks below the blowhole. He checked his watch. It was too late to return to the cavern even if he wanted to—and he did not. He had seen enough. This had to be the cave described by Juan Francisco, the Spanish captain, where his crew was killed. He remembered one more thing—in addition to the human skulls, the rock was covered with dark stains, as if from blood...

*

Earl woke with a start, threw his blankets off, and swung his legs over the side of the bed. He was breathing hard and sweating, and his hands were shaking. There was the taste of bile in his mouth. *Damn! Chris Zauner found the cave! He worked it out, checked the blowhole, and discovered a passageway to the cave that can be entered at low tide. Oh man, what other secrets are there on Destruction Island?*

He stared at the clock radio on his nightstand and saw that it was just after 2:00 a.m. Sally was sound asleep, so he sat on the edge of the bed until his breathing slowed. *It ought to be a cinch to find the cave, but will there still be anything in it? Can stuff like that survive over 240 years? They can, if properly preserved. The things in King Tut's tomb in Egypt survived for over three thousand years.* Earl snuggled up to Sally and went back to sleep. What he didn't know was that there was more to the story about Chris Zauner and the cave…

*

Chris was light-headed and shivering. He clutched the front of his slicker as he climbed the steep path back to the top of the cliff. A breeze was stiffening, and larger waves were pounding the rocky shoreline below him. As he reached the rim, Chris heard a thump as the blowhole resumed its role in responding to the wave surges with the rising tide. Checking his pocket watch, he figured he had been away from the house for about two hours, maybe less. Opening the door, he smelled fresh coffee brewing. Hermine was busy with preparing breakfast.

"You are up earlier than usual, Chris. Anything wrong?"

"No, dear," he replied. "I just wanted to check the bearings under the lens while it was still operating. They sounded a bit noisy last night. Once I was satisfied, and not wanting to disturb you, I took a little walk along the cliff. It is so refreshing after a rain squall clears out and is followed by some clear weather."

For the next two days, Chris couldn't get the visions of his venture down into the blowhole, the passageway behind it, and the cave out of his head. He thought about returning, but his courage failed him. Chris knew that his performance during his work shifts was suffering as well. He'd forgotten to make his morning entry in the log book because he was slow to clean the lamp black from the panes of glazing. All because he was letting the things in the cave fill his mind. He had not looked for the golden mask mentioned in the note. He should have examined the stone altar, or whatever it was, more carefully. He should have looked for something that might provide some clue as to who these people were or why they left everything in place. Of course, he would never know. He had panicked, and he wasn't going back in there. There could have been a hundred reasons why the cave had been left undisturbed for 125 years. And it was going to stay that way.

Chris resolved not to mention his exploration in the keeper's log. There would be no more entries about it. He would not discuss it with his staff or with Hermine even though she suspected that something was wrong. She knew it immediately when he walked back into the house after running from the cave. His facial features must have told her something. But she did not bring it up again even though he had been forgetful as to the chores he had to perform for her around the house. Hermine simply did not need to know about the existence of the cave and its awful contents.

*

On the night of the next full moon, Chris took the early morning shift at the lighthouse. At full light he shut down the lens and made a brief entry in the keeper's log that simply stated that one ship had been sighted headed north and all that was well. Olle Olsson entered Chris's small office just as he finished making his entry.

"Mornin' Olle, Chris said to the big man. "Do you mind if I help replenish the oil and clean the mirrors?"

"No, sir," Olle replied. "I'll take up the oil if you would tackle the glass. That narrow walkway 'round the lens is always a problem." Olle was big and brawny. It was incredible what the man could lift. Carrying the large cans of oil up more than a hundred narrow steps that wound around the interior of the lighthouse to Olle was like a child playing with blocks. While this was not Chris's chore, it felt good to help, and it seemed to make up for things he had been forgetting to do over the past few days.

It was after nine before he returned home. Abigail's books were scattered over the table when he sat down but she was not seated doing her usual schoolwork. Hermine brought him a hot cup of coffee.

"Thanks, Hermine. Where is Abigail? Is she still sleeping?"

"No. She's been up for quite a while. I thought maybe she went to the lighthouse to find you. You didn't see her?"

"No, she never came in," replied Chris, his face showing his concern. He picked up a drawing that lay on the table among Abigail's books and other papers. It was a drawing of a man standing by the blowhole at the bottom of the cliff. Chris groaned and stood up in such a rush that he spilled his mug of coffee. "Oh my God! She's gone down to the blowhole! She must have seen me go down there."

He grabbed his hat and a lantern and rushed out the door toward the cliffs as fast as he could. As he reached the edge of the cliffs, he searched the area below for Abigail. He couldn't see her, but deep inside him was the dreaded feeling that she must have gone down and maybe even gone inside the blowhole. Chris started down the trail. On the rocks below, a large wave crashed, and seconds later, he heard a thump as the blowhole began to sound. Without hesitation, he climbed up and checked the interior. It was half-filled with water. Abigail was not inside. He glanced around and was looking back up the trail when he heard a scream come from under the ledge.

"Help me! Help me! I can't get out!"

"Abigail, honey, I'm here! I going to get you out of there," Chris hollered into the chamber. His shouts were drowned out by water rushing out of the slit in the side of the blowhole and rising halfway up the inside of the basin. Ignoring the incoming water, Chris set down the lantern and slid down the edge of the blowhole. He waded toward the overhanging ledge, struggling to stay on his feet as the water surged and then started to drain away.

Chris heard Abigail's frantic voice, choked with sobs, and figured she must be inside the passageway to the cave. "Papa...Papa...the water is coming in and things are crawling all over me! They're biting me!" she screamed again and again. "Help me!"

The chamber opening was still flooded, and with the swirling of the water in the basin of the blowhole, Chris figured it wasn't going to get any lower. He took a big breath, dropped to a prone position and half-crawled/half-swam under the ledge and into the chamber. His back scraped the barnacles along the top of the chamber as the swirling water tugged at him. But seconds later, he was inside, and the receding water let him struggle forward to stand up.

Abigail's screams were much louder as he emerged in the passageway. In the darkness, Chris waved his arms in front of him until he touched her. "I'm here, honey!"

She grabbed his waist tightly in a hug. Chris immediately felt something crawling up his arms and pants legs. It was the copepods. He ignored them and knelt beside the little girl, brushing her face, arms, and clothing in an attempt to knock off as many as he could.

"Listen to me, Abigail. I will get us out of here, but we have to go under the water. All you have to do is hold your breath for a few seconds. You can do that, right?"

Abigail stopped screaming, but her body was still shuddering uncontrollably. Finally, she uttered, "Uh-huh."

He didn't hesitate. He grabbed Abigail, tucked her in front of him, and walked backward until they were almost submerged. He waited until the cavern flooded with water again and started to recede.

"Now! Hold your breath!" Chris held Abigail with one arm and used the other to feel the bottom and walls as he pushed backward, letting the receding water carry them out into the basin of the blowhole. Their heads broke the surface of the swirling water as he tried to gain some footing. Abigail was sputtering and coughing, but that was a good sign. A strong hand grabbed Chris's arm and yanked both of them up over the rim. It was Olle, and behind him stood Hermine, with a wool blanket in her arms...

CHAPTER 35

Jake Dixon hated tourists. Worse than tourists, he hated losing. He had missed his target with the explosives in the boat and failed to find the cave. When he was in the Marine Corps, there had been several occasions when Jake had gotten into a fight, and his opponent thought he had beaten him. But something inside Jake had triggered a will to win, and he had fought back, leaving his opponent wondering what had happened as he lay on the floor bleeding. He was determined to finish is job for Juno Betar.

On the long trip back to the harbor at Victoria, Jake had spent hours with his boss going over everything they knew about Destruction Island and its hidden cave, which presumably held the golden mask. To find the mask they had to find the cave. Juno had expressed his concern over the unfortunate loss of Knute, but that did not deter him from wanting to continue the search. He seemed more determined than ever.

When Jake talked about the Pence brothers being familiar with the island, his boss came up with a new course of action—perhaps an easier way to finding the cave. Juno decided that if the Indians on the coast had been going to the island for generations, then they must know a lot more about the place than he and Jake did. So their tactics shifted, and Jake was ordered to learn what he could about the island from local Indians by any means that he needed to employ.

The town of Forks wasn't exactly a hotbed of such information, but it was a commercial center near several coastal tribes. The small community was sprawled along the Pacific Highway and, after World War II, had become a major center for the timber industry. Now it was vampires that kept the town's economy going. After a series of best-selling novels that had been made into movies and involving teenage vampires, the town became a tween girl's mecca.

Jake parked his sedan in front of a tavern near the intersection of the turnoff to the Quileute Indian Reservation and went inside. The place smelled of stale beer and cigarette smoke. Jake moved to the bar and found a vinyl-covered stool that wasn't too badly torn up, ordered a Coors Light, and surveyed the room. There were a couple of Indian men and one woman talking loudly at a table on the far side of a pool table. Most of their conversation was swearing about good-for-nothing relatives. On the other side of the bar, there was a small dance floor and four booths set along a wall full of neon beer signs. A young couple sat in the booth closest to the front entrance, while in the last booth a lone man sat with his head in his arms on the table and a half-dozen longneck beer bottles lined up in front of him. He had dirty gray hair tied into a single braid. Jake watched him for a few minutes, and, as if sensing Jake's stare, the man lifted his head and peered at the empty bottles. His head wavered as if he were trying to figure out if any of them still contained any beer.

Jake smiled. He ordered another beer, this time in a long neck bottle, and took it over along with his own and sat down across from the man. The Indian looked up at him.

"This one's full. Try it." Jake pushed the fresh bottle toward him.

The man reached for the bottle, almost knocking it over, got a hand around it, and took a long pull. "What do ya want, white man?"

"Just being a friend," Jake replied.

"Got no white friends. Go away and let me drink by myself," the drunk said.

"Hey, I just brought you a beer. Is that any way to be friendly? I just need some information." He sat and stared at the man, with his senses recoiling. The smell of beer and urine was overwhelming.

"Yeah, like what, white man?"

"Ever heard of Destruction Island? Ever been there?" Jake asked firmly.

"Where? Destruction Island? Ain't hardly anyone goes there anymore. It belongs to the damned government."

"I know, but Indians can go out there, right?" Jake anxiously pressed his question while the man was alert.

"There's a few families from the res that do. Don't know 'um. You might ask Oscar."

"Oscar? What's his last name, and where do I find him?"

"Everyone knows Oscar Persson. He's an officer with the tribal police. He likes to drink at the Cedars. Ya can't miss him—he's got a big belly. Now get the hell out of my face, white man!"

The Indian took another swig from the new long-neck, put it in the line with the others, and laid his head back down in his arms. Jake was glad to slip out of the booth.

A few minutes later, Jake was cruising south on the main drag, watching for another watering hole called the Cedars. He found it just north of a small airstrip near the visitor information center. In front of the information center was a replica of the red pickup from the *Twilight* films that had put Forks on the map for tourists. The Cedars had a new sign, but the building wasn't in much better shape than the first bar. It had fresh paint and a newly paved parking lot, which was half full of pickup trucks and beat-up cars. He parked next to one of the pickups that had mud caked up to the windows. The bed of the truck was littered with empty beer cans and fast-food wrappers.

Jake entered the pub, half expecting the waitresses and bartender to have fake fangs in their mouths. To his relief, there were none. There was music, and it was loud. Two couples were using the dance floor. The room had a shuffleboard table and a couple of dartboards at one end. The furniture was newer than stuff in the last place, and the bar had comfortable chairs with backs instead of stools.

Jake sat at the bar, ordered another beer and checked out the other customers. No one looked Indian, and none of the guys had big bellies, like the drunk had mentioned.

So he waited.

Eventually, it occurred to him that he would need to take a different approach with someone who was in law enforcement. Roughing the man up to extract information probably was not going to work.

At five minutes after nine, a man fitting the description walked in, hitched up his pants, and took a seat at the other end of the bar. He ordered a glass of whiskey and a beer. It was called a boilermaker and was a popular drink with those who wanted to get a buzz on fast. Jake decided to let him drink for the next half hour or so, hoping that the man wasn't just making a quick stop. He looked like he was stewing about something and needed a few drinks. When the cocktail waitress, a perky little redhead, sauntered back by Jake, he caught her attention.

"Excuse me," he said, "Is the fellow at the other end of the bar a state police officer? I think his name is Persson. He pulled me over south of here on my last trip out to the coast."

"That's Oscar Persson all right. He's tribal police, not highway patrol. Comes in here three or four times a week after his shift."

"Thanks."

Jake smiled, not for the cute waitress who smiled back, but because he knew that he had found his prey. He waited another five minutes and then moved in. Making contact was actually easier than he thought it would be. Oscar Persson was a talker.

"Hi," Jake said as he slid onto one of the seats next to the man. "The waitress told me you are a police officer, and I'm supposed to meet a friend at the Quinault Lodge. Is that far from here?"

"Lake Quinault?" Oscar asked. "It's down on the Quinault res, maybe an hour or hour-and-a-half drive. You gotta keep an eye out for deer and elk on the highway down that way."

"Great! My buddy and I are freelance writers, mostly for travel magazines and such. We're down here to write an article for the *New York Times* online edition."

Jake took a sip of his drink. "So are the local police tourist-friendly? You know, to college kids on spring break, as long as they don't bother the locals or other tourists?"

"What do ya mean? Yeah, I guess so," replied Oscar. "Neither the tribal police nor the county sheriff's put up with any of that *Girls Gone Wild* partying or drugs—stuff like that. But it's okay to let off some steam and drink a few beers. Hell, I like a beer once in a while."

"Yeah, me too," Jake said. "That's why I stopped here in Forks. I felt like having a beer. Say, I think I read in the Tacoma newspaper that it's been quite a summer down here. Some guy washed up on a beach and a boat blown up, killing another guy, and then all the tsunami debris covering the beaches. Sounds like the coast could use some good publicity." Jake paused and finished his bottle of beer. "Want another beer? I'll buy."

"Sure, if you're buyin'. I'm a bit pissed at my supervisor. He gave me a reprimand for makin' remarks about one of his reports. Hell, he wrote it up like he did some big investigation and hardly talked to nobody." Oscar banged his fist hard on the bar causing Jake to flinch. "And yeah, we sure could use some good press for a change. You know, them law-enforcement folks down by Aberdeen also found a dead college kid a few weeks back? Figure it might be related."

"No kidding! Wow!" Jake faked his surprise. "I haven't seen or heard anything about that incident." He raised his hand to attract the bartender and showed two fingers, implying two more beers. The bartender nodded back and opened the drink cooler to grab two more longneck Buds. "Any of them from around here?" he added.

"Sure are. Them Pence brothers are from just down the highway. Will Pence was the guy who washed up on a beach down by Westport, and his brother Leon had his fishin' boat blown up." Oscar looked at Jake with a questioning look. "You gonna write about them? Most of it has been hashed over pretty good in the papers."

"Naw, I don't write about the sensational stuff. Too much competition, and no money in it for freelance writers. I prefer to stick to little-known things like who serves the best damn cheeseburgers on the Washington coast or places of interest that no one ever has heard of before. Like I read about this island off the coast with some old lighthouse. I can't remember the name. You know the one I mean?"

"Destruction Island?" Oscar answered.

"Yeah, that's the one. I didn't even know there was a damn island out there. Does anyone go to the place?"

"Not anymore. There used to be an operating lighthouse on it, but it's been abandoned for a long time. Now it's a bird refuge. Hoh and Quileute people used to go out there, but now it's restricted. Why they would bother beats me. It's a bitch to get to. You need good weather and a boat, and there ain't a very good spot to go ashore." Oscar paused to take a long sip of the fresh beer that the bartender placed in front of him. "Strange you asked about that damned island. I went to a meetin' with some law-enforcement guys down in South Bend, and they were talkin' about it, too."

"Is that right?" answered Jake, this time with a truly surprised look. "Now I am thinking of a story— *Mysterious Island Subject of Investigation*. If I may ask, why would an island in the middle of nowhere that hardly anybody hears about suddenly be the subject of an investigation?"

Oscar took another long swig of his beer, nearly draining it. He made some obvious motions with the bottle to indicate that another would be welcome. "Well, off the record, of course, I had to drive down to South Bend yesterday to attend some damn meeting where they were looking into Pence's death. The detective heading up the investigation thinks there may have been a murder...that his death wasn't accidental. My boss told me to attend because our office did a report of Pence's brother's boat accident—the report that got me in trouble. If someone hadn't died when it sank, everyone around here would have laughed. Why that old wood-hulled boat was still floating is a wonder in itself. Pence never did any maintenance on it. My boss figured it was just a coincidental accident."

Jake smiled. "Old boats never die. They just sink or rot away on some mudflat. Here's to Pence's old boat." He raised his bottle and then took a long sip. "So how does the island of mystery get to be part of this guy's death?"

Oscar shook his head. "That's where things started getting really weird. They had Leon Pence there for questioning. He's the brother. Him and some other fellow, a forester I think, were on the boat and survived, along with this other guy's wife, when it sank. Supposedly they were going to spread the brother's ashes out at sea. The way Pence told it, he went out to Destruction Island looking for evidence that his brother was out there. He found the proof and also reported that some pot hunters had been doing some digging. We get reports of illegal diggin' around here all the time 'cause of so many old Indian settlements and burial sites. It keeps our cultural resource people pretty busy cleanin' up after them." Oscar gripped the bar with both hands and stood up unsteadily. "Order me one for the road while I make a visit to the men's room, will ya?"

Jake watched Oscar weave through the tables and chairs to the restrooms at the back of the pub. He went over in his mind what the inebriated patrol officer had mentioned. *So Pence did find something to indicate his brother was on the island. And he saw where we were digging for the old bottle. No matter, we're finished with that job. We found it, and there is no way the digging can be tied to us. So what else do they know? What a break to learn that Oscar was present at the meeting.*

Jake was lost in his thoughts for a few minutes when a heavy hand suddenly clamped onto his right shoulder. His reflexes kicked in as he grabbed the wrist and turned so quickly that Oscar, who had come back to his barstool, nearly fell down. Jake grabbed his wrist in a vise grip and held it against the bar.

"Easy there, man!" Oscar exclaimed. "You sure got some moves for a writer."

"Sorry. Oscar. My mind was elsewhere, I guess. You came up behind me, and I was surprised. Spent two years in the Helmand province in Afghanistan, where I had to stand night watch. You never get over being a bit jumpy after that."

"Ah, that I can understand. I did a tour in Iraq during the first war myself." Oscar rubbed his reddened wrist and got his overweight frame situated back on his barstool. There was another beer in front of him, which got his attention.

Jake wanted to get Oscar talking again and pressed him for more information. "So why were these people so interested in this island?"

"They weren't until this forester fellow, Earl Armstrong, piped up and stated that there could be a reason for the pot hunting, or at least something really old that might be of interest to a collector. He said that the object could have been buried on the island near the old lighthouse for a long time. Apparently his great-grandfather used to be employed at the lighthouse. Armstrong started talking about some old bottle left by a Spanish explorer that his great-grandfather had found and reburied. That there was a message in this bottle referring to some kind of treasure hidden in a cave on Destruction Island." Oscar snickered and shook his head. "Doesn't that beat all? That island is nothin' but a pile of rocks pounded by waves. There's no way some treasure could survive for hundreds of years. I bet there is somethin' collectible out there now that the tsunami debris is hitting the coast. Destruction Island had to have taken a big hit."

Jake ignored Oscar's remark about the tsunami debris. "Well, maybe there are caves out there. Could that be a possibility as a hiding place?" Jake asked halfheartedly. "Yeah, that would make quite an article that I could sell to one of the tabloids. Kind of perpetuates the mystery, you know? I can see the banner now—*Investigators Search Elusive Island Cave for Clues to Recent Murder.*"

"Ain't no caves on that island that I ever heard of, but I guess anything is possible," Oscar mumbled, with his speech beginning to slur a bit. "This Armstrong fella sure seemed convinced that there was one and his great-grandfather seen it once. Said he could find it. What I hear is that they're gonna make a trip out to the island to take a look around. I think they said it would be in a few days. I don't care what the hell they do as long as I don't have to go. I hate helicopters and boat rides. Both make me sick."

Jake glanced at Oscar's big belly and heard him belch. He nodded as he looked at his wristwatch. "Gee, I better get moving. My friend down at the lodge will be wondering where I am. Maybe I'll continue down the coast and see if I can find this Armstrong fellow. A historical tie-in to a travel article about this mysterious island sounds like a good idea." He gave Oscar a pat on the back "See ya around. Maybe I'll be back up this way."

Jake headed for the door, pulled out his cell phone, and punched in a number as he walked to his vehicle. Juno Betar answered.

"I think I know who is going to help us find the cave. There's a guy down in South Bend by the name of Earl Armstrong who claims his relative is the very guy who made the entry in the log and was the one who found the bottle. I don't know how this Armstrong guy knows more than we do, but I'm going to find out. I might have to find a way to persuade him to share his information."

CHAPTER 36

E arl Armstrong woke up shivering, disoriented, and with aching muscles. His blankets were wrapped tightly around him again, yet he felt cold and his hair and face were damp with sweat. It took him a few minutes to decide that he wasn't sick and to get his bearings. He was in his bedroom, and Sally was still sleeping quietly beside him. He swung his feet over the side of the bed and sat up. His muscles really did ache. Then he remembered hauling bags of debris and loading drop boxes the day before. *Or was it from crawling around in a cave?* He shivered at the thought and realized that he had again had a dream that associated him with Chris Zauner. The big question on his mind was why. *Why am I having a series of dreams about Chris and something that happened on Destruction Island over one hundred years ago? Gosh, it's been over fifteen years since I've had this kind of dream. Why me? I've got to get some help. Maybe Johnson Wewa will know the answer.*

*This is really crazy, going to an Indian shaman rather than
a psychiatrist.*

After breakfast, Earl decided to look up Johnson
Wewa's telephone number and called him before leaving home.
"Johnson, how are you doing?" Earl asked as the old shaman
answered the call. It was hard to hear him, and Earl began to
talk louder. "Where are you?" Johnson's response sounded as
if he were speaking in a tunnel that had a slight echo. "Okay,
let me repeat that," Earl said. "You're in Astoria?"

Earl nodded as he listened to Johnson explain and
then ask how Sally was doing.

"She's recovering just fine. We think the doctor
will let her go back to work in another few days. Right now
she's anxious to do anything, and if it weren't for the kids,
she would be climbing the walls. At the moment, she and
the kids are watching a movie. Say, I'd like to take you up
on your standing offer to visit the sweat lodge. Are you
planning on using it anytime soon?" Earl waited for a reply.
"Great, late this afternoon fits my schedule. This is kind
of important, Johnson. I'm having vivid dreams again."
Through the static of a poor cell signal Earl finally understood where to meet Johnson and he nodded a couple more
times in agreement. "So I'll meet you around 4:00 down on
the beach below the cliffs at Stony Point."

*

Earl took the kids to their summer classes then drove south on the coast highway. The path to the pebble beach below the cliffs started in some tall cedar trees and was steep but well used. There was a county park with campsites less than two miles away, and, at low tide, people could park along the highway, walk down to the beach, and go out onto the tide flats to dig for clams. The flats were mostly covered as Earl reached the bottom of the trail and began to hike to the point using the beach. He picked his way around several drift logs and in another hundred yards reached a small alcove in the cliffs below the point that was tucked out of view from the more highly used stretch of beach. Johnson Wewa's sweat lodge was behind a couple of bleached logs, up against a massive old stump. Despite being close to the highway, the site had a remote feeling and a beautiful view of Willapa Bay and Leadbetter Point off to the west.

The sweat lodge was constructed of driftwood that was tilted inward and covered in a hodgepodge of old wool blankets and elk hides. There was a small hole at the top, and Earl could see a wisp of smoke rising and drifting into the trees above the cliffs. Earl was not surprised that Johnson was already ensconced in his sweat lodge, even though Earl had not seen any other cars at the trailhead along the highway. But that was Johnson's way. He kept to himself and could appear and disappear without anyone noticing. Johnson Wewa, while highly educated, was a shaman and kept to traditional Indian ways. Earl assumed that the man was in his late sixties or early seventies. No one knew for sure how old he was; he was the kind of person whose physical features didn't show his age.

Johnson was a short, stocky man with strong arms and legs, bordering on dwarfish, but he could move nimbly. His face showed a few wrinkles and his hair, worn in long braids, had turned white. What impressed Earl, and others, too, was the man's wit and sharp mind. He never forgot a face or an event. Johnson could remember conversations that took place twenty or thirty years before and describe them as if they had occurred yesterday.

Earl noticed that Johnson's clothes were neatly folded and placed on one of the large roots of the stump. It was a custom that a person wore little or no clothes into a sweat lodge. As Earl approached the lodge, a voice from inside called out. "Better peel off them duds if you're coming in, Earl. I've got it pretty warm in here right now."

"Hey, Johnson," replied Earl. "I'll do just that. How did you get here? I didn't see any vehicle on the road."

"Don't have one right now," answered the voice from inside the lodge. "My darn car just decided to stop running. I'm afraid it's going to take a lot stronger medicine than mine to fix it."

Earl chuckled as he undressed, folded his clothes, and placed them next to Johnson's. He walked to the small entrance of the lodge and felt the acrid heat hitting his face as he pulled aside a flap of elk hide to enter.

There was a small fire in front of the man. When Earl drew the flap closed, it was fairly dark inside—the only light came from the glow of embers and from the hole at the peak of the lodge where the smoke drifted out. Earl made himself as comfortable as he could on a reed mat just inside the entrance. Sweat was already starting to bead profusely on his forehead and chest. "Whew! You're right about it being warm. What's that I smell?" Earl asked the man, who was sitting completely naked and cross-legged on another reed mat on the far side. His face glowed red from the fire.

"I added a little sage and sweet grass to the fire," Johnson replied. "The aroma and heat will relax your tired muscles."

"How did you know that?" Earl asked the shaman.

"Not hard to know, being that nearly everyone around here has been laboring for several days removing the debris that has attacked our precious shores. Surely you would be one of the volunteers."

Earl had to agree as he rotated his shoulders and upper arms. The soreness in his muscles was already easing. They both sat there, staring at the glowing embers of the fire for several minutes. Johnson had placed several hot rocks on top of the embers and was sprinkling some water over them when Earl finally broke the silence. A cloud of steam obscured each of them.

"The dreams are back, Johnson," stated Earl in a calm voice. "Not about my great-great-grandfather, Ben Armstrong, like the first time. I haven't dreamed about him in over fifteen years. But a couple of weeks ago, I took Christine and Bernie to the Westport Maritime Museum. I read some of the old archived logs that were kept by my great-grandfather, Christian Zauner, including about a strange event he experienced. I also handled an old Indian basket that once belonged to him. Handling the ledgers caused my fingers to tingle just like last time and then the dreams started."

"And you have full recall of events in your dreams?" the shaman asked Earl.

"Exactly." Earl told Johnson about Chris Zauner. "Something traumatic happened to him, Johnson. He was troubled by a particular event. As far as I know, he kept most of the details of what happened a secret, even from his wife. But no one in the family since has ever discussed what happened."

"And you dreamed about the details—am I right?" Johnson asked while using a small piece of cloth to wipe beads of sweat from his brow.

"Yes. More details than I care to remember. Then something happened recently that seems to be related to what took place over a hundred years ago on the island."

"On Destruction Island? I understand it's quite a beautiful place. Have you ever been there, Earl?"

"Yes—I mean no; I haven't been there, but it looks like I will be going there tomorrow. That's why I wanted to discuss the dream event with you. Maybe you could tell me what I should do."

"We'll see. Tell me about what you know about what happened on the island."

Earl proceeded to explain to Johnson about the entry that Chris Zauner had made in the keeper's log, the bottle that his wife had found accidentally, and the contents of the message left by the Spanish explorer just as Chris had presented it in the log. He wanted Johnson to have a clear understanding of the facts. Earl also told him about finding the body of Will Pence, the homicide investigation that Detective Eddie Shaw was conducting, and Will's brother, Leon, finding a cooler on the island that belonged to Will.

Johnson raised a hand. "Let's back up a bit. Try to remember exactly what the message said. You say it was in Spanish?"

"I think so. Christian Zauner was born in Austria, and his father was an officer in the Austrian army. So he must have had a fairly good education prior to immigrating to…"

Johnson interrupted him. "The message, Earl. It is important. What do you remember about it?"

Earl paused and drew a breath. "Lieutenant Juan Francisco de la Bodega y Quadra left the message on the island in 1775. He was the captain of a Spanish sailing vessel called the *Sonora* that was exploring the Northwest coast. The sole survivor of the crew that he sent ashore for water reported everyone being killed by a man wearing a *mascara del oro*—a mask of gold. Then he reported that the message was resealed in the bottle and it was buried where it was found. For some reason, the log entry did not include the full translation. I know why, however. My dream about Zauner described…"

Johnson interrupted him again. "Hold on. I know you have a very unique ability, and I want to hear all about the dreams, but first I must think about the facts, at least as they were set down."

For several minutes, Johnson said no more, and Earl focused his senses on the sights and sounds close by. His hearing was sharpened, and he could hear the crackling sound as beach pebbles rolled in the waves of the incoming tide. Two crows were cawing to each other somewhere in the trees above the cliff. He pushed several partially burned branches back into the fire and watched them burst back into flames. His body no longer felt hot, and he was sweating less.

Finally, Johnson spoke. "To my knowledge, the coastal tribes never killed strangers unless there was a reason. But they could become aggravated to the point of taking revenge if something was stolen from them or if one of their people was killed. Furthermore, the coastal tribes were not known to have ceremonial masks representing their spirit figures. So I have to conclude that the natives that the Spanish vessel encountered were not from this area."

He sprinkled more water on the rocks in the fire pit and continued. "The existence of a golden mask, as you described it, is also unlikely in this region. The highly developed tribes farther north might have used gold, but not the tribes in this area. My guess is that it was a sun mask and not rimmed in gold, maybe copper, but the date is a little early for tribes to possess trade copper. So the crewman could have made this mistake as to what he saw. The sun mask was very common in ceremonies of the Kwakiutl people from the north. It represented a spiritual being who, when descending to earth, shimmered like gold."

Why were these people from the north in this area?" asked Earl.

"The Kwakiutl were known to come south in search of slaves and were greatly feared by the indigenous people along the coast. They were a powerful and warlike group in those days. The Spanish captain and his vessel could have stumbled upon a slave-hunting party that used the island as a staging location. Unless your great-grandfather knew a great deal about early Native American culture of the Pacific Northwest, he would not have been aware of such things."

"Wow, what you have just said makes sense," replied Earl. "Now can I describe my dreams? They are even more fantastic."

CHAPTER 37

The helicopter chartered by US Fish and Wildlife flew north from the airport in Aberdeen at an elevation of one thousand feet over the waters of the Pacific Ocean, just off the coast. The steady drone of the huge rotors and whine of the turbo engine prevented the four passengers aboard from talking to one another. Three of the occupants had nearly forgotten that the primary purpose of their trip was to investigate the apparent illegal digging on Destruction Island and were totally absorbed by watching the continuous line of tsunami debris on the beaches that stretched northward from Grays Harbor. They could see thousands of people working together to gather up the debris and load it into containers, pickup trucks, trailers, and dump trucks. The human effort being expended to save the beaches was impressive beyond anything imaginable.

The sandy beaches of the coastline gradually gave way to rocky stretches. Still, there were hearty souls struggling to collect the tsunami debris. Then the helicopter swung away from the coastline and Destruction Island came into view. A brisk wind and moderate ocean swell were driving waves onto its rocky shoreline. The island had not escaped the invasion of tsunami debris, and everywhere along the high-tide line a broad band of debris had collected.

The fourth passenger, Earl Armstrong, ignored the tsunami debris and focused on the island. He had a strange feeling like he was going home. Yet, nearly everything he knew about the island was due to what others had told him and from his dreams about his great-grandfather. He thought about the discussion he had with Johnson Wewa in the sweat lodge. Ultimately, Johnson had encouraged him to go to the island if he had a chance. Earl smiled in his excitement—first, to be able to set foot where Christian Zauner had spent many years, and second, to confirm the stories from his dreams.

While Johnson had urged Earl to go to the island, he cautioned him not to have too much hope, particularly about finding the cave and especially the mask. Time could have changed many things physically, and the cave may no longer be accessible. Its contents could have been removed or decayed beyond recognition. Johnson also felt that Earl's great-grandfather had acted falsely and, as a result, had

carried a great burden for the rest of his life in not revealing the truth about what had taken place or the existence
of the cave. Earl had disagreed and stuck to the belief that
Chris Zauner had a deep respect for the friendly natives that
visited his island, and his hope that someone in the future
would rediscover the bottle and would unravel the event and
deal with the contents of the cave. Earl was set on being the
one to have this opportunity.

Their chopper touched down on the old helipad a
few hundred yards from the abandoned lighthouse. The
cracked concrete sections looked like a crazy quilt stitched
together with a profuse crop of weeds. However, it was
still serviceable and was used by the Coast Guard and the
Fish and Wildlife Service when they made rare trips to the
island.

Lori Williams was the first person to climb out,
and she did so even before the main rotor blades had come
to a stop. She removed her communication helmet, tossed it
back inside the helicopter, and trotted quickly away, keeping her head low. Lori was wearing all of her regulation
field gear, including her bulletproof vest and a fully loaded
sidearm. She carried a VHF radio and was already in contact with someone. Eddie Shaw and Earl dropped to the
ground, grabbed their day packs, and hustled after her.

There were numerous openings in the brush just
off the landing pad; old concrete sidewalks that led off to

forgotten buildings that once made up the lighthouse complex, some almost overgrown with vegetation. Earl tried to identify some of the buildings that they passed. Most were old foundations; others were collapsed wooden structures covered in blackberry vine. The building foundations, no longer recognizable for what they once were, and the old sidewalks were like a maze.

Even with brush towering over their heads, Lori seemed to know where she was going and had taken one of the paths that headed toward the southerly bluffs that they had just flown over. Eddie and Earl had to walk fast to keep her in sight. Earl noticed more than a few rabbits scurry away into the underbrush—ample evidence that the island had an ecological problem. The tall white tower of the lighthouse was visible off to his right. Earl was determined not to leave the island without visiting the tower and the keeper's cottage.

In another five minutes, the brush gave way to a cleared area that stretched to the edge of the cliff. They could see the lighthouse, the ocean beyond, and several old buildings a few hundred yards off to their right.

Lori Williams stood in the middle of the cleared area, surrounded by potholes. She was whirling around, waving one arm and speaking into her radio. She broke off as Eddie and Earl approached her. Earl could see that she was steaming mad.

"This isn't some random dig. It was methodically organized. And look there—tire tracks. They used some type of backhoe or mechanical excavator in their work. It's going to take a huge effort to restore this area. Look at all of the burrows that have been destroyed."

"It was probably the same equipment Leon Pence and I saw strapped to a helicopter, Lori," Earl stated. "They used an old farm up near Oil City as their staging area, flew the equipment out here by helicopter, did their digging, and, when they finished, took everything out."

"With such an organized search, just what the hell were they looking for?" Lori asked in dismay as she took in the whole scene. She was struck with the immensity of what they were witnessing: a near-total disturbance of the area as both a historical site and as a natural resource.

Earl pointed toward the lighthouse and the foundation of the keeper's cottage. "I...I think if we walk over to that building location, we may learn more." Eddie and Lori looked at him with blank faces. Before letting them respond, Earl turned and started walking toward the old lighthouse. They had to watch their footing so as not to step on auklet burrows as they approached the site. A few seabirds rose out of the grass and took flight. As they got closer to a building foundation, another area of disturbed land, which Earl had alluded to, became visible. Its surface was much smaller, but it had been methodically scraped and dug with some type of excavator. There were tire tracks and areas where the removed soil had been randomly discarded. The entire area behind the foundation had been neatly scraped to a depth of maybe six inches. Closer to the foundaiton, the depth was about twelve inches. Then it stopped.

Eddie and Lori lagged behind as they studied the massive earth disturbance and scanned the area for anything that the diggers may have left behind. While he waited for them to reach him, Earl stepped inside the foundation. He smiled and waited for the others to reach him.

"They dug that area down to one depth and then started over again, going deeper just like an archeologist would," Earl said as he pointed at the excavation. "They didn't go any deeper over the entire excavation site, meaning that they probably found what they wanted."

"You are referring to the old bottle, the one you described at our meeting in South Bend?" Eddie asked.

"This is probably the garden area where the bottle was originally found, and where Hermine and Chris reburied it. If the thieves who stole the keeper's logs read the entry about the bottle carefully, they most likely figured that out."

"Then it's too late, we'll never get them," Lori stated as she looked around for clues someone was there recently, anything they might have been left behind.

"Not exactly." Earl said simply as he gazed toward the westerly shore of the island. "You still have a chance to actually catch them red-handed."

Eddie and Lori had puzzled looks again, trying to figure out why Earl was so sure of himself. "Okay, Earl," said Eddie. "Would you mind letting us in on why you are so confident we have a chance to catch these guys?"

"Because once they translate and fully interpret the message that was in the bottle, they have to come back to the island. Maybe they already have, but I doubt it. They are probably deep into carefully planning stage two of their scheme, since they now know that their first little operation has been discovered."

Lori looked at Earl with an expression of surprise on her face. "You think they are coming back?"

"Yup, to get the golden mask out of the cave," said Earl as he continued to stare at the cliffs west of them. "It's not going to be easy for them because they probably don't know where to look for the entrance to the cave. But I do. We just have to wait a few days until there is a period of low tides." Earl paused, and over the raucous cries of a flight of gulls overhead, he heard a dull boom—the sound of the blowhole below the westerly cliffs.

"I kind of missed something in what you said, Earl. There's artifacts in a cave here on Destruction Island? "Lori asked, confused.

Before Earl could respond, their attention was drawn to the noise of a helicopter approaching from the south and making a sharp swing to the west side of the island. Lt. Bo Phillips's voice boomed over Lori's radio. "This is Sea Air Rescue two niner zero. Switch to twenty-two alpha secure."

Lori responded and adjusted her radio frequency setting. "Coast Guard Rescue, this is Lori Williams with Fish and Wildlife. Do you copy?"

"Roger that," answered Lt. Phillips. "Just checking on what you nice folks were up to."

Lori pressed her radio close to her ear because of the noise of the rotor and engine from the passing chopper. "We're investigating some vandalism and possibly the site of a homicide. Over."

"Roger," replied Phillips. "Be advised that NOAA has posted a major weather change. A hurricane that was headed for the coast of Mexico has shifted north and could affect weather all the way to Vancouver Island. Strong winds and heavy rain are predicted within 24 hours. We're finishing our tsunami survey with a swing around the island to check on debris accumulation then heading for the barn."

"Copy that. We're about finished down here and should be departing the island in a few minutes. This island is not a place I would want to be during a blow. We'll be heading back to Aberdeen shortly."

"By the way, Lori, I hear you ran down a couple of real bad boy's singlehandedly recently. If you pass through Astoria, can I buy you a cup of coffee and hear all the nasty details?"

"Who can resist an offer from such a charming fly-boy?" Lori responded coyly. "Sure, we can chat about guns and chasing bad guys."

*

In the small cove at the north end of Destruction Island, the waves were pounding a once-pristine beach that was now piled with a blanket of tsunami debris several feet deep. The cove had the special characteristic of being a collector. Ocean currents that swung around the north end of the island would shed their drift material, which would then wash into the little cove and be trapped.

Half-buried in the accumulated pile of debris near the south end of the small beach was a large object, dull orange in color, with algae and other sea growth clinging to it. The object was cylindrical in shape with a dome at one end that was battered almost beyond recognition. The lashings along its sides, including its rudder, small propeller, and radio antenna, had all been stripped away. On one side were the, faint and scratched white letters *KANJI MARU*. Dave Ramsey looked out the side window of the H65

SAR helicopter, recognized the orange object and snapped another picture.

*

It was late afternoon when Earl and Eddie returned to South Bend from Aberdeen. Lori Williams had driven back to Seattle. Before she departed, she had informed Eddie that she needed to obtain approval from her boss for their plan. They had all talked at length about how to catch these men. Eddie and Lori were both uncertain that the men would be returning to the island, but Earl was very adamant that the killers, as he referred to them, would certainly be returning to the island to complete their search. Earl had assured them that they had maybe three days, depending on the behavior of the hurricane off the coast of Mexico. Even if the men got to the island sooner, the tide and wind wave conditions would prevent them for gaining access to the cave, if they found the entrance. This suited Lori because after her plan was approved by superiors she had to arrange for support from several agencies, including Phillip's detachment at the Astoria Air Station.

Both Lori and Eddie had been curious about how Earl knew so many details about the island, but Earl remained vague. He simply told them that there had been stories passed down within his family about a cave on the island, and the only known entrance was through a blow-hole located on the west shore during a low tide. The thieves could search as hard as they may but it was unlikely they would find another way into the cave until the tide was low enough to expose the chamber within the blowhole.

Lori Williams planned to ask the Coast Guard to make daily flights over the island to watch for a boat or aircraft activity and to monitor aircraft movements along the north coast. What they had no control over was the pending tropical storm. While it was risky, whoever was attempting to find the cave might be able use the storm to their advantage and reach the island without being detected. They had to hope that the thieves would be forced to wait it out as well.

CHAPTER 38

Jake Dixon spent the better part of the morning driving around and familiarizing himself with the town of South Bend. Traffic along the main street was heavy due to the beach cleanup activity. Jake liked this situation because it made him less noticeable. There were quite a few vehicles in front of the D & D Café where he stopped for breakfast. Inside the door was a stack of newspapers. He grabbed several and took a seat at the end of the counter. After ordering, he started flipping through the older papers and found what he was looking for—an article on Earl Armstrong being involved in a boating accident at La Push. The article mentioned that Earl was married with two children and employed as a forester with a local Indian tribe. Apparently, he had an office in South Bend. The article also mentioned that his wife, Sally, was a doctor on the local hospital staff. She was currently recovering from her injuries as a result of the accident.

Jake mentally thanked the hometown journalist for being so thorough with the facts. He would have had to ask a lot of questions to get the same information. He asked the waitress for a copy of the white pages and looked up the numbers and addresses for the tribal forestry office and local hospital.

Back in his car, he first dialed the number for Earl's office. A woman answered. Jake explained that he was a freelance reporter and wanted to interview Earl Armstrong. The woman said he was out of town and when asked for Earl's cell number provided it. Jake gave her a fictitious number, hung up and dialed the hospital number to get in touch with Sally Armstrong. The answer he got was that Dr. Armstrong was out on sick leave and due back to work next week. Jake hung up again and decided to park near Earl's office and watch. Just before ten o'clock, he observed an Indian woman come out and walk in the direction of the post office. Jake dialed the office number again and got a recorded greeting. He concluded that Earl was indeed not in town. In a few minutes, the woman returned, carrying a bundle of mail.

He decided to check out Earl's home and found that it was on a hill overlooking the downtown area and the bay. The street was quiet, with very few parked cars, and there was a Volvo station wagon in the driveway. He jotted down the license plate number and a description of the vehicle and then kept driving. He made several more calls as he headed back toward Aberdeen. His boss was relying on him to plan the next phase of their search for the mask and Jake was bound and determined this time to be thorough in every detail. He had to persuade Earl Armstrong to help, and there was one way to make it very convincing to the forester—which would be more important, the mask or his family?

*

While Jake Dixon was making his calls and developing his plans, less than one hundred miles north in Seattle, a tall Asian woman had just deplaned Delta Flight 156 from Narita Airport and was waiting quite impatiently for her first-class luggage to arrive on the carousel. Norika Edo's flight was late leaving Tokyo due to mechanical problems. Her stateside search team was waiting for her to clear customs and when she exited, they quickly exchanged greetings and hustled her into a hired Mercedes sedan. Suitable accommodations had been arranged at a small boutique hotel in Tacoma near the Museum of Glass, where Norika was briefed by Hiroko Takahashi on his team's latest source of information.

In the small hotel restaurant Hiroko set down his cup of tea and began his briefing.

"Madame Edo, I am very glad you are here because I have some positive information to report. My sister has been most busy taking calls regarding large objects washed ashore, but, unfortunately, this effort has failed to locate the escape pod. However, our offer to assist with the cleanup of tsunami debris and to provide special crews and equipment has been widely acknowledged by the local people. Edosan Corporation has received much praise from government officials. Some of them are quite anxious to meet you and thank you personally."

"That is very thoughtful of these elected officials, but we have no time to shake hands and pose for photographs. Besides, they are just looking for publicity and a means to take credit for the cleanup work that I am paying for. We must focus on the pod. It has to be out there somewhere."

"I do have some information that is encouraging," responded Hiroko. "I made arrangements with the manager of a café in Astoria to hire one of my men as a kitchen helper. The manager couldn't understand why someone would want to do this but agreed to the arrangement—no questions asked when I offered a large sum of money. This restaurant is frequented by members of the government's coastal defense agency, called the Coast Guard. They have helicopters and ships that have been tracking the movement of the tsunami debris because of the potential impact on commercial ship navigation. There is a helicopter crew stationed near this city that conducts frequent visual surveys and tracks larger objects of tsunami debris. My man was to make every effort to listen to the conversations of the flight crew whenever they had coffee or ate meals at this café. He was to give them special service and, if he could, make casual friendships with the crew."

"Yes, yes," Norika said, showing some impatience in her voice. "Get to the point. Did he get any information as to the whereabouts of our pod?"

"Very possibly, although it was purely from the standpoint of their curiosity. One of the Coast Guard crew members was showing pictures he had taken during their overflights of the debris to a group of friends who had joined them. The officer had photographed an escape pod much like the one we are looking for. The pictures showed the pod washed ashore on a beach somewhere. I was fortunate to see the picture myself and it looked encouraging."

"Have you learned when and where this picture was taken so we can recover it?" Norika asked.

"No, not yet," replied Hiroko. "And I hate to disappoint you, but we must have patience for a little while longer. There is a storm expected to hit the coast in the next twenty-four hours, and there is nothing we can do until it is over. Hopefully by then we will learn of the location."

Norika tried not to let her emotions show to Hiroko. Somehow she would have to control her impatience. The recovery of the pod was almost within her grasp. *Would the remains of her husband be on board? Did he have the funds with him? They had to be or she was dead. Matasuba will not let this go.* "Hiroko, we must move quickly. We must be ready when we know where the pod is located. Have the man at the restaurant keep pressing members of the flight crew for more information, including the location, Then have your sister at the call center issue a notice to all public agencies involved in the tsunami-debris cleanup that the Edosan Corporation will make available a helicopter and a salvage ship for removal of large objects suspected of containing hazardous materials."

This new plan began to form in Norika's head. It was going to be a formidable task to recover of the pod without her true intention being discovered. But if they disguised the recovery as a major hazardous waste cleanup operation, it just might work. She would have possession of the pod before anyone else opened it, recovery the bonds and diamonds and pay off Matasuba and his associates. She would survive.

*

Earl arrived home late and parked his 4Runner next to the family Volvo. Sally had just gotten the kids off to bed and was getting ready for bed herself.

"You are looking much better," Earl said as he gave her a hug.

"I feel much better, Sally replied. "How did the trip go?"

"We did what we could on the island, but the threat of a tropical storm coming our way cut our time short."

"Is it bad? I mean the damage caused by these men? Do you think they found what they were looking for?"

"I'm pretty sure they did. The area around the old keeper's house had been methodically excavated. By the looks of things, they had been searching for some time. Leon's brother probably caught them in the act which got him killed."

"What will happen now? Asked Sally.

"If the found the bottle, they have letter that is in it, which means now they know about the cave. Whomever is behind this isn't going to give up, Sally. They'll keep searching until they find the cave and steal the artifacts."

"You make them sound like desperate men, Earl."

"They killed three people, Sally, and almost killed us. But now that it's known what they intend to do, we'll be ready for them. Catch them in the act, so to speak."

"We'll be ready for them?" Sally asked pointedly.

"Not me. Federal agents will apprehend them. Yeah, I'd like to be there. I would give anything to see the inside of that cave. You know, when I stepped out of that helicopter onto the island, it was like I had been there before. And there really is a blowhole on the west side of the island. I heard it. If it exists, then I bet the entrance to the cave exists too."

"Then let the federal agents and Eddie Shaw deal with it. These are dangerous men."

"You are right as always, Sally. I was lucky to get invited along. And my approach to catch them is what they will use. So I should feel good about that, I guess. Leon should too. And I need to tell Johnson Wewa about my trip. So why don't we invite both of them for dinner tomorrow evening?"

"What about the storm? There could be problems driving if it hits the coast."

"It's just a possibility, Sally. Might not even happen."

CHAPTER 39

The summer weather held through Saturday afternoon and provided a splendid evening. There was an alpenglow on the hills around South Bend when Johnson Wewa hiked up from Main Street to Earl's home. His awe of the light conditions gave him both pleasure and an uneasy feeling. To Johnson, being trained as a shaman, an aural glow was a sign and meant that an extraordinary event was about to happen. While the TV weathermen were refining their prediction of a violent storm hitting the Washington coast in the next few days, Johnson could not put aside the feeling that the impending storm would have a dramatic impact on him and on the family who was expecting him. To Johnson, it was like knowing you had to stand and take a second punch. The tsunami debris had been the first hit and had deeply affected Johnson's sense of balance with Nature. He had been amazed at the resiliency of common folk and how they fought back each time their pristine shoreline was covered with debris. The worst was over but now he was worried that something else was about to commence. For a shaman, this was troubling. He was powerless, and, while he could caution Earl Armstrong and Leon Pence, he could not predict or change their future.

He found the two men sitting in the front yard with Sally and the kids enjoying the last of the alpenglow.

"Hey, Johnson!" Earl called. "Isn't this a glorious evening? Look at the effect the light has on our recovering patient."

There was an obvious blush on Sally's face as she rose to give Johnson a hug. "I think I owe my quick recovery to you, Johnson," she said, and then broke away with a smile as Christine and Bernie rushed over to give him hugs as well. "At least the kids believe so. You showed up at the hospital, and from that point on, everything was going to be all right. You chased away their fears."

"I may be a shaman, but I think I had a lot of help with your situation," Johnson said with a chuckle. "You are a strong woman, and I knew that you would recover just fine. Has the doctor let you return to work yet?"

"Monday...thank goodness! I can't wait. I mean, the time with Christine and Bernie has been wonderful, but you know me. I want to help people. There have been thousands helping with the beach cleanup, and I have had to stay here at home. The hospital emergency room has been

overwhelmed. Every doctor, nurse, and technician is working overtime, and I haven't been able to be of assistance.
That part has been truly frustrating."

"We're so glad you came to visit, Mr. Wewa,"
Christine said as she clung to one of Johnson's arms.

"Me, too!" Bernie yelled as he tugged Johnson's
other arm. The two of them led Johnson up to a swinging bench on the front porch, pushed him into it, and then
joined him, one on each side.

"Hey, it was your father who invited me," Johnson
said looking first a Bernie and then Christine. "We have a
lot to talk about. But…I suppose I have time for one story.
Okay?" Johnson put an arm around each of the children.

"Yeah!" Christine and Bernie exclaimed in unison.

The bright alpenglow had quickly faded and was
replaced with dusky shades of gray. It was a sign that the
predicted storm was coming, but the scene on Earl's porch
remained cheerful. All heads turned toward Johnson with
the expectation of hearing one of his legends. Johnson was
about to start his story when he noticed a black sedan driving slowly up the street toward Earl's house. No one else
noticed the car with its darkened windows, which seemed
to be out of place in the small community of South Bend.
Johnson frowned as he watched the car turn the corner, but
he then quickly put on a smile and started his story.

"Up on his mountain, Coyote got to wonderin' what the little people were up to in their village down by the river. So he decided to pay them a visit..."

*

Later in the evening, after Sally had shooed Bernie and Christine off to bed, everyone made themselves comfortable in the living room to hear what Earl had to say. Outside, the rain had commenced, accompanied by a steady wind that occasionally shook the house. Johnson had spied the big easy chair and sat sipping a cup of tea that Sally had prepared for him. Leon took a seat on the hearth of the fireplace and didn't seem to mind leaning back against the rough bricks. Sally chose the couch beside Earl and anxiously slipped a hand into his.

"Leon, thanks for driving down from La Push," Earl began. "We've been through quite a lot since your brother was found dead down our way at North Cove. I believe something far bigger than I, and quite probably you, could have imagined is taking place on Destruction Island. You said that you are convinced that your brother Will was killed out there. Based on what I saw on my trip out to the island yesterday and what I am beginning to understand took place, you may be right. But Will's murder is not the beginning. The story began nearly 250 years ago with another murder, actually several.

Over the years, Destruction Island has been called the Isle of Sorrow. Will's death unfortunately ties in with the island's reputation. Your family has visited the island for generations, and there was a time when your grandmother, as a little girl, came to know my great-grandmother. The principal keeper, meaning the person in charge of the light-house, was my great-grandfather, Christian Zauner. He was stationed out there for nine years. He had his wife, Hermine, and their daughter, Abigail, with him.

Times were tough back in the 1890s for Indians and white homesteaders alike. Chris Zauner and his family had a pretty good life even though they lived in isolation on a small island four miles off the coast. The *Columbine*, a lighthouse tender, arrived at the island every two months to deliver supplies. They shared some of their supplies with the visiting Indians. Hermine gave them sugar and flour to take back to La Push. A friendship developed between the Zauner's and the Indians, but that was not always the case, as Johnson described to me recently.

The Indian villages along the coast were unfriendly to outsiders, and they had a right to be. Other Indian tribes further north raided their villages from time to time and took their people as slaves. So when the Spanish and later Americans explored the Pacific Northwest, it often resulted in a battle. Destruction Island figured into several of these accounts. There is documentation from back in 1775 that tells of some of the crew of a Spanish ship called the *Sonora* were sent ashore to obtain fresh water and were nearly wiped out by hostile Indians. The captain of this ship left a record of the event on Destruction Island.

By happenstance, Hermine Zauner found that record, which was contained in a bottle. Chris Zauner was able to translate it and made a brief entry about its contents in the lighthouse log. Until recently, those logs, on loan from the National Archives, have been at the museum in Westport. I had the occasion to read some of the entries last week. I noticed that the page referencing the discovery of the bottle had been marked, and I realized that someone else had read about it. When Leon and I had a meeting with Eddie Shaw at the county sheriff's office, we heard a report that those logs were later stolen during a robbery at the museum. The logs were the only items removed."

"What's the value of some old journals to a thief?" Sally asked.

"It's not the books themselves. It's the message— the one I happened to read. This person was interested in recovering the bottle and learning what the actual message said because the entry Chris Zauner made in the log was very brief. I think this was intentional."

"Why would he do that?" Sally asked again.

Johnson held up a hand. "Ah, let me try to answer that question for you, Sally." Earl let Johnson go ahead and speak, knowing that he would answer it better. Besides, Johnson was the one who had told him what he knew and understood his dreams about Chris Zauner.

Johnson continued focusing his attention on Leon. "Earl has informed me about his dreams. He has a gift— a very unusual one. It is almost like a relative from the past is reaching out to him for help. Some fifteen years ago, Earl came to see me about some confusing dreams about his great-great-grandfather. His dreams seemed to be triggered by handling several objects that had belonged to the man. Earl told me that it happened again after he read from the log entries written by Christian Zauner. After what happened fifteen years ago, I have no reason to doubt what he told me. There were things revealed to him through dreams that he would never have discovered on his own."

"So you believe that what Chris Zauner wrote in the log was intentional as well?" Leon asked.

"It's more what he did not write in the log," replied Johnson. "The local Indians were not friendly during the time that the lighthouse was being built and began opera-tion. In fact, they strongly objected to its construction. While they did not commit to violence, they did blockade the beaches, delaying the unloading of building materials.

When the Zauner family moved to the island, they faced a difficult challenge in befriending the Indians who frequently visited the island to gather traditional foods, but they succeeded, probably due to Hermine's focus on the Indian women.

Earl told me that after knowing the content of the message written by the Spanish captain, the Zauner's faced a major dilemma. If they informed Chris's superiors with the Lighthouse Board, which was the predecessor to the Lighthouse Service, the true story of the crew of the Spanish ship being killed in a ceremonial sacrifice, would become public knowledge, and the local Indians could suffer reprisals for something that happened many years before. Even in the early 1900s, Indians were often referred to as savages out of ignorance. Without professional help, Chris Zauner wouldn't have had any way of knowing that the Indians who murdered the crewmen in the cave probably were most likely not local Indians, but a slave-gathering party from the north.

Through Earl's dream, the objects in the cave were only vaguely described. I believe they may be of Kwakiutl origin from Vancouver Island or even further north. What is in the cave has to be preserved and studied. Only then will we know the truth. But if the people who stole the logs and recovered the same message that Chris Zauner found, and then find the cave before anyone else, they will certainly remove all of the artifacts and we will never know what happened.

"Wow," exclaimed Sally. "If someone is successful in robbing the cave, the whole story could become a myth, right?"

Johnson Wewa's response to Sally was interrupted by the ringing of the telephone. Earl took the call in the kitchen. "Hello?" There was no response from the caller. Earl stared at the raindrops driving against the window in the kitchen door, waiting for someone to say something. "Hello?" Earl said again. There was an audible click as the unknown caller hung up.

*

The black SUV with tinted windows was parked in the shadows, away from the bright lights of the all-night Raymond service station off Highway 101. The driver had gone in to grab some snacks while Jake Dixon made his first call to the Armstrong residence. Jake smiled to himself, having sensed some concern in Earl Armstrong's voice. He would call the residence several more times and hang up. Then tomorrow morning he would make a call to the man's cell phone and present him with the threat to his family. It would indeed worry Armstrong that someone had both his home phone and cell numbers —thanks to the

Indian secretary in Earl's office. If you say you are a journalist, everyone tries to pass you on to someone else rather
than answer your questions themselves.

He made another call and Juno Betar answered
immediately. "The game is in play. We'll make the snatch
tomorrow. When you arrive at the farm at Oil City, we'll
inform Mr. Armstrong why it is best for him to fully cooperate with us in finding the cave."

312

CHAPTER 40

Norika was getting very frustrated with having to wait out the storm. As predicted, the summer storm hit the coast of Washington with such ferocity that weathermen and news reporters in Seattle and Portland were quite busy with their storm reports. There were swollen streams with minor flooding on some of the coastal rivers, trees down, and power outages. The rain and wind created massive traffic tie ups all around the Puget Sound.

Norika remained in her Tacoma hotel room except to join Hiroko for dinner in the small restaurant off the hotel lobby. Hiroko insisted that she not leave the hotel and while he had not mentioned it, he appeared to be uneasy about something. He knew she was in danger from members of the Yakuza and they should be extra careful even in the United States. Yuri Matasuba could easily order associates located in Seattle to assist in finding her if he desired.

It was late Sunday evening when Hiroko took a call on his cell phone from the man he had placed in the restaurant in Astoria. The man could hardly contain his excitement as he now knew the location of the *Kanji Maru* escape pod.

"Are you sure it was our escape pod?" asked Hiroko. "Everything hinges on the information being correct."

"Yes, Hiroko san, I have no doubt of it," the man answered. "I asked if I might look at the photos out of interest in the tsunami debris problem, and, not revealing my curiosity, was able to identify some markings partially visible on its side. It is from the *Kanji Maru*. I asked where the photos were taken, and the man informed me the photos were from a place called Destruction Island."

CHAPTER 41

S ally gripped the old wool blanket and tucked her legs close to her body trying to stop shivering and be comfortable lying on the hard dirt floor. She was frightened more than she had ever been in her life. The old barn where she and the children had been confined seemed to become a living creature. As the storm raged and then blew itself out, the sides and roof groaned with every gust of wind, and at times the sound of the rain hitting the roof of the old building was deafening. Boards banged and creaked. Rain dripped from holes in the roof where shingles had been blown away and rivulets of rain water ran across the dirt floor. Earlier in the night, Sally tried to comfort Christine and Bernie as best she could until they finally fell asleep. Afterward, Sally could not fall asleep herself as her mind dwelled on why they were being held and what the morning would bring.

It wasn't the storm that frightened her. It was the men that snatched them out of her car. *Who were they? What did these men have in store for them? Could she somehow escape?* There was little she could do but wait for daylight.

After dozing for several hours, Sally rose stiffly and placed her blanket over Christine and Bernie who were still asleep. While she had slept, the wind and rain had quieted down. She had to examine their surroundings and moving around might help lessen the aches in her arms and legs still sore from the boat accident. While she walked around looking at the walls of the old barn, she went back over what had happened the day before.

During the evening with Leon and Johnson, the telephone calls had started and occurred repeatedly all night, and then Sunday morning the unknown caller had given Earl a disturbing message—his family was in danger and only he could prevent it. She could tell Earl was distraught when he told her. The caller had made threatening statements and informed Earl that he knew where they lived in South Bend. Sally and Earl had discussed calling the city police or sheriff's office but knew there was little likelihood of assistance because nearly all law enforcement personnel were either involved with the tsunami debris cleanup or storm problems.

They had concluded that Sally should pack a few things and drive to her parents' home in Seattle. Sally thought it was more than that but couldn't get Earl to elaborate further. He was emphatic that Sally, Christine, and

Bernie had to be out of harm's way, and her parents' place would be fine. Earl had also said that he would be more comfortable if they were in Seattle, away from the direct path of the big summer storm. Sally had finally relented and informed the kids that they were going to Grandma's in Seattle. While they were packing, she called Sam Reynolds at his home and told him that she had decided to take a few more days to recuperate.

As Sally had driven north toward Aberdeen late Sunday afternoon, she had listened to the radio for reports on the storm. There were a lot of warnings of high winds, possibly up to eighty miles per hour on the coast. Heavy rain was predicted as well, and flood watches were posted for some rivers. She had planned to use Interstate 5 by taking the cutoff to Montesano instead of going all the way up to Aberdeen.

Shortly after beginning the climb up the last long grade before the Montesano cutoff, Sally had come up behind a dark SUV that had passed her just outside of Raymond. It had slowed while she passed it and then stayed close behind her. A few minutes later, two other cars had passed them both at high speed then slowed and remained in front of her. Bells should have gone off after the warning Earl had given her earlier.

The highway climbed several hundred feet in elevation along the side of Scar Hill before dropping into a series of sharp curves. Christine and Bernie both had been reading library books, and Sally had been focused on the twisting highway. She had dropped back from the two passing cars and no longer saw them up ahead. As she came around a sharp bend, she had noticed a car up against a guardrail with its lights flashing. Another vehicle was positioned sideways, halfway across her lane. There was room to go by, but not much. She had slowed down and come to a stop when she saw a person slumped over the wheel of the car in the center of the highway. They were the same two cars that passed her minutes earlier. That was her second mistake. She should have passed on by and let the police deal with the accident, but her medical instinct had kicked in. Before she could react, she noticed in her rearview mirror the headlights of the SUV as it came around the curve. It weaved a little, as if it was attempting to stop, but then Sally had realized that it was going to hit her car. Bernie and Christine screamed with the impact, and Sally's Volvo slid a few feet toward the other two vehicles. A man jumped out of the SUV and approached the driver's window. He wrenched open her door and pointed a gun at Sally's dazed face. The man had spoken to her in a firm voice. "Please get out of the car, Mrs. Armstrong. You and the children are coming with me."

The next few hours had been like being in a trance. Sally could no longer hear the voices around her as she and *the children were pulled from the Volvo and hustled into the back of the SUV. The man with the gun was in the front seat with the driver, and the SUV backed up and drove around the makeshift blockade. She looked back just in time to see the other two cars and her own damaged Volvo turn and start to follow the SUV.*

Sally and the children had been asked to put on blindfolds and remain silent. If they did not comply, they would be gagged and forced to lie on the floor. None of their captors had spoken to one another. How many captors were there? She knew there were two men in the car and at least three others who were driving the other vehicles. After a few minutes of quiet crying, Bernie grew silent, taking strength from his older sister, who sat quietly, holding Sally's hand in a steel-like grip. They had assured each other that they would be all right by squeezing each other's hands.

When the vehicle had finally stopped, the three had been ordered to remove their blindfolds and get out of the car. There were hustled through the wind and rain into an old barn and locked up for the night.

The wind, which had howled incessantly all night, had now calmed considerably, and Sally could hear the sound of a river nearby as well as what she thought was ocean surf. She took a deep breath, and the salty smell convinced her that they were near the ocean. Sally did some stretching exercises and tried to remember any sounds and unusual movements of the vehicle during the trip that might help her pin down where they were being held. Given the radio news reports she had heard after leaving South Bend and the time on her watch, which she had been able to check once she and the kids were alone, she figured that they must have traveled for about two and a half hours. She estimated that they must have driven 120 - 150 miles. And they were still on the coast, so their captors must have driven north on the coast highway. For the last part of the drive, they had been on a gravel road for maybe twenty minutes.

She tried to visualize a map of the coast in her mind. There were not many access points to the beaches north of Aberdeen. The Ocean Shores area would have taken less time to reach. When Earl and she visited La Push for Will's funeral, it took about the same length of time to get to Forks. But the roads were all paved, and at the end of the road there was an Indian reservation. Sally could not remember being in such a place, and she began to worry that she was on private land, far from the highway and anything else. Her hopes of being rescued dimmed.

Earl would know. He always remembers places. His forestry work takes him all over this coast. He was just up this way to help Leon Pence investigate something. Sally smiled and shook her head. *Maybe our captors brought us to the same location: to Oil City on the Hoh River. Earl told us all about his kayak trip and their narrow escape from a helicopter. It was an old farm with a barn. That must be where we are being held! It must be the place. The guys said it was really isolated.*

Then there was the time Earl and I took a beach hike out of La Push. Wow, that was a long time ago. It was awful and I told him I would never do it again. If we are near the ocean, we must be close to the southerly end of that dreadful trail. What else was there? Not much. On the south side of the river is another Indian reservation. We can go there and get help. I've got to see whether we can wade across the river, if I can find a way out of this barn.

Her thoughts turned to their captors. *These men are not very smart. Or are they? To use the same location must mean they don't intend to be here long. And when they do leave, what do they plan to do with us? We have got to try to escape. Earl will figure it out, but it might be too late by then.*

Now that she knew fairly certain where they were being held, she focused on escaping from the barn. Christine and Bernie were still asleep, so Sally started to explore its interior. She started with the large double doors where they had been forced inside. She tried to open the doors. There was a chain with a lock on the outside. There was another set of doors at the opposite end, so she crossed quickly, only to find the same situation. She looked around. There were no windows at ground level. There was a row of windows up high, but they were covered in cobwebs and dust and did not look as if they could be opened even if she had a way to climb up to them.

Sally turned and looked up at the hayloft, which ran half of the length of the barn over several livestock stalls. There was an access ladder attached to one of the support columns, and Sally climbed it into the loft. There were quite a few bales of hay stacked in the loft, some tumbled over, and hidden just beyond were the small doors that were used to bring the bales up into the loft. Sally worked her way over the bales towards the small doors when she suddenly heard a racket over her head. It startled her, causing her to fall over one of the bales. She recovered in time to see a pair of barn owls flutter through one of the holes high up in the roof. Sally smiled as she scrambled the rest of the way and examined the set of double doors. *Those owls got out of here and so will we!* She peeked through a crack and saw that the doors faced a field away from the house. The doors were held closed with a simple wooden latch, and when she turned it, one of the doors released and swung open with a slight squeak. She grabbed the door and re-latched it.

Just above the doors was a track with a block and tackle. The rope was still in place and looked to be in good condition. It should be easy to lower Bernie and Christine to the ground the same way that hay bales were raised to the loft. She could then shimmy down the rope herself.

Sally climbed back down the ladder and went back to the main door closest to the house. She peered through the crack between the two sections of the large door. She could not see anyone moving around, but with the rain still falling and the wind still whipping the trees beyond the house she felt there was little likelihood of anyone standing watch outside. She figured it wouldn't be long before their captors started stirring and came to check on her and the kids. If they were going to try to escape, the time was now. She was worried about the rain and wind but more so about what they might in store for them. She hoped that they would not have to be exposed to the elements for too long.

First, Sally needed a plan for what they would do once they were free of the barn. She decided that crossing the river was the quickest way to safety. If she remembered correctly, there was a paved road from the main highway into the Indian village somewhere on the other side. There were also people there. Her second thought was to backtrack on the gravel road to the highway and flag someone down. It was quite a few miles to the highway, though, and if the men discovered that they were gone, there was a good chance that they would be followed and recaptured. Her backup plan, which she hated to think about, was the Hoh Head Trail along the beach, the one she told Earl she would never do again.

CHAPTER 42

After a final check at the main barn door to be sure there was not any activity in the yard or at the farmhouse, Sally woke Bernie and Christine. She was relieved that their captors had simply locked them in the barn rather than tying them up or holding them into the house.

"Wake up, kids! We are getting out of here."

"Where are we, Mom?" Bernie asked as he rubbed his eyes.

"We're a long way from home and Dad. I think we are quite a way up the coast, maybe in the national park, or at least very close to it. I think the beach is not far away. If I am right, you should hear the ocean after we get outside."

"Can we go home now? Christine asked.

"We are going to try. Remember, they locked us up in an old barn. So first we have to get out. Then we are going to run as far away as we can and get help."

"What about the men who kidnapped us? Are they still here?" Christine asked.

"I don't know for sure. Our car is still here, along with the one we rode in, but the other two are gone. So maybe only two or three men are still here.

"But Mom, it's still raining, Bernie said. "I can hear it on the roof."

"I know, Bernie. But we can't stay here. It's too dangerous. Unfortunately, they took my car keys as well as my purse, so we are going to have to make do with what we are wearing. Look around and grab anything useful that we can carry. Bernie, find some rope and roll up the two blankets you and Christine have been using. Make slings so we can carry them on our backs."

"You mean like we're going to go hiking? Neat!" Bernie said, beaming.

"Could be," answered Sally. "But we are going to have to move fast. Hopefully the rain will stop soon."

Christine began prowling around as Sally requested and came back carrying some old jackets.

"These were hanging on some nails over beside the big door. They are too big for Bernie, but you and I might be able to wear them," Christine said.

Sally examined the coats. One was a long-sleeved denim jacket. It would not help much once it was soaked. Sally thought about that for a moment and wondered if there was something in the barn they could use to water-proof it.

"Christine, check those shelves over that work-bench and see there is anything we can put on these jackets to help them shed water."

While Christine ran over to search the shelves, Sally examined the other two coats which were extra-large, winter farmer coats. They were filthy and musty but might keep them warm. She took the denim jacket, laid it on the floor and stepped on it, then grabbed a sleeve and pulled. It ripped off. She did the same with the other sleeve.

"Put this on, Bernie. It will keep your body warmer and you will have use of your arms."

Christine came back with a small can and showed it to Sally. "This is beeswax, Mom. Will it work?"

"That's perfect. You rub some on the back and shoulders of Bernie's new vest and then on the other two jackets. I'll see if there is anything else useful around here."

On the workbench, Sally found an old rusty knife with a six-inch blade. She rubbed it on a whetstone to sharpen the blade. The only thing else useful was a couple of old coke bottles. Sally decided that they may work for carrying water if they had to. If they could cross the river—and that was a big if in Sally's mind—their escape could be over quickly. *But what if they had to hide in the forest or hike the beach trail?*

"All right, kids, time to go. From now on, no talking until we are safely away from this place. First, we have to climb up into the hayloft using that ladder over there."

"All right!" Bernie exclaimed with a big smile. "Hay lofts are neat."

"It's just the way out. We won't be there but for a few minutes." Sally replied.

Bernie was first up, followed by Christine. Sally looked toward the main barn door once more before climbing up herself. There were still no signs of their captors. She climbed. The three of them clamored over the hay bales to the loft loading door. This time, Sally unlatched both doors and let them swing open. Sally readied the block and tackle and made a loop at the end of the rope. She showed Bernie how to put his feet in the loop and hold onto the rope. He didn't show any fear as she pushed the overhead pulley out on the track a few feet and lowered him to the ground. Christine was next. She, too, showed no fear. But now there was no one to lower her.

Sally left the rope extended to the ground from the pulley and tied her end off to a beam. She reached out with both hands, grabbed the rope and swung out, trying to quickly wrap her legs around it. She kicked back and forth, trying to feel it with her thighs. The bulky coat kept getting in the way. Her hands were burning from slipping slightly when she finally got the rope between her legs and feet.

With the pressure off her hands, she began to let the rope slip through both her hands and legs. Moments later, her feet touched the ground.

"That was cool, Mom!" Bernie told her. "How did you learn to do that?"

"My dad built my two brothers and me a tree fort. It had a rope to climb down." She didn't' mention that she was always too scared to use it like her brothers did. Sally looked around to get her bearings.

The river was off to the right, and there was an old fence covered in blackberry vines leading toward it. She grabbed each child by a hand and trotted off in the direction of the river. When they got to the riverbank, the situation was as bad as Sally thought it might be. The river was flowing high and muddy, its surface full of brush and small logs moving swiftly downstream. This option was not going to work.

"Okay, kids, looks like this is not the way to go. There is a road on our side of the river. That's how they got us here, but it's a long way to the highway, and if we use it, they would probably recapture us quickly. Which leaves us with only one option—the beach."

The trio reversed their direction and, using the brush along the fence to hide their movement, walked quickly back by the barn and on toward the trees at the end of the field. They climbed through a fence and up a bank to the gravel access road. There were no fresh vehicle tracks. Sally turned left away from the highway.

"Now we're going to have to run, kids," she said to them. "I want to be a long way from here when they find out we're gone."

They were leaving tracks in the muddy road, but there was no alternative. They followed the road to the beach. The tall, second-growth forest gave way to storm-twisted brush. They could hear the sound of the ocean surf up ahead. There was a side road, and as they approached it, Sally saw a sign marking the way to the Third Beach Trail. She slowed their pace to a fast walk, wiping her rain-drenched hair from her forehead and eyes. She didn't know how far it was to the start of the trail, but at least with every step they were farther from their captors.

They walked for close to twenty minutes and still had not reached the trailhead. Sally kept glancing back down the road, expecting to see a vehicle rushing toward them. If that happened, their only option would be to scramble into the thick vegetation along the road. Then she saw it—the trailhead sign. The beach was less than a quarter-mile mile ahead, but the end of the trail—and safety—was fourteen miles farther. She couldn't bear telling Christine and Bernie how very, very treacherous that fourteen miles would be or that chances were they would never make it.

*

In the kitchen of the old farmhouse, Jake Dixon was fixing some eggs and hash browns. After sending one of his men to collect Juno Betar at the Forks airfield, and two others to grab Earl Armstrong in South Bend, he only had one man left to guard the Armstrong family and wait for Betar to arrive.

"Sloan, get your butt out here and take this food over to the barn for that family!" Jake hollered.

"Huh?" There was a groan from one of the bedrooms, and a few minutes later, Mike Sloan appeared. He buttoned his fly and pushed his wild hair back.

"The key to the barn door is hanging on a hook by the door. Be sure to lock it when you come back."

"Ain't you coming with me?" Sloan asked. "What if they jump me and try to escape?"

"They're just a woman and two little kids, for cripe's sake. Get out there!"

Sloan peered out the window in the back door and mumbled something inaudible about the rain, and then he grabbed a jacket hanging on the back of a chair. He put on a hat and then picked up the tray of hot food and snagged the key off the hook as he tromped out. He was mumbling some more as he splashed through the mud and puddles of rainwater in the barnyard. A few minutes later, Jake heard

Sloan hollering and through the kitchen window saw him running back toward the house, splashing through the puddles as he ran.

"Jake! Jake! They're gone. They ain't in the barn. I looked everywhere."

Jake grabbed his jacket and hat and started for the door. He stopped and went back to a table and grabbed his Glock, checked to be sure it was loaded, and dashed for the door just as Sloan reached the porch.

"They ain't in the barn. I even checked the hayloft. There was a door open on the end. I think they climbed down somehow."

Jake ran to the far side of the barn with Sloan trying to keep up. He looked up to see the open doors and the block and tackle swinging freely in the wind. Below it were a bunch of tracks that led over to the fence. He noticed where the tracks headed toward the river and then came back and went off toward the trees on the hill.

"Take a weapon and use that Volvo to drive back toward the main highway. If they're trying to make it to the highway, we should be able to catch up to them. You only have to grab one of the kids. The woman won't leave one of them behind. If someone gets hurt, then it's too bad. And look for their tracks, damnit. We have to get them back, or Betar's plan isn't worth a plug nickel!"

Jake Dixon trotted back to the main house. He had to tell Juno Betar what had happened, and he needed to call Earl Armstrong sooner. He called Juno first.

"The woman with the kids escaped from the barn," Jake said.

"Damn! She did what? Juno asked.

"She lowered the kids and herself from the hayloft while the storm was still raging. I've got to give her credit for that. Then they tried to cross the river to the Indian village, but the water was too high. So they doubled back to the road, but it's too far to the highway. We'll get them back."

"No matter! It doesn't matter whether they are locked up, on the run or dead. The husband has no way of knowing we don't have them. You have proof they were taken and still have two men watching him, right?"

"Yeah, I sent two guys back down there last night."

"Good! They are to grab Armstrong and take him to the airstrip across the river. My helicopter will pick him up there. Tell Armstrong he's to cooperate. You'll make it very clear to him why he should, correct?"

"Yes, sir!" answered Jake. "You can be assured that he will get the message, and we'll have him waiting for you at the airstrip."

"He better be. I'm growing tired of this playing around. We're moving up the schedule. After picking up Armstrong, I'll fly directly out to the island without you, retrieve the mask, and then fly to the farm. Once I arrive, we'll clean up the loose ends and be done with this. Now, take care of that woman."

"Yes, sir!" Jake barked once more.

"I may have to deal with Mr. Armstrong while on the island. It would be very unfortunate if his fate adds to the Isle of Sorrow legacy!"

Jake was disappointed that he would not take part in the search for the mask but understood his part of the plan. He retrieved his shoulder harness from the kitchen table, strapped it on, and then placed his Glock 9mm in the holster. It was time to place the call to Mr. Armstrong and then go after that woman and the kids. He picked up Sally's cell phone and searched for Earl's number.

CHAPTER 43

Latonya Baker knew something was disturbing Earl the moment he arrived at the office. She had offered a pleasant good morning, but he had hardly acknowledged her. Instead he walked straight to his desk and began checking his messages. She was staring at him when his cell phone rang. Expecting another message from the unknown caller, Earl glanced at the caller ID on his phone as he answered. It was Sally. "Sally? I thought you were going to call last night. What is...?

"Listen closely, Armstrong," the caller stated. "We have your wife and kids. In fact, you made it too easy by sending them to us. To prove it, I'm using your wife's phone."

"You listen!" Earl replied. "I don't know how you managed to get Sally's phone, but this has gone far enough. I'm going to report these crank calls to the police."

"Not if you want to see your family again. So shut up and listen!" Jake held his own phone close to Sally's and replayed a recording he had made the night before. Earl could hear Sally protesting and Bernie crying.

"Is that clear enough, Armstrong?"

Earl was stunned. He had thought Sally and the kids were safe and sound at her mother's home in Seattle. Nothing could be further from the truth. Whoever these people were, they must have been watching the house, and Earl had done just what they expected.

"Just what are you up to? Why are you involving my family?"

"It's just a little insurance policy, you might call it. You fully cooperate and provide us with a little assistance in finding what we are looking for, and they are no longer needed and will be released."

"Just what are you looking for?" Earl asked, and then it dawned on him, and he knew the answer. "You're looking for the golden mask that is supposed to be hidden on Destruction Island!"

"Then you know we are serious about finding it," the man replied.

"I'd say that killing for it is serious business," Earl answered. "And why would you stop at killing three people?"

"Come, come, Mr. Armstrong. If your favorite pie is sitting on a picnic table and a few ants are trying to get to it, you have to squash them. That's life."

"Well, my family is not a couple of ants to be squashed. If you need my help in finding the cave, then you better release them right now," demanded Earl.

"Sorry. We figure you'll work in earnest if there is a little reward in it for you. Right now, we are wasting valuable time, Mr. Armstrong. So listen. A car will be waiting for you around the corner, across from the café. Leave now and don't tell anyone about our conversation, or we may just have to cancel our insurance policy."

"Okay, but I can't help you alone," answered Earl. "I don't have all of the information necessary to find the mask. I...I need to bring someone with me who lives only a few minutes away."

"Very well. You have five minutes to reach this person, Mr. Armstrong, so hurry. If my men see any police, consider our insurance policy destroyed." Jake hung up.

Earl stared at his phone. Who could he ask? Leon was back in La Push, which was hours away. Eddie was in Astoria helping with the plans to go back to Destruction Island with Lori Williams and other Fish and Wildlife agents. The only other person who could help him enter the cave and find the mask was Johnson Wewa. That is, if he was at his home in Raymond.

He still had a few minutes before he had to walk out. He glanced over to where Latonya was sitting at her desk. She had been watching him. Now she pushed back her chair and began to walk over to his desk. Earl dialed a number. He needed to reach Leon.

Leon's phone rang several times, and Earl began to panic. Then there was a voice. "Yeah? What's up, Earl?"

"Thank God I was able to reach you, Leon. They've got Sally and the kids." Latonya was now beside his desk, listening.

"Who's got them?" Leon and Latonya asked simultaneously. "What the hell happened, Earl?" Leon added.

Earl raised a hand for Latonya to wait before saying anything else. "Whoever is after the mask kidnapped Sally, Christine, and Bernie as they were driving up to Seattle. They took them to force me to help them find that cave out on Destruction Island. I've got to do it, Leon. I don't have a choice here."

"You can't do that, Earl. They'll kill you. These people are murderers. They killed my brother and tried to kill you and me."

"I know there's a risk, but they made it very, very clear. They really have my family, and I don't want them harmed."

"Earl? What's going on?" Latonya could no longer keep quiet. "What do you mean by your family might be hurt?"

Earl waved his hand again, motioning for her to be quiet. "I don't have time to explain, Latonya! Just listen to what I'm telling Leon. Then I've got to go." Then he closed his eyes and spoke into the phone slowly. "I am going to take Johnson Wewa with me."

"Take Johnson to the island?" Leon asked.

"If he's home, yeah. I think I can find the entrance to the cave, but Johnson's got to help locate the mask once we are inside. That is, if we can get inside. I kind of know how to do it from my dream about Chris Zauner, but…"

"Earl?" Leon interrupted. "Earl, you're crazy to do this. Call the authorities. Let them deal with it."

"I can't, Leon. I have to go. Somehow I think it was meant to be. I feel that my great-grandfather wanted me to be the one to deal with this golden mask, or whatever it is. Whoever kidnapped Sally and my children has all the cards. I just have to do this!"

"Okay, okay, but let me help. If these are the same guys, I think I know where they took Sally."

"You do?" Earl answered.

"Yeah. I think they're being held at that old farm at Oil City. Play along with them, Earl. I'll get Sally and your kids. Just don't get yourself and Johnson killed. Okay? Let them take the mask. Don't worry about your family. I'll get them out of there."

"Thanks, Leon. I owe you one."

Earl hung up the phone, feeling a little bit better about the situation. He turned to Latonya, who, for once, couldn't think of what to say. "You heard what I said to Leon Pence. I can't say anything more, Latonya. Do what you can to reach Eddie Shaw and tell him what I am about to do. But for God's sake, don't talk to anyone else about this. And give me an hour, okay?"

Earl grabbed his hat and jacket and ran for the door. Latonya still stood by his desk, staring after him with her mouth open and her left hand grasping her chest.

*

After the call from Earl, Leon Pence took a moment to think things through. He didn't want his emotions to make his decisions for him. He now had more than one reason to seek his revenge against those who were holding Earl's wife, son, and daughter. They had killed his brother, sunk his boat, and nearly killed him. If they were going back to the island with Earl, they had a longer trip ahead of them by helicopter, and it was not likely that they would drive all the way back to the farm at Oil City. But once they had finished their business on the island, Oil City was the most obvious destination.

Leon didn't want to think what they might do with Earl and his family once they arrived at the farm. His first decision had to be to rescue Sally and the children. That might take some pressure off Earl to cooperate. Getting them out of harm's way also made it easier for the authorities to deal with these guys once they landed on the mainland. He wasn't worried about how many men might be holding Sally. He had been trained in reconnaissance and extraction operations while in the Marines.

Leon swallowed the last of his now-cold coffee and went into his bedroom. In his closet, he pulled back some clothes, uncovering a large gun safe. He dialed the combination and opened the door to reveal his gun collection. Leon took out his pride and joy—a Sako long-distance competition rifle, a civilian version of a military sniper rifle. The rifle had fantastic accuracy. He dry-fired the rifle to check the trigger pull and then grabbed several clips of special .338 Lapua Magnum cartridges that he had loaded himself. He could hit a two-inch circle at 1,000 yards. Then he donned a pair of camo pants and a camo shirt and strapped his tactical survival knife to his right leg.

It took Leon less than thirty minutes to reach the turnoff to Oil City. He took the graveled road fast, sliding through some of the turns, which were muddy from the storm. When he caught his first glimpse of the farm field through the trees, he pulled over and started on foot. Earl and Sally's Volvo was parked at the turnoff to the farm. It was empty. He examined the road surface for tracks. There were lots of footprints and he squatted down and studied them. For an experienced hunter and ex-Marine, the tracks told him all he needed to know. There were three sets of smaller tracks coming up from the farm and headed toward the beach. The prints were deep, meaning that whoever made them were running. Two larger sets of tracks also went the same way.

So Sally has taken the children and managed to escape. Leon grinned and shook his head. He knew the woman had some smarts. She was headed for the Third Beach Trail, and Leon knew every foot of that route. Keeping his rifle at the ready, Leon started off at a trot, following the tracks toward the trailhead. The hunters were now the hunted.

CHAPTER 44

The storm had blown itself out around dawn and all that was left was a light rain. At the hotel in Tacoma, Hiroko Takahashi gently rapped on the door to Norika's room.

"So sorry to disturb you, Norika-*san*," he whispered. "We must leave right away."

Seconds later, the woman opened the door and replied, "You have not disturbed me, Hiroko. I have been up for some time conducting business with my partners in Asia and Europe."

The man bowed his head in respect, and as he raised it, there was a worried look on his face.

"Is everything okay?" she asked.

"Perhaps not," Hiroko replied with some hesitation.

"What is it?"

"I have had two men standing guard continuously. One of them reported to me that someone was watching the hotel yesterday and all night."

"Yuri Matasuba! Or his spies! I knew I could not make this trip without him being informed and having someone follow me."

"I think we can slip away, but we must leave immediately. They will be keeping an eye on the car we used from the airport, so we will use another car that I rented late last night. It is now parked in the back of the hotel."

"Good! Are the preparations for recovery of the pod underway?" Norika asked.

"Soon, Norika-*san*," Hiroko answered as he bowed his head once more. "There is a helicopter that will be waiting for us in a town called Forks, but it is a long drive. The man I left on the coast in Astoria is now on a salvage vessel, which I have chartered. It is proceeding up the coast and will be standing by, awaiting our arrival. The helicopter will fly us out to the vessel and then assist in locating the pod. Once it is located, the salvage vessel will attach a cable, tow it off the beach, and take it on board."

"You have done well, Hiroko. This unfortunate event is almost over. Now give me a few minutes to pack my things and we can be on our way."

Hiroko went to talk to his partner since arriving in the United States to search for the pod. "Yuki, we have to protect Norika Edo and you need to give us time to get away by staying with the first car we rented. Later this morning you can sneak away and wait for my call."

"Yes, Hiroko *san*, I know what to do."

The drive from Tacoma to Port Angeles took several hours. Hiroko Takahashi had chosen to drive the second car himself. Throughout the trip he kept on the lookout for any vehicle that might be following them. Norika sat beside him in the passenger seat, with two bodyguards in the backseat. They slept the whole time, having been on duty the night before. In Port Angeles, Hiroko pulled into the large parking lot of an Asian restaurant and sent one of the men inside for hot tea and noodle soup for them to share on the rest of the drive. They were still nearly two hours from Forks, where the helicopter would be waiting at the small airfield on the south end of town.

They were pulling back onto the highway when Norika's cell phone buzzed. She looked at the number and recognized it. It was a number she could never forget, as she rubbed the tender stub of her pinky finger.

"Yuri Matasuba! You bastard! Why are you calling me?"

"Oh, again such an impolite greeting for such a fine Japanese lady to offer a business associate," Yuri replied.

"You may have been a business associate of my late husband, but you are most definitely not an associate of mine. What do you want?"

"Why, my share of the diamonds and bonds, of course, Norika. I understand you are very close to obtaining them. At least you should be, if you place any value on your life."

"Maybe I am. Whether you believe it or not, I do want to recover the diamonds and finish this business with you and your associates once and for all."

"I know, I know," Yuri said. "And I also know all about your tsunami debris recovery sham. It is a nice touch of diplomacy but means nothing to our government or to you, for that matter. Sending teams around here and there to look at tsunami debris is such a farce. At least I realize now why you are doing it. The diamonds are somehow part of the debris that drifted across the Pacific, am I right?"

Before answering, Norika took a moment to turn on the speaker of her phone so Hiroko could hear the conversation. He needed to know so that he could respond accordingly when the time came.

"That information is for myself alone to know. It is not to be shared with you, Yuri."

"Well, I certainly wish you all the success in your recovery efforts. In fact, we expect to be on hand to offer assistance, so to speak." Yuri said with a slight chuckle in his voice.

"Then you better hurry. We left your spies sleeping next to some hotel near the international airport. You might as well call them home so they can feed your cats or something."

"Norika, your tea is getting cold, and I do know where you are headed."

Norika nearly spilled her Styrofoam cup of tea as she, Hiroko, and the two bodyguards turned to look behind their car. They were being followed by a black sedan, the same one that Hiroko said had been watching the hotel all night. The bodyguards pulled out their automatic pistols and checked their clips.

"Like me, my men have many talents, Norika," Yuri continued. "I do not have to be there. Yuki, the man you left behind, sang like a turtledove in the bright dawn when one of my men sliced off one of his testicles. Ah, this town of Forks. I believe it is quite small and close to the ocean, is it not?"

"I hope your men enjoy it, and may they encounter the vampires that are said to reside there," Norika answered furiously. "Goodbye, Yuri Matasuba, and good hunting!" she said as she turned off her phone.

Hiroko had subconsciously increased his speed as if he could outrun the other vehicle. However, the road conditions made it impossible to drive at high speed. While Norika was talking to Matasuba, they had reached the east end of Crescent Lake, a long, deep lake along the northern boundary of Olympic National Park. The highway ran extremely close to the south shore, with the edge of the pavement sometimes only a few feet from the water's edge. The highway grade was flat and also just a few feet above the surface of the lake. The problem was the curves. The highway turned in and out, following the shoreline, and was narrow. Several large tractor-trailer rigs had passed them, heading back toward Port Angeles and adding to the driving risk. Hiroshi analyzed the situation and then announced to Norika what he intended to do.

"I think I can rid us of Matasuba's men," stated Hiroko. "However, it is a very dangerous driving maneuver, and we could end up in the lake. Please, everyone, tighten your seat belts and brace yourselves for whatever happens."

Hiroko kept his speed as high as he dared and hoped that the black sedan would do the same. He also kept checking the highway farther ahead and finally saw what he hoped for. Another tractor-trailer rig was headed toward them, several curves away. He wanted to gauge the point when they would take a curve to the left and momentarily be out of the following vehicle's sight.

The tractor-trailer disappeared up ahead as it followed a curve to the right to go around a small corner of the lake. Hiroko increased his speed further, and, as he went around the bend to the left, he let his left wheels cross the center line by several feet, putting them well into the lane of the oncoming truck. The truck driver, who was shocked to see them approaching in his lane, blasted his horn and swerved to the right, away from their car and the lake. His trailer started to swing out. Hiroko yanked the steering wheel back to the right, putting two tires on the gravel shoulder and barely squeaked by the advancing rear end of the trailer. He glanced in the rearview mirror to see that Yuri's men were not so lucky. The truck's trailer had not sufficiently straightened out to provide them with enough room to pass. It had continued to swerve to the right, and to avoid a collision, the black sedan drove over the bank into the shallow water of the cove. Hiroko relaxed and smiled to himself.

"All is well, Norika-*san*. Matasuba's men have decided to stop for a swim in the lake and will not be catching up with us anytime soon."

CHAPTER 45

Sally, Bernie, and Christine hurried as fast as they could across a stretch of open beach. They had rested briefly upon leaving the road. The rain was slackening and a hint of clearing could be seen in the sky off to the southwest. The sea was still rough, with twelve- to fourteen-foot breakers hitting the shore and running up the beach, leaving huge rows of foam as it retreated. This forced the trio to stay close to the drift logs, some of which blocked their way, requiring them to climb over.

Now and then, Sally would glance back to see if anyone was following their trail along the beach. Up ahead, she could see Hoh Head rising into the low clouds that seemed to cling to it. Even in good weather and with low tides, there was no beach at Hoh Head. The cliffs tumbled in a sheer drop, right into the ocean. In the distance, Sally could see waves crashing hard on the rocks as if they were trying to climb to the tree-lined top of the cliff, only to fall back and try again.

As Sally marched along the sand, everything that she knew about the Hoh Head trail started coming back to her. It was a well-defined trail that partially followed the beach from the Hoh River to La Push, a distance of more than fourteen miles. What was unique about the trail was its rope ladders. To get around the point, the trail climbed more than a thousand feet, part of that climb with the help of ladders made of logs and a single rope used to assist in climbing hand over hand. Once above the first set of ladders, the ascent was so steep that hikers had to use other ropes to climb the cliff. Then the trail entered the rainforest, which would be nearly impenetrable if not for the maintained trail that passed through boggy areas and crossed streams using logs for footing. For these reasons, the trail was considered difficult even for experienced hikers who were in good shape. For Sally and the kids, it was going to be much worse, but it was not a matter of choice—it was a matter of survival.

Sally stumbled in the soft beach sand. The rain-sodden coat she wore was heavy, but she dared not leave it behind. Unless they were very lucky, they probably would spend at least one night somewhere along the trail, if they could stay ahead of their pursuers. Sally glanced back at Christine and Bernie. They seemed to be handling it well, but they played sports, and Sally had just spent a week in the hospital.

She kept an eye on the waves breaking on the beach. The tide appeared to be ebbing, which would help them get around the first set of cliffs to Jefferson Cove. It had a broader sand beach, which unfortunately did not last—it ended at the base of Hoh Head. From there, they had to climb the infamous rope ladders.

It took them over an hour to reach the beach at Jefferson Cove. The waves ran up close to the base of the cliffs in an area filled with large boulders. Several times they had to stop and wait for periods of smaller waves and then run.

As they trudged across the sand beach to the cliffs at Hoh Head, Sally could see the first set of ladders. They were steep but should be manageable. Bernie and Christine noticed the ladders as well.

"Are those ladders up ahead?" Christine asked as she stopped to stare at the cliffs.

"Yes! That's our trail. It goes up over the point, and not around, I'm afraid," Sally replied. "Keep moving. We'll rest when we get to the top."

"Can't we stay on the beach?"

"Not unless you are able to swim around that point. And I don't think it's possible even on a good day."

Bernie got to the bottom of the ladder first. "Can I climb up?" he asked as he put a hand on the first rung and looked upward. The rungs were each cut from tree limbs and lashed about three feet apart to longer poles leaning against a steep dirt and rock bank.

"We are all going up. We can't go back," Sally answered, and as she had done dozens of times since they escaped, turned to check behind them. This time she saw movement. Someone was coming along the beach not far from the trailhead. "Darn! They've found us. They can't be more than an hour behind."

Sally pointed at the ladder. "We have to climb. Bernie, you first. Then you, Christine."

Bernie grabbed the rope and scrambled up the first rung and then the second. "This is fun! It's just like at the school playground, only way bigger."

Christine hesitated but then started to climb after Bernie, carefully hanging onto the rope with both hands as she moved from one rung to the next. Sally checked to see if the old knife she had taken from the barn was secure in a coat pocket as she waited for the kids to get a little ahead. As she grabbed the rope and started up the ladder, she had an idea as to how she might slow their pursuers down.

The climb left Sally breathless, and when she reached the last rung, she asked Bernie and Christine to relax for a minute while she took care of something. Sally pulled the knife out of her pocket and examined the rope they had just used to help them climb up. It was braided nylon line like the type used to anchor a small boat. There were knots every few feet to prevent the climber from slipping. Sally pulled the line over to the side support next to the topmost rung and then took the knife and sawed through two of the three braided strands of rope.

"Christine, hand me one of those good-sized rocks in the bank beside you."

"What are you doing, Mom? You're destroying part of the ladder system. Someone could get hurt if it breaks."

"I hope so."

Sally used the rock to drive the blade of the knife as deep as she could into one of the poles next to the top rung, where the line was secured. Then she draped the remaining strand of rope around its sharp edge. What she hoped would happen was that the weight of a person climbing would cause the blade to cut through the last strand before he got to the top.

"Alright, let's hope this works. This should at least slow that guy down," Sally stated as she studied her sabotaged rope ladder. She put a hand on a knee and forced herself to stand. Her muscles were complaining from their run and now the climb. She looked back down the beach and saw that the man had made it around the rocks and was trotting across the broad beach of Jefferson Cove. He would be at the base of the ladder before long. Looking farther back down the beach toward the trailhead over a mile away, she saw that another man had taken up the chase.

"Time to go!" she hollered and started up the steep incline, using another rope that was tied off somewhere above.

Sally and the kids reached the top of the cliff and were running along a flatter section of the trail just as Sloan got to the bottom of the first ladder. They were now several hundred feet above him, and he saw them cross an open section at the top of the cliff before disappearing into a patch of trees. Sloan took a moment to sling the rifle he was carrying onto his back, and then he leaped up onto the first rung of the ladder, ignoring the rope and climbing hand over hand. He was halfway up when his right foot slipped and he had to catch himself by grabbing the rope. He hung on to it, swung his body out slightly away from the ladder, and resumed his climb, using one hand and then the other to pull himself up.

The weight of the man's body on the rope had caused the knife to bend downward, almost pulling it out of the ladder support. The rope started to slip along the blade toward the haft. Then the last braid parted. Above the sound of the surf, the wind carried the man's wail up the cliff and into the timber as he fell down the ladder. His left leg slipped inside one of the rungs, breaking just above the ankle as he fell backward down the ladder and the force of his body ripping off three of the lower cross pieces. His wail turned into a painful scream as he tumbled thirty feet to the bottom of the ladder, where he lay unconscious, covered in coils of rope.

Jake Dixon could see Sloan lying motionless at the bottom of the rope ladder as he ran across the last open section of sand beach. By the time he reached the cliff, Sloan was sitting up and rocking back and forth, holding a badly twisted leg.

"My leg! It's broken!" Sloan yelled with gritted teeth. "The damn rope broke."

Jake pawed through the coils of rope, found the end, and examined it. "It didn't break. She sabotaged it by partially cutting the strands."

"What are we going to do?" Sloan asked between moans. "You gotta help me get back to the car and to a hospital."

Sloan screamed as Jake pulled his blood-soaked pant leg up to look at the break. It looked nasty. A jagged end of the tibia bone protruded through the flesh. Jake found a couple of sticks of driftwood. "Gimme your jacket," he said to Sloan as he used his Ka-Bar knife to slice off some of the rope and unbraided it. Then he wrapped the leg with the jacket and used the sticks and rope to splint it.

"There are some longer pieces of driftwood along the beach to use as a crutch. You can drag yourself over there and then walk out by yourself. I'm going after that woman."

"What? You're leaving me to get out of here all by myself? I can't make it over those rocks!"

Jake inspected the broken ladder. There was a large gap and without the rope to help scale the cliff it wasn't going to be easy to get to the top.

"Well, I could shoot you," Jake stated, shaking his head and putting one foot on a ladder rung to start up. "Your choice!"

Jake stepped back and grabbed what was left of the rope. He found a short, heavy piece of driftwood and tied it to one end. Then he tried to flip it up over the first intact crosspiece which was a good fifteen feet above his head. On the second attempt the stick went over the rung and he played out the line to let it slip back to where he could grab it and then tie it to the bottom crosspiece.

"Jake, don't leave me! Jake!" Sloan shouted as the man grabbed the rope and began to climb.

CHAPTER 46

As the crow flies, the closest general aviation airport to South Bend was located less than a mile from city center, just across the Willapa River. But to users, its location felt surprisingly remote. It was surrounded by tidal marshes and required driving several miles upriver and back on the other bank. The airfield was generally unattended, and refueling was self-serve. It was the perfect place for Betar's chartered helicopter to land and pick up a special passenger without much notice, as well as refuel for the flight out to Destruction Island. In fact, hardly anyone noticed the sleek Bell 429 slip over the Willapa Hills from the north and quickly set down next to the airfield's small building, which housed a lounge for pilots. The only other building on the site was a small, semi enclosed hangar with several private planes tied down inside. There was not a person around.

Juno jumped out and walked over to a bench next to the building and lit a cigarette. He had spent much of the last hour of the flight on phone calls, dealing with business matters. He had hardly even noticed the beautiful scenery that they had flown over on the trip from Seattle. Little stirred around him, and a rank smell of salt marsh vegetation and mud flats filled the air.

In the distance to the south, Juno could just see several huge shell mounds of processed oysters in front of the downtown businesses in South Bend. On the side of the airfield building was a poster promoting this year's fly-in and an all-you-can-eat oysters fundraising event and touting South Bend as the "Oyster Capital of the World." Betar just shook his head and snapped his wrist up to glance at his expensive Bulgari watch. His impatience was growing. He wanted this trip to be over, to be as far away from this stinking place as possible.

The pilot busied himself with refueling the helicopter while Juno's bodyguard, Mirko Rifi, checked out the lounge. Mirko had worked for Juno longer than Jake Dixon. He had been a friend of Juno's since Juno was a young businessman starting out in Eastern Europe. As he exited the lounge, Mirko shrugged his shoulders in a sign that there was no one else around. Juno nodded his head toward the hangar. Mirko was about to walk across the tarmac when he heard a car approaching the airfield on the access road. He walked over to meet it, cautious and ready to draw a semiautomatic pistol from inside his loose jacket, if necessary. The car's driver signaled by raising a hand and pulled up next to him. Mirko opened one of the rear doors and motioned for the backseat occupant to get out. He was surprised when he saw two men and looked at the driver then Juno with a confused look.

"All I know is that Dixon told me to bring two guys," the driver stated.

Betar dropped his cigarette to the ground, smashed it with a booted foot, and walked over to where the three men were standing.

"Bring both of them over here, Mirko," stated Juno. "Jake informed me that there would be two guests to take with us." He assumed that the younger of the two was Earl Armstrong and addressed him without extending a hand. "I'm glad you see it our way and decided to join us on this little business venture. Who is your friend?"

"You can fly to hell—it's right out that way!" replied Earl, pointing toward the ocean. "We are not here of our own free will and…"

Earl's response was cut short by Mirko's clenched fist in his stomach—hard enough to take away Earl's breath.

"Let me make this clear," Juno continued. "I am a businessman, and you are going to provide me with what I am seeking. If either of you try to delay our task or attempt to escape, Mirko here will make it much more painful for you. Now answer my question: why have you brought this fat little man?"

Earl slowly straightened up, rubbing a hand over his stomach. "Th...this is one of my closest friends, Mr. Johnson Wewa. He is an Indian shaman and knows more about the culture and artifacts of the Northwest coast than anyone I know. I need his help in locating the golden mask. That is what you want, right?"

*

The activity around the airfield at Forks was quite different than the South Bend airfield. Norika Edo and her men found the runway filled with people strolling around row upon row of classic cars. Attendees were parked along the shoulder of Highway 101 well back into town. The parking lot of the visitor's center was occupied with half a dozen food booths operated by the local Boy Scouts, church groups, and civic organizations. A bluegrass band called the Broken Down Jugs played in one of the small plane hangars as people danced or sat on bales of straw just outside the hangar doors. There was no helicopter parked anywhere around the airfield.

Hiroko Takahashi drove slowly through a gate and around the north end of the runway to where a helipad was marked on the pavement. He turned off the engine and opened his car door. The amplified bluegrass music blasted across the field. He put a hand over his brow and scanned the sky in every direction. He could neither see nor hear the sound of a helicopter approaching. Hiroko looked at his watch. It was supposed to have met them ten minutes ago.

He made a call to his man, who was now on the salvage vessel. The ship had a possible fix on the *Kanji Maru* escape pod and was headed for the location. But there was no word on the chartered helicopter to ferry them out to the ship. There was nothing to do but wait.

CHAPTER 47

Sally Armstrong was getting extremely tired as she pushed the children and herself to keep moving northward along the forested trail high above Hoh Head. There was only one way to go, and that was to continue on toward La Push. She knew that they had a long way to go, and there was a good chance that their pursuers might catch up with them. But she wasn't going to give up. As long as they had some energy, they would push on. Unfortunately, the lack of anything to eat since the night before was taking a toll on how fast they could move. She felt the exhaustion setting in and tried to ignore it.

Neither Christine nor Bernie had complained. They appeared to fully understood the seriousness of the situation—if they slowed down, then the bad men they saw on the beach would be able to get them. Sally figured that the men had been slowed down some at the rope ladders. Scaling the first forty-foot ladder without a rope would not be easy, and the scream they had heard must have meant that one of their pursuers had fallen due to her booby trap.

Sally and the children were now deep in heavy timber. The path was gradually sloping downward, and the sound of ocean swells crashing on the shore meant that they were getting closer to another section of beach. The trail suddenly leveled out and turned into a section of constructed boardwalk. They were in a marshy area, which, after several hundred yards, ended at a stream. Unfortunately, there was no bridge, and the water level was still high from the rainstorm. They would have to wade.

"Well, we were almost dry, and now, I'm afraid, we are going to have to get wet again," Sally said to Christine and Bernie. She looked upstream and downstream. There was no easier spot to cross than right at the trail. The current was swift, but the water didn't look to be much higher than Sally's thighs. Still, there was a risk that they, particularly the kids, could lose their footing or slip.

"We have to cross this stream. Bernie, you and Christine will hold hands very tight; Christine, you and I will hold hands. My body should break the current and make it easier for the two of you to stay on your feet."

"That's okay, Mom. We can make it!" Bernie said.

"I know you can. But we're all tired. Ready? Let's go."

The three of them stepped into the stream. At least the water wasn't frigid. The other bank was only about twenty feet away, but to keep their balance, they had to move slowly and place each foot carefully in front of the other. The water rose on Sally's right leg to the middle of her thigh and pushed hard against her. If she stumbled and went down, they all would.

Foot by foot, they moved across, holding on to each other's hands. When they were only four feet from the other bank, the force of the water eased, and they quickly reached the bank. Sally took a Coke bottle and filled it using part of her blouse to screen out debris. The water was still cloudy but they each took a drink, and then she filled it again to carry with them.

"You two are real troopers. I'm so proud of you," Sally told them.

"Are those men going to catch us and hurt us, Mom?" Christine asked.

"Not if we keep ahead of them. There's a town and people at the end of this trail. So let's find the next beach."

Minutes later, they broke free of the timber, wound around several drift logs, and ended up on a broad sand beach that stretched ahead of them for over a mile. About halfway to the end of the beach, and another cliff, was a ridge of rock that extended out into the surf. They would have to climb over it.

Sticking to the hard sand just of above the reach of the breakers, they made good time and came to the bottom of the rock ridge. Several stacks of stones marked where the trail climbed over the top before dropping back to the beach on the far side. Sally estimated that it was only fifty feet or so to the top and started up the steep trail followed by Christine and Bernie. She immediately felt the pain in her leg muscles return. She stopped at the top and looked back the way they had come. A man had just emerged through the pile of drift logs and had seen them. He started running along the beach toward them.

"Oh no! Come on, kids! I think the trail goes back into the trees up ahead. Maybe we can find a place to hide."

Sally, Christine, and Bernie dashed down the far side of the rock ridge and began running along the final stretch of beach, which ended at another cliff a half-mile away. As she ran, Sally tried to see where the trail went up. Then she saw it, and her spirits dropped. There was another rope ladder to climb. Maybe they could get to the top and pull the rope up before the man reached them.

She looked back. The man had also dropped down onto the sand and was closing the gap. He caught them just as they reached the ladder. Sally slumped down to the sand, feeling defeated.

Jake Dixon was breathing hard when he called out to Sally. "Hold it right there! If I have to, I'll shoot one of the children."

"You don't have to shoot one of us. You've won," Sally replied.

"This has been a stupid attempt to escape, Mrs. Armstrong. It really doesn't matter what you try—your husband is now on his way to the island with my boss. He will do what we want, regardless of your silly games."

"The island?" said Sally. "You have my husband? You don't know that for sure. And you don't know my husband. It won't be easy to gain his cooperation."

"Oh, he will cooperate. I talked to him earlier. He and Mr. Wewa are cooperating fully."

"Wewa...is he with my husband?" Sally asked, puzzled.

"Yes. Your husband insisted that Mr. Wewa accompany him to the island to help him find what we are looking for. Now get up! We're headed back to the farmhouse."

Sally slowly got to her feet and looked at Christine and Bernie. Both of them were sobbing quietly. They had used up all their energy with the last desperate run and looked like zombies. Sally wasn't sure that they would be able to make it all the way back. She wasn't sure that she could make it back herself. She felt like she was wearing lead boots as she took each one of the children by the hand and slowly started back down the beach. She glanced out at the ocean. If it had been better circumstances, the view would have been extraordinary. There were sea stacks everywhere. They were beautiful in the sunlight, with the ocean waves dashing against them. Sally didn't know it, but she was looking at the Devil's Graveyard.

As they walked, it suddenly dawned on Sally why they were being taken back to the farmhouse. The man intended to kill them, and it was probably easier to dispose of their bodies by burying them in the floor of the barn or in a field rather than out here on the beach, along a well-known hiking trail. With that thought, Sally was suddenly surprised that they had not encountered anyone hiking or camping along the trail. No matter—help or no help, she couldn't give up. She had to come up with another plan before they got back to the farm.

Sally grew more furious with the thought that this man intended to kill Christine and Bernie. Leon Pence had expressed his concern over these men when they had met at their home in South Bend. Their leader would stop at noth-ing to find the golden mask, including the deaths of two innocent children.

Sally squeezed each of her children's hands. They squeezed back. The sign gave her renewed courage. She was not giving up. She would fight this man with her last breath. No one was going to get the chance to kill her chil-dren. The children had to escape. They had to live, no mat-ter what happened to her. Sally glanced back at their captor. He was trailing them about ten feet back and looked tired, having run hard for several miles to catch up with them. She looked down at Christine and Bernie as they walked and spoke softly to them.

"When I say so, I want each of you to run for the rocks as fast as you can. I want you to keep going until you find help. I'm going to delay this guy the best I can. He's tired and won't be able to keep up with the two of you. Now nod your heads that you will do just as I have said."

Sally glanced at both of them and saw that they were still frightened, but they nodded nevertheless. She looked back at the man once more. He was trying to make a call on his cell phone and appeared annoyed. She made a weak smile and let go of Christine and Bernie. "Now! Go!"

Sally turned and rushed at Jake Dixon with her head down and tackled him. They went down together. Jake was clearly caught by surprise, and Sally started punching him and scratching at his face. Jake let go of his phone and threw a punch at Sally's face, which hit her just below her left eye. She fell to one side, her body twisting away from the man. Jake noticed the children running, so Sally launched herself at him again and took another punch as he fought back. She bit her lip and momentarily lost her vision with the blow. When she opened her eyes, the man was standing over her and had pulled a pistol out from under his jacket. He was breathing hard. She looked toward Christine and Bernie and guessed that they were out of pistol range. She attempted a slight smile with her bleeding lip.

Jake Dixon shook his head. "That was another stupid, failed effort, Mrs. Armstrong, and, regretfully, the last attempt you'll have. I was going to kill you anyway, so I might as well take care of it now and save myself the trouble of taking..."

Sally's eyes went wide as a red spot appeared on the front of the man's shirt and begin to spread as she heard the sharp crack from a rifle echo off the cliff. The spot spread slowly, down to his waist. Jake Dixon looked down at his chest with an incredulous look on his face. He slipped to his knees and then fell over onto the sand without uttering another word.

Sally turned quickly and looked down the beach, searching for the children. At the sound of the rifle, they had stopped and now stood staring at the top of the rock ridge. Sally tried to make out what they were looking at, but her left eye was beginning to swell shut. Out of her right eye, she saw a man with a rifle stand up and walk slowly down the hill and approach Christine and Bernie. They didn't attempt to run away. As the man reached them, he slung his rifle over a shoulder, took each of them by a hand, and started walking toward her. Sally struggled to stand but found she was too weak, so she tried to wipe away the sand, blood, and tears from her face as she waited. Sally managed a smile when she recognized the man.

It was Leon Pence, and he was smiling, too.

CHAPTER 48

The bluegrass music was beginning to wear on Norika as she paced back and forth next to the rental car. She looked at her watch and then at the sky for the hundredth time.

No sign of the helicopter.

Hiroko sent a bodyguard for some soft drinks while they continued to wait.

Norika watched the man as he disappeared into the crowd near several food concessions. "Where are we headed from here?" Norika asked.

"Our chartered salvage vessel should be nearing the location of the rescue pod photographed by the Coast Guard where it washed ashore with the tsunami debris."

"Is it there?" Norika asked.

"They believe so. But a Coast Guard patrol boat will not let them approach the island and without the helicopter they cannot confirm it is the pod from the Kanji Maru. Still, it is very encouraging though not absolutely positive."

"After so many months of searching, I am both happy and afraid. It has to be the one. Are we very far from the ship?"

"No. It is a short flight from here. Once we are airborne, we will fly directly to the coast and out to the ship. It has a helipad."

"That is good. I would like to be there when the pod is recovered."

Norika had turned her phone back on and it buzzed. It was Matasuba again. She refused to answer it and became concerned that his men may have found a way to catch up with them after being run off the highway. She scanned the crowd on the far side of the runway and noticed her bodyguard scurrying back toward them. The noise of an aircraft filled the air. It got her attention as well as that of the crowd at the car show. A small Bell 212 helicopter swooped over their heads, flew low along the length of the airfield, and then began to drop onto the helipad.

Three men burst through the crowd on the other side of the runway and began running toward them, following the bodyguard. Hiroko saw them first.

Matasuba's hired boys. Our helicopter is just in time.

"We must get aboard immediately, Norika-*san*!" Hiroko hollered over the noise of the chopper's engine.

He rushed to the car and grabbed Norika's travel bag. He then took her arm, and together they ran to the helicopter's door, keeping their heads low to avoid the spinning blades. The pilot observed their urgency to take off and immediately increased his engine speed. The two bodyguards stayed by the car, ready to defend their employer by facing the three pursuers. But Matasuba's men stopped short of the helipad and could only watch in frustration as the Bell helicopter lifted into the air and turned toward the west.

Minutes later, Norika and Hiroko were leaving the forested mainland behind. The rugged coastline was below them. The helicopter pilot began chattering on his radio and then made a sharp turn southward along the coast, flying over dozens of sea stacks. It was a picturesque sight of breathless beauty, reminding Norika of the Shirashima coast of her own country with its sacred island of Okinoshima. She made a little promise that if she were successful in her quest, she would make the trek to the sacred island and offer a prayer to Buddha.

In the late afternoon sun, an island and a large ship appeared in the distance several miles offshore. It was the salvage vessel, which had spent the better part of a day cruising northward from the Columbia River and now drifted about a mile off the eastern shore of Destruction Island. The pilot circled and then deftly dropped the helicopter onto the helipad near the stern of the large vessel.

Norika had a chance to freshen up, and then the captain invited her to the bridge to talk about the recovery of the lost pod. She was impressed with what she saw, taking in all of the instruments and human activity. In a large captain's chair sat a large man with graying hair. He wore a khaki uniform shirt and matching trousers.

"Mrs. Edo, it's a pleasure to welcome you aboard my ship. I'm Captain Strong, and my ship and its crew are anxious to be of assistance. However, I am afraid I have some disappointing news. We need to delay the search. About an hour ago, we were radioed by the Coast Guard to assist in an emergency operation. We do not have a choice and have to respond."

"I was hoping we could begin the search immediately, Captain," Norika replied. "What is this emergency all about?"

"Several days ago, a tour boat collided with a large concrete dock, which most likely is part of the tsunami debris from your country. Several people drowned and others were seriously injured during the collision. The Coast Guard wants to remove this navigational hazard as soon as possible, and we have been requested to take it in tow into Grays Harbor. Under the terms of our contract with the government, we have to render assistance at the earliest opportunity when there is an incident resulting in risk of life or an immediate hazard to navigation."

"How long will this take?" asked Norika.

"Well, even if we were to locate your rescue pod this afternoon, we would not be able to begin the recovery until morning. There are too many hazardous rocks around the shore of the island, and we prefer not to begin a job such as this only to have to abandon it and start again the next day. It puts my men at risk. So we plan to tackle the recovery of the dock first. The Coast Guard has placed a light beacon and a GPS locator on the dock. We are underway to the location now and should not have any difficulty finding it, even at night. With any luck, we should be back here in the vicinity of Destruction Island by early morning. We'll keep the helicopter on board and can commence the search as soon as there is sufficient light."

"Can we remain on board? Can you accommodate us?" Hiroko asked.

"We have a couple of guest staterooms. They're pretty basic but comfortable. I'm making my own cabin available to Mrs. Edo because I will probably be up all night anyway. My second in command will show you to your cabins. And please join me for dinner at seven, Mr. Takahaski."

Hiroko smiled and made a slight bow.

"Oh," the captain added. "The two of you are welcome to come up to the bridge and observe us putting a towline on the dock. But it is going to be the middle of the night and pretty boring."

Hiroko bowed again to acknowledge the generosity of the captain and then took Mrs. Edo by the arm and followed the second officer down into the ship, away from the bridge. If he had bothered to look out the starboard windows, he would have noticed another helicopter flying close to the coastline, headed toward Destruction Island.

CHAPTER 49

Thermal uplift currents blasted Juno Betar's helicopter as it flew at near maximum speed along the long sand beaches and cliffs of the Washington coast. It was flying well under one thousand feet, an elevation that was illegal for that part of the northern coastline because of a marine reserve designation. It was also dangerous. Some years back, a Coast Guard helicopter had violated the rule and struck a power line to an island off the community of La Push and crashed into the sea.

Juno liked the thrill of flying close to the terrain at high speed and sometimes took over the controls himself even though he did not have a pilot's license. For Earl and Johnson in the back of the helicopter, it was all they could do to stay in their seats. It was a rough ride with the cliffs and coastline forests slipping by very closely in a blur. The security man, Mirko, who was sitting between them, somehow slept through it all with his mouth wide

open and head lolling side to side from the bouncing of
the helicopter.

Earl was relieved when the helicopter finally
banked westward and the low profile of Destruction Island
became silhouetted on the horizon in the late afternoon
sun. The white tower of the lighthouse on the cliff at the
southerly end stood out against the dark, rocky mass. Earl
occupied the seat behind the pilot and glanced out his window. He noticed a ship headed away from the island at
about the same time that Juno Betar and the pilot began
talking through their headphones. Judging from the pilot's
gestures, apparently they were talking about the ship and
a small helicopter that Earl could see sitting on the stern.
There was another boat further to the north. Moments later,
the pilot heard a radio message.

"This is United States Coast Guard. Unknown aircraft near Destruction Island, you are entering a restricted
area. Please identify yourself."

The pilot pointed out the Coast Guard vessel to
Betar who gestured emphatically with several thumbs-
down jerks toward the island. The pilot waved him off, nodded and ignored the radio call even when it was repeated.
He took time to circle the old concrete helipad to check it
out before descending. Earl noticed some anger or disagree-
ment between the two men. As they passed over the cliffs on
the east side of the island, Earl glanced at the swells hitting

the rocks and smiled to himself. It was well above low tide and large waves were hitting the rocks. *At least some things are in our favor. The longer this takes, the better chance we have at being rescued. Sure hope Eddie understood Latonya's message.*

The pilot dropped the helicopter onto the concrete pad and shut down the engine. With the soft sound of the whirling rotors slowing, the quietness of the island hit Earl's senses with a soothing feeling—like hitting a soft mattress—after the jarring ride northward from Willapa Bay.

Juno Betar jumped from the helicopter, stretched, and turned to face the three men in the backseats.

"Mirko! Get your butt out here!" Juno shouted at the still-sleeping form in the center seat.

Mirko woke with a start, confused as to where he was. He struggled to respond to what his boss was hollering at him. He was hemmed in by Earl and Johnson—neither of whom were in a hurry to unfasten their seatbelts to climb out.

"Armstrong! You, too!" Juno hollered again. "Climb out of there. It's time for you to do what we're here for—to find that damn cave."

Earl moved as slowly as he could. He undid his seatbelt, worked his legs around, and found the ladder rung on the side of the fuselage. He then took his time climbing down. Once on solid ground, he stretched a bit and looked around, trying to get his bearings from his last flight out to the island with Lori Williams and Eddie Shaw. Juno walked over and got in Earl's face.

"Well? Which way do we go?"

"Relax, Mr. Betar," Earl said as he finished stretching the cramped muscles of his arms and legs. "We aren't going anywhere for a while."

"What the hell do you mean by that?" Juno screamed at Earl. "You know what I can do to your family if you don't cooperate. Now quit stalling!"

"What I mean, Mr. Betar, is that we have quite a long wait before we can gain entrance to the cave for the simple reason that its opening is now underwater. I'm guessing that the tide is still rising, which means we have to wait at least six hours, maybe eight or nine. That is if the tide will even go low enough and those ocean swells out there don't settle down some more."

Juno's fist hit Earl on his right cheek, knocking him down. Earl groaned as his shoulder hit hard on the rough concrete of the helipad. He rolled onto his side and rubbed the side of his face and then his shoulder.

Johnson Wewa had been watching the confrontation between Juno and Earl while still in the helicopter. He scrambled down and hurried over to Earl.

"Are you alright?" Johnson asked.

"Yeah. I'll live, at least for another six hours or so." He managed a slight grin that Johnson saw but Juno could not. Johnson's face brightened. He realized that Earl was working on a plan.

"Mirko, get these two on their feet," Juno commanded. "They're going to show us where the entrance is, and I'll be the judge as to whether we can get inside the cave."

Juno Betar said something to the pilot that Earl couldn't hear as Johnson helped him up. The pilot shrugged as he took off his headset and relaxed in his seat. Mirko came over and started pushing Earl and Johnson away from the helicopter although he didn't have the slightest idea where they were headed.

"Okay, Mirko. I know the way," Earl told the man. "First, we find the old residences of the lighthouse staff. I suspect you know where those are, right? Did you enjoy digging in the dirt and helping find that bottle for your boss, Mirko?"

"Shut your mouth, or you just might take a flying leap off the cliffs like the last guy that interfered with us."

"Just like Will Pence? You threw him off the cliff?" Earl asked Mirko.

Mirko pulled out his pistol and pointed it at Johnson Wewa.

"How about we start with your friend right now?"

"Easy, Mirko!" Earl replied, raising his arms with his palms down. "Your boss is going to need both me and my friend to find what he's looking for. You wouldn't want to spoil his one chance to get his prize, now, would you? We're also going to need all of our physical abilities, so hands off. You'll score more points with your boss if you cut us some slack. Look around you. We're on an island. Where would we go?"

Mirko's face reddened from Earl's jabbing words, and Earl could sense that he had judged the situation correctly. Mirko busied himself by removing some things from a storage compartment in the tail of the helicopter, including a battery-operated lantern and some flashlights. He also took out a large backpack, which he placed on his shoulders. He gave a headlamp to Juno, gave a flashlight each to Earl and Johnson, and carried the lantern himself.

Led by Earl, the four men walked single-file along the same sidewalk used on his earlier visit with Lori and Eddie. The sidewalk was overgrown with vegetation and partially covered with dirt and sod. They had to brush away blackberry vines as they made their way to the building complex at the south end of the island. Earl could see the lighthouse up ahead and to their right. He led the way, followed by Juno, then Johnson, and Mirko last.

They were still in heavy brush nearly twice their height when Earl took another path to the right. They came to the old duplex house used by the assistant keepers. It was still in fair condition, having been largely rebuilt during the Second World War, when an army observation unit had been stationed on the island. Earl led them right past the old wooden building.

After another hundred yards, they came to the foundation of the principal keeper's house. Earl's heart took a leap again, and he felt an odd sensation as they proceeded around the foundation and walked toward the western edge of the island.

The old sidewalks that connected all of the buildings of the abandoned lighthouse complex ended at this point. They pushed through the brush and finally broke out on the edge of the cliff. Earl's sense of direction was uncanny. He had managed to guide them right to the top of the crevice leading down to the blowhole even though he had never been there before.

They peered down toward where the waves were breaking onto the rocks below. Some of the waves were breaking eight to ten feet in the air before crashing back into the sea. Over the sound of the breaking waves was an unmistakable thumping sound. The blowhole was singing its tune like a kettle drum in a symphony orchestra. Earl watched the waves for several minutes. There were exposed barnacles on the rocks, and he figured that his guess was a pretty good one—the tide was rising.

"Down there is the only entrance to the cave," Earl told the others. "If you want to attempt it now, be my guest. But if you don't want to drown in the process, we need to wait until the tide is a lot lower. Then you'll need my help to guide you in, and then you'll need Johnson's help once we are inside. The way the ocean is acting right now, we'll have maybe two hours to find the mask and get back out, or it will be a death trap. Once the tide starts to turn and come back up, the surge will block the entrance, and we will be trapped inside for another twelve hours. That is, if there is enough oxygen in the cave for us to live that long."

"Just why do I need this old man?" Juno asked with a sneer. "What's so difficult about locating a ceremonial mask once we are inside the cave?"

"Because the cave was used for ceremonies by a group of Indians," Earl answered as he started back toward the old lighthouse complex. He stopped and turned to face where Juno and Mirko still stood at the edge of the cliff. "There may be hundreds of objects, all carefully stored inside sealskins to protect them from the elements. Johnson is a shaman, trained to know about ceremonial artifacts."

"Okay, but just how do you know that these artifacts are in a cave that no one else knows exists?" Juno demanded.

"Because of old family stories, that's all." Earl said, hoping that his voice did not provide any sign that he was lying. "But it would be a waste of time to discuss them. First, we have to get inside; second, I have no idea where to look for the mask."

Juno just shook his head, clearly showing his exasperation with the whole situation that they were in.

"You might as well find a spot to get comfortable," Earl added. "We have more than six hours to kill. And when the evening mist rolls in, it's going to get very damp and chilly."

Johnson smiled weakly at Juno, shrugged his shoulders, and then hurried to catch up with Earl. Juno let them go.

*

Just as Earl had predicted, a mist settled over the island landscape just after sundown. The wind calmed down, and the sound of the waves seemed to have lessened. The seabirds that nested on the cliffs below the lighthouse had also settled down for the night, their raucous cries and flights having ended for the day. Earl had found that one of the doors to the assistant keeper's dwelling was unlocked, and he was able to force it open despite being swollen in its jamb. There was an old mattress in one of the rooms. It didn't smell too musty so that was where Earl and Johnson settled down to wait out the tide. He didn't know where

Mirko and Juno were at the moment, and he didn't care. He and Johnson could have run off and hidden somewhere on the island, but it would have only delayed the inevitable. It was best to play along with Juno Betar and avoid anyone getting hurt. The man had his cell phone, and Earl had seen him use it, so there had to be coverage out on the island. The last thing Earl wanted was a threatening call that would result in harm to his family.

Earl and Johnson shared a bottle of water and some energy bars. Mirko had found where they had settled in and tossed them the stuff before stomping back out to find his boss. Earl chewed on a bite of one of the bars as he explained things to Johnson.

"Sorry for getting you into this," Earl said, keeping his voice down in case one of the others was somewhere close.

"I probably would have done the same," answered Johnson. "That's what friends do."

"Well, I don't want to get stuck in that cave while Juno and Mirko tear everything apart looking for that mask. I don't want to get trapped and die in some old forgotten cave that no one knows about. I'm probably the only person alive who can figure out how to get inside. So I needed some way to ensure that the job was quick and that we would have a chance of getting back out. In my dreams, Chris Zauner panicked and wasn't inside long enough to discover everything that was there. He thought he was running out of air, but it could have just been an anxiety attack from recalling his own dream about being part of a ceremony with an awful end—having his heart cut out or something."

"I don't think that the Kwakiutl Indians did that sort of thing—the killing part, yes, but removing the victim's heart? That's another culture, Earl."

"Well, whatever they did down there, if there are still things in the cave, that's where I need your help." He sat quietly, eating the last of the energy bar, and then got to his feet. "There was something else that Chris knew concerning the existence of the cave. Let's take a short walk and see if we can find it."

Earl took out the flashlight that Mirko had given him and walked outside. It was fully dark, and the moon had not yet risen. He found the short walkway over to the other keeper's house, where only the foundation remained. Minutes later, they were standing in the middle of the foundation. Earl used the beam of the flashlight to search the ground around them. While most of the surface was dirt and weeds, there was some evidence of an old wooden-plank floor that had long since collapsed.

"Just what are we looking for, and what does it have to do with the cave?" Johnson asked.

"Chris's wife, Hermine, had a root cellar just below her kitchen. It was a trap door in the floor with a small crawlspace. It's where she kept things cool—like her potatoes and canned fruits and vegetables."

"I'm not following your logic. How does a root cellar have a connection with a cave?"

As Johnson said the words. Something clicked with him.

"Oh, I get it!" exclaimed Johnson. "There is an actual connection. That's how the root cellar stayed cool."

"Yup. If I'm right and it does exist, we may have nothing to fear about lack of oxygen in the cave. But it will be our secret, one that we might use to our advantage. Now we need to prove that for ourselves."

Earl began to scrape the dirt with the side of his right foot.

"Remember that trap door you found that helped us escape from that old mill building before it came down on our heads years ago? Well, now we're searching for another one that could also save our lives. We need to find that door and try to open it."

The two men scraped away the dirt, starting in the center of the foundation. After about twenty minutes, they had searched over half of the floor. Earl was beginning to think that they wouldn't find it. *It's got to be here somewhere. My dreams have never been wrong.*

Johnson was the lucky one once more; he made a little whooping sound when he found it. Earl flashed the light on Johnson—he was pushing away the dirt with his hands. Then he grabbed something with his fingers and pulled. He had found the iron pull ring to the cellar door.

Together they scraped and dug until the full outline of the door, including its hinges, was exposed. The hinges were rusted and falling apart, but there was a possibility that they could lift the door anyway. They sat for a few minutes, staring in awe at the exposed door. Finally, Earl stood and gave the word.

"I'm going to try to lift one side using the ring. Hopefully it's bolted through and won't pull out. If I can get the door up a few inches, you try to get a grip on the edge and help me lift."

"Let's do it," replied Johnson.

Earl tugged at the ring. The muscles in his shoulder that had been bruised when Juno hit him screamed. He relaxed his grip, took a deep breath, and pulled again. There was a scraping sound as the door inched upward. Johnson grabbed the lip with both hands and heaved. A blast of cool air hit them both as they collapsed onto the floor with the old wooden door between them. Earl brushed off some dirt, picked up the flashlight and shone it down into the opening. It was empty. The sides were wood lined, and there were traces of what looked like sawdust, which must have served as insulation. One side of the small chamber was exposed rock with a dark, narrow crack. Johnson reached down and could feel cold air emanating from the crevice.

"Remind me never to doubt your dreams ever again, Earl," Johnson said with a grin. Earl grinned back. Then he searched his pockets and found a scrap of paper and a pen. He wrote a short note, folded it, and tossed it into the hole.

"What did you write?" asked Johnson.

"Our rescue plan for whoever finds it—we're in a cave connecting to this spot through the blowhole."

"So they can retrieve our bodies?"

"Maybe. Let's go back and get some rest. In a couple of hours, it will be time to take a good look at that blowhole."

Earl patted Johnson on the back and kept his arm there as they walked together back to the old house. The beam of his flashlight lit up several pairs of eyes on the side of the path. Earl moved the light to see what it was. A few of the island's many rabbits sat frozen in the bright light. Earl shook his head as he pictured Johnson and himself sitting in the dark confines of the cave somewhere below them. *Now if only we can figure out how to not be frozen for all eternity in the depths of that blasted cave!*

CHAPTER 50

The Coast Guard Air Station at Astoria had been on alert for over a week. Tsunami patrols, navigation patrols, and far more emergency assistance calls than in a normal summer had all of its personnel working overtime to the point of exhaustion. Nevertheless, when Lt. Bo Phillips got the word that Lori Williams from Fish and Wildlife had made a priority request though the district office, he was more than willing to be assigned to support her mission.

The Flight Operations Room was the nerve center from where all missions were dispatched. For the last twenty-four hours, Bo and his flight crew had been using it to prepare their support for Ms. Williams's request for a flight out to Destruction Island. They were monitoring weather reports, sea conditions, and air and ship traffic in the area of the island.

Lori Williams was due to arrive at the station within the hour and would be joined by another Fish and

Wildlife agent plus Detective Eddie Shaw with the Pacific County Sheriff's office in South Bend. Bo was accustomed to taking part in joint agency operations, which usually involved high-priority interdictions for drugs and DEA guys. This one was different; he didn't think it concerned drugs—maybe contraband, though. Whatever it was about had been flagged as serious with weapons authorized.

Everything that Bo knew about the operation so far, and that wasn't much, was that it involved a major criminal act and the perpetrators could be armed. Lori was scheduled to brief everyone later that evening. He didn't understand why the mission wasn't scheduled for tonight, but apparently Lori Williams wanted full light because of the necessary "boots on the ground," as she referred to it, nature of the mission.

Based on secure radio transmissions that Bo had received, the Quileute River Station had already dispatched its two 47-foot motor lifeboats to Destruction Island to stand by in the event that their assistance was required. No communication regarding the mission was to occur on open channels except to advise traffic north of Grays Harbor of a restricted area near Destruction Island. There had already been one unidentified aircraft incident reported by one of the motor lifeboats which they had been ordered to monitor but not intervene. Phillips was puzzled by the order but apparently it had something to do with the mission.

It was 2100 hours when Lori Williams began her briefing. She had everyone's attention the moment she walked into the room. Even with a bulky bulletproof vest and her equipment belt, it was obvious that she was a gorgeous woman. Her dirty blond hair was pulled back into a simple ponytail, and she wore no makeup or jewelry. All the men in the room had heard the rumors regarding her reputation—she was tough, buff, and all business. At five feet eight inches tall, she could get in a person's face and often did. She had handled some rough cases and been successful because she was also smart.

At the podium, Lori took a moment to focus on each of the men in the room. "Evening, gentlemen. I'm Agent Lori Williams with the law-enforcement branch, Seattle Station, US Fish and Wildlife. I know that you are all tired from putting in long days due to the tsunami debris. However, I need your assistance for an extremely important mission. This investigation, which started as a run-of-the-mill case involving willful disruption of protected wildlife and government property, has escalated into murder, possibly multiple murders, kidnapping, and potential theft of historical artifacts. Whoever committed these crimes, or is behind them, is unknown. How many people are involved is also unknown.

"At this point in time, all illegal activity appears to be isolated to one location—Destruction Island. You know the island as the site of a formerly important lighthouse. The island also served as a military installation during World War II. All of the buildings are now abandoned, and no one lives on the island. The place is part of our north coast marine sanctuary because of its importance as a bird nesting site. As crazy as it sounds, there may be other important, yet to be discovered, historical resources on the island, and I'm not referring to the abandoned lighthouse complex.

"I'm going to let Detective Edward Shaw from Pacific County explain some of the recent criminal circumstances, and then we'll discuss the actual operation, which is planned for early tomorrow morning."

Each man in the room followed Lori with their eyes as she moved away from the podium and over to a side wall. She crossed her arms over her breasts. Their staring was interrupted when the person who now stood at the podium cleared his throat and spoke.

"I'm Detective Eddie Shaw and as, uh, Lori stated, I'm with the sheriff's department up in Pacific County. Earlier this month, the body of a man washed ashore near Grayland Beach State Park, just north of Willapa Bay. Recent investigation into the cause of death led me to believe that this man was murdered on Destruction Island when he stumbled upon persons unknown, possibly pot hunters, digging near the old lighthouse. We believe they were searching for information that would lead them to a hoard of Native American artifacts located somewhere on the island.

"A good friend of mine, Earl Armstrong, who happens to be the great-grandson of the first keeper of that lighthouse, believes that there is actually a cave on the island where these artifacts have been preserved. The thieves somehow discovered this, and yesterday they kidnapped Mr. Armstrong and another man, an Indian by the name of Johnson Wewa. We believe that they were forcibly taken to the island to disclose the location of this cave.

"To gain Mr. Armstrong's cooperation, they took his family hostage and were holding them at a location up north on the Washington coast. I say this in past tense because, late this afternoon, I received a call that his family is now safe. One of their captors was killed and another taken into custody. However, we have no way of knowing whether either Mr. Armstrong or those who are holding him are aware of this fact. So, at the moment, we have to conclude that the lives of these two men are still at risk and the clandestine operation to steal the artifacts is proceeding."

Bo Phillips raised his hand to ask a question. Eddie paused and nodded.

"Is it possible that they are no longer on the island?" Bo asked. "This could be a recovery operation for two bodies—Mr. Armstrong's and his friend's."

"I think I can answer that question," said Lori as she walked back to the podium. "A salvage vessel operating in the area reported seeing a Bell 429 helicopter on a course for the island at about 1700 hours yesterday. Your station at La Push also reported an unidentified aircraft in the vicinity of the island. We believe it is the men we are after. I put in a top-priority request for the next military satellite flyover to take a couple of infrared pictures. While I have not seen the photos, a report I received by telephone indicated that one hour ago, there were five major heat signals on the surface of the island—one near the helipad, and four in the old lighthouse buildings. There are deer on the island, but given these locations, we have to assume that these are our targets."

"So three black hats and two white hats that apparently are still alive due to their heat signatures." Bo stated.

"Yes, I believe so," Lori responded. "We may get another flyover report just before we reach the island, which will help us when we hit the ground."

"What about the guy near the helipad?" someone else asked. "He'll see us approach and could alert the others."

"I'm not indicating that this will be as easy as politely requesting that they raise their hands and let themselves be arrested. Detective Shaw said that they have probably killed several people already, so they may choose to fight. Our first objective is to prevent them from leaving the island. We want to keep their helicopter on the ground, and the Coast Guard patrol boats will see that they can't escape by boat."

Eddie Shaw had been nodding in agreement but now had a question for Lori.

"What about this salvage vessel that's in the area? Do we know whether they are involved or just what they are doing?"

The Coast Guard duty officer raised a hand and chimed in without waiting to be recognized. "We have reports on that vessel because it is currently conducting a navigation-hazard operation under our command. The vessel departed Destruction Island earlier this evening and will be operating in the Grays Harbor area until after midnight, at which time it plans to return to Destruction Island to complete another recovery operation for a company called the Edosan Corporation."

"Edosan Corporation?" Shaw said. "That's the Japanese company that has been assisting with the coastal cleanup of tsunami debris. I wonder why they are chartering a salvage vessel."

"I think they are trying to recover a rescue pod that is part of the tsunami debris," stated one of the Coast Guard flight crew. Heads turned toward the man. It was Lt. Dave Ramsey.

"Lt. Phillips and I have been flying debris survey missions for several weeks. I usually snap a few photographs of the floating debris. It's pretty impressive. One of the things that I happened to take pictures of was an orange rescue pod that must have broken loose from a ship and become part of the debris mat. My last photo showed it on a beach up in some cove at the north end of Destruction Island. I happened to be showing the photos to some of the guys over at the café when a Japanese waiter recognized the pod, got very excited, and wanted to know where I took the picture."

"Looks like the Edosan Corporation folks have ulterior motives," commented Shaw. "Their willingness to assist with the cleanup must have been a cover for something they desperately wanted to find."

"They sure have been getting good press coverage," Bo Phillips stated. "They must have spent a couple of million bucks helping with the cleanup of the beaches."

"Yeah, but they haven't been entirely honest with the public and the political officials from whom they asked for cooperation." Shaw said. "They were always the first to know when any large objects washed ashore, and sometimes they would send out a cleanup crew that would check it out but then leave it for others to deal with. All along they were looking for the rescue pod. Whatever is inside it must be pretty important for them to get back."

Lori listened to their conversation and then turned to the Coast Guard duty officer. "Can you get in touch with the salvage vessel? Their presence at the island could complicate our plans. We're going to require them to stay clear of the island and give us their cooperation until we're sure it is safe for them to move in and recover the rescue pod."

"Yes, ma'am," responded the duty officer. "We can hail them on the marine frequency and then request that they call us by cell phone. Do you want to talk to them?"

"Sure. Just let me know when you're in contact," Lori replied. "Okay, gentlemen, let's talk about what we are going to do tomorrow morning. Commander Phillips, you'll be taking us all up to the island?"

"Yes, ma'am! Liftoff is at 0400. Uh, I assume that you and your other agent are going to be well armed? Like carrying assault rifles?"

"We are hardly a SWAT team," Lori answered, "but, yes, we will be prepared to neutralize them if we are fired upon."

"What I mean, Ms. Williams, is that we have certain protocols for loaded weapons while in the chopper—like no rounds in the chamber," Bo Phillips stated as he got up to refill his coffee mug.

"That's fine, as long as we're not taking fire while still airborne."

"I hope it doesn't come to that," replied Phillips. "We're not looking to make this a combat mission."

"Detective Shaw, you will hold on board the helicopter until Agent Thornton and I have secured the area around the helipad. Agent Thornton will take charge of the man at their chopper. It's probably the pilot. The rest of us will check out the buildings and try to locate the remaining men."

"Ms. Williams?" The duty officer beckoned to her from the door of the operations room. "I've got the captain of the salvage vessel on the phone. You can take the call in my office."

"Good. Everyone needs to have a description of Mr. Armstrong and Mr. Wewa. I'll let Lt. Shaw handle that while I take this call."

Lori followed the duty officer down the hall and into his office and then sat down at his desk to take the call.

"Captain, this is Agent Lori Williams, Fish and Wildlife Law Enforcement Division. How are you tonight?"

The captain acknowledged Lori's greeting and told her that it was going to be a very long night. He also explained that his client, the owner of the Edosan Corporation, was there with him on the bridge and requested that she be part of the conversation. He asked if it would be all right to use a speaker phone. Lori agreed.

"Agent Williams? I'm Norika Edo. My company is assisting with the tsunami debris cleanup. I understand we both have very important business on this island. Ah, what is its name, Captain?"

"Destruction Island, Mrs. Edo," the captain answered.

"My people have learned that my husband's remains are quite likely on this island, and I very much want to recover them. I have chartered this ship to assist in the recovery, so time is very important to me. I have been delayed already and am quite upset that you are asking us to wait longer. I really don't understand why anything can be more important than what we are doing."

"My condolences, Mrs. Edo. I am truly sorry, but the lives of two men are at stake. We need your cooperation. I can have the United States Coast Guard notify your captain as soon as it is safe for your people to go ashore. Until then, it will be quite dangerous. The men we are trying to take into custody are suspected in the deaths of several people. They have willfully caused destruction in a wildlife reserve and may be engaged in theft of historical artifacts."

"But, my husband has been…"

"Yes, I fully understand, Mrs. Edo. Your country values it historical resources, does it not? I'm sure the destruction of historical resources in your country would not be tolerated for a moment. So, please help us do our job. We are requiring the salvage ship to remain at least one-half mile off the island until our mission is complete. You can also be of assistance by reporting any unusual activity to the Coast Guard by radio."

"We have a helicopter on board," the captain stated. "Can it assist with aerial surveillance?"

"Until 0500, no aircraft or boat will be permitted within one thousand feet of the island and under no circumstances will aircraft be allowed to land on the island until we believe it is safe to do so."

"Very well, Agent Williams," Norika stated. "I hope you catch your man, as your American TV shows always say."

CHAPTER 51

Whether it was the bright light in his face or the kick to his right side, Earl wasn't sure which caused him to groan and wake up. He had slept fitfully, both from worrying about his family and from the discomfort of the damp conditions in the old keepers quarters. The voice that accompanied the action was unmistakable.

"It's time to get moving, Armstrong!" shouted Mirko. "The tide ought to be low enough, so wake up your friend and grab your flashlights. We got work to do."

Earl clicked on his flashlight and looked at his wristwatch. It was a few minutes after two in the morning. While he hated to agree with Mirko, the time had come to see if they could enter the cave. He nudged Johnson and struggled to his feet. He felt stiff all over, and his pants and jacket were damp from the moist night air, adding to how miserable he felt. It had taken him a long time to doze off as he tried to figure out what they should do once inside the cave. No real plan had come to him. They would just have to take it one step at a time. He hoped that they would get out of there alive, but at the moment he was far from sure about anything.

Juno was talking quietly with Mirko when Johnson and Earl walked outside. It was unearthly quiet, and the mist over the ground hung like a low curtain, hiding everything around them. Juno gave the men a moment to relieve their bladders and then motioned for them to head back toward the crevice that led down to the blowhole. Earl was fairly certain that neither Juno nor Mirko knew the way.

Earl had to be careful as he led them, not wanting to slip and fall off the cliff. When they reached the spot from which they had surveyed the area of the blowhole the afternoon before, Earl stopped.

"So what do you want me to do now?" he asked.

"Get your ass down there," Juno replied. "You're supposed to know the way. And you better be right, or someone is not coming back up."

"Okay, but I have to warn you that this is not going to be easy. The darkness and the fog will make it difficult to see how to climb down. It's not easy to see even in broad daylight. So, watch your footing. Use your light to see where the person in front of you puts his feet and follow suit."

Earl started down the cliff. He surprised himself by finding the first part of the descent to be fairly easy. In his dreams, Chris Zauner had done it by the light of a full moon. Chris had felt that the moonlight revealed the places to step. Earl tried waving his flashlight rather than shining it directly on the rocks. Despite the fog, a few of the depressions carved by someone in a forgotten era still appeared in the weaker beam of the flashlight.

It was hard for Earl to judge how far down the slope they were traveling. The ocean waves had calmed, so there was no clue from the sound of them hitting the base of the sea cliff. The flashlight beam didn't penetrate far enough to reflect off the water.

As Earl moved slowly down the slope, he could hear the shuffling footsteps of the other three men behind him. No one slipped, which was a relief to Earl. If someone fell, that person might throw the person in front of him off balance, and they could all end up falling. When Earl estimated that they were about halfway down, they had to wedge between several outcroppings. *This must be the spot where Chris was attacked and knocked unconscious.*

Earl kept his thoughts to himself. Johnson would understand and believe him. The others would think he was crazy. Another five minutes went by, and then another five. They kept descending, foot by foot.

"Armstrong, you sure you know what you're doing?" Mirko hollered from the back.

"You want to find that cave? Then shut up and let me do this."

Eventually they arrived at the blowhole. Its surface was damp but contained no pool of water. Earl shone his light around its interior. There was a dark crack in the bottom on the far side. Again, Earl was relieved to see this. Everything from the dream for finding the cave entrance had been correct so far.

"This is called a blowhole," Earl informed the others. He used his flashlight like a pointer and waved it around the rim, the interior, and then at the crack. "Over there is a crack that leads out to the sea. When the tide comes up, it surges up through that crack and fills the whole basin with seawater, and then it slowly drains back out."

"So where's the entrance to the cave?" Betar demanded.

Earl moved his light to shine on the overhang along one edge of the blowhole. "It's just under that ledge. If you look where my light is shining, you may be able to see some slight steps carved into the edge of the basin leading up to it."

"Okay, enough with the geology lesson. Let's get down there!" Juno said. He took a step towards the blowhole.

"Wait a minute!" Earl shouted. "This is where it gets real tricky. I need to explain what to do and what may happen at this point. First, like I said, when the tide comes back up, the basin will fill up. The water level also reaches well into the opening, enough so that it becomes fully submerged. Attempting to get out under those conditions means you're going to have to hold your breath and swim out underwater. If the surge is strong, it might be impossible to get out, or you could get hung up and drown. So, going in and out, it's one at a time, not crowding the person in front of you.

"Once inside the passageway, you'll find that it is quite narrow, and there's a low ceiling. You'll have to stoop—except for maybe Johnson here. We will be going up a slope where the passageway eventually widens into a large cavern. That's where everything is supposed to be located."

"Humph, don't seem that difficult," Mirko said with a smirk. "We got lights. We get in and get right out with the mask before the tide turns, right?"

"Yes, it seems simple enough. But nothing is ever simple," Earl added. "For one thing, I'm not going to lie to you and say that the cavern is full of historical artifacts, things left behind by some forgotten people, who most likely carved these steps. Everything could have been removed from the cavern decades ago."

"All right, all right! Enough talk," Betar said. "We'll know for ourselves shortly. You first, Armstrong."

Earl gritted his teeth and turned to shine his light into the blowhole. Like he remembered Chris Zauner doing, he checked the ominous dark crack for a surge of sea water and then slid down to the bottom. Looking up under the overhang, he saw the dark opening to the start of the passageway. *Damn! There really is a cavern here.*

He used his light to find where to step as he crawled up and into the passageway. Small crabs and copepods skittered away from the light and his feet. Earl kept moving until he was a few yards beyond the section of the passageway that was perpetually wet from each tide change. The others followed.

At this point, Earl remembered the half-human, half-animal figure painted on the side of the passageway. He played his light on the walls and found it exactly where it should have been before the passageway took a bend.

Earl could hear the others coming up behind him. Mirko was swearing something about bugs crawling up his pant legs.

"Johnson, what do you make of this?" Earl asked as he waved his light over the figure.

Johnson Wewa stood by Earl and studied the design painted on the rock.

"Well, doggone! Whew!" Johnson exclaimed with his eyes wide. "This is strange. You should know what this symbol is, Earl."

"A Watcher?"

"Maybe. More like a figure intended to guard the entrance to something important—like a warning sign."

"What is that thing?" Mirko asked nervously. He waved his light at the figure and then up into the darkness, half expecting something to come charging out at them.

"It appears to be some type of transformation figure that is part animal and part man," said Johnson. "I'd say that it is Kwakiutl in origin. Figures like this appear in a lot of their legends and paintings. Some, like this guy, are pretty frightening—kind of like ogres in our campfire stories. Wander off into the woods at night, and you'll get eaten by one."

"We don't need any archeology lessons, either," Juno said. "Let's keep moving."

"I might disagree with you on the importance of archeology," Johnson replied. "Understanding what is in here could help us find what you are looking for."

"Hold it a sec!" Earl asked.

In the beam of his flashlight, he found something lying on the floor of the chamber, near the figure. Earl reached down, picked it up, and examined it. It was a hat with a simple insignia of a lighthouse on the front.

"Holy smoke! This hat belonged to my great-grand-father. He lost it when he was leaving the cavern."

Earl put it on. It felt good, and he took it as a good sign as he resumed walking. The walls of the passageway soon widened, and after another hundred feet, they were in the main cavern. Four lights began to wander over the ceiling and walls of the cavern. *It's exactly like Chris described it.*

Earl could make out some type of platform along two sides of the cavern holding dark, formless bundles. It was probably as Johnson had guessed. They contained things that had been carefully packed and stored, but no one had ever come back to collect them.

At the far end of the room, near the center, was a large rock with a flat surface. Chris Zauner had referred to it as the place of sacrifice. Johnson Wewa stepped forward a few paces, anxiously looking at how things were arranged. He turned and faced the others, who were still exploring the chamber with their lights.

"Oh my god, Earl," Johnson sighed. "You know what this place is?"

"What?" Earl asked.

"This is a burial chamber—a tomb," Johnson said gravely as he played his light over one of the platforms. Human skeletons were stacked on top of each other. There must have been a dozen of them. "My thought is that these were slaves sacrificed to be with some important person, probably a chief, who is somewhere in this chamber. Nobody was planning to come back here. Whoever made the sacrifices and placed things in here did so as gifts to honor the person who died."

Juno Betar walked over the opposite side of the chamber, where the platforms were stacked high with bundles. Mirko hesitated and hung back, close to the exit, ready to bolt at a moment's notice. Juno shifted several of the bundles. Some were heavy; others light. All were sewn tightly closed. He ran his hand over the surface of one of the bundles.

"It's some kind of hide with a smooth surface, like hair."

"They are probably sealskins," replied Johnson. "The tribes that traveled by canoe used to wrap their possessions in sealskins. It was kind of like our modern-day dry bags."

Juno took out a pocket knife and started cutting the material used to stitch one of the sealskin bundles shut. He pulled it open to reveal a number of wooden bowls, spoons, and large pots. Each object was beautifully made, with painted relief designs. Museums and private collectors would beg for such objects for their collections. But there was nothing inside that resembled ceremonial regalia like the mask that Juno was searching for.

Earl looked at his watch. It was after three o'clock. They had maybe two hours at the most before they had to get out the cavern or be trapped by the incoming tide.

"Mirko!" Juno Betar's voice echoed from the far end of the cavern. "Get over here and start cutting open some of these bundles."

The two men used knives to open bundle after bundle as Earl and Johnson stood by and watched. Earl nudged Johnson in the ribs and nodded toward the side of the cavern nearest the entrance. It was where Chris Zauner had discovered a cache of weapons. Earl made a quick flash of his light—just enough for Johnson to see what was there. The man acknowledged his nod, realizing what Earl was thinking.

While Juno and Mirko were busy, Johnson slipped over to where the weapons were stored, stooped, and grabbed a war club. It was hefty and felt good in his hand. He held it by his side and walked back over to where Earl stood in the semidarkness, watching the two men work. The shadows of the two men danced on the ceiling in grotesque forms as Johnson crept over by the big stone and hid the club in a dark niche behind it.

It took Betar and Mirko, working together, over an hour to check each of the bundles that were stacked on the wooden platforms. Each time, they dumped out the contents of the bundle and moved onto another one. Scattered in their path were drums, capes, headdresses, shields, tools, fishing hooks, and other objects, including some small masks. The large sun mask was not among them. Juno turned and scanned the interior of the cavern, looking for other places where the mask might be located.

"I told you that we would need Johnson's help," Earl said to Juno. "Now do you believe me?"

Juno took his pistol out of his belt holster and walked over to where Johnson and Earl had been sitting. He was sweating profusely. There was a gleam in his eyes like that of a gold prospector so focused on finding the mother lode that he failed to notice the flakes of gold in the rocks he had tossed aside. Juno put the pistol right in Johnson's face and pulled back the hammer. He held it for a moment and then swung his arm so that the pistol was pointed at Earl.

"That right?" Juno said with a sneer. "Got any bright ideas, or do I just shoot Armstrong and then you?"

Johnson tried to be as calm as he could. He removed his glasses and rubbed some dust out of his eyes. He stood tall and made a slow, circular turn, examining the perimeter of the cavern with his light. He avoided looking at the area where the weapons were stored, not wanting to alert Juno to their presence. The beam of his flashlight settled on the sacrificial stone and the dark confines of the cavern beyond it. The area was strangely bare. There were no wooden platforms. The surface of the cavern wall looked slightly different. Johnson walked around the large stone and ran a hand over the surface of the wall. Parts of it crumbled and dropped onto the floor of the cavern.

"As I suspected when we entered the cavern, this place is not a ceremonial or living area but probably a burial chamber. I think we will find what you are looking for with the remains of the principal occupant behind this wall."

"Oh, man, you mean we have to uncover some ancient corpse like King Tut or somethin'?" Mirko asked.

"We'll let the shaman and Mr. Armstrong do the digging, Mirko. After all, they have enjoyed a nice rest while we searched the rest of the stuff."

"Ah, sorry," Johnson replied. "But disturbing the graves of my ancestors is not something I'll help with. It cuts against one's traditional values to disturb a grave unless done in a proper way. Mr. Armstrong does not follow the traditional ways, but he carries Indian blood in his veins. I would leave it up to him to decide what he will do."

"He's not going to decide," Juno said. "I've got the gun, and I make the decisions. Armstrong, find something to break down that wall and clear an opening so we can see what's on the other side. Mirko, you help Armstrong by moving the debris out of the way."

Earl took a moment to make it appear like he was looking for something to use to break through the wall and then accidentally found the war club that Johnson had hid in the wall niche. He gave it a confident slap with his left hand and then walked over and took a swing at the wall. The club vibrated in his hands but did the job. A chunk of the wall fell away. He took several more swings at the same spot, and the end of the club went through. As Johnson had suspected, there was a void on the other side. A few more swings, and several bigger chunks of the wall gave way.

Mirko started grabbing the pieces and throwing them aside as Earl widened the hole. Dust generated by their action drifted around them. After another ten minutes, he was satisfied that a person could climb in. He moved back a few feet and set the war club down, back alongside the big stone. Juno and Mirko kept their eyes fixed on the opening, but neither seemed anxious to take a closer look.

"I guess the next step is up to me as well." Earl said. "Mirko, give me the lantern. I'm going to need more light in there."

Earl stuck the lantern inside and then his head. Like the outer cavern, there was a raised wooden platform against the back wall. Only this one was different. It was covered with animal skins on which lay a lone skeleton. It had to be some prominent tribal figure, such as an important chief of a clan. At the foot of the skeleton was a large, round object.

"I think we found it," Earl said as he stepped inside. "At least it looks like some kind of a mask. Sure is a big one."

He stood over it. It was circular, with a round humanlike face protruding from the center. Instead of a man's nose it had the beak of a bird, maybe an eagle. Around the edge were four other faces painted in bright pigments. But the most striking feature was the metal inlay around the whole circumference. The inlay reflected the light of Earl's lantern. There was only one metal that could do that after lying exposed for hundreds of years—gold. This was what Juno Betar had been searching for, no matter the cost. Earl's mind raced. *Now that he has it, will he decide to kill us?*

Earl set down the lantern inside the walled-off chamber and picked up one of the smaller pieces of animal hide and wrapped the mask in it. He then tucked it under one arm and climbed out to join the others. Instead of handing it to Juno, he walked over to the sacrifice stone and placed the wrapped mask in the center. Earl stepped back next to Johnson so Juno and Mirko could examine it.

"Now's the time," Earl whispered to Johnson. "Switch off your light and use the club. I'll go for Juno's pistol."

The next few seconds were chaos. Juno was unwrapping the mask and holding it with both hands to admire its craftsmanship in the beam of his headlamp. Both Earl and

Johnson switched off their flashlights. Mirko's lantern was still behind the wall. Johnson grabbed the club and swung it hard at the back of Mirko's head. The blow sent Mirko flying into the stone dais, his body then slipping to the floor.

Juno was fast. He let the mask drop back onto the piece of hide and spun around, bringing out his pistol. It discharged just as Earl tackled him. The shot echoed in the chamber, followed by a grunt from Johnson. Juno's arm with the pistol chopped downward, hitting Earl on his right temple. Earl fell to the floor, dazed and unable to see clearly. Juno Betar ignored his fallen friend, turned to the stone dais, and grabbed the mask. He then ran for the entrance to the cavern. Earl could hear him running down toward the blowhole. Then it was silent.

Struggling to a sitting position, Earl felt around for the flashlight that he dropped when he attempted to stop Betar. He found it and switched it on.

"Johnson, Johnson!" Earl shouted. "You okay?"

"Ah…not so good, I…I'm afraid," Johnson said, his voice breaking. "Betar shot me. M…my left leg is numb and I…I'm bleeding pretty badly."

Earl crawled over to Johnson. In the beam of his flashlight, he could see that Johnson's left pant leg was soaked in blood. The bullet must have hit the femoral artery.

Earl ripped off his shirt, tore some long strips, and began wrapping them around Johnson's leg near the wound. He pulled out his handkerchief and stuffed it under the strips of cloth over the wound and then tied the strips of cloth tightly around the leg.

"Johnson, we have to get you out of here," Earl said. "Stay with me now. Keep your left hand pressed on the bandage. It will slow the bleeding."

Earl helped the man stand and put his right arm around Johnson's waist. The two of them hobbled across the chamber and down the long passageway to the entrance. The last few feet were the hardest because Earl had to stoop and partly drag Johnson. They half-crawled, half-slid into the blowhole, which was partially filled with water. After several hours in the darkness of the cavern, the early morning light was both blinding and a blessing.

Earl lay beside Johnson for a few minutes to catch his breath, but they couldn't stay where they were. Already another wave surge brought more seawater into the basin. Johnson was only semiconscious from the loss of blood.

Earl was struggling to stand and push Johnson out of the blowhole when he heard someone shouting his name. It was Eddie Shaw. He looked up toward the top of the cliff. Eddie was scrambling down, with Lori Williams right behind him.

Covered in dust, scraped up, and with blood on his face, Earl had to look a sight. Still, he managed a big grin as Eddie and Lori reached the edge of the blowhole and slid down beside him and Johnson.

"I'm alright. Johnson needs some medical attention. He was shot in the leg by Juno Betar. The bullet hit an artery."

"Where are the others?" Lori asked.

"Juno ran out. He had a helicopter. He might have…."

"No one's leaving this island, at least not by helicopter. We have it in custody," answered Lori. "Are there any more of them?"

"Juno's bodyguard is still in the cave. He could be dead. I dunno. Johnson clobbered him pretty hard with an old war club. Those things are pretty nasty weapons."

"How…how did you get into the cave?" Lori asked, looking around.

"The entrance is just under that overhang, here in the blowhole. But don't attempt it. The tide is coming in, and it won't be long before this whole basin and part of the passageway is flooded. If the guy is alive, he won't be going anywhere soon."

"Nice hat, Earl," Eddie commented, seeing Chris Zauner's dirty blue cap askew on Earl's head. "Looks old. Where did you get it?"

CHAPTER 52

On board the salvage ship, the Bell 212 lifted off precisely at 5:00 a.m. to fly at one thousand feet elevation and begin searching the island's coastline. It had been a long night, but nothing unusual occurred with the dock-recovery operation. The experienced crew on board the ship was accustomed to working in shifts. The crew that had handled the dock recovery had been supervised by the captain, and his first officer was now in command while the others were grabbing some sleep before they had to commence the recovery of Norika's rescue pod—if it could be found.

Hiroko flew with the pilot and assisted in the aerial search for the pod. He knew what to look for, but the task was not easy. Passing over the island, they noticed another helicopter on a helipad near the south end of the island. They circled once and saw no human activity, so they proceeded to start an aerial survey of the rocky coastline, beginning

with the eastern shore. It lacked any beaches, consisting
mainly of a low, rocky cliff that fell directly into the sea.
There were exposed rocks offshore, but these were swept
clean by every incoming swell.

The helicopter moved over to the western shore and
flew as low and close as it could. Again, there was no dis-
cernable beach where large debris could accumulate. Every
five minutes, Hiroko radioed his report to the salvage vessel. There was considerable tsunami debris washed into
every possible part of shoreline that had a beach. After an
hour of searching, Hiroko grew concerned with the possibility that pod had already been found. *What if some fisherman found it and towed it away?*

*

Being a ship owner, Juno Betar recognized the
orange object among the driftwood and debris on the beach
for what it was—a totally enclosed rescue pod. All of his
ships had several on board. If a crew had to abandon ship
due to disaster, such as an uncontrollable fire or collision at
sea, they deployed the pods. Some could hold a crew of up
to a dozen men. This one was fairly small. It was also badly
damaged and lodged among tsunami debris and several
large logs. Juno half-slid, half-leaped down to the pebble
beach and worked his way over the logs to get to it. If he

could open the pod, he might be able to use it as a temporary hiding place until he could arrange a way to be taken off the island. He still had his phone.

The pod lay tilted to one side. It was made of fiberglass, and one end had been crushed but appeared intact. These pods were made to be almost unsinkable. The one in front of Juno had suffered heavy damage. The fenders had been ripped off. The rudder and propeller, with its protective cage were missing. While the small windows in the conning tower used by the helmsman for visibility was intact, the tower itself and its hatch were partially crushed. Juno wondered if it might be filled with water and unusable as a hiding place.

He could hear the sound of a helicopter searching the island for him and knew he needed to get out of sight or they would discover his position. He ran to the far end of the craft. There was another hatch almost completely enveloped in a mass of kelp and debris. Juno set down the animal hide containing the mask and tore away at the debris that was blocking the hatch. When he had cleared the hatch area, he tried to twist the latches. They were dogged tight and refused to budge. Hoping they weren't secured from the inside, Juno grabbed a rock off the beach and tapped each of the latches. They moved. He was able to turn them the rest of the way by hand and then lift the hatch cover. It was dry inside, but the escaping odor almost caused him to vomit. It was the smell of death.

Juno turned, picked up the mask, and set it inside. He then climbed in despite the wretched odor. He left the hatch open to let the chamber air out as long as he dared. At some point soon he would have to close it. There was also very little light inside the pod, and what came through the open hatch revealed a repulsive scene. The sides of the craft were lined with seats and harnesses so the occupants could be strapped in. All of the side seats were empty. In the position used by the helmsman was a human form strapped to the seat and slumped over the controls. The man's skin was drawn taunt from desiccation.

Tying his handkerchief over his face, Juno approached the skeletal remains. The figure appeared to be Asian, partially bald, and well dressed. The expensive clothing struck Juno as odd. If a crewman had managed to gain the safety of the pod only to become trapped inside, his clothes should be that of an ordinary sailor.

On a seat beside the dead man was a black briefcase. It had been carefully lashed to the seat with one of the harnesses. Juno crawled over the seats to reach the briefcase and undid the buckles of the harness used to secure it. The case was unlocked. Juno flipped the latches and opened it. Inside were several fat manila envelopes, and under the envelopes were a large number of plastic bags embossed with the name "De Beers." Juno realized that he was looking at a small fortune in uncut diamonds.

He ripped open one of the envelopes and found it full of bond certificates—another small fortune. Juno looked over at the corpse and pictured the desperate man attempting to escape some shipboard disaster, taking his valuable possessions and boarding the rescue pod, and then discovering that he was without power and adrift. He had to endure the beating that the pod had experienced and was left trapped inside and floating in a sea of tsunami debris. He must have resigned himself to his fate—starving to death.

Hearing the sound of an approaching helicopter, Juno scrambled back to the opening and quickly closed the hatch cover, securing it from the inside. It would be a while, maybe even several days, before he could plan his next move. He would manage. Juno smiled to himself, realizing that he possessed not only the sun mask but now the added bonus of a fortune in diamonds and bonds. They were his under international salvage rights of the sea. Was it luck or was it survival skills that had led to his success throughout his life? Juno didn't care, but he liked the rewards.

CHAPTER 53

After helping Earl get Johnson back to the helipad, where he could be airlifted to the hospital in Aberdeen, Lori Williams and Agent Thornton began the search for Juno Betar. They started with a search of the lighthouse and buildings without turning up the missing man. While waiting for Lt. Phillips' helicopter to return and assist, she used her radio to contact her superiors and was surprised to learn that Juno Betar was a billionaire businessman with no criminal record. They had his helicopter, so Mr. Betar had to be hiding somewhere on the tiny island. After the Coast Guard helicopter returned, they commenced a thorough ground search starting at the south end and moving northward.

The thick brush made Lori nervous. It was like hunting a dangerous wild boar. Suddenly, a half-dozen rabbits burst from a clump of vines, scattering in every direction. Lori jumped back and then shook her head. *Rabbits?*

What if it had been a boar or Betar? I wasn't ready. After the rabbits, the two officers moved more slowly, not knowing whether Betar would jump out of the brush or from behind a rock and fire on them.

"What if he had some other way to escape and is already off the island?" Thornton called out to Lori.

"The Coast Guard patrol boats are on alert for anyone attempting to leave the island. So far, no one has reported any other boats in the area."

Since neither Lori nor Thornton could see very far while moving through the high brush, Bo Phillips guided the search from his helicopter five hundred feet above them.

"Johnson Wewa is going to be okay. He has a pretty serious wound." It was Bo's voice on her handheld radio.

"That's good to hear," replied Lori.

"Any sign of the other man?" Bo asked.

"Not yet. The thick brush is making the job rather tough. I'm sure glad you got back here quickly to lend a hand."

"You know our motto—Always Ready. That's us."

"Really? Is that 24-7?"

"Yup," replied Bo. He was about to explore her quip further when he saw something that concerned him off to their left. "Say, there are some crevices along the west shoreline just ahead of you. I can't get a good visual without getting closer and risking taking fire. So you better proceed carefully and check them out."

"Roger!" Lori replied. "Keep an eye out for him doubling back."

"Will do." Be careful down there and don't fall off a cliff. I don't have my rescue specialist with me."

Under other circumstances, Lori might have smiled and responded to Bo's remarks. But she wanted Betar. She didn't care who he was or how important he might be. Somehow, Betar was behind several murders and a dozen other crimes. Lori motioned for Thornton to swing further left toward where Bo had said to check. Then she spotted some fresh tracks on the trail. *He ran through here.* Lori abandoned her cautious movements, increasing her pace and swatting branches aside to follow the tracks as she conveyed the information to Bo.

"I've got fresh tracks. One person headed northwest. What's up ahead of us?"

"You're almost to the end of the island, Lori," Bo answered. "There's a cove and the bluff drops down to a pebble beach covered in driftwood."

"All right. Do you see anything?"

"Yeah, we got a problem. That helicopter from the charter vessel is headed toward the cove, too. I'll radio and tell its pilot to back off. I think they pushed the throttle a little too fast and didn't wait for us to give them the all clear."

Lori broke out of the brush and could see the helicopter chartered by Mrs. Edo circling over the north end
of the island. She looked over the edge and saw the small
cove, with its beach jammed with drift logs and tsunami
debris. The cleanup effort had obviously not reached as far
as the island. Mrs. Edo's helicopter hovered just off the cove
but showed no sign of attempting to land. As much as Lori
preferred it wasn't in the area, she had to admit it was not
violating the conditions that had been required of the Edo
Corporation. The helicopter wasn't the only problem. The
tracks she had been following ended at the bottom of the
bluff, and the man was nowhere in sight. She was going to
need more people to help with the search.

*

Aboard the small Bell helicopter, Takahashi
scanned the drift logs and debris in the cove, trying to
locate the rescue pod. The pilot beside him responded to
the radio message from the Coast Guard asking them to
back off a little while longer. He pointed toward the salvage
vessel and hand signaled that they needed to return. The
pilot was about to break off from where they hovered when
Takahashi grabbed his arm and pointed down below them.
A splash of orange paint was visible near the south end of
the cove. It was almost obscured by the debris. He nodded

to the pilot and motioned for them to return to the salvage vessel. Now it was up to the shore crew to use a boat to get a tow cable attached to it. Takahashi had a big grin on his face as they touched down on the helipad.

*

Lori Williams and Agent Thornton searched the beach and brush on the bluff for over an hour without finding any further trace of Betar. The man had disappeared. Just offshore, a workboat from the salvage vessel bobbed in the waves. It would drift off and then motor back to the same spot as it waited for authority from the Coast Guard to finish its recovery operation.

"I just got another message from the salvage vessel, Lori." Bo Phillips said over his radio. "They are getting super-anxious to get a line on something buried in debris before it gets too rough. If they wait much longer, they may have to cancel. Apparently, the Japanese company that is paying for the charter is making all kinds of threats."

"Well, we're not having any success," Lori answered. "Maybe they can do better. I guess it can't hurt to let them go ahead. Thornton and I can observe everything from the top of the bluff. What are they after?"

"It's what is left of a totally enclosed lifeboat. Some call it a rescue pod. The owner of the company is on board the ship and she says that the remains of her husband are inside."

"Yeah, I talked to that woman. She's a real piece of work. Glad she's not my boss. All right, give them permission to come in, but let them know that we'll be monitoring everything they do. It's got to be costing thousands of dollars per hour just to recover a corpse! I suppose we might as well let them finish their work and clear out of here."

Bo Phillips passed on the go-ahead authorization to the salvage vessel. Minutes later, as Lori watched from the bluff, the boat motored into the cove, and a man carrying the end of a coil of rope jumped nimbly onto the rocks, climbed over some of the driftwood, and stopped at a large pile of kelp and debris. He began pulling on the line, which was attached to a wire cable. Lori hadn't noticed the cable before, but now she could tell that it wasn't actually secured to the small boat. It must have been pulled to the shore from the salvage vessel.

When he was finished shackling the cable to the object, the man on the beach made some circling hand signals, and after notifying the ship, the workboat picked him up and backed off to observe. Lori saw the cable quiver as it went taut, sending a spray of water into the air. There was a series of thuds and groans as several of the drift logs moved. Then an orange object behind them rode up over the logs and nosed down deep into the pebble beach before sliding on its side into the water. It was totally submerged and then bobbed up, shaking off kelp and other debris like a bronco throwing its rider and saddle. Then, like a playful dolphin, the rescue pod repeatedly dove into the ocean swells and reemerged as the cable was reeled in from the salvage vessel with the workboat in pursuit.

CHAPTER 54

With the first yank on the tow cable, Juno Betar was thrown ten feet to the bow end of the pod, bruising his right shoulder and striking his head against the fiberglass bulkhead. The only thing he could imagine had happened was that a huge wave had lifted the pod off the beach. In a panic, he tried to grab the harness for the nearest seat, but the steep incline of the pod prevented him from getting a good grip. On the second pull, he was dumped aft toward the dead man as the pod reversed its slope. Then it rolled onto one side and began sliding. It was with the screeching of the hull along the rocky beach that Juno came to the realization that someone was actually pulling the pod backward out into sea.

His panic subsided when he saw that the pod wasn't sinking, but what was happening roused his anger because someone was trying to claim what was now his. The rescue pod had been abandoned, a derelict when he had found it, and now he, Juno Betar, occupied it. They couldn't do this, yet it was happening. Somehow he managed to strap himself into one of the safety harnesses attached to the seats along the port side of the pod. Juno could now hear the faint throb of an engine and an occasional shout from somewhere outside. A few feet from his position was a tiny porthole, so he stretched himself to peer out and saw an open workboat occupied by several men who were tracking the course of the pod.

Knowing at some point that these men, or whoever was pulling the pod, would endeavor to open it, Juno needed a plan. He took out his pistol and checked it. One round had been fired—the one in the cave, which actually had been accidental. Juno knew very little about firearms and was wearing this one to give him a sense of bravado. He left the messy things to those he hired.

Juno looked around for the whereabouts of the briefcase, which was now his as well. It was lodged under one of the aft seats. He was unclipping his harness to retrieve it when the pod bumped into something hard. Someone jumped onto the pod and was walking along the top of it. Then he felt another jerk and the pod swayed and swung back and forth. Moments later there was another bump as the pod was set down. The moment of truth had arrived. Juno undid the lashing that secured the aft door, gripped the briefcase tightly, and waited.

*

Hiroko Takahashi had waited a long time for this moment. The search for the missing rescue pod and answers to the mystery of whether Mrs. Edo's dead husband was inside. The answer now sat in front of him in a cradle on the deck of the salvage vessel. Mrs. Edo, the captain, and many of the vessel's crew stood close by, waiting for several of the deckhands to secure the pod and finish removing strands of kelp and other debris that had become attached to the hull. Norika Edo had changed clothes and was wearing a plain black dress that she had brought from Japan for this proper occasion—the recovery of her husband's body.

Hiroko walked around the battered orange vessel to inspect it. It was a miracle that it was still afloat, but these rescue pods were designed to withstand extreme conditions. There was an access hatch on the top of the little conning tower, which was mangled and inoperable. At the bow was another hatch, which looked as if it might still function.

Now Hiroko waited patiently for the captain to give the okay that the craft could be breached. The deck crew backed away and he saw the captain say something to Norika and then nod in his direction. He used a short ladder provided by the crew to reach the bow hatch. He examined the dogs that held it closed. They could be turned from either the inside or the outside. He frowned as he noticed the fresh scrapes next to each one. *Had the hatch been opened recently?*

Hiroko hurriedly released each of the four latches and pulled the hatch cover to one side. A man's hand holding a pistol extended out and pointed right at his face. He froze. Then he saw the face of the man behind the pistol.

Hiroko backed slowly down the ladder as the man emerged and looked around. There was a loud murmur from the people gathered on the deck. Norika emitted a short scream and had a hand over her mouth.

"Surprise, surprise, folks," the man with the gun said. "I want to thank you all for assisting me and my vessel. My name is Juno Betar, and I hereby declare this to be my property by the international laws for salvage at sea."

"Like hell you do!" Norika screamed as she ran forward. "This vessel belongs to me!"

Juno Betar stepped down onto the deck and moved the muzzle of the pistol to point it at Norika. He had the briefcase in one hand and the wrapped mask under his arm. He held on to the mask but set the briefcase between his legs on the deck.

"And just who might you be?" Juno asked.

"I am Norika Edo, owner of the Edosan Corporation, and this rescue pod broke loose from one of my husband's ships, the *Kanji Maru*. That name is painted on the side of the pod. Plus, I believe my husband is on board."

"Oh he's on board all right," Betar replied. "However, I would say that he is no condition to make an appearance or any such claim."

Standing amongst the tight group of men watching, the captain knew that the Coast Guard had to be notified immediately. He whispered a few words to his first officer, who had hung back, then slipped inside a door, dashing for the radio room.

"That briefcase also belongs to my husband. I demand that you hand it over to me," Norika said. The expression on her face changed from anger to disgust. "You are Mr. Betar? We already know about you. You are a thief and a murderer. What do you plan to do now? Kill me, too? Look around you. You are on a ship and the only way you are going to get off is in the hands of the authorities."

"Those are lies, and like the vessel I have claimed, the briefcase also is now mine. You see, I took a look inside it. I'm guessing you want this briefcase more than you want to recover your dead husband. So it is my ticket off this ship. We're going to make a little trade. You deliver me to my helicopter, which is over there on that island, and I might just share the contents of this briefcase. I think 60-40 is a fair split. After all, you did come all this way to claim it, and your husband's body. Then there are the expenses, such as paying the captain here and his crew."

Hiroko took a step toward Betar, who again pointed the pistol at him. "No, I wouldn't shoot you, Mrs. Edo, but your bodyguard might have to take a bullet if he gets any closer. That's what he is, right?"

"Mr. Takahashi is a trusted employee. He will do what I say, and you do not need to fear that he will attempt to attack you."

"Fine, then do we have a deal? I am in a bit of a hurry. I'll tell you what. You can have this little orange tub. I have no further use for it. Besides, it is rather smelly inside from the mess your husband made of it."

"Mr. Betar, in my country, if you made such insulting remarks to me, you would be dead seconds later. As much as I loathe admitting it, I accept your offer. We can leave immediately in my helicopter. However, my bodyguard, as you refer to him, accompanies me."

CHAPTER 55

None of the search crew on the island was very pleased when Bo Phillips passed on the message from the salvage ship that Juno Betar had slipped off the island right in front of their eyes. Lori Williams was fuming over her the decision to let the pod be pulled off the beach without checking it out first. Thornton apologized over and over to her for not giving it any serious consideration as a possible hiding place while searching that end of the beach. At the time, he didn't recognize that it was an intact vessel and assumed it was only a large piece of junk, heavily encased in seaweed and debris.

Lori and the others were gathered around the Coast Guard helicopter, which had landed on the helipad next to Juno Betar's helicopter. The pilot had been questioned but refused to cooperate, so they had no additional information as to what Betar was planning to do with the mask or where he would go once off the island.

After Johnson Wewa had been evacuated for medical treatment, Eddie Shaw stayed with Earl, who took his time going over the events from the time he and Johnson had been taken hostage and flown to Destruction Island. They sat with their backs against the old lighthouse unaware of what was being played out on the helipad and salvage ship. Earl was relaxed and quite willing to replay the events after learning about the rescue of his family. He had talked to Sally on Eddie's phone and had also thanked Leon Pence for what he had done to rescue them. A weekend hike on the Third Beach Trail would never be the same for his family—that is, according to Sally, if they even decided to go there again.

Phillips had passed out energy bars that he had picked up in Aberdeen after flying Johnson to the hospital. Lori had just finished hers when Phillips took another call from the first officer on the salvage ship. He had everyone's attention when he disclosed its content.

"Listen up everybody!" Phillips announced. "You're not going to believe what's about to happen. It seems that Juno Betar wants his helicopter back, and we're supposed to give it to him and let him fly away. If we don't, he will kill two people who are with him."

"What?" Lori Williams shouted at Phillips. "Juno Betar is on his way here, and we are supposed to just let him fly away in his damn helicopter? No way! That's just not going to happen."

"I know how you feel, Lori, but it is the hostage who is asking us to do this as a matter of international relations."

"International relations with who?" Lori asked. "No other country is involved."

"Unfortunately, you're wrong," Phillips replied. "The hostage is Mrs. Norika Edo of the Edosan Corporation. She's asking our government for its full cooperation and trusts that we, as representatives of our government, will honor her request."

Lori raised her hands in disgust. "When will it end? We can't make a deal with a hostage-taker!"

"From what I was told, the deal is not with Betar but with Mrs. Edo," Phillips replied. "She wants us to free Betar's pilot and back off so they can land and transfer to his helicopter. She is willing to go with Betar."

"That's like making a deal with the devil," Thornton commented.

"Well we've got maybe five minutes before they get here. What's it going to be, Lori? This is your operation."

Lori shook her head and kicked at a stub of grass growing out of a crack in the helipad. "All right!" she finally said. "But I want that helicopter watched so closely that we can count the hairs on Betar's head."

"One more request from Mr. Betar. One of you needs to loan him a pair of handcuffs, and I don't suppose he plans to wear them himself."

They had visual contact with the small helicopter from the ship within four minutes. Two minutes later, it was on the ground, and three people climbed out. Betar actually grinned and waved as he boarded his own helicopter as if he were a celebrity going off to ski in Colorado. Norika Edo and Hiroko nodded to everyone as they followed Betar to his helicopter and boarded.

*

Once his helicopter was airborne, Juno relaxed. Norika appeared to be calm and sat in the seat behind the pilot. Hiroko sat beside her in Eddie Shaw's handcuffs. Juno occupied the seat beside the pilot but kept the pistol trained on Norika. He had the briefcase and the sun mask close to his seat.

"Mr. Betar, I would like to see the contents of the briefcase," Norika stated calmly as she eyed the case. Her husband's initials were embossed next to the clasp, but she had not seen what was inside, though Betar had intimated that what Norika wanted badly was inside. Betar must have had a sense about her interest, or else they both played the same dangerous games. "I only have your word that the contents are something that I desire to have."

"That seems fair enough," Juno answered. "Our deal was 60-40, and I am surprised that you were agreeable and did not negotiate. I might have considered other offers, being that I have what I came for."

"You do have the law to contend with. From what I was told, they have a long list of charges."

"And I have several attorneys who will have a long list of arguments. I pay them well, and my share of what is in this briefcase will likely be more than enough."

Juno placed the briefcase on his lap and moved the pistol out of the way to work the clasps with the other hand.

"You see, Norika? Your husband was indeed a wealthy man when he died. I think I will be satisfied with the diamonds, and you may have the bonds."

"On the contrary, Mr. Betar. You see, there really was no point in negotiating, as I intend to have everything that is mine."

Juno was startled by her response. He was slow to realize that the fountain pen Hiroko had removed from his shirt pocket and been toying with was actually a deadly weapon. Hiroko, still wearing the handcuffs, stabbed Betar at the base of his skull, moving so quickly that the motion was a blur. The casing of the pen contained a kubotan, a pointed stick commonly used by ninjas. The point of the kubotan killed Betar instantly. His pistol slid to the floor, and Norika quickly recovered it and pointed it at the pilot.

"You will remain on course and maintain radio silence if you want to live to see your family again. Since Mr. Betar feels ill and no longer desires to be flown anywhere, I think we will say good-bye to him."

Hiroko reached across Juno's slumped body and opened the door of the helicopter. He undid Juno's seatbelt and pushed the body out. The helicopter was not quite to the coast, and Juno Betar's body fell at least a thousand feet into the ocean. At that moment, Norika happened to notice the unusual rock formations scattered along the shoreline below. It was the same scene she had admired on the trip out to Destruction Island. Enjoying the view, she sighed and relaxed fully for the first time in many months.

"This is such a beautiful place," she said to the pilot. "Does it have a name?"

The nervous pilot glanced down through his side window and then replied, "It's called the Devil's Graveyard."

CHAPTER 56

Destruction Island; August 1899

The Zauner family stood at the starboard rail of the lighthouse tender *Columbine,* staring back at Destruction Island and recalling memories of their nine years living on the island. Some were dark, such as the time that their daughter nearly died in a cave, but many of their memories were of good times. It had been a fine life on the island, and it was a beautiful sunny day for their last memory of the place.

The transfer of their meager household belongings to the tender was going smoothly. The sea was calm, and the workboat moved back and forth easily from the ship to the small dock on the island. On this particular trip, the *Columbine* carried a group of tourists taking a day trip out of Aberdeen to enjoy the scenic coastline and a visit to Destruction Island. Music blared from somewhere in the vessel. The group included several children who were enjoying watching the antics of two young sea lions in the water alongside the ship. They chattered and laughed. Their parents and other adults lounged in deck chairs or stood by the rail, watching the unloading of supplies for the lighthouse, and the trunks and boxes containing the Zauner's household goods being brought back to the ship for the return to Aberdeen.

Captain Christian Zauner had gotten his wish for a new assignment where their daughter Abigail could attend school. Hermine was pregnant again, and he was glad that the child would be born in a safe place rather than on a remote island. Chris had been the principal keeper of the lighthouse had applied for the position of principal keeper at a new lighthouse that had just been finished in Westport, at the entrance to Grays Harbor. It would probably be his last assignment, with retirement approaching in a few years.

Chris felt both contentment and a bit of uneasiness with their departure from the island. He was putting behind him part of the tragic history of the island and the secrets hidden in the island's cave. He shuddered every time he recalled the fear he had experienced entering the cave himself and how he had almost lost his daughter. With their departure, these dark memories would remain like the island itself—shrouded in black and white clouds of seabirds by day and curtains of mist by night. Perhaps someone else in the future would unveil the island's secret and share it with the world.

Hermine tugged at Chris's shoulder, disrupting his thoughts. She smiled at him without saying a word. Chris patted her arm tenderly as they enjoyed their last view of Destruction Island together...

EPILOGUE

The sun warmed the backs of the group of people sitting in folding chairs in front of a small portable stage and the banner-draped museum building. It was a pleasant summer morning for the small, coastal community of Westport. Near the back of a crowd numbering over 350 people, one particular man had fallen asleep in his chair. Children shouted and giggled as they played on the lawn. The raucous calls of seagulls came from the nearby harbor, where fishermen were busy cleaning their early morning catch. Adding to the noisy scene was the cacophony of the local high school band warming up and getting ready to play for Westport's biggest event in quite a few years.

"Dad, Dad, wake up!" Christine called as she tugged at her father's left arm. "You've been dozing, and the ceremony is about to start."

Earl Armstrong opened his eyes and, just for a moment, didn't recognize where he was. *Have I been dreaming about Destruction Island again? Oh, yes, the dedication of the island's artifacts.*

The Armstrong family had been surprised and a bit overwhelmed at being asked to be the guests of honor for an important ceremony to dedicate a new addition to the Westport Maritime Museum. The addition had been built to house part of the large collection of Native American artifacts removed from the cave on Destruction Island plus other donations. An anonymous donor had given a sizable gift to the museum for the purpose of constructing the new wing, which would be devoted to early Indian cultures on the Pacific Northwest coast.

Earl stood up to stretch and looked at his watch. Christine was right. The ceremony should be starting in about five minutes. He glanced around and saw Sally chatting with Leon Pence and Eddie Shaw. He walked over to join them. It had been a year since their adventures together surrounding the events on Destruction Island. Earl was glad that they were all together again for the dedication ceremony. The only person absent was his favorite Indian shaman, Johnson Wewa. He looked around the crowd and frowned. *Why didn't Johnson show up for this event? That's not like him.*

It was Eddie Shaw's voice he heard talking first as he reached where his wife and friends were standing. "Sally, I haven't heard anything about who contributed the money to pay for the museum addition. Have you and Earl found out who the donor was?" asked Eddie.

"We've heard nothing," replied Sally.

Putting an arm around Sally's waist, Earl added to what she said, "From what I learned from talking to the director about the agenda for the ceremony was that even they don't know. The funds were wire transferred from an international bank in New York without identifying the source. Whoever it was must not need a charitable contribution record, I guess." Leon laughed at Earl's comment. "Maybe it's not exactly clean money but some Mafia guy with a conscience."

"Yeah!" Earl responded with a chuckle. "I wonder if it was….nah, it couldn't be."

"Couldn't be who?" Eddie asked.

"I was thinking maybe it could have been that Japanese woman we met on the island last year. I don't even remember her name."

Oh, you should remember her," Eddie answered." That was Norika Edo. I still remember her bravely climbing into Juno Betar's helicopter.

"Yeah, a woman of mystery," Leon commented. "One of the Seattle newspapers in doing a follow-up story tried to find out more about the Edosan Corporation and its owner. There were speculations she was part of the Japanese mafia."

"Well she was one tough woman," Eddie added. "She stood up to Betar and never flinched at what he did— planning to steal the sun mask, killing several people and kidnapping you, Sally and your kids."

"And Johnson Wewa, too," Earl added.

"You know it's still an open investigation?" Eddie stated. "Not for me, but for the feds. Since Leon shot that guy on national park land when he rescued Sally, a federal marshal was assigned to the case. Juno Betar's body washed up on the very same beach. They never figured out how his body got there. We all saw him take off with Norika Edo."

"Well, I don't have an ounce of remorse for that guy after he had Sally kidnapped and intended to have her and the kids murdered." Leon replied.

Their conversation was interrupted by the high school band beginning to play and the museum director's voice over the portable PA system, reminding everyone that the ceremony was about to start.

For the next thirty minutes, Earl and the Armstrong family sat on the stage while the museum director, the mayor, a county commissioner, and a representative from the state historic preservation office all took turns speaking to those gathered. Earl had to force himself to listen, or he would have dozed off again. The event program listed Earl as the last person to say a few words, and when the time came, he figured that the director would introduce him. To his surprise, Johnson Wewa was asked to come up onto the stage.

Johnson Wewa smiled at Earl with a twinkle in his eye as he approached the microphone. Earl knew he was up to something. Johnson said a few words about the importance of the cultural artifacts to be displayed in the new area of the museum. Then he directed a couple of museum staffers to bring a large wooden crate up onto the stage.

"Folks, at this time, I have a letter to read, and when I'm finished, I want Earl Armstrong to assist me in opening this big box. I think we'll all be thankful that this is the only thing Earl has to do today and we don't have to hear one more speech."

The crowd laughed. Johnson cleared his throat and read the letter, which was handwritten in a neat script.

Mr. Earl Armstrong,

I have read the newspaper articles about your adventures involving a place called Destruction Island. From this island, I was able to recover things precious to me and felt it only proper to return this

*object to the people of your country. I
hope that the museum project being dedicated today, with the funds that I contributed, will be a suitable home for it and
other artifacts you helped to recover.*

*Norika Edo, President
Edosan Corporation, Tokyo, Japan*

The audience clapped as Earl stood up and joined
Johnson Wewa to open the crate. The people quieted and
watched their every move intently. They lifted off the lid,
set it aside, and then began to remove volumes of straw
packing material. Inside was a large, round object wrapped
in Japanese silk cloth. Johnson lifted it up and set it on a
table placed on the stage. Earl used his pocket knife to cut
the bindings, and together they unfolded the silk wrapping.
Inside it, they found something wrapped in animal hide.
After carefully undoing more ties, the two men held the
object up for everyone to see. It was a beautifully carved and
painted mask trimmed in hammered gold—the Kwakiutl
sun mask, the *mascara del oro.*